# One Verse Multi

## By the Author

Best of the Wrong Reasons

One Verse Multi

# One Verse Multi

*by*

Sander Santiago

2022

**ONE VERSE MULTI**


**ISBN 13: 978-1-63679-069-5**

This Trade Paperback Original Is Published By
Bold Strokes Books, Inc.
P.O. Box 249
Valley Falls, NY 12185

First Edition: January 2022



---

**Credits**
Editors: Jerry L. Wheeler and Stacia Seaman
Production Design: Stacia Seaman
Artwork by Nikoli Shaver
Cover design by Jeanine Henning

## Acknowledgments

This book owes a lot to Nikoli. Thank you for supplying the beautiful cover and making a masterpiece out of my disjointed thoughts.

Thank you, Bold Strokes Books. You would think I could come up with a more powerful way to convey my gratitude.

Thank you, Katy Y., for being a solid first reader.

For
Nikoli
Mariah
Laura

# Part One

## *Trying to establish the hypothesis*

# Section 1

## *Give a horse a flying test*

The video on the screen looked more like B-reel of a desert flyover, just vast, vacant dunes. Only it wasn't. My remote quantum drones were only flying three-ish meters off the ground. According to the report, this place wasn't a desert of sand but of ash. Each pile of dust had been something. The chances were too high it had once been a person. Before the event, the city had been home to nearly nine hundred thousand people. Now it was a dead zone.

"Martin, move your ass," Tamar Garcia ordered. She kicked my foot with her clunky boot. I guess I was in her seat. I moved over as much as I could on the couch. I smiled and tried to look forgivable. She was tall—tall enough that people asked her constantly if she played basketball. She would never play basketball. And her *chola* aesthetic made her all the more intimidating. She pulled her hair over her shoulder and hugged it as if she were trying to protect it, scowling at the screen.

When the drones arrived at the coordinates I had been given, I set them to hover, typing the command into my laptop. I didn't want to look at the dead landscape. Instead, I looked at the ends of my locs, pulling at loose hairs pretending I wasn't impacted by my own imagination of the horrible event that must have occurred. When that wasn't distracting enough, I looked around the room.

The research lab was more like a science-themed apartment, with a workroom, a living room, and dorms. The couch Tamar and I sat on faced the couch our other two teammates sat on. With the armchair, the three pieces of furniture formed a C, with a table in the middle. The C faced the door connecting the living room to the workroom. Beyond the armchair was the hallway to our rooms. The couch Tamar and I sat on faced the video screen.

"This is what they are calling ground zero," Hugo Del Mar said, flipping through the hefty folder that contained our research assignment. The folder had the name *Multi-verse Protection Corporation (MVP)* stamped on it in harsh-looking red ink.

Hugo was a sandy-haired Frenchman from a universe in which the French had kept their territories in the Americas and fully colonized the western half of the continent. He would have been from what was generally considered Wyoming in most verses, which made him something like an American cowboy with a French accent. My name out of his mouth was all "m" and "t" instead of "m" and "r" the way my mom said it.

"Nice and ominous," I said.

He looked at me over the top of his folder and rolled his eyes. He was sitting with his back to the screen and had yet to turn around and look at it.

"Six years ago, a universe-multi man named James Dugan was the focal point of a massive multi-verse disaster," Hugo continued, his tone too scientific for an event that destroyed a city of hundreds of thousands of people, at least in the ground zero universe. "This was the site with the most impact. The blast radius is roughly three kilometers, but the radiation reaches at least one hundred kilometers."

I typed commands that rotated some of the quantum drones. The visual on the screen broke into five different views of ash piles, chemically damaged sky, and inky distant horizons. Not a plant or animal in sight.

"This is very interesting to see," Wei said. Wei was from a sleepy A-class universe where khaki was considered the lux color, so everything from Teslas to tuxedos were all shitty tans and beiges. He was a round-faced, Chinese territory man, who wore a "long on top" crew cut and had been adopted by an elderly couple in what most universes called Ohio.

Hugo looked back at the screens for the first time. Up to that point, Wei hadn't said a word. He was getting over strep throat. He had spent the last four days constantly chewing extra-potent CBD lozenges from some B-class verse, twenty years behind the nearest A-class. They must have been working. Looking at me, Wei pointed to the laptop. "I didn't get to watch you work at the rift closing we recruited you at. How did you develop the code?"

I was about to answer when Hugo cleared his throat. "Wei, you can nerd out with Martin later, focus."

Wei winked at me and faked some bashful pose, then turned back to the screen.

"Anyway, Martin, if you want to go to the next verse, I'll read the event description," Hugo said.

I tuned the quantum drones into the next verse. The images on the split screen were of trees, grass, and a clear blue sky. I adjusted the drones to get better images, then buzzed them around to get a feel for the area. I felt relieved by this verse, mostly because stuff was alive. We were in a park roughly the size of a city block, a cozy square of grass sliced by brick walkways. The paths were lined with trees and benches. The sun hadn't moved from where it hung low in the evening sky, but it was bright and warm and unobscured by ash.

"This is San Jose. At approximately three in the afternoon there-verse time…" Hugo started to read. I flew the drones around as he talked, looking for I don't know what. The park was empty of people. A car passed, and a cat jumped out of a trash can chasing a squirrel.

"…a man named James Dugan stood at these coordinates. In other verses, other James Dugans stood in the exact same place at the exact same time. That marks the start of the event. In the first verse, Dugan was last known to be at work in a power plant deemed the source of the explosion. That is all we know of his actions. In this verse, witnesses reported seeing the here-verse Dugan get up from a bench and walk to this section of the park."

As my drones wandered, one set came upon a statue at the north end of the park. It was a stone statue of an angel holding a rose with names carved into the base. It stood out because the park had no other statuary.

"Witnesses say Dugan started moving his arms, silently gesturing in what looked like a performance. A crowd gathered. Dugan didn't respond to any of the questions asked by onlookers. At three fifteen p.m. here-verse time, Dugan's pantomime became erratic and panicked. Three minutes later, the James Dugan of this universe erupted in a sudden and peculiar explosion."

"Fucking unreal," Tamar said.

"Seventeen people and Dugan in this verse were killed in the explosion. The authorities would later say Dugan had a bomb, but none of the eyewitnesses reported seeing one. The autopsy reported Dugan's body emitted an extreme, unexplained level of radiation. He also had unexplainable chemical burns and was perforated by an excessive volume of shrapnel, including unusual metals and glass. The same inexplicably large quantity of debris was found in the other bodies. However, some key bits were missing. Someone on the ballistics team wrote in one of his reports there was no bomb because fragments from the bomb itself were not found."

"Did this Dugan guy converge with his counterpart in the ground zero verse?" I asked. I looked hard at the statue, realizing it was a memorial. Seventeen names were inscribed on the base along with a date. James Dugan wasn't listed.

"Do you think?" Hugo asked. His voice was more like a teacher giving a logic test than a researcher looking for a hypothesis. I guessed he might have had an answer of some kind he wanted me to figure out for myself. I thought about it. People converged often enough. The degree of damage was unpredictable and could have been responsible for a quantum event that mimicked an explosion. The difference between this event and others was that the damage was uneven.

"There's too many universes involved," Wei said, getting to the mystery before I did. He got up from his couch and came to my laptop. "Make this thing take quantum pictures."

"Also, it says here some Dugans survived with minor damage as the event occurred in their universe," Hugo explained.

"People don't survive convergence," Tamar said. Hugo gave her a resolute nod.

I was actually curious now. There were two ways convergence happened. The first was rifts, or a weak spot in the quantum barrier between universes that could allow things to pass between them. If a universe-multi person crossed the barrier into a verse where they had a counterpart, that was the end of both. Convergence also had the power to destroy whole universes. It had been my job in MVP for the last decade to locate and close rifts.

The second source of convergence was tuning, using a quantum drone or a Multiverse Encounter Sequencer (MES). A sequencer was a universe-unique Nokia E70 series cellular phone MVP had modified to create quantum consonance and dissonance and allow for travel between universes, among other things. It didn't make calls. My sequencer was connected to the laptop. The quantum drones were controlled through the sequencer, and the laptop just gave me more power to access more drones.

MVP had virtually eliminated tuning convergence by having only universe-unique people like me as technicians and most research staff. We only existed in one universe. A convergence event at MVP hadn't happened the last eighteen of the twenty years the company existed. That meant if it was convergence, a rift must have happened. Wei was on the right track. The way to spot a rift was to look at the area from a quantum perspective.

"Wei, move so I can do it," I said, pushing his head out of the way of my laptop screen so I could type code. He leaned in eagerly anyway.

The quantum drones could collect data on pretty much anything. They were a swarm of near-microscopic computers that could act as a collective or as individuals. So, I switched the drones from video to quantum and pulled up the quantum visualizer. The sequencer would process the data from each drone and build a map of the area. I programmed the drones to look within a ten-meter cube of the Dugan coordinates. The image of the park became a blank canvas. Anything that had a quantum frequency for the there-verse would be depicted in white. Anything with a different frequency would be a different color based on its home-verse.

We watched eagerly waiting for colors to change on the screen. Slowly the drones chased down a few thousand particles from other verses. After ten minutes the program beeped to let me know there was nothing left to find.

"That was anticlimactic," Tamar said dryly.

I could hardly believe the image. The data showed the area had less than five percent particle contamination from another universe. Any square meter of any verse had an average of eight percent due to natural forces. Any zone that had a rift at any point in history would have a contamination rate of twenty to seventy percent. "Not only was there no rift," I said, "but this place is almost quantum pure."

"Isn't that something?" Hugo said as if he already knew.

"If it wasn't a rift, what was it?" I asked.

"That brings us to our assignment," Hugo said. "The file suggests it had to do with universe-multi people, so we're going to study what impact they have on the multi-verse."

"Great," Tamar said even though she didn't make it sound that great. "I need some food."

"Go to the other verses," Wei said to me, trying to type on the laptop himself.

Hugo looked at Tamar. "Okay, what's the matter? This is actually some really interesting stuff. Tam?"

"It's fine," she snapped, clearly annoyed. She stood and crossed to a phone on the wall of the lab. "I just want some food."

Hugo stood and followed her. "Tam, *qu'est-ce qu'il y a*?"

Tamar shrugged off the hand he had placed on her shoulder. "Nothing."

"Aren't you excited for a new project?"

"Not like we didn't have plenty of old projects."

Tamar and Hugo had been with MVP for thirteen years, research teammates almost from day one. Wei had been with the company the least amount of time and, at twenty-one, was also the youngest. Wei had been on Hugo's team for a year.

"Tam."

"All right, fine, Hugo. I don't trust it."

I let Wei have the laptop so I could watch the drama between Hugo and Tamar.

"Tam."

She growled at him. "Why now? MVP has only cared about finding universe-unique things and closing rifts until now? The point of the whole company is to protect all the universes from rifts. Why bother with this one guy and this one event?"

Hugo puzzled it out, linking his arms behind his head. He looked like an anime protagonist. The plaid cotton button-down and denim jeans threw off the image a little. His long, wavy hair was pulled into a ponytail and shoved under his cowboy hat. It was funny watching him next to goth princess Tamar.

"Don't you think a recurrence of this event would be equally as threatening as any rift? Maybe more threatening?"

"Not if it's only been one time in the whole history of the universes," Tamar said.

"We won't know until we study it."

"Well, Hugo, I don't think it's just some interesting project. It's too specific."

"You're such a skeptic, but I guess that's a good thing in our line of work." Hugo tried to make a friendly show of putting his arm around Tamar. She just jabbed him in the ribs.

I didn't say it, but I agreed with her. The file had the name Don Brady on it. Brady was the company's director of marketing. What did he want with this information? He didn't do anything unless he could sell it. He had observed me once, thinking he could capitalize on my rift closure technique. All technicians used the sequencers, but only I used the laptop. I was the fastest, most effective technician the company had. Brady, however, figured the cost of finding universe-unique computers was too high compared to the benefit of the work, or at least work that could be effectively done with a sequencer. Other technicians had come to me to learn my technique, but most stuck to the company plan. I didn't trust that. If we could do our jobs better and faster, why not invest?

As far as this project went, I had a feeling Brady already knew what he wanted to do in the multi-verse, and this research would somehow give him the means to do it. Or worse, it would give him the means of covering his ass when something happened. The wording was almost too specific:

> *CLASSIFICATION GRADE: ALPHA. Discover the reason for the event. Provide an accurate and thorough understanding of the quantum forces that linked the James Dugans during the event and the cause of the connection between the counterparts. What impact do universe-multi humans and human-intelligent animals (H-HIA) have on the total multi-verse? What would happen to the multi-verse should one or more of the universe-multi H-HIA be removed from their respective universes, with special interest in A-class universes?*

I didn't say anything. I just listened to their argument.

Tamar tried to dodge Hugo by pulling the phone around a pile of boxes. The stuff all over the room was mine. I was new to the team and had to be relocated from rift technician quarters to the lab. I hadn't had the chance to unpack.

"Can we eat first?" Tamar asked Hugo. She gestured at him with the phone. It only connected internally to headquarters' concierge. The whole system was run like a hotel with a full staff to clean, cook, and launder. And it *was* lunchtime.

"*Bien.* Order my number five. I want to write some things down before I forget," Hugo said, going to his desk in the corner.

"What about the rest of you fucks?" Tamar growled at me and Wei. We shouted a number at her. There was a set menu for each person: fifteen items—three breakfasts, five lunches, and seven dinners. This helped Headquarters' inventory since we had to go to the verses to get food. HQ floated in an ocean in a dead-verse, a people-less verse with less than habitable shores.

As Tamar placed the orders, I walked over to my boxes. One was labeled *Desk* and should have had my stash of Cheetos, but it didn't. I had not been the one to pack, so I had to hunt it down. I found a box labeled *Misc* and gave that a quick sift. No go. I ended up finding them in a box labeled *Snacks*, which shows you how much food I had hidden in my dorm. I took the Cheetos back to the couch and watched Hugo scribble away. Then I looked at Wei. He was looking at me.

"Should we be taking notes?" I whispered to him, waving the Cheetos his way.

"Can I see your gear?" he whispered back.

"Is that an invitation?" I laughed as I stood up and pulled tech out of the boxes. I passed him five laptops and a handful of tablets.

"Why is it all broken?"

"Sometimes the parts converge when I go to a different verse. I did an experiment to see how bad convergence would be before I started using the laptops. Since it was never more than damage to the device and I could replace that, I figured it'd be fine."

"How did you conduct your experiment?" Wei asked, his voice straining enough to toss another CBD lozenge into his mouth.

"I rolled a few through some rifts on a skateboard," I said. He laughed and moved couches so he could better inspect the tech junk.

"How do you make your selections?" Wei asked, pulling two busted computers closer.

"I usually pick older generations or new versions that are missing modern features."

"Why?"

"In the A-classes, the counterparts of older computers are less likely to still exist in a form capable of connecting to the sequencer. The newer ones without the modern features are less likely to be multi because no one really wants a brand-new laptop that isn't even a touchscreen or one you need a mouse for."

He nodded as if he agreed and picked up a particularly mangled laptop by the corner of the screen. The bottom half separated and fell to the floor just in front of Tamar's boots as she came back to the couches. He looked at her. "We call that downloading."

Tamar didn't laugh, but I did.

"Right," Hugo said, slapping down his pen. He shuffled some loose, lineless papers together and stood. "We're about to be busier than an E string in a fiddle contest."

"No," Tamar said.

"I really think—"

"Food, Del Mar. Food before science."

"Mastication before education," Wei said.

I added, "Ingest-igate before you investigate."

"*Tu te fous de moi?*" He sighed and rubbed his head. "Okay, we'll eat, then we'll work."

Tamar gave Hugo a triumphant smile and folded up on the couch so that she was almost an egg next to Wei. Wei and I shuffled the drones through the other verses in the file and repeated the same map-building process. I was surprised the results were pretty much the same, even in the ground zero verse.

The food arrived, and Hugo passed out our boxes. I had completely forgotten what I ordered, so I was damned happy to see a bowl of five bean chili with cheese and a side of tortilla chips. I might have moaned as I took the first bite. I didn't look up again until Hugo cleared his throat. To my horror, he was already throwing his waste into the receptacle and brushing crumbs from his hands. He had eaten so fast I couldn't even say what the food had been.

"Right. The cows won't herd themselves, so let's get to it." The rest of us whined, but Hugo just waved us down. "Y'all can finish. I'll write while you eat."

Thanks to the button Hugo pushed, I learned there was a dry-erase board behind the screen we had been watching. The projector clicked off automatically. Hugo picked up a blue marker and wrote *The Plan* in barely legible cursive.

"Let's set up what we are going to do, then we can assign duties," Hugo said. He wrote *universe-multi* on the board near the middle. "Our inspiration is James Dugan and his fifteen counterparts. We must find a way to observe universe-multi subjects. What we need is to determine how to find them."

"Well, how do you find universe-unique people?" I asked. "I mean how do they do it generally?"

Wei leaned toward me. "We listen."

"To what? It can't be listening at a quantum level because everything is tuned to the universe it originated in. I mean, how do you distinguish any one thing in a whole verse?"

Hugo crossed the room to a grand piano. He sat on the bench as if it were just an ordinary chair or piece of furniture. I was definitely interested in the piano. It had been years since I had gotten to play one. Most rooms in HQ had some odd thing someone had brought from a verse. In the common room of my old quarters, we had two grandfather clocks. They didn't tell time, of course, but there they were.

"We listen to voices and communications for people living in small regions," Tamar said. "We also take photos and compare them. It starts big, but then we narrow our parameters with statistics."

"Voices…" I repeated. "Well, that's it, then."

"Is it?" Hugo asked.

I munched more Cheetos. "Sure. Instead of having computers eliminate the voice if there's a match, have it eliminate the voice if there isn't one."

"Across all verses?" Wei said.

I just shrugged. I really didn't know.

"No," Tamar said. "We can start with a sample of parallel verses."

"This is great," Hugo said. He jumped up and crossed to the board to write. "This also naturally provides us with some parameters and brackets to put people in."

He drew a line on the board, then another parallel to that, with about five centimeters between them until the board had nine rows. Then he marked the lines with brackets that linked the two outer lines, then the next, then the next leaving the center line unbracketed. He labeled the innermost bracket *V zero*.

"We can start with a naught verse, v-naught, and find a person within that verse. Then we can determine two groups, those who are not multi in verses immediately parallel to v-naught, and those who are. Then we can break out those who are I.P.M.—I made that up. It means Immediately Parallel Multi—"

He kept talking, but my head was swimming. I looked at the piano. I wondered for a moment if this was a mistake. I was already lost, and it was only step one. I felt eyes on me. When I looked up, Wei winked at me and gave me a thumbs-up. Hugo's back was still to the room. His diagram became suddenly and unsettlingly three-dimensional. I looked back at Wei. Wei pretended to sleep then wake, wiping fake drool from his chin. I laughed.

"Wei, if you're already distracting Martin, I'm going to be mad," Hugo said.

"Who's Wei?" Wei said, winking at me again.

"I think we need a few people in a few brackets to start. Dugan was known to be in sixteen verses. We know there's about three thousand stable A-Class universes, but I suppose that might be putting the cart before the horse. We'll select two people from each bracket and observe them. Then when we have some parameters, we can build a bigger survey from there. No reason to give a horse a flying test, I guess."

I laughed and three faces turned to me.

"Oh, shit. Wasn't that a joke?" I sighed, feeling embarrassed.

"It was. Just no one finds me funny."

"I think you're funny," I said. "And a genius, because what the actual fuck is that diagram?"

I watched him think about it. Then I watched him blush. He turned back to the board and continued talking. "So…"

And with that, I lost track of the experiment. My brain went back to combing the maps I had made for any clue as to what was happening. Wei fell asleep for real. An hour or so later, when I was on the verge of dozing off myself, Hugo clapped.

"Anything else?" he asked. He put his hands on his head, marker and all.

Tamar said, "I have some research on H-HIA who have encountered rifts and other multi-verse phenomena. I can look through it and see if I can find anything we can use as a variable."

"Any other research points?" Hugo asked Tamar.

She seemed to sense me staring and glared at me through narrow eyes, black with eyeshadow. I didn't look away. I just smiled. She rolled her eyes and looked back at Hugo.

"I also want to look deeper into James Dugan," she said. "Maybe a journal exists. Maybe one of them is still alive."

Hugo wrote it down, and then he turned and stared at her. She glared at him. He looked at her with more intensity. Finally, she said, "I promise not to investigate the motives of the founders."

Hugo smiled and shook his head. "I hate that I don't trust you."

"I'll work with Tamar on the Dugan thing. I want more readings," I said. It was only half a lie. I really wanted to know why Tamar was so suspicious. Hugo beamed, and Tamar rolled her eyes again.

"What else?" Hugo asked.

# Section 2

## *Outpaced for a while*

"Right, so when we get in there…" Tamar said, turning in my direction and blinking a few times. It had been three days since the planning meeting, and Tamar and I had been sent to discuss progress with the data team. It was my first time meeting them. Hugo and Wei had gone to the Hub to formally file the plan with the research coordinator and get more equipment.

"You know what?" she said. "I was going to tell you to be cool. But you probably can't, so just try not to do anything embarrassing."

"What am I gonna do?"

She rolled her eyes. "This team is amazing and I won't stand for fuckery."

"Uh…okay."

She focused on me again.

"What's the problem? What am I doing?"

"Nothing—yet."

She pressed a code into the keypad by the door. It wasn't a lock since her code didn't let us in. We had to wait for someone to open the door in person. I didn't like being on the gangway. The Department of Universe-unique H-HIA was in the third dome of HQ. The whole drifting city was like a spider web with the Hub in the center. Eighteen more domes were arranged in three rings connected by six main arms and several interconnecting hallways. And the whole complex just floated along like the ocean wasn't the scariest part of any verse.

The gangways connecting the domes were like the enclosed tunnels at aquariums, only it was sky overhead instead of fish. Looking through the curved plastic made me nauseous. I tried to look at anything else. A door is a door, so I looked at Tamar. She looked at the black paint chipping off her fingernails. She was nearly as tall as the Plexiglas. If she put her hand up, she could have reached the ceiling.

"How tall are you?" I asked. She turned a stare so cold and unapproachable on me that I might have actually shivered.

I took a breath and counted, trying to ease some of the nausea. It wasn't so bad when I was inside because I couldn't see the rise and fall of the horizon. Watching that straight line at the edge of the world tip to one side, then leap up, then tip to the other always made me want to vomit.

"You look like shit," Tamar said, pulling her black and white flannel around her as if I was going to barf on it.

"Believe it or not, I get pretty seasick."

"Good thing you live on the ocean."

I wanted to retort, but a guy opened the door. He had dark brown skin, a flattop haircut, and a silver cross dangling from one ear. He also had his septum pierced and was wearing sunglasses. He whipped the glasses off in a hurry when he spotted Tamar. Grinning stupidly, he let us in.

Tamar glared at him. She shouldered past and marched down the hallway. I guess she knew where she was going. The building was arranged in a circle with the hallways forming a wraparound porch. The rooms jutted into the circle like pie slices. It gave me the impression of a circular motel rather than a computer supercenter. Tamar stopped at a door marked fifty-six and waited. The guy stopped behind her, prompting Tamar to clear her throat. He jumped at the sound and used his keycard to let us in.

"Mason, who is it?" a voice called from another room.

"It's Tamar," Mason said.

"You dusty, messy-headed, big-eyed, Brussels sprout breath. You look like a garage sale hanger," a young person said, coming from a back room.

"You can take your scrawny, bald-headed, chapped lip, dresses-like-my-grandma's-couch self, and kiss my ass, Kiki," Tamar said with a smile.

And then they hugged. I waited to be introduced.

"This is Martin," Tamar said when they parted.

"I'm Kiki, they/them." Kiki grinned at me. They held out a hand. They had a soft voice and matched Tamar's goth style, only their color of choice was red instead of black. They were short with coppery tan skin and had bleached, cropped hair.

"Martin, he/him," I answered, feeling a sense of kinship.

"And I'm fucking done," Tamar said, echoing our tone.

"Why are you like this?" someone said from the doorway.

I was so surprised by Tamar and Kiki, I didn't notice Petite, Tan, and Handsome standing there. He looked at me, and I looked away. The room we were standing in was some sort of anteroom and had conjoined chairs along the walls like a stadium. Mr. Handsome was standing in the first interior doorway.

"Don't be mad, Luca," Tamar said. "I love you too."

She bent in a sexy, girly way and kissed him.

"Stop," Luca said without meaning it. Then he looked at me.

"Ugh, this is Martin. This is Luca, he's in charge," Tamar said.

"Hi, I'm Martin King," I said, holding out my hand. Luca gave me the usual questioning look. "Nope, I'm not him. My middle name is Logan, and the rest is just my mom getting remarried when I was ten."

That didn't seem to change the look he was giving me, though. I got the feeling he knew me.

"Well, *MLK*, I'm Luca, and that's Mason. We're your data team."

I nodded and followed him into a room stuffed wall to wall with computers. Think sci-fi movie from the sixties instead of middle school computer lab where you learned to type. Huge towers and processors lined the walls. It seemed for every two computers, there was a monitor. It was warmer in this room by a few degrees, with the noticeable and constant purring of many small motors.

"Hugo sent us the parameters you outlined. We're just waiting on the green light," Luca said to Tamar.

"*We're* the green light," she said.

"Fun."

He actually rubbed his hands together and bounced on the balls of his feet. He was dressed like the love interest in a women's fragrance ad, a white shirt, nice jeans, and immaculate shoes. I considered being embarrassed by my black joggers and Denver Nuggets jersey, but I thought I looked good so I wasn't.

He got a stack of laptops off a cart and moved them to the empty table in the middle of the room, arranging them into a neat row of four. All of them were labeled with our names. Tamar and Kiki huddled in a corner together, lost in a conversation they were having in Spanish. Mason went to a bank of computers and plopped into a high-backed chair.

"Since Tamar is busy, I guess you can just explain it to her later," Luca said to me.

"Right," I said, stepping closer to the table.

He turned on the computer with my name on it. "So, this was Hugo's framework, right?"

I looked at the model he opened on the screen. It was a three-dimensional map similar to the one Hugo had drawn on the board. The gray depiction of the universes stretching in both directions of time looked like thousands of wires running through black electrical tubing, branching and breaking across a gridded plane.

"That's it," I said, familiar with the shape of the A-class universes.

"He said you're the one who suggested we reverse the UU algorithm to find UM people."

"Uh, yeah. I'm the genius," I said with a laugh, trying for a fake brag.

"Not bad," he said, giving me a smile. He stopped and stared a moment, then blinked and started to walk away. It was *that* look.

"Why'd you look at me like that?"

Between him and Tamar both staring at me, I was beginning to think I had something on my face. My scraggly beard was grown out more than usual. If I had Cheeto dust in it, it wouldn't be the first time.

"Sorry, it's just really cool to meet you." He ran a hand through his fluffy, neat black hair and gave me a dimply grin.

"Bet," I said.

He laughed. "I guess if I were you, I wouldn't be modest either."

"Exactly. Though what about me makes you say that?" I really didn't know. My bravado was mostly fake, but I knew people talked about me. I was curious about what they said.

"You're kind of a legend among the data people."

"Sounds fake."

"Naw, look." He pointed to a picture hanging on the wall. It looked a little like the first X-rays of DNA but in swirls of blue and green.

"What's that?"

"That's a still from the Juno rift closure you did last year. Well, it's really the shape of your drones exactly three seconds before the rift was sealed."

I felt my mouth hanging open, so I closed it.

"Look, we aren't fangirls or something. Well, I mean we are but—I mean—wow! No one handles the drones like you. Analyzing your data is like reading a good book or hearing great music."

I looked from the photo to Luca. I felt the same about my work. The act of doing it felt like those things. "Thanks. Didn't know anyone was a fan."

"Hell, yeah. I think encounter management needs more guys like you. Or gals too, I guess. Or NBs."

"Well, now they don't even have me, so they'll have to figure something else out."

Luca looked at me with sincere shock. "I know, right? I mean, can you believe it? With everything going on."

I honestly had no idea what was going on. I was new to research, and I knew they had more information about MVP and the universes, confidential stuff ordinary techs didn't know. I hadn't been told anything beyond the project. Luca seemed to think I knew as much as he did. If I played this right, I could get information.

"I've been out of the loop for a few days, playing catch-up on this project," I said. "Any updates?"

"Naw, nothing new."

"Fair, I guess. Then again…Well, first, what have they told y'all about it?"

"Nothing more than you probably know. Rift opening rates aren't news to MVP. They only care about closure rates. All my warnings go unanswered."

That was a good segue. "*Your* warnings?"

He nodded and snapped a finger gun at me. He went to a lone computer at a desk in the adjacent room.

"See, this was the latest projection I sent. I guess I can tell you since you're you. Maybe if you tell them, they'll listen."

I leaned around Luca to look at the screen. I felt some guilt at not clearing up how little power I actually had, but I wanted to know, and he wanted to tell me. The graph he showed me was clear enough. It charted two relationships. The first was the relationship between time and total rift encounters reported. That line went up in a steep parabola. The second was a more linear line depicting the relationship between time and the number of rift closures. New rifts were way outpacing the closures. The lines intersected some time three years ago, meaning MVP had been outpaced for a while.

"Geez," I said, authentically surprised. "I knew it was bad, but not like this."

I had no idea it was like this and only learned how bad it was in that moment. The rate of rift formation was increasing, and we weren't keeping up. Most people knew what damage an open rift could do—missing flights, the whole of the Bermuda Triangle, unexplained car crashes, and missing persons. More rifts meant it was getting worse.

"We've been lucky so far," Luca said. "No huge disasters, and the increased rates have been concentrated to a few universes. But at this rate, it won't be long before something major happens."

He pulled up a map with dots on it. It gave me the nostalgic impression of a wireless phone company's data coverage map, but for the whole universes. The rift dots were concentrated around a few A-class universes.

"See, most of the activity is here," he said, pointing.

"Weird," I said. "I wonder if any of the increases are correlated with hotspots in those verses, you know, like Florida, Alaska, Area 51, parts of Norway, the Tianzi mountains…"

He smiled at me.

"What?"

"Talented, cute, and smart. You're a real triple threat," he said. Then he pressed a few keys, and a table came up detailing rift rates by hotspot. I didn't look at the table, though. I just grinned back at him.

"Can I have this report?" I asked on a whim.

It was the first time Luca looked suspicious. "Really?"

I shrugged and stood, moving locs off my shoulders. I thought for a second about what I could do with this information. "These past few months I was teaching some of the rift techs how to close rifts the way I do. With what I know, I think I could use your numbers to make a case for keeping that training going, improving our rift encounters."

Luca beamed. "I would be honored."

"Well, you know where to send it," I said, feeling suddenly embarrassed. "Let's get back to it?"

"Right. These eight computers here are dedicated to your project. The programs and equations are already in them, so we just hit run. Hopefully, the UM possibilities will start rolling in. We'll categorize them according to Hugo's parameters and send you reports every Monday until you tell us to stop."

"That's pretty kick-ass."

"Right? Then when you're ready to observe, we have those computers set up to transmit quantum, audio, and visual data from any subject you choose." He pointed to the computers on a second wall.

"What do those computers do?" I was looking at a third wall, broken only by the door to the other room. Luca pointed to the computers on that and on the remaining fourth wall.

"Those and those will continue collecting and analyzing rift data. If there is a rift anywhere in the known multi-verse, we're watching it."

"You watch them all?" I asked, amazed.

"Well, specifically we're an acoustics team. Unless one of us gets bored and looks for something else, we look for disruption patterns across barriers."

"Why?"

"There are many ways to understand rifts. If one's on the water, they usually look for a physical change in the hydrodynamic property at the barrier points. If one's in the air, it's the wind. We have a natural area focus, forests mostly. Some animals are intuitive and can avoid crossing the universe barriers. Some not so much. People especially."

"Huh," I said.

"We observe a lot of lost cows."

I snorted a laugh.

"Do you have any questions?" he said. "About the project, I mean." He seemed embarrassed to talk about his work. I really did think it was cool, but I moved on.

"Naw, not yet," I said, "but I'm sure we will once the data starts rolling in."

He talked me through the program, explaining how the computer would randomly select a voice signature in one universe and compare it with every other universe, terminating only if the voice didn't have a match within the first one thousand sampled universes. If the computer found a match, it would start over on a new voice.

"Are voices really that unique?"

"Yep, but we have other ways of ensuring it really is a match."

"Like?"

Luca pointed to different variables in the equation he was using to code the program. "Location is a good one. Usually someone gets discarded by a counterpart who lives in the same one hundred kilometer radius. Even my own counterparts live in the same city as my parents."

"You aren't unique?"

"Naw. I don't travel much, so it doesn't matter."

"I didn't become unique until I was eight," I said.

"Right. I knew that. We use old data to train new analysts."

"Smart."

"You seem surprised by a lot of this. It's ordinary multi-verse stuff."

"I'm surprised by you," I said, unable to stop myself.

He laughed and shook his head. "Anyway, another parameter is phone number. Most people's cell phones are within a few digits of each other, assuming they've had the same number for a while. Parents, parents' locations, and social media screen names are also weirdly similar."

"That's a lot."

Luca sighed. "Thinking about how un-unique I can really be keeps me up some nights."

"Huh," I said.

"Are you almost done? Hugo wanted us back by four," Tamar said. Her voice made both Luca and me jump.

"Didn't mean to interrupt the love fest," Kiki added, crossing their arms.

"Hey, you're as big a fan as the rest of us," Luca said.

Kiki gave him a hard look, then shrugged and sucked their teeth. "It's true."

"Great. Love knowing that everyone loves Martin. Bye," Tamar said. I followed her, waving as I left.

# Section 3

## *Close enough for jazz*

"This is it," Hugo shouted, practically kicking open the door to the living room.

"What the hell?" Tamar jumped at the sudden sound and spilled half the popcorn from the bowl she was holding. Angrily, she went over to the automatic vacuum and turned it on with her foot. The small robot beeped to life and started rolling around the room.

"I'm sorry," Hugo said, his enthusiasm diminishing only slightly. "*Excusez moi.*"

He was carrying a heavy-looking filing box. His face was flushed and red around his ears and cheeks. He bumbled into the room, trying to take off his denim jacket and carry the box at the same time. I sat up from where I was half lying on the couch just in time for Hugo to plop down right where my feet had been. He finally shook the jacket loose and put the box down on the coffee table.

"We have it. It's finally here. Where is Wei? Wei!" Hugo shouted down the hallway.

"What is that?" Tamar asked, the crunch of popcorn accenting her words.

"I'll tell you when Wei gets out here." He pulled his hat off and threw it on the back of the couch as he snapped open a pocketknife and started slicing the tape holding the lid of the box down.

"*Wei Miller*," Hugo shouted again. I muted the TV.

"I'm here," Wei said, strolling out of his room with a huge tan comforter wrapped around his shoulders. He made a show of flapping around the room before landing gently on the couch. When he was finally seated, he pulled the blanket around himself and turned a bored gaze on Hugo.

"Right, the data team came through. We can make selections for observation."

The rest of us cheered with limited energy. It was almost midnight. Tamar and I had been watching a movie. Well, she watched the movie. I fussed with my locs. I had seen a version of the movie before, but that was one of those funny things about the multi-verse. In this version of the movie, the chick picks the brunette, which was bananas. In the other I had seen, she picks the blonde. Many a great debate in either verse could be answered if they could just watch the other version.

"Martin," Hugo said.

I blinked at him.

"Were you listening?"

"Naw. What?"

"I was saying how the guys in data—"

"They aren't all guys," Tamar said.

"Okay, how the data *people* generated a small sample of nine categories. I was thinking we can review it now."

"Whoa, wait. We're doing this now? Like, *now* now?" I asked.

"Yes…no…maybe. The data comes when it comes, and it came."

"It did take a week and a half," Wei said without any malice.

"Right. Longest analysis yet, and they aren't even done. This is just the first batch so we can start observations. They'll send more." Hugo moved the box from the table to the floor and started placing stacked and bound papers where it had been. Hugo looked at me, his face equal parts giddy and unsure. "Shall we?"

I looked at Tamar and Wei.

"I don't sleep." She shrugged.

Wei looked at me blearily. "I'm already awake."

I shook my head. "Carry on, Del Mar."

Hugo brightened and unloaded more paper. We watched him divide the stacks into small piles. I looked over the sheets as he arranged them according to the color coding on the covers. The front of each packet had a name on it and a designation I didn't yet understand. The pages were also tabbed. They looked like reference texts for college.

"Okay, here's how it breaks down." Hugo crossed to the switch and flipped on the overhead lights. The rest of us groaned. Then he went into the workroom and wheeled in a dry erase board, placing it right in front of the original plan board.

"The data team was able to find people that fit into nine distinct categories. Category One is the selection of one hundred universe-unique people for a control group."

I wondered if I'd actually need the calculus I pretended to learn in high school. I squinted at the black smears on the board that passed for Hugo's writing. "I guess that's what that says."

Wei laughed. "It looks like *battery one u.u. pine poles.*"

Hugo paused and glared at us.

"Sorry," I said.

Wei didn't say anything. He just stopped laughing.

"Anyway, each universe-multi group has a control, and the categories are based on parallelness, and distance is measured by the MVP scale of distance. We have seventy-six *pine poles*," Hugo said good-naturedly, "in this category."

Margo, my recruiter and mentor, and a cartography junky, explained the multi-verse to me as colored pencils in a box. Every here-verse is like the middle-most pencil. Some pencils lie exactly parallel and touch, then some others are parallel and next to the middle one but there is a gap between them, not another pencil, just space, so that would be parallel and not touching. All the other pencils get more and more distant as you move away from the center one. It's way more complicated, but that visual always helped me.

Eventually Hugo had everything detailed out on the board in a less than neat but readable table. "Any questions?"

"Wait a minute," Wei said, his face brightening for the first time since he had been a blanket butterfly. He stood and went to the board. He pointed at the last number in the range of universes for category nine, the ones who were most multi.

"What?" Hugo asked, excited.

"This number means that someone exists in all A-Class universes?" Wei asked.

All our attention snapped to that number with almost audible force. At least one of the people listed was multi across all three thousand eleven stable A-class verses. That was like finding a unicorn. It was the statistical extreme opposite a pure-unique.

"I need to see this," Tamar said. She set her popcorn aside and read over the covers of the packets in the piles.

I looked too, the designations on the cover now understandable. Each cover listed the name, the group category in shorthand, and the number of universes that person was in. Wei and Hugo watched, leaning over the couch. I found the packet first.

"Tidus Avery, category nine, distance factor five, n equals three thousand eleven," I read.

I tried to pass the packet to Hugo, but he just grinned and said, "Open it."

I opened to the first page. "Tidus Allen Avery. Twenty-four years old, lives in—"

There was a list of cities and county designations based on universes the Tiduses lived in. It looked like they mostly lived in what most A-class verses called Florida. If not there, then they lived in the Texas region. After the location list, there was an index of the packet's contents. I turned to the first page, which was labeled "profile."

To my surprise there was a photo taped to the page. It looked like a candid photo of a barista from over the shoulder of a patron at a coffee shop. He was a Caucasian guy, average looking aside from the rainbow hair. Well, averagely attractive. He was tall, but otherwise had an ordinary build. His smile was stunning, though. The most distinctive thing about him was that he looked familiar.

"Oh shit," I said.

I felt three sets of eyes on me.

"I know this guy."

"What?" the three of them exclaimed together.

"Naw, not *know* know, but I met him once. At the rift you recruited me on, actually."

"Really?" Tamar asked. Taking the book from me, she flipped through the pages and passed it back. "You met Tidus of A-Class Universe 2940FOX?"

I looked at the photo. It was the same face, only the hair was lavender and the store was one-third coffee shop, one-third bar, and one-third bookstore. He was leaning this time, looking out at something that seemed far away.

"Yeah," I said, feeling a sense of dread.

"Well, that's interesting, I feel like—" Hugo started, but I didn't listen. I told them I had met him, but there was so much more to it than that.

❖

I heard Wei's voice. "We have thirty seconds until the first fire trucks arrive."

His update broke my concentration, and I blinked a few times. I was focused on the complex pattern I was building with the drones. They swarmed in three dimensions, pulling the rift's edges together. It was like sewing at a quantum level. Wei and Tamar were at their stations around the rift site. They were communicating to me and Hugo through devices in our ears, which meant any comments they made went straight into my head, making it hard to focus.

"*Merde*," Hugo swore. "Right, so we have thirty…twenty-nine… twenty-eight…seconds to get the rift closed. At this rate, we'll fail by two seconds."

"I can do it," I said.

Hugo leaned down suddenly, and I grunted as he rested some of his weight on me. He peered over my shoulder to observe the progress of the rift seal from the perspective of my laptop.

"You're only at sixty percent closure."

"More than half," I said, going for hopeful.

I remembered being annoyed I had been assigned to a new rift team twenty minutes before an encounter. I didn't know this guy, and he didn't know me. I tried not to fault him for his nerves. Then I refocused. I split the drones again, from eight groups to sixteen. I heard Hugo gasp. When people made groups, they usually stopped at four or six. The more groups, the more commands you had to be able to type. Six was pushing it on the sequencer alone, but using the laptop, I could do more. The trick was knowing when the rift was closed enough.

"Martin, even at your fastest we'll need one more second than predicted."

"Close enough for jazz."

Neither of us said it, but the rift decay was exponential, and it would be close. I needed to get out in front of it. I had never seen a closure decay so quickly. It was like particles were being pulled off the edges as quickly as I could get them placed, like they were being sucked into the rift. Rifts had spillage, but this felt so much more alive. I didn't want to tell Hugo, but it was a weird rift. It resisted.

"That increases the risk of H-HIA interference to almost seventy percent," Hugo said, showing irritation toward me for the first time. People were usually irritated with me within the first five minutes.

I sighed. H-HIA percent interference probabilities were almost like predicting rain in South Florida. If the chance was over fifty percent, it might as well have been one hundred percent. Protecting people from rifts was why I got into this business.

"I can buy some time," Tamar said.

"That's all I need to hear." I laughed.

"Tamar, keep it sane," Hugo said.

She groaned.

I took a breath and thought about every aspect of the encounter area, the people involved. The drones made a sloppy circle around the edge of the rift, wavering as my concentration wavered. I sent them in opposing directions, creating counter looping circles that looked like a depiction of a large atom. The rings looked suddenly puny as I considered Hugo's calculations. I needed a bigger atom.

"Okay. Wei, how much time do I have?"

"Fire truck in ten seconds."

The rift was in the upstairs office of a building in Fort Lauderdale. We had cleared the building by setting off the fire alarms, which meant people were wandering close to where Hugo and I were trying to work. Fortunately, we blended well. Hugo and I were sitting on a bench near the intercoastal water inlet, looking no more interesting than ordinary Floridians.

"I'm going to give you a controlled disaster on the first floor near the front doors. It'll put people in the way as they try and see. I'm also going to block the three nearest sets of stairs. Minimal damage, I promise," Tamar said.

Her promise marked the arrival of the first fire truck and the detonation of the first of a series of explosions inside the building. Tamar's plan worked, though. With the other doors impossible to open, the first responders had to rush in through the front of the office building. The mesmerized crowd was slow to get out of their way.

I divided the drones again. The atom morphed with each

division. Sixteen groups had been a flower, thirty-two became a dense triacontadigon, the sixty-four made a pattern I couldn't name.

"Martin," Hugo said, barely catching my attention.

I ignored him. I understood why no one broke the swarm into so many groups. It hurt, for one. I only had ten fingers and they only moved so fast. The commands were just patterns on the keyboard, and I practiced that pattern enough to be able to do it quickly. But I had never done this many. I knew I wouldn't be able to hold the sixty-four groups for very long. The harder I typed, the more the pattern wobbled. But the rift got smaller and smaller, disintegrating.

"Count…till…sealed," I requested, not daring to divert even an ounce more of my attention from the complicated process.

"You have seal in six, five…" Hugo read.

"H-HIA encounter in six…five," Wei started.

Their voices smashed together in a dull echo of each other, only Wei's countdown was close enough to Hugo's that his numbers got caught up in the tail end creating a disturbing syncopation. *TwTwo… OnOne…*

With a last command, I sent all the drones to the floor for maximum invisibility against the industrial carpet just as the firefighters pushed into the room.

"Fuck, was it enough?" I gasped. I hadn't realized I had been holding my breath until I tried to speak.

"Well, if you ain't just eat the devil with the horns on! That's the best driving I've ever seen," Hugo said. He nearly jumped up and down. I was shoved forward suddenly by the force of him slapping me on the back. I had to catch the laptop before it hit the cement. I replayed the last seven seconds of data transmitted by the drones. The rift was closed and holding.

"What in the fucking hell, how?" Tamar said. "I've never seen… Damn!"

"Damn," Wei echoed.

I blew out a breath. "All right, all right, at least we got it done."

I didn't want to process how close I had come to real failure, but a closed rift was a closed rift.

"Come on," Hugo said, seeming to sense my thoughts. "We succeeded, even if it's not how you wanted to do it."

I sighed and slowly swam the drones back to me, avoiding the firemen and the crowd. I could have passed out from relief when I got them zipped in my backpack again.

"That really was impressive," Hugo said as he slipped his gear back into his bag.

"Yeah."

I rubbed my wrists, stiff from the effort of the last few seconds. I heard a twig snap just a hair closer than I would have liked. It made me jump, and I turned to see the rest of the crew approach. Tamar and Wei joined me and Hugo by the edge of the water.

"You really don't suck," Tamar said, flipping her braid over her bare shoulder.

She looked as casual as you could imagine, in a bikini top and shorts. No one in this world would guess she didn't belong there. Wei didn't say anything. He just shook my hand with both of his.

"Can we leave now?" Tamar asked.

"*Oui*." Hugo grinned.

Once the on-site aspect of the job was over, crews usually hightailed it back to headquarters. I always wanted to see how the encounter cleaned up, so I lingered.

"I'll stay," I said. "Meet you guys back at HQ for post-op."

"Right on," Wei said.

He started walking toward downtown. Tamar waved as she headed opposite Wei. They were out of sight by the time the news vans showed.

"I'm glad to have you on my team," Hugo said with a grin, shaking my hand.

"Is that a formal offer?"

"Wouldn't jump the gun and say yes until you have all the details, but it's a welcome on my end," he said. He had finished packing and shouldered his bag. I think he wanted to say more, but he didn't. I wondered if I should say something, but I didn't. I watched him walk away with a wave.

It took me a long time to come down from a job. The adrenaline high powered me through the work, but I hit some pretty solid lows once it wore off. I was slow to get the computer in the bag and my sequencer in my pocket. I thought about the rift and how unstable it had been. I—

"Oh shit! What happened?" a husky voice said beside me.

I turned. It was a purple-haired giant and his huge dog. It felt weird to encounter someone who hadn't witnessed it all, jarring almost. I felt like I had been alive for days working to clean up the mess he was walking up on, yet to him the experience was just a simple walk with his dog amongst the Fort Lauderdale high-rises.

"Oh…um," I stammered as his eyes landed on me.

He gave me a warm smile, half genuine greeting and half amused camaraderie. "You see what happened?"

"Aliens," I said, unable to help myself. That was my go-to answer when people asked about my involvement in things. I didn't like lying, but I could abide some flagrant fiction.

He shook his head. He had a sort of modern Steven Tyler vibe, big mouth and creamy skin. His clothes gave the impression of being too small, but it was because he was so tall, which also gave him the illusion of thinness. He was wearing tight jeans and a sleeveless, blue tie-dye shirt that was almost a crop top on him.

"The grays?" he asked, faking a gasp.

I hadn't expected him to answer. I shrugged, suddenly feeling super dumb. But I tried to play it cool, flipping loose locs out of my face before I crossed my arms. My whole ponytail was probably seven or eight kinds of messy, but I pretended it looked the way I wanted.

"I mean, there were explosions," I said, going for aloof. "So, maybe not them."

He raised his eyebrows in a way that suggested he was impressed. His billowy purple curls were practically in his eyes. Then his face scrunched as he asked, "The grays don't blow things up?"

"Naw. I think only the green ones like to catch that much attention."

"Fair enough." He looked like he was considering it as he surveyed the building. His humongous Great Dane nuzzled my backpack. I watched the dog while its owner watched the crowd.

"What's your dog called?" I asked at the exact moment he asked me something.

"What?" we asked in unison.

A laugh played on his mouth.

"I said, what do you think happens to the ghosts?" He leaned slightly toward me, his question becoming private in the action. I felt my mouth drop open in surprise. He shrugged in a way that read as bashful, but his eyes were light with confidence. "When a building burns down, I mean. They're suddenly homeless, right?"

I laughed and shook my head. The only thing I could really think about was that I needed to get away from him as fast as I could. I wanted to stay and talk to him. Just having his eyes on me made me feel warm and tongue-tied. And that was a problem since this wasn't even my home-verse.

"Would it matter?" I shrugged. "Ghosts who haunt office buildings are probably boring."

He crossed his arms. "Oh, so only interesting ghosts can have homes?"

"I mean if the ghost is interesting enough, people turn that home into a tourist site. So, maybe they need to get their shit together, exploit their afterlife a little."

He laughed. "I'm Tidus," he said.

"Martin."

He held out his hand, and I shook it. We stood in an awkward but not unwelcome silence for a few minutes. His dog sat by him but kept his big dark eyes on me. I wanted to pet him.

"I…did you work there?" he asked.

"Naw, I don't."

"What—"

"Hey, it's been nice talking to you. I have to…a place I was going, so…" I waved as I shouldered my backpack. Both the dog and the man looked disappointed.

"Good luck," Tidus said. "His name is Bowser, by the way."

I waved again and tried to walk away from the encounter site.

And that's where I should have left it with Tidus. But it wasn't. I turned back, and I said something clever and gave him my phone number. He thinks I travel a lot for work, which I do. We have messaged each other every day since. I knew things about this guy. Things I liked. I tried to focus on what Hugo and the others were talking about, but I wondered if they needed to know what Tidus and I had said to each other.

I looked at my phone, my real, capable of making calls and receiving messages phone. And I looked at the messages he sent me. *Hi. Bowser says hi. Do you think dogs can see the ghosts of other dogs? I like tacos more than pizza but pizza more than hot dogs. Hot dogs are not tacos, Martin.*

I knew it would be an issue if I kept talking to him. But what could I do? I was a romantic, sure, but I wasn't dramatic. I couldn't risk everything the team was working on for more conversation with him. I liked my job, worked hard, and I had ten years with the company. Tidus had his role to play. I had mine.

I typed out a message quickly and hit send before I could change my mind. It was some generic and horribly disguised lie about work taking me away from communications. For both our sakes, I shut off the phone. Then I focused, really focused, on what Hugo was raving about.

# SECTION 4

## *Too many trains, not enough stations*

"Open your shit and let's do this. I'm only gonna explain this once," Kiki said, tossing their backpack onto the nearest table. They pulled a laptop out and connected to the smart screen. I felt suddenly like I was in a college lecture I hadn't prepared for.

"Kiki, thank you—" Hugo said.

"Naw," Kiki said, holding up a well-groomed hand, decorated with gold rings. They looked less the goth and more trendy mechanic. They had on gold jewelry, an army green jacket with a gold sequined shirt beneath it, and matching green joggers. They also made an easy show of gold stilettos and huge gold shades, which they didn't take off. They said to Hugo, "Don't start with me, Del Mar. Now—"

The rest of us popped open our laptops in a hurry.

"Click this," Kiki said, clicking on the network button for MVP.

"This is your project dashboard link."

I clicked the designated link, and it took me to a program that at first looked like a minimalist social media site. There were eighteen photos on the page. The photos were our respective observation subjects. It had taken most of the night, but we had worked through the initial packets the data team had sent, and we were able to select a core group of subjects. Hugo assigned each of us two people per category. No one acknowledged the irony or the issue of me being assigned to the Tiduses.

I avoided looking at the Tidus circle. Instead, I looked at the Peter Rogerses. The Peters existed in only four universes, so the four photos cycled slowly within their circle. He was in his seventies and didn't give me the same gut bubbles as Tidus did.

"Each circle links you to the observation profile. On their group page, each individual has a link that will automatically bring up an observation log. It'll then catalog it, store it, duplicate it, and feed the data to us for analysis. Got it?"

"Got it," we all said.

"Okay, so let's go in." Kiki yawned and clicked one of the links for the fake profile on their mock dashboard. The screen opened on a video feed of the data lab. Mason was sitting at a computer, bobbing his head along with whatever music must have been playing. Luca wasn't in the shot.

"The video comes up automatically. Click this to switch to audio and click this to switch to quantum."

"You already set up the video feeds?" Hugo asked, his voice a little disappointed. He was clicking accusingly through the links for one of his subjects.

Kiki shrugged. "There's only one. We put 'em in the living room of each person's house—or equivalent, since not all of them live like that. We figured you'd want to move them or add some or whatever you do. We had to start somewhere."

Hugo must have gotten a burst of inspiration because he was scribbling on the blank paper he likes to write on. I leaned into Wei a little to see what Hugo was writing, but I couldn't read it.

"It says that if we can stay awake through the whole lecture, Hugo'll buy us drinks," Wei pretended to translate. "Kiki included."

"Thank God! I'm fucking fading," Kiki said, running a hand over their brow.

"It doesn't say that," Hugo muttered. He just kept writing.

I asked, "Why do you write like that, bro? Can you read that?"

"It's not poorly written," he snapped, his accent rising with his indignation. "It's in French."

"A-hem," Kiki said, purposefully over-pronouncing the syllables.

"Sorry."

"Anyway, try to break the site if you can. It's not like we ever fucking leave, so come to the lab if you have questions or if something doesn't work. Whatever, whenever, I guess. Are there questions?"

Hugo was the only one to raise his hand.

I looked back at the computer. In following along, I was now on a video feed of Peter Rogers of A-class universe 239ACE. He was sleeping in an armchair. I opened the audio and heard him breathe, the sound almost imperceptibly delayed from the image on the screen. It made him seem like he was breathing from far away, and in a way, he was. I opened the quantum data screen, but nothing interesting presented itself. I sighed. I wanted to tell Peter to be more interesting, but there was no way to do that and also science. I switched to the other Peter Rogers feeds, and they were all in the middle of equally uninteresting tasks.

"What if it's not a quantum issue?"

"What?"

The room was looking at me, and I shrugged. "Nothing. Never mind, my mouth was answering my brain."

"Your brain answered itself *using* your mouth," Wei corrected.

I glared at him. "Keep that shit to yourself, guy."

He just laughed.

"All trains and no stations," Hugo teased.

"Sure, buddy."

The meeting went fast after that. Hugo asked a handful of questions, most of which Kiki said we could figure out. Hugo wanted to have another meeting to set up observation schedules, but we talked him into giving us a break first. We were packing up when Luca came into the room with a rolled-up poster.

"Hey," he said, waving to the room generally.

We either answered or waved.

"I just brought something for…uh…Martin." Luca pointed the poster a little in my direction.

I guess my surprise showed on my face because Luca grinned at the floor. Kiki and Tamar cackled, passing by him arm in arm. Hugo was still scribbling away on his pages as he walked, using his laptop as a hard surface. Wei gave me a deep bow as he left. He flashed Luca a heart shape, and then it was the two of us.

"I thought you'd like this," Luca said.

I unrolled it carefully. Printed in ombre triangles was the thirty-two-sided atom-like shape I had made at the Fort Lauderdale rift closure.

"Wow," I said, amazed. "How do you make these?"

"We can map the location of each QD on a three-dimensional plane because they all feed us longitude, latitude, and elevation coordinates."

"This is really cool. Thank you."

"You're welcome."

I remembered talking about how the rifts were forming more frequently and the weird way that particular rift seemed to reopen.

"Luca, I have a few questions. Would you wanna go to the cafeteria and eat with me?"

I had asked the question with purely science in mind, but I wondered for a moment if he would read something more in it. The light behind his eyes at the idea of spending a dinner talking science told me he was in it for the science too. Or maybe he was more a fan of mine than I understood.

The cafeteria was a basement plaza in the Hub with several restaurants and shops. The restaurants were really just places where food was stored, reheated, and served. Each was categorized by source universe, since everything that came in had to go out. The shops were storerooms where you could get equipment, entertainment, clothes, and other things, again labeled by universe for return when done. It was vaguely like the student union of a college. I went to the endless gyoza restaurant. Luca went for cereal. We met at a table near the middle of the room, surrounded by other MVP employees.

"It's been a while since I've eaten in here," Luca said, opening the box of Honoy-Os cereal. I watched him dump it into a bowl then add a box of Froze'n Flakes on top.

"Same."

He looked around. And so did I. I didn't recognize any of the faces.

"I never realized how many people are here," I said.

"Right, way more than I remember."

I popped a few of the dumplings into my mouth.

"So, MLK, what are your questions?"

"Oh…well, I was wondering if you noticed anything weird about the rift?" I gestured at the poster, safely rolled up again.

He nearly spit out his cereal. "Of course I noticed."

"Tell me."

We talked about how the rift was reopening quickly, and it was impossible to know why. He said he had tried to run some analysis on the data by area, region, time, and people, but nothing seemed to hold. It was a normal enough rift on all bases the drones could measure.

"That's all I know," Luca concluded.

"Well, I messaged a buddy of mine and told her to keep me up to date on rifts other techs reported as weird. I also sent her your report, so we'll see what she thinks," I told him. I had sent the report and the message to a coordinator I trusted.

"Really?"

"Yeah, I mean I said I would."

He grinned and ate his cereal. After a few minutes of silence, I opened the conversation back up.

"Have you ever looked in on your counterparts?" I asked.

"I know what verses they're in." He shrugged. "One is a TV star."

"I don't even know where mine is." I then amended, "Was."

"What happened to him?"

I ummed and watched Luca's face. "Mikyea Winslow drowned when she was eight. That's all I know."

He blinked at me, his expression carefully passive. I wouldn't have been surprised if he was surprised. I had transitioned years ago, more than half my life.

"Bummer. Drowned? And you didn't?" he said finally.

I couldn't tell if he had questions or if his idea of me had changed. I guess that was half the point of passing, or better yet, of finding people you didn't need to pass with. Time would tell what Luca really thought. It always did.

"Naw, I did drown. Or at least I started to, but my stepdad saved me. Mom was only dating Apollo at the time. Then when I was ten, they got married, and he adopted me. I took his name when I was thirteen, for his fortieth birthday. I changed my whole name to Martin Logan when I did that—made the paperwork easier."

"Back up. You have a dad called Apollo King?"

"Right. He…uh…is exactly what you would expect a guy named Apollo King to be like."

I wondered why I didn't know where my counterpart had been from. I had been so surprised to learn I was universe-unique, I hadn't thought much of why.

I asked Luca around a mouthful of gyoza, "Could you find that universe?"

Luca looked confused. "Your home-verse?"

"Naw, Mikyea's. I mean, can you find the verse of someone who's dead?"

He squinted at me, concerned. "Why?"

I was brewing an idea, but it hadn't fully come together. "I don't know. If I had to think it through—and I'm just spitballing ideas—we're all doing this research because James Dugan did the thing, right? Well, that was what, six years ago? And they only found sixteen verses with him in them. What if some of his counterparts had died in some other way? Did anything happen in those verses?"

"Can the dead impact the multi-verse?" Luca said.

"I dunno. But we *are* studying universe-multi people, so I feel like it bears asking."

"Bet. Well, write up the question and run it through Hugo. He's the leader, so I can't go on a project without his say-so."

"Bet," I said. Then I remembered the lab meeting. "Oh shit, what time is it?"

Luca flashed me his wristwatch. I was late.

"Shit, I have to run," I said, jumping up. "Luca, I—"

"I get it," Luca said, standing too.

I grinned at him and grabbed my poster. "You know, I need a frame for this."

"Good luck, it's a weird size."

I laughed and ran from the Hub.

Hugo and the rest weren't mad I was late. Hugo was translating his notes onto yet another white board. Tamar was filing her fingernails into points like lime green talons. Wei was sitting straight up but was literally asleep, his eyelashes perfect lines on his cheeks.

"Hey all," I panted.

"You okay?" Hugo asked.

"Fine, I can't breathe 'cause ran," I gasped. And like the unfit chubby guy I was, I tried to breathe less loud so they would really believe I was fine. By the looks on their faces, it must not have been working. "God, why am I so out of shape?"

"Well, it's good timing."

# SECTION 5

## *The project is restricted*

I was surprised by how complicated the observation schedule was. I had eighteen subjects, which was two people per category. And according to Hugo's plan, we were to work eight hours a day, six days a week. Not that Sunday was a day off—we just only worked six hours. I tried not to groan and reminded myself that I liked my job.

"Everyone online?" Kiki asked when all of us were ready and settled at the table in the center of the lab. They sat in a swivel chair near a bank of computers looking at us. Luca and Mason were walking around, half looking at our computers, half watching the progress of separate programs they were running.

"Ready," Hugo said.

"I love this part," Tamar said, genuinely excited. "I love H-HIA. They're all so weird."

Wei made a whistling sound and flapped his hands imitating a bird. His hand-bird fluttered off over his head.

"What was that?" I laughed.

"Take-off," he said, looking at me over the taupe sunglasses he was half wearing. "The bird took off."

"I would've gone with—" I made an engine sound and launched my hand off the table like a rocket.

"How about," Luca said, pretending to take off his shirt. Wei cheered, and I gave him a few risqué clicking noises.

"Luca wins," Tamar said. "The rest of you, three out of ten."

"Three?" Wei and I said together.

"*C'est le bordel*," Hugo said, rubbing his temples. "Can we move on?"

We laughed and turned back to Kiki. They walked us through the site again and had us pull up our first subject. I chose to start in on the Tiduses. Tidus of A-Class Universe 2940FOX was who Hugo had assigned to be the base Tidus, so I would be observing him the most. Not like it wasn't already an issue—let's just make sure I got to stare at him every other day. I reconsidered telling Hugo about texting Tidus, but the video screen popped up. And the room was empty.

"FOX Tidus isn't in his house. Or at least isn't in this room," I said, turning the image of his empty room to the group.

"Oh, this is exciting." Hugo grinned, leaning toward the screen.

"I like sectionals as much as the next guy," I said, "but I don't think this is how it works."

"This is our chance to problem solve," Hugo said. He clapped me on the shoulders and shook me a little.

"There's information in your packet. Maybe we can find him?" Luca said, pulling his chair next to me at the table. I opened the Tidus book and turned to the index, making an unhappy sound. Luca patted my shoulder.

"Yup. I hear ya," he sympathized.

The rest of the eight hours of the first day of observation was actually painful. Luca and I spent three hours trying to figure out where FOX Tidus might be based on his data. We had it narrowed down to work and school, but he also had several friends he visited, he went to the gym, and he liked to hang out at parks with Bowser. We were just about to scrap him when he walked in the door. I was able to observe him take Bowser out, bring him back in, and feed him. Then he left the room and didn't come back. By the end of the day, I had observed seven empty rooms across four subjects. Hugo didn't think my ranking of their living room sets was very funny.

Tamar had similar visibility issues with several of her subjects, one of whom sat in his living room the whole hour, but she could only see his left foot. Wei was successful with his first subject, but his second group had a few counterparts who looked like they were moving out of their houses. All of those would have to be reset. Hugo spent the whole time helping us and didn't actually get to any of his people.

It was nearly seven before Kiki called it. They had been watching the data feeds and was unsatisfied by the information coming in. Finally, they announced, "I can't do any more of this. I'm leaving. I suggest the rest of you leave too."

"Wait for me," Tamar and Wei said, standing.

"Come on now," Hugo said. But even he was spent. I yawned, and then he yawned, and then Luca yawned.

"Okay, we start again tomorrow," Hugo said. He made no move to leave, though. He sat and pulled some paper and a pen out of his backpack. By the time I looked up from what Hugo was doing, the other three were gone.

"I need food," Luca said, turning to me. "Want to eat with me?"

"Sure." I grinned, noticing Mason sitting in a chair. His beanie was pulled low over his eyes.

"Is he asleep?"

"Mas?" Luca said.

Mason started and stood up.

"You wanna come get dinner?" I asked.

"Me?"

"Sure, me and Luca are going."

Mason gave Luca a wide, toothy grin.

Luca looked at him carefully. "We'll probably eat in the Hub. You up for that?"

"I think I can handle it."

"Hugo, you wanna come?" I asked, even though I knew what he would say.

"I will soon." He dismissed me with a wave.

"Let's go then," Luca said. I followed them out of the room.

We ate tiredly, then Mason wanted to see the stars, so Luca and I walked with him to the observation deck on the roof of the Hub.

"Gentle winds," a guard said as we passed his station. They were there to protect HQ from dangerous sea life and weather. Looking at the rocking horizon, I didn't envy them.

"Come this way," Mason called, leading us to a lounge area.

The three of us lay down on separate metal benches bolted to the surface of the building. Lying down, even on the metal, felt phenomenal. I hadn't realized how tense and exhausted I was until I was horizontal.

"Dude, that was rough," I sighed. "Is it always like that?"

"Never," Luca said with a laugh.

"Really?" I half sat up to look at him.

"We don't have to *observe* universe-unique people. When we do make observations, it is usually of stationary events like rifts," Mason said. His voice was soft and low, melodic.

"So, you can see why nothing we have done has worked," Luca continued.

"I had fun," Mason said.

I literally stared into space. For all I understood about the multiverse, space was still mysterious, beautiful, and scary.

"We have to fix the relays," Mason said.

"What?" Luca asked.

"The data relays. They aren't strong enough. They're being spread too thin. Our model underestimated."

"What does that mean?" I asked.

Mason sat up. "In order to get data from one verse to here, you have to set up a communication relay. A receiver on this end, coded to this verse, communicates with a transmitter on the other end, coded to that verse. Set up in between is a relay station coded equally for both verses."

"How can something be in two verses at once?" I asked, sitting up.

"Carefully and artificially. We carefully balance the quantum resonance by forcing particles in and out at random. It's basically rapidly tuning particles, bouncing data from the there-verse to the here-verse."

"Sounds bananas," I said, not really knowing where to put that information in my brain. "I have faith you can figure it out. What we really need, though, is a way to keep drones trained on a subject no matter where they are. The stationary thing isn't going to work."

"Amen," Luca said.

"Maybe you could do it, Martin."

"What do you mean?"

"Well, in order to keep the QD on a moving target, there would have to be someone commanding them where to go. You're the one who can control the largest number of drones, even if it's only at one one-hundredth of the capacity we would need for the project."

I thought about the cramp in my hands from controlling sixty-four groups at the last rift closing. One one hundredth sounded like it would kill me. "Ouch."

I turned back to the sky. It was a clear night. I felt sorry for most people whenever I was on the station roof at night. The sky was unlike anything most people would ever see in their lives, especially in advanced verses. There was no smog, no light pollution, distortion only from the water, which amplified everything. A shooting star crossed, and I half expected the sky to ripple like water.

"Why couldn't we get a team of drone techs and make it their job?" I asked.

"The project's restricted," Luca said.

"What?"

"Why do you think the data team is so small?"

I looked at him, and he looked back. Then his expression changed, and he shrugged. "I forget you're new to this. Yeah, so it really is just the seven of us. The founders don't want the project public. That's why you're on a closed network."

"I didn't know that." I added that to the pile of suspicions I had about the project.

"It was a good idea," Mason said, sounding sleepy.

I went home about an hour later. No one was around, so I sat at the piano. I played and thought about my mother. She had taught me and my brother to play, but for very different reasons. She wanted him to get involved with an art because she thought it would help him find peace and focus. Me, she wanted to be like her. I saw myself like I saw my brother.

"Lint," I said suddenly, into the music.

"What?" Tamar asked.

I jumped, banging my elbow on the piano.

"Sorry. I was listening. I didn't mean to scare you."

I breathed. "You're fine, I was just…"

She nodded and moved closer. She put her elbows on the piano and leaned in to look at the strings. "Why'd ya say lint?"

"I was thinking about my brother. He used to call me lint because I would follow him around so closely. I'm so small compared to him. He's a big dude, like our biological father, tall…meaty."

She smiled. "Sounds hot."

The huff of air that escaped me was more gasp than laugh. "Gross. Besides, what about Mason?"

She squinted at me. "What *about* Mason? What do you know?"

I laughed. "Nothing, I was just talking to him—"

"What did he say?" she demanded, getting closer to me.

I put my hands up. "That the communication relays were weak."

She sighed. "He's such a nerd."

"A nice nerd."

"We aren't friends, Martin, so mind your business."

I squinted at her and whispered. "Are we friends enough to talk about how sketchy this whole project is?"

She narrowed her eyes on me. I couldn't tell if she was trying to talk herself into talking to me or trying to talk herself out of it.

"What do you know?" she finally said.

"Well, I was talking to the guys about how the observation points were irritating because the drones were stationary. Then I said let's get more people and Luca said…"

My train of thought derailed. Everything said tonight dropped into my head, stirred around like soup, then solidified into a single idea. A solution, to be specific.

"We don't *have* to control them all," I shouted.

"Um." Tamar blinked.

"Holy shit, I have to go," I said, jumping up from the bench.

"What about—"

"I don't know. I was just thinking out loud again," I said.

"You're so dumb, Martin."

"Sorry, keep talking. Here…sit," I sighed, then I made a few expressive gestures with my eyes.

She still looked annoyed, but she sat. I started to play, whispering urgently, "I didn't want them to overhear us."

"Who?"

"Anyone, Hugo, I don't know. Jeez, don't you know anything about villainy?"

"You watch too many movies."

I laughed and leaned toward her. "Anyway, why would the bosses restrict this project? As techs, we're told we have access to all the information from the research being done at HQ. But then we don't, because Luca said his reports about rifts are being suppressed. And so is this. I had no idea they restricted research."

"Really?"

I nodded. "So, they have to be up to something. They're hiding our work and Luca's."

She narrowed her eyes at me. "How do I know I can trust you?"

I grinned. "Because up until three weeks ago, I was a tech. The founders don't even know our names. Wanna know how I know I can trust you?"

She made an *I'm waiting* gesture with her head.

"Because you're an asshole."

She smiled at me. "I didn't know they're suppressing Luca's work."

I stood again. "Listen, we can talk about this more later, but I had an idea—a fucking epiphany. I have to tell them, wanna come?"

She shrugged. I hurried from the room with her striding behind me, boots loud on the tile. We crossed HQ in record time. I pressed the code into the door four times before anyone came to it.

"For fuck's sake, can't you wait for a person to get their happy ass down a hallway?" Kiki snapped.

"I need to talk to everyone," I said.

They blinked at me. "You know people sleep, right?"

"Hey, bitch," Tamar said, kissing Kiki on the cheek.

"Hey, bitch back."

I moved past them and started running again.

"That boy's lost his mind," I heard Kiki say.

I practically kicked open the computer room door. Luca was cleaning up some of the debris from the failure of the day. He looked horrified to see me.

"Martin, what is it? Did something happen?"

"Yes," I shouted, actually hugging him. "I had a fucking idea."

Because he was so petite, I nearly lifted him off the ground. I set him right and then asked, "Where's Mason?"

"He went to bed." Luca grinned, and then he took a step away from me.

I probably shouldn't have hugged him. "Sorry."

"It's okay…I…what is your idea?"

"Go get Mason." Luca left, and I went to the board and drew a diagram I thought Hugo would be proud of. I added a few lines of drone code that could achieve what I wanted.

"What's all the commotion?" Hugo said, coming into the room. He looked like he had been asleep.

"Martin has an idea," Tamar said. She leaned against the table where we had been working. I watched her pick something out of her teeth, the green on her nails bright against black lipstick.

"*Bon travail*. What is it?"

"Where'd you come from, man?" I asked.

He pointed and rubbed his eyes like that was answer enough. I guess it was. In my excitement, I must have run right past him sleeping in the anteroom.

"All right, Martin," Luca said. Mason followed him, wearing only pants and a beanie.

"Come over here, look."

Mason was pretty hot shirtless. As everyone moved around, I caught Tamar's eyes and gestured subtly to Mason. I flashed her all my fingers to say he was a ten out of ten. She rolled her eyes, considered him, and flashed me eight of her fingers. I gave her a *good enough gesture.* She gave me the middle finger.

"Martin, I want to go to bed, so…please," Kiki said.

"Is that an invitation?" I said with a wink. They looked at me like my life was temporary, so I surrendered and moved on. "The problem we're having is that no one's in the cameras when we're ready to observe them, and the search cost is astronomical, right?"

There was assorted agreement.

"Okay, so Mason said I'm great with drones. I was thinking we could move some of them around, but it would take one hundred of me to be able to track each person."

"Wait," Hugo said. "I'm not following."

I blinked, breathed, and started again. "Basically, the whole observation portion of the experiment is set up as if we were watching rifts, *stationary* things, which is y'all's background, right?"

They agreed.

"*But* the cameras are in the wrong place, or the subject is in the wrong place."

"Okay," Hugo said.

"See, for me the rifts and the drones are never stationary. They both move in some way. They are flows and mixes of particles. As a good tech, you have to be able to anticipate where a particle will be, right?"

"Right."

"But as a great tech, you attach the drone to the particle as soon as you find it and leave it attached until you need it. Then you don't spend your time looking for shit." It felt weird to have the attention of people who were smarter. I hoped I was explaining this enough.

"Oh, I get it," Mason said. "Instead of attaching the drones to the wall and then searching for the subject, we attach them to the subject directly."

"How would we see them if the damn thing is on them?" Tamar asked me.

"When the time comes to observe, we can just move that single drone. We don't have to move them all at once."

Mason smiled. "That's brilliant."

"We can make the laptops use the drone operating system in the sequencer—honestly you could use my program. The drone lives on the subject, collecting whatever passive data. Then we move them around for observation purposes when we need to see the subject."

"The signal won't be strong enough for commands that complicated or for that much data," Luca warned.

"We're going to boost the signal anyway," Kiki said. "So—"

"So I get to build a better antenna," Mason shouted. He stood and actually high-fived me.

"Put a shirt on first, buddy," Hugo suggested. Then he stood and looked at me. "This is a really good idea, Martin."

"Yeah, I'm impressed," Kiki said, shaking my hand.

"What do we need to execute it?" Luca said.

"Coffee, because I know we aren't getting any sleep," Tamar sighed.

I blinked. "Wait, I still want to go to bed."

"That an invitation?" Kiki said with a wink.

Hugo laughed and flung an arm around my shoulder. "Science waits for no one."

"Calm your spurs. Can't science wait till morning?" I grumbled, trying to get out from under Hugo's arm.

Apparently, it couldn't.

# SECTION 6

## *The joystick doesn't make it any more fun*

It took seventy-two hours, with a few necessary breaks, to complete the changes I suggested. Mason and Kiki were able to boost the relays enough that we could send multiple commands to every drone in every subject group and still get complete data back from each. After we got the system set up, I spent a day training both research and data teams to control the drones. It felt weird moving only one drone at a time. The others caught on fast enough that I was able to show them advanced maneuvers for the fun of it. Mason, in his infinite genius, managed to snag some joysticks that turned it into something more like a video game.

For as much as we achieved, we were exhausted. Hugo decided to give us a day off. I told him to throw a party in our common room to celebrate. To my surprise, he agreed. It was weird at first having the data team in the lab, but it was nice to just be people for once.

"I'm very proud of everyone here. I think we've pushed the envelope in our respective fields. I have no regrets selecting everyone I did for this team, and I know we're an honor to our company, to each other, and to ourselves," Hugo said, toasting.

We cheered and sipped whatever was in our glasses.

"I can't wait until we actually get data we can use," Hugo said more quietly to the three of us standing in his vicinity. It was Tamar, Kiki, and I. Luca, Wei, and Mason were picking at the food table across the room.

"Hopefully it answers Don's questions," Tamar said with only a small bitterness.

"I think it might answer more questions than that," Kiki said.

"What do you mean?" I asked.

"I think it might answer Luca's, too." They shrugged.

"How?"

"What are Luca's questions?" Hugo asked.

"For the past few years, rifts have been popping up more frequently. Some are in locations where we've never charted one. For all we know about rifts and tuning, we can't explain the new occurrences."

"Who knew there was still so much to figure out?" I said. "From the tech world, the rules are pretty set and what they tell you about the multi-verse is pretty consistent."

"So we all thought, but then we lost 345BGH and 346BGK," Kiki said. The glint in their eye was obvious.

In 2012, A-Class Universes 345BGH and 346BGK collided, forming one universe. The theories around it are conspiratorial. Some say it was because a baseball team in one verse defied statistical probability and won the World Series. Some say it was because the other universe elected an unlikely president. Either way, we aren't allowed to talk about it, so everyone talked about it. It was treated like a black spot on the reputation of MVP because it couldn't be predicted or prevented.

"Multi-verse collapse happens," Hugo said. I forgot some people also say it was just the natural order of the universes.

"I can't even imagine the chaos in 346BGH still," Tamar said. We toasted to our relief at not having to be involved in that verse very often.

Hugo looked around, and then said softly, "I think we should work on Luca's question. But I think we need to be careful."

"Why?" Tamar asked.

Hugo looked at her, his gaze steady. "Because if MVP *wanted* it researched, they'd put a team on it. We work for them, and that is the end of it."

It didn't *feel* like the end of it, but I didn't say anything.

"Hey," Luca said, stepping up.

"Luca," Kiki said, shrugging off the tension. They draped their arm around him. "What side do you take on 345BGH and 346BGK?"

"It was the baseball all the way."

Kiki practically shrieked. "How can you say that? The president—"

I watched them argue. Techs had crews we worked on, but we were generally isolated. I hadn't felt close to anyone I worked with in years. My connections were always outside MVP, back home with my parents and my brother and sister. I had a few friends back there too, but no one I kept in touch with. I had even considered a chance with Tidus, but that was over.

My people believed I worked in a special division of the FBI, and that I traveled a lot and was sworn to secrecy. Occasionally, I would watch crime TV in some other-verse and go home and tell my family that story and pretend it was part of the work I was doing. Looking around the lab, however, I felt a part of something. Wei and Hugo were talking by the food table. Mason was investigating the piano. Tamar and Kiki were facing off against Luca, who stood alone defending the baseball side of the debate. Then all three turned to me.

"Martin?" Luca said.

"Uh, what…?"

"Which do you think it was?" Kiki said.

I laughed. "I think it was the actor winning his first Oscar."

They erupted.

"How—"

"That's the least surprising thing—"

"Martin, be serious—"

I laughed. "It's the only thing that happened in both universes."

They just bombarded me with evidence against it. I laughed so much my eyes watered.

Turns out the party was the last fun I would have for a few days. The next morning started off surprisingly depressing. I got a message from my coordinator friend, Fern. It was a note plus a link to a memo from her supervisor.

Her message read: *Thanks for the heads up. Probably accounts for a lot.* And the memo detailed the collapsing of a bridge near a school, killing three. The news would report it as a construction issue. The memo, however, explained that a rift opened at one end of the bridge and it lost enough ground to the there-verse that it finally collapsed.

I went to the data lab feeling low-key impacted. I showed the notice to Luca when I arrived, thinking it would give him a sense of justice. He quietly showed it to everyone else. And no one spoke about it. Hugo roused the group with a pep talk that worked well enough. After that, we started observations. The new system worked so perfectly, the few glitches went almost unnoticed. We were all so focused that it was silent for a few hours.

Unfortunately, it was boring. We started on the current day in Hugo's schedule, which meant we were on the Friday subjects. The Kaydee McPhersons were four years old, and I spent two hours watching one watch cartoons on her tablet and the other throw a fit because she didn't want to eat waffles for breakfast. I moved the drone around the room at first, looking at the house, trying to note anything out of the quantum ordinary. Then I just positioned it and watched.

By the end of the day, I was disappointed. The urgency of setting up the experiment and making sure everything worked had given me the false impression that universe-multi people were on the brink of destroying the multi-verse every single minute of every single day. But that proved wrong when the only interesting thing that happened in the whole eight hours was that Wei farted so loud and it smelled so bad, we had to leave the room for five minutes.

"Good lord, James Dugan might have been the only interesting one," I said, standing and rubbing my eyes when Hugo's alarm went off, concluding the day.

"He was only interesting when he exploded," Wei corrected. "He might've been just as boring."

"Well, we'll find out soon enough," Tamar said.

Hugo picked up his hat from the table and put it on. "What do you mean?"

Tamar glared at him. "I told you I want to investigate them more."

"Tamar, I don't think—"

She crossed her arms. "The founders want us to figure out if any of these people will pull a Dugan, right? Well, we need to know more about that guy."

Hugo didn't flinch under her harsh voice, but he didn't posture either. "Who will do your observations?"

"Kiki can do mine," Tamar said.

"Luca can do mine," I added.

Tamar's head snapped around to me. "What?"

"I told you, I'm going with you."

"Kiki and Luca can do what now?" Kiki asked, Luca behind them.

"Hugo is letting Martin and me investigate James Dugan more, maybe find some history, but we need someone to watch our groups for those days."

"Naw, I don't want to do that," Kiki said.

"Sure," Luca said.

I cheered. "My man."

He grinned at me. I liked that grin. Maybe I had a weakness for dimples.

"You'll do it," Tamar said to Kiki.

"When? I have other shit to do."

"Not for a while," Hugo said. "We need base data on everyone before you go off, so maybe not for two weeks."

Everyone mumbled some answer but didn't discuss it further. The crowd dispersed to finish what they were working on so they could go home.

"How was it?" Luca asked as I put finishing touches on an observation.

"Boring. I like reality TV, but this isn't it. The joystick doesn't make it any more fun." I laughed.

"Sounds like my ex," Luca said with a wink.

I giggled. "Ditto."

"Maybe tomorrow will be better," he said, patting my shoulder.

It wasn't. Saturday and Sunday were just a rapid-fire stroll through all sixteen base subjects. We didn't observe the universe-unique ones. I also got another memo from Fern, detailing three more losses to unexplainable rifts—a kid on a bike and an elderly couple in a car. Feeling a low-grade horror for the general multi-verse under the tedium of observations was like having a near fever, like 99.5. Not well but not sick.

Things didn't get interesting until Wednesday. My first subject was FOX Tidus. I found him in the coffee shop. It was seven in the morning, and according to the reference book, he would have been there for about an hour already. He looked settled in, cleaning an espresso machine and talking to a customer. I clicked into the audio.

"I wish there was more I could do, but the offering depends on the bakery," he was saying, "We sell what gets sourced, and today it's Fay's."

"When will you source from Mario's again?"

"I'm not sure. You know how sporadic the local movement can be. When they volunteer, they volunteer."

"Fay's is in Georgia, so I wouldn't call it local," the customer snapped and started walking away.

"Have a good day?" FOX Tidus said. He ran a hand through that lavender hair. It looked like it had been touched up.

I typed some notes in the appropriate section of the form. *Does his work location overlap with any other Tidus? Does it depend on the volume of H-HIA interactions a person has?* I thought about that last one more. We couldn't say James Dugan was charismatic, likable, charming, nothing. FOX Tidus was charming. I remember being drawn to him that day in Fort Lauderdale, and his messages always left me buzzing with some feeling I couldn't place. He had an energy around him. But who was Dugan?

"Tidus, I finished last night's spoilage. Would you mind dumping the garbage?" a man asked. His name tag said Manager Cody.

"Sure."

I followed him around to the back of the shop. The spoilage turned out to be several boxes of old pastries. I half expected Tidus to put them into the trash bins in the room, but he hoisted one and started out the back door. I followed. I watched him dump the box into the trash compactor across the alley and then head back to the shop. He did this with two more boxes.

It was the last box that surprised me. As he was carrying it out, a homeless man, woman, and dog crossed into the alley. They watched Tidus but didn't say anything, though you could see the question they wanted to ask. They wanted the pastries. Tidus didn't look at them, but he left the box on the ground by the compactor instead of putting it in like he had done the others. Then he went back inside. Manager Cody was waiting there.

"I saw that," Cody said.

Tidus just shrugged and tried to walk past him.

"Tidus, you can't give them food. It encourages them to stick around."

Tidus turned and said in a tone that was practical and impassioned but not loud, "Cody, they are *people*, not stray cats, and it's danishes, not gold."

"I still have to tell Gwen."

Tidus waved a *so be it* hand and went back to the front of the store. The person called Gwen was taking customers, and Tidus fell in line with her, saying nothing about it. I felt that pull again, that want to know more. Charming and kind. I wrote *kind* in the box on his form marked "characteristics." The bell went off, and I had to switch to the next Tidus.

Tidus 44AAD was also at work. He was a clerk in a law office across town from where the coffee shop would be located. I just watched him file reports. His hair was the natural curly brown that FOX Tidus must also have under the dye. I wrote the differences into his chart. If the multi-verse was created by the actions of people, this choice or that choice, branching into every possibility, I had to wonder what choice AAD Tidus had made or hadn't that FOX Tidus had or hadn't.

Halfway through my observation, AAD Tidus pulled a single-serve box of Honey-Ohs cereal out of his desk and snacked on it. Honey-Ohs was analogous to the cereal Luca'd had for our first dinner together, Honoy-Os. I wrote that in the chart. A person came into the room just then, and I switched on the audio.

"I'm sorry," Tidus was saying.

"Isn't that just the worst, though?" the person responded.

"You won, Di. Try to stay positive and focus on that. The kid'll be in a better home because of us."

"Yeah, I guess it just goes to show you how messed up those parents were. Why'd they keep the dog? It was the only decent gift that kid had ever got from them."

"I agree, it's fucked up. We can hand the dog's case over to animal rights and maybe someday…But for now, Jason was our biggest concern, and we helped him."

The Tiduses were two for two in the heartstrings department. I finished up AAD Tidus's forms and clicked away from the Tidus group. It was on to good ol' Peter Rogers.

# SECTION 7

## *You will make sense of this*

I was standing behind Tamar as we got on the bus. It was a cold day in the town of San Jose. The air felt thick and still, like a storm was coming. I pulled my backpack straps and tried not to think about this verse being blown apart like the ground zero verse.

"Pass?" the driver asked Tamar. Tamar nodded and inserted her pass into the reader. She wouldn't tell me why she wanted to take the bus across San Jose. Maybe it was a part of some observation she was making. Maybe she just wanted to see it. Either way, I was down for her plan.

"Pass?" the driver asked me. I pulled my backpack over my shoulder.

A security guard on the bus stood from where he sat behind the driver. I rummaged for my ticket and then put the pass into the reader. The security guard sat.

"Keep that in your pocket," the bus driver warned.

I saluted her and plopped into the seat across from Tamar. For some reason she was fuming.

"Did you see that?" she said.

"No…maybe?" I wasn't following.

She glared at me. "You know that guard only did that because you're black, right? He assumed you'd have something in your bag."

"Oh yeah."

"Doesn't it piss you off?" she said.

"It would if I let it."

"Well, fuck that and fuck them. I can't believe it. This is a fucking bus, not a bank or something. Also how dare they not search my bag? I mean if you're going to be racist, be racist equally and do me the honor. I'm Chicana, after all."

"You can get the next racism, I promise," I said, smiling.

"Why are you like this?"

I laughed. It took a week of searching and annoying Hugo, but we were finally able to get permission to visit the Dugan verses. Mason uncovered seven more James Dugans on top of the sixteen known. Minus the dead, there were ten we could visit. We submitted a proposal to the research coordinator and were given passes to visit the B-class verses.

Our whole HQ was A-class universe focused, from our clothes to our food to our entertainment. By definition, B-class universes were twenty years or more behind the progress of A-class verses. Which put my twenty-eight-year-old ass in a place that reminded me of when I was in elementary school. Tamar and I were pretending to be high schoolers.

I looked at Tamar across the city transport, funnily named The Zip. She was chewing gum and kicking her crossed leg gently. The man next to her pretended to read the paper, but really he watched her boot get dangerously close to grazing his slacks. She was still her goth self but with the energy of the early 2000s. She had on tight, red plaid pants with black hanging suspenders. She had on a black denim vest, detached fishnet sleeves, and thick, smeared black makeup.

I felt like what I was wearing was pretty damn close to the skater vibe I always wanted but wasn't allowed to have. When I was young and wanted to bury my body under a pile of clothes, hoodies and wide-legged pants were a godsend. I was kind of a chub as an adult, so the skinny jeans they tried to put me in made me sad. I opted for baggy shorts, a hoodie, fat lime green skateboarding shoes, and a beanie.

"What are you looking at, Martin?" she said, whipping her face toward me.

"What made you suspicious of MVP in the first place?" I asked.

She popped her gum. "What made *you*?"

I stared at her until she rolled her eyes. She dug into her backpack and handed me a folder.

"I'm pure-unique," she said.

"Weird flex, but okay," I said. Pure-unique were people who had never had a counterpart, living or dead. They were statistical anomalies, the rarest of people in all the multi-verse.

She just rolled her eyes. “Since I can go basically wherever I want, I sometimes go to a random verse. Mostly for hook-ups.”

I nodded, not an uncommon story.

“One day I found this.”

She gestured for me to open the folder. The topmost item was a magazine with an older black man with a square jaw and trim physique on the cover. He had on an exceptionally well-tailored suit and was shaking hands with someone while accepting a plaque.

“Senator makes history, works with judges to eliminate prison time for minor offenses,” I read. I looked at her. “Sounds like a good guy.”

“I guess, except the alternative is to be forced to pay two hundred dollars a week to rent an ankle monitor from his family’s company,” she grunted. “That’s not the point. Do you recognize that guy?”

I shook my head.

“Look at the next photo.”

It was of three men and a woman standing against the ocean horizon. One of the men was the guy on the magazine cover, and the other was Don Brady. I didn’t know the third man, and the woman’s big glasses obscured her face.

“Are these MVP founders?”

“More or less. I’m not sure who started when, but they’re top MVP execs. Turn to the next thing.”

It was a magazine with the same black man on it, seated behind a podium at what looked like a press hearing. “CEO Steps Down, Names Housekeeper’s Son Successor.”

“I thought he was a senator,” I said.

“He is…in the first verse. In this one he is—*was* a CEO.”

I was speechless. It was a basic understanding that MVP founders were all universe-unique. They also told everyone they were almost exclusively MVP now, so even in their home-verse, they shouldn’t have been so important to warrant being on magazine covers. My mind flooded with questions.

I set the first cover on my left thigh and the second on my right. Side by side, the man was as distinct as he was the same. The senator had a fade and was clean-faced. The CEO had a five o’clock shadow and a forearm tattoo. But they were the same man—Carl Payne. I closed the folder.

"What do you make of it?" I asked.

Tamar shrugged. "I don't know, but my gut tells me it's not good."

"Wow."

That was all that was in the folder. I handed it back. She put it in her backpack and looked at me sternly.

"What about you?" she asked.

"What about me what?"

She grinned. "Martin, you're so dumb. When did you become suspicious of MVP?"

"I think it's suspicious that a company who says their top priority is to protect the universe from rifts only gives twenty-eight percent of their resources to the Tangential Encounter Management Group."

"That's it? Where does the rest go? Research?"

"Research and Monitoring are only thirty-two percent combined."

"What's left, HR?"

"Right, but even with the employee compensation programs and equipment, there is still thirty percent unaccounted for."

Tamar nodded as if she agreed it was strange. "What do they do with the money?"

"No, not just money, Tam, *resources*. There's a labor budget that exceeds compensation, there's logs for equipment that can't be accessed by any department. There's accounting lines labeled weird things like *Universe Expansion Preparation*."

"That sounds useful to have."

"Yeah, but why then is it listed as inventory?"

"You know what? I don't understand how MVP makes money anyway."

"That's half the problem, most of the employees don't. MVP makes money by investing. They put money into financial markets of specific universes. They also provide microfinancing services in said universes, which means they offer small short-term loans to individuals through an app called Peanuts. But that's it. And even that portion of the business is less than three percent. They shouldn't have some of the financial line items they have."

"How do you know all of this?" Tamar asked.

"I read the financial statements."

She stared at me.

"They're a corporation only because employees need a familiar structure to operate under, which means we're the only ones who can hold it accountable. It's not like there's a multi-verse government to investigate corporate malpractice."

"You get your compensation, so what's it matter what they do with the rest?" Tamar asked.

"So, what does it matter to you that the founders claim they're universe-unique but might not be?" I said.

Tamar just nodded and shrugged. I understood. We both had the same voice in the back of our heads that said something was wrong. Now we had each other's information but couldn't reconcile the two.

"You ever ask anyone about it?" she asked as the bus took a hard turn around a traffic circle.

"Yeah. I got a form letter and a financial statements for beginners packet. They basically said, 'Keep at it, Mr. King, and you will make sense of this complicated financial information with time and practice.' "

"Brutal." Then she asked, "How do you make sense of them?"

I laughed. "We all nerd out on something."

We didn't say anything for the rest of the ride.

# Section 8

## *I feel bad for the guy*

The retirement home was a sprawling complex of four-story buildings that could have passed for apartments. We had to walk a block from the bus stop to the estate entrance. The gate was open, and I followed Tamar up the quarter-mile driveway to the front desk. We gave the receptionist our names and our fake teacher's note from Mr. Del Mar. She gravely wrote out our visitors' passes and pointed us in the direction of Dugan's room. I set up my drones before we went in. I thought about Luca back in HQ, waiting for the data I would send. He would also be watching me and Tamar on drones assigned to us. When I was ready, Tamar knocked.

"Come on in," the man behind the door said.

James Dugan looked like Santa Claus, with a thick, white beard and balding head. He had a pleasant demeanor and offered us tea as soon as we plopped down on his brown sofas. Tamar conducted the interview while I tried to investigate the room with drones, hoping Dugan wouldn't think too hard about the cell phone I was holding. I told him it was a tape recorder, and he seemed to trust that. From what I could see on the sequencer, nothing here suggested a rift event or any other multi-verse phenomena.

He had a lot to say about any subject Tamar brought up, but very little of it was about the multi-verse. She was easing her way in. We didn't land on anything good until Dugan mentioned having strange dreams. He was calling them dreams, but it seemed more to me like he was walking through the multi-verse without knowing how he was doing it or what had really happened. When he said it gave him inspiration for his paintings, Tamar asked to see them.

As soon as Dugan was out of the room, retrieving his paintings, my sequencer beeped with a message from Luca: *Scans complete. No quantum variance, cept you and T. Cute green blob man.*

"Stop flirting with Martin and focus," Tamar said to Luca through the drone, reading over my shoulder.

"You can stop too," she said, glaring at me.

I rolled my eyes and put the sequencer back on the table. I wasn't flirting. I was being flirted with. There was a difference.

James was shuffling back down the hall, explaining as he walked. "Some years ago, seven maybe eight, I started having dreams like I was living whole other lives. I was me but my home or my job or friends would be different. Or I was watching myself live my life. They weren't always bad, but it *did* distort my sense of reality. The doctors diagnosed it as a sort of schizophrenia."

"Oh?" Tamar and I both said as he sat.

He sighed. "I think that was their best guess, really. Nothing they did helped, but I didn't care much for evaluations and such, so for a while I would lie and say their medication helped."

"Interesting," Tamar said.

James had morphed from jolly to grave. He seemed to be studying our faces, trying to land on our reactions. He put a pile of papers and sketchbooks down on the coffee table between us. I scooted closer to Tamar. She opened the book. The first few pages were just self-portraits. Well, they appeared to be self-portraits at first glance. The more we saw, the more I realized he had been drawing counterparts. One stood out. I pulled the loose page out of Tamar's hands.

"What's going on here?" I asked.

"That was one of the first dreams I remember."

It was a picture of a Dugan looking down at his reflection in the ice. The image had been rendered with what I guessed was watercolors. It gave the ice a realistic wetness. You couldn't see the face of the man standing on top of the ice, but the other was Dugan.

Tamar asked him to explain the inspiration for some of his work. He talked about them and how each dream episode would be in a world just like the one he knew, only different. While it sounded like multiverse, there were some missing pieces. He couldn't have possibly visited a universe with a counterpart. They would have converged.

Second, there were no rifts in the area he could have walked through. And finally, there was a clear tell when someone tunes, traveling the MVP way through the multi-verse.

For some people it was a sound or feeling. For me it was a smell. It was just the way a brain would come to interpret the act of changing universe frequencies. I always smelled peanut butter when I tuned. Try as she might, Tamar couldn't get Dugan to admit to some consistent thing that would have meant tuning.

In all, it left us with more questions than answers. When it was over, Tamar and I left in near silence. We walked to where James said he had lived and the several locations around town where he worked. I couldn't stop thinking of the photo of Dugan under the ice.

"I feel bad for the guy," I said.

"Me too."

I think in that moment we both abandoned the idea of visiting other Dugans.

The Dugan experience was the first event in a chain leading to a melancholy that came over the group. Shortly after returning, we got a report of a plane gone missing because of a rift, three hundred plus people lost to a dead-verse. The week ended with Hugo reporting that all our hours of observation so far had concluded nothing. We weren't making progress. Of course, that was exactly when the founders started sending messages to Hugo, demanding results. Hugo became very grumpy about the structure of the experiment.

Tamar sulked around the lab and quietly did her observations. Wei fell ill again and was cooped up in bed. Luca agreed to take over Wei's subjects, so we only saw each other at the worktable. And since the data still poured in, Luca, Kiki, and Mason were busier than ever, even if it amounted to nothing. I found it hard to work, to draw my focus away from my friends. I mentioned to Hugo I had noticed a depression creep up on everyone. He said it was normal—starting projects was exciting and kept the adrenaline high and the brain focused. When that started to wane, the collective low was expected.

I knew it was more than that. I didn't tell him I couldn't let go of Dugan. Who would he have been without the multi-verse travel? Living in the dead-verse was like stepping out of a party and looking back in through a closed window. I had been a tech with MVP for ten years, what else did I know? Or maybe I knew too much.

Thinking about living in a verse made me think of Tidus. The Tiduses were my favorite subject to observe. They seemed to span the full gamut of living. It was simply a matter of asking what if you were a doctor, or an actor, or a bookstore clerk, and there was a Tidus for almost every reality. Worse still, I liked every Tidus I observed. They were all good guys, fun guys. Thinking of him made a few hours of my week bright.

I also caught myself staring at Luca from across the room. He was clearly impacted by the people lost to rifts. I tried to stop showing him Fern's reports, but he would ask and ask. I watched his beautiful face fall with sadness every time I gave in to his request. I wanted to reach out to him, to comfort him, but we were never alone. It never seemed appropriate. And I would dream of Dugan's drawing. The man on the ice staring down into his own face. When I couldn't sleep, I played the piano softly. None of the rest of the team complained. Sometimes they came out and listened.

The malaise and quiet lasted weeks. There was always more bad news. Wei healed enough to get a different illness, and Mason had a pretty scary panic attack when a large chain of relays collapsed. Kiki stopped dressing up and resigned themselves to a set of teal sweats for a few days. I mentioned it all to Hugo, and he finally agreed it seemed like more than just the lull of science.

"Go home," he announced at the end of a particularly dismal Thursday. It was raining hard on the ocean, making everything dreary.

"What?" we all said looking at him.

"Go to your home-verse and see your parents or friends or whoever you have. We'll pick it up on Monday."

We looked at each other.

"What about observations?" Wei asked.

"I have a plan for that."

We gave a collective groan.

"*We* can't do it," Kiki said, crossing their arms defiantly. They gestured between themselves, Mason, and Luca. "We want to go home, too."

Hugo put up his hands in surrender. "I know, I know. I have an idea I want to try starting Monday. But that plan can wait, and so can our subjects. For now, *relaxez vous et profitez*."

No one knew what to do for a moment. It was technically quitting time, but I had two more hours of observation I needed to finish since my day was interrupted when Mason asked me to help him test the new relays.

"I'm already gone," Tamar said.

"Ooh, girl, come home with me," Kiki said, grabbing Tamar's arm. "We can get drunk."

"*Sí, por favor*." Tamar laughed.

They were out of the room before the rest of us could say bye.

"Mason," Luca said, his voice a warning.

I looked over to where Mason was trying to sneak away.

"I'm going to leave. I just have to check on the—"

"No checking," Luca said. "Here, I'll help you, but you need rest."

They left the room.

"Martin, are you going to work all weekend?" Wei asked me. "You could come to my verse if you have nowhere to go. You can eat something other than gyoza."

"Like what?"

He blinked at me. "Actually, I bet my mom could make a casserole out of gyoza. She only owns casserole dishes."

I laughed. "I would, but I owe Mom and Apollo a visit."

"Hugo?" Wei asked.

"*J'irai par la forêt, j'irai par la montagne. Je ne puis demeurer loin de toi plus longtemps*."

"What does that mean?"

"In short, I'm going camping."

We talked for a few minutes, then said good-bye. I looked at my schedule and then at the clock. The last two observations for any Thursday were Sade Sawyer and Fleur Rooney. One was a thirty-three-year-old stay-at-home mom of four; the other was a twenty-one-year-old army recruit. The two hours passed faster than I expected.

"Monday morning," Luca said, his voice suddenly loud. I jumped a little. I forgot he and Mason had gone into the other room. Mason had a bag slung over his shoulder and was holding an umbrella. Luca was leading him to the door out of the data lab. As they passed, Luca smiled at me.

"I think it'd be better if I came back Saturday night," Mason said.

"Sunday."

"Luca—"

"After lunch."

"Fine." Mason waved at me from the door. "Bye, Martin."

"See ya."

Luca shut the door behind him and laughed.

"Some days I wish he could be bribed so I could pay him to go away," Luca said, crossing the room. I watched him come. His smile for me was wide, and his eyes soft, but I could see how tired he was. I didn't know what to say.

"What're you still doing here?" he asked. "I mean, what're you up to?"

"I had to finish my obs."

"You haven't seemed quite like yourself. Are you okay?"

I was surprised by the direct question. But then again, I wasn't. "I haven't felt like myself," I said. "Have any of us?"

He leaned against the table near me, just the way he usually did. He nodded as if to say *fair point*. Tamar said we flirted. I couldn't deny that when I let my mind wander, it went to Tidus. But I also couldn't deny that when I focused, I found Luca.

"Martin," he said, shoving my arm slightly.

"Um…what?"

"I asked if you wanted to talk about it. For someone with perfect pitch, you don't listen very well."

"Fuck off."

I stood and leaned against the table. His shoulder rubbed against my upper arm. We hadn't come in much physical contact, but it felt familiar when it happened.

"I feel like the Dugan experience was hard on me. I guess maybe I've been thinking about Mikyea dying. I know it's more complicated than that, but…"

"Would it help to know which verse was hers?"

My expression must have been surprise because he raised his eyebrows in response.

"You found her?"

"Yup."

"How?"

"Martin, we're a rifts and universe-unique research team. We've been looking for needles in haystacks for the last seven years as a group and fifteen on my own. It wasn't until you showed up that we were suddenly looking for the fucking hay!" For emphasis, he threw his arms out and gestured to the total sum of computing power in the room. "If I couldn't find someone, I'd fire me."

He laughed. His eyes crinkled at the edges, showing his age. Luca was one of the few of us over thirty. His height and bright, warm complexion gave him a sense of being young. But he was older than me by six years. His age was in his voice, his way of carrying himself, and in those fucking beautiful eye wrinkles.

"Where was she?"

"We shared a universe, actually. She lived in my home-verse."

"She'd be lucky to share a universe with you."

Luca squinted at me. "She's dead, buddy. Not much luck there."

I felt my mouth fall open in embarrassed surprise. I decided to play dumb. "Wait…she died!"

He elbowed me, exasperated. He didn't rake his hair like most guys—he fluffed it, lacing perfect, long, fingers into the strands at the base and pulling gently. And I enjoyed watching him do it. I must have really missed something about him because all of my attention honed in on his presence.

"Is it weird or wrong?" he asked, suddenly sheepish, "To call her a 'she'?"

I thought about it. "Not to me. I don't know how she identified. I didn't really know until I was older. I wouldn't be bothered if someone referred to baby me as she, but everyone is different, so…I don't know. Does it change how you think about me?"

"Fuck no. Shit, Martin, that's not what I meant. I didn't—don't—" The look of panic on his face was endearing.

"Luca, breathe. It was a metaphysical question, you're fine."

He nodded, but he was probably going to overthink it. I decided it was better to keep talking.

"Well, *they*'ve been on my mind a lot. One of the Dugans caused the death of a counterpart or two, and he may have never known they existed. But does knowing about mine, about M, matter or change anything?"

"Think I understand," Luca said. "My counterparts are all alive, four total—all some *me* I might've been. I sometimes wonder if they've ever accidentally stumbled upon the idea of me, of this. I feel like if something happened to them, I would wonder about all the possibilities missed."

I looked at him. That was part of it how I'd been feeling, but there was more: the loss of life, the rifts, the Dugans, the work. But there was also that. Possibilities with Luca, or in a verse, or with someone like Tidus, some other life than this one.

"That's it," I said. "I'm hung up on possibilities."

Luca nodded. "When I started with MVP, the leader of my team was a woman named Shawnna. She said once that the quantum world was just probability and energy waves, and all of reality is just the product of chance and energy."

I was still looking at him. And he looked at me. He gave me a half-smile.

"She also said that measuring quantum particles changes them, so in a way there's also choice. I think what she was trying to say was in life you just have to try, you have to hope, and you have to choose."

"I like that."

I had no idea how that applied to what I was thinking about, but I liked listening to him talk. And I liked watching him talk. I felt drawn to his mouth.

"Luca?"

"Martin."

"I don't know what it would mean, but I want to kiss you."

His eyes went wide, but his smile didn't seem surprised. I could see his practical brain thinking it over, and in that moment, I lost a fraction of my nerve. I was about to back out when he snickered and said, "Go for it."

His eyes were closed before I even moved. I studied his clear, silky, light brown skin, framed by his dark hair. I looked back at his mouth and leaned in. I was relieved when our lips came together. To my surprise, Luca relaxed into the contact. A brightness started where his mouth met mine and spilled back into me. I almost laughed when I remembered that most people called that *a spark*. I wanted to chase that feeling, but Luca pulled away.

"See you on Monday?" he asked.

"Bet." I watched him leave before I turned to finish shutting down my laptop.

# Section 9

## *It started out as a good idea*

I walked up to my mom's house and knocked. I had slept in and caught a flight late Friday night, arriving in Denver early Saturday morning. I took a cab to my parents' house. I knocked a second time.

"Come in," Apollo called.

I entered the landing on the split-level, breadbox style home. It was a cold morning, but it was also September in Colorado. I shouted into the house, "Lo, you can't keep doing that, bro. This isn't the nineties. You just gonna let anyone walk into your home—"

I didn't have the chance to finish my rant because he came marching up the stairs, his arms wide. He wrapped them around me, laughing.

"My boy, what are you doing here? We weren't expecting you."

I liked to tease him that he had a Santa laugh but he just told me to fuck off. Apollo was a barrel-chested, second-generation Greek, standing over all our heads at six feet tall. His hair, near-perfect ringlets of salt and pepper, was to his shoulders and his thick beard completed the halo of hair around his hazel eyes.

"I got some time. We broke a case early."

"Is that my baby?" my mother, Andrea, cried coming down the stairs. Her hair was a half freshly twisted half pile of locs. She had on a black T-shirt that must have been Apollo's because she was swimming in it. Her makeup and jewelry was gold and on point. She had on navy blue slacks and house shoes.

"Hey, Ma," I said with a laugh, letting her hug me too.

"Brother!" bellowed Quintavius, from the top of the stairs. I went past Mom and gave him a half hug, half handshake.

"Shit, is everyone here?" I said, feeling overwhelmed and loved.

"Bitch, we might be," my little sister said. She sat in the living room. She was playing a game and didn't look up. She was barely twenty, Apollo and Andrea's only full biological kid. She was the reason I said yes to the job with MVP. I had never told anyone that.

"Nichelle, don't say that," Mom said.

"Why's everyone here? Someone die?" I asked.

My mom shook her head. "You're as bad as her."

"Hello," a final voice called from the kitchen.

I looked at Apollo. "Is that Geegee?"

He nodded and took my bag.

"Geegee," I shouted, rushing around the corner and into the kitchen.

She was stirring a pot on the stove. Apollo's mom was the best. I loved that short, beautiful lady. She let me wrap her in a hug. She just patted my arms.

"You're looking skinny, my dear," she said.

"'Cept your fat head," Nichelle teased.

"At least people can see my head. Looks like you got a pimple on your shoulder and put some hair on it."

She gave me an air high five.

"Well, you ain't been here but five minutes, and I'm ready to send ya back. Take Nichelle with you," Mom said.

I followed my mom around for most of the morning, sitting in the bathroom while she retwisted her locs. I ran away before she could get hold of mine, promising to let her do them before I left. Then I caught up with Apollo and Quin. They liked to hang out in the lower level of the house, watching fishing TV or talking shop. They asked me about work, and I enthralled them with a story I stole from a newspaper in the Dugan verse. Then I went to hang out with my sister. She was still playing video games.

"Let me play," I said, grabbing another controller.

"No, I'm trying to beat this level."

Like a brat, I stood in the middle of the TV pouting.

"Fucking shit, Martin. Fine, dummy. Move."

I sat by her on the couch and watched as she took her avatar to a save zone and navigated to the main menu. I knew that game because we played it nearly every time we were together. It was a semi-cooperative shooter game where the goal was for one or more of your team to be the last team standing. Hundreds of other players from around the world were out to kill you. It was bright and goofy looking.

"Fort-nite?" I said, reading the title.

"What, you don't want to play this?"

"Naw, it's fine…I just…was it always called that?" I asked. It didn't feel right saying it. It felt so wrong, in fact, that I wanted to look it up on my phone. Some of it was right, but… "Was it always hyphenated?"

"Pick a skin, Martin," Nichelle sighed.

I tried to shrug it off and selected an anthropomorphic bear. We played an hour, which meant we pissed off noobs around the world for an hour. At some point, I fell asleep on the couch. Mom didn't wake me until dinner. We sat at the table while Geegee and Apollo dished up some of the stew Geegee had made. She had also made bread, a salad, and sweet tea. I nearly cried at the first mouthful.

"You look tired, Martin," Mom said as she piled more bread on my plate.

"I am."

"Work going okay?"

I shrugged. "It's all right. I got put on a team in a new division, so it's hard to adjust."

Not to mention that it was hard knowing that the universes were under threat of collapse at a rate higher than we had ever measured, and the one organization that could do anything about it was ignoring the evidence. I tried to think of a way to say that without saying that.

"Sometimes a job has more weight to it, feels more important, you know. It feels like the world will end if you don't get it solved."

"That's stressful," Mom said.

"Maybe you need a vacation?" Quin said.

Nichelle grunted. "Maybe you need therapy."

"You're both probably right. Trust me, I've thought about it."

"Something bigger than that, son?" Apollo asked.

It was both annoying and affirming that Apollo called me son as much as he did. He called us all son or daughter. I think he just loved the idea of having kids. I wondered about kids sometimes. Can't raise kids in a dead-verse.

"Martin?"

"What?"

"Something else going on in your life?" he said.

"Naw."

"Well, since Martin's boring, I heard that some of the professors are going to sue the university," Nichelle said. Her eyes roved the table, gauging everyone's reactions.

"Why?" Mom asked.

Nichelle shifted in her seat, preparing to launch into a juicy story. "They found out the school had installed cameras in their offices. They say it's a violation of their privacy. The rumor is that the university did it because they wanted evidence the professor was committing a crime."

"What crime?" Quin asked, his face scrunched in confusion.

"Sleeping with students."

We all stared at her.

"What? I bet plenty of them do it, but that's not the point. The university says they have the right. The professors say it's a violation of their *human* rights."

"I guess…But what does it matter if they aren't actually committing crimes?" Quin said, slurping his soup.

"It's disgusting. I can't even imagine being filmed against my consent," Nichelle said.

"It's a public office," Apollo said.

"It doesn't matter, people should know. Especially if that place is given to them under the impression of privacy."

"How'd they get that impression?" Mom asked.

"The doors all lock."

"What does the school want with hours of bland footage of nerds at desks?" Quin said.

I listened to them debate the ethics of filming people against their will. I didn't say anything. Hugo had sent us home to relax, and up until that moment it had worked. Fundamentally, I agreed with Nichelle, but professionally, I violated people's privacy over and over again.

I ate as much of Geegee's soup as I could, and I felt my mood sink, feeling homesick for something unnamable. As I tried to fall asleep that night, I couldn't stop thinking about the name of the video game, Fort-nite. It was wrong somehow. The internet wasn't helpful. I added an alert for it anyway.

I also couldn't stop thinking about the conversation at dinner. If people are going to be spied on, it should be for the greater good. But I was losing faith in my greater good. Maybe I was just looking for an excuse. Maybe if I distrusted MVP enough, maybe if I added one more straw on the ethical ambiguity pile, the camel would break. Maybe I just wanted things to be different.

Sunday brought on a deeper gloom. I woke up slowly and tried to land on something I felt good about. I thought of Luca, but he seemed veiled by the smog of MVP. I tried to think of FOX Tidus, but that just reinforced the idea of how deeply complex and secretive our work was. I knew things about him only people invited into his intimate world should know. I knew how fast his heart beat when he was watching his favorite part of his favorite movie or when he beat a boss in his favorite video game. That seemed too private. And for all the stress of it, we weren't making progress.

"Martin, you have to keep your head up," Mom said, yanking my head back by my locs. She was halfway through retwisting them and weaving them into a protective roll that would let the new growth settle.

"Sorry."

"Boy, what's the matter with you?"

"I was just thinking about the conversation at dinner yesterday."

"Why? Don't let your sister get to you."

"I can't help it." I tried to look at my hands in my lap, but Mom yanked my head again. "It's part of my job to watch people, but sometimes they don't know it."

"You look for criminals."

"Not all of the people we watch are criminals."

She looked at me. "Do you think you're helping people?"

I nodded.

"Well, then that either has to be good enough, or figure out what to do about it."

I sighed. "You sound like my friend Tamar."

"Who's that?"

"A woman on my new team."

"Well, if I sound like her, she must be smart."

I laughed.

"Ma," I hissed as she yanked on my baby hairs.

"Martin."

"Do you know what a Mandela effect is?"

"I do."

"Have you ever seen one?" I asked. "Or do you know one?"

She looked at me and whispered conspiratorially, "I think it's the government."

"Ma, I asked if you know one, not why they happen."

She went off then and talked for the whole rest of the time I sat on the toilet while she did my hair. She rattled off common Mandela effects and some I hadn't heard of that I would have to look into later. Tapping into a surprise special interest of my mom's made me feel tenfold better. I didn't know we had something like that in common.

I made it back to HQ Monday morning feeling not great. I wasn't alone. Both Kiki and Tamar had on dark sunglasses, slumped in their chairs. They both looked flushed, like they were trying to fight the urge to vomit. Wei was dead asleep at the table, but that was pretty usual for him. Mason was the only one who was busy.

"Y'all were supposed to use this break to rest, not to make yourselves worse," Hugo said, surveying the room. He looked at Mason, who was at the computers, wheeling between four monitors, quickly typing at each for a few seconds before moving on to the next. "Even he looks more stressed."

I wasn't interested in anyone there. The one person I wanted to see most had yet to show up.

"He had a family emergency," Kiki said, looking at me from over their glasses.

"What kind?"

They shrugged and leaned away from me. "He'll be back when he can."

My mood dropped that little bit more.

"Well," Hugo said. "I have some new ideas."

"I'd like to say something," I said, putting my hand up.

Hugo alone looked well rested. "Go on."

"I feel weird about monitoring people. We don't have their consent to study them. I mean, I get that it's for science—that it's beyond any one person, but people deserve more."

Hugo's eyes were bright with what I could only assume was pride. I couldn't imagine what he was proud of me for. I was standing against everything we had done so far.

"What brought this on, Martin?" he asked, sitting.

"I've been thinking about how wrong everything feels," I said. I crossed my arms and looked at the floor. "I don't like looking into people's lives without them knowing."

"I second that," Tamar said. "I mean, there's some shit I don't care about because anyone with a computer could find it, but it's a little too far at this point."

My head whipped up. In a look, I understood she didn't want to be one of the bad guys. We all started with MVP for the generalized reason of helping people. Now it felt like we were part of the problem, or that maybe our help was doing more harm than good. She felt it too. The Dugan visit made it clear to us both.

"Well, I feel like the ethics of science is always a worthy discussion," Hugo said. "And I won't argue with you. I've redesigned our experiments anyway. You see, nothing we've done has gotten us any closer to an answer."

"The data doesn't say anything," Mason said. He took his beanie off and rubbed a crop of surprisingly blue hair. "Kiki, Luca, and I have been analyzing the data in any way we can. It's all been useless or confusing. For one person, gender is correlated with location. For another, location is correlated with occupation. Any model designed finds all included variables significant, but those variables become insignificant as soon as any one is removed. It's almost impossible to decipher. Even the rift models are starting to look less than predictable. It would be nonsense if it were even remotely consistent."

"Great," Wei said.

"It started out as a good idea," Mason said.

"Is that why you asked me all those questions?" Tamar asked. "To try and find a pattern?"

"Yes, but either the problem is bigger than we're measuring or smaller."

"If smaller mattered, then the frequency scans would turn up something," I said.

"I agree," Hugo said.

"So, what, it's bigger?"

"Right. I feel like the closest thing we have to any insight was from the Dugan interview. Dreams are an emergent property of the interactions of the complex systems we're made of. Maybe the phenomenon of synchronizing in the way the Dugans had was an emergent property," Hugo said.

Then he looked right at me. "I think you're right, Martin. These are people, not a heartbeat or a longitude. So, let's learn from it. I propose we interview our subjects. Let's see if the Dugan Interview Method gives us a direction to go in. This will require more of Tamar's expertise, helping us navigate culture and social nuances. Mason and Kiki, we'll need a creative solution to capture the data."

"I think it'll still be important to keep measuring at certain levels… frequency, vitals, so on," Mason said. "I'm not willing to give up on all variables."

"Okay," Hugo agreed.

"Won't this make it harder?" I asked. The room stared at me. "We're going from defined things like elevation to what? *Feelings?*"

"Qualitative data can inform how we access quantitative data," Hugo said.

"I…I don't think I know what that means."

"If everyone is on board with the new direction, we can get started," Hugo said, not bothering to explain.

We all groaned.

"Fine. We ride at dawn. But will you please rest?"

Before they left, I flagged down Kiki.

"What's up?"

"Is there a way to look up a Mandela effect?" I asked, thinking of my sister's video game and the conversation with my mother.

"Kind of, but it's hard because once a verse updates, there's usually no trace of it other than what people remember."

"What about a comparison across verses? It might not tell me anything, but I want to know."

"We can try," Kiki said.

# Section 10

## *FOX*

Over the next two days, we pieced together a game plan. Hugo decided it made sense to focus on the most multi subject we had. Which meant all our attention was about to focus in on the Tiduses. I was also thinking about Mandela effects. Kiki had looked into the game, but it didn't reveal much. I tried to do a cross-reference for the effect in past reports, but there was no mention of the game.

After that, the rest of my attention went to Luca, who still wasn't back by Wednesday. We scheduled the first interview for that night, but Luca's absence pulled my thoughts away from the project. I worried about him. I thought of going to his home-verse to check on him, but I chickened out. If he needed someone, wouldn't Kiki or Mason be with him? Were he and I even on that level? I didn't know. I took my cues from Kiki and tried to focus on what Hugo wanted me to do.

"You want me to do *what* now?" I asked.

"You're the best choice to interview FOX Tidus," Hugo said.

"Why?" I wanted to run out of the room and right into the ocean.

"You've already met. It'll ease the burden of trying to build context," Tamar said.

*Build context?* Yeah, sure, I built context with the guy. I all but ghosted him, now I'm just going to show up. *And* everyone else will know. I debated again telling them about the texts. But I didn't. I guess I was just going to chicken out of everything.

"I wouldn't even know what to say."

"You got through the Dugan interview," Hugo said.

I pointed at Tamar. "She did most of the work."

"She'll be with you," Wei said. He walked over with a com. "In your mind."

The design of the interview process was that two people would go to the verse and engage the subject. Someone else would be live relaying questions or advice, watching from the drones with the addition of communicators. The rest of the team would either manage the data coming in, which meant managing the drones, or they would run interference as needed while the interview teams were in the verse.

"Who's going with me?"

"Me," Wei said, flashing me a few dance moves.

"Y'all are going to trust this guy and that guy," I said, pointing between me and Wei.

Wei laughed. "On my business card, *scientist* comes before *ladies' man.*"

I laughed and Tamar groaned. "He's just there for support and to take pictures. We need you to focus on getting the info."

"This is a bad idea," I said, mostly to myself. To the others, I said, "He'll be at work. He won't want to talk to me."

"Wednesday is the slowest day for the shop," Mason said.

I glared at him because he wasn't helping. He didn't seem to notice.

Hugo approached, his boots loud on the tile in the computer lab. He put his hands on my shoulders. "Even a foal has its own legs to stand on."

"I don't know what that means."

It was full steam ahead anyway.

❖

Wei and I decided to walk through the queer community that was a part of Fort Lauderdale and where FOX Tidus's shop was. It was late in the evening but hot still, the steamy air doing a lot to increase my nerves. Wei was busy taking photos, cooing over the colors and exuberance of the community. I was trying to forget everything I knew about Tidus. I had been observing FOX Tidus and counterparts for two hours a week for over a month. And while it was only a few days' worth of texting, I had texted him a lot. But I needed to figure out how to avoid all of that, especially with Tamar listening in. Maybe he forgot about me.

The coffee shop/bookstore/bar was cozy and bright. It had once been a garage, and they had the steel door rolled up to let in the evening. Sea-stressed wood lined the walls and the bar. The floor was an oceanic swirl of blue cements. A handful of people sat at the mismatched tables. Mostly it was gay couples and loud groups of friends.

"I love this place," Wei said, snapping a photo of the books lining one wall. They were all used books, repriced for sale in the shop.

"It's cool."

The area behind the bar was empty. I found a free stool near the cash register, but the location was weird. Sitting there would mean having my back to the rolling garage door, and I was under the full intensity of a low-hanging lamp. But I had seen Tidus at work enough times to know he would pass that stool a hundred times a shift, more than any other place in the bar.

"I'm going to look around," Wei said, patting my shoulder.

He went immediately to a table of women. I picked up the menu. It was simple and had been handwritten, then photocopied. All of the drinks were literary puns.

"Hi," a voice said loudly near me.

I almost leapt off my stool. FOX Tidus was looking down, trying to unwrap a new package of cocktail napkins.

"Hi," I said.

"What can I get you?"

I ummed and watched his large hands unpack the small, white squares and place one in front of me. He looked up, and our eyes met. His expression went from politely disinterested to familiar surprise, his big mouth spreading into a wide smile.

"Martin?"

"Tidus?" I said, trying to sound like I really didn't remember.

"Correct." I didn't miss the slight disappointment in his expression. "You're back in town?"

"I, uh…kind of…um, what's good here?" I already felt in over my head.

"Um." He thought about it, running a hand through his lavender hair. He leaned on the bar and cocked a hip, looking at the menu I was still holding. "If you want coffee, then Murder on the Orient Espresso, and if you want a beer, Ale of Two Cities. It's a beer mixed drink."

"I think Orient Espresso," I said with a smile.

He nodded, took the menu, and walked away.

"*Well done, Martin,*" Tamar said in my head. "*Nice and boring. What did he mean by back in town?*"

I couldn't talk back. I looked over at Wei, and he gave me a thumbs-up.

"You want any food?" Tidus asked, crossing back down the corridor behind the bar, food menu in his hands.

"Naw…thanks."

I must have done something that gave him the impression I was tired because he asked, "Long day?"

"Kind of," I said. And it had been. "Why do you ask?"

"You're getting a triple shot of espresso at eight in the evening."

"That much? I didn't read it, I just took your word." I half laughed.

He laughed too, throaty and low. I remember feeling he was laughing through our messages. I remember hearing it for the first time. I watched him beat a tournament on a video game he had been playing for six hours. It was better in person.

"I guess I wasn't looking to go to bed early anyway."

"*Is that an invitation?*" Wei said. He was snapping photos across the bar.

"*Give me something to work with here, buddy,*" Tamar said.

"Oh no?" Tidus asked. He worked as he talked, punching an order into the register.

"Naw, I have to go over questions. For work. That's what I meant by *kinda*. I'm here but only for a few days. I'm trying to help Florida prepare its census."

He narrowed his eyes. "Didn't we just do that? Do you do the interviews or something? Aren't you with the FBI?"

"I help troubleshoot data collection processes for the government. I was working with the FBI on the last project. Today was the first day with the census. I'm literally here to help pick the questions."

"*Wow, that is creative. Would you even know where to start with a job like that?*" Tamar said.

Tidus gave me an intrigued look. "I guess I didn't realize people picked the questions."

"They do if people on the committee are messing with the integrity of the survey. I was at a regional meeting reviewing question submissions all day. It was awful."

"Oh?"

I studied him. He blinked back at me, genuinely interested. That made me feel more nervous. Why hadn't he asked about my contacting him? Was he waiting for me to bring it up? Or were we supposed to just ignore all that? I mean, I knew I should for the sake of my job, but…

"*Tell him that people want to add weird questions to the next survey.*"

I swallowed. "The problem is that this year several reps have offered up really weird question suggestions."

"Huh. 'How many people in your household?' not good enough anymore?"

"*Jackpot.*"

"That would still be on there, but the next one proposed was, 'Have you or anyone you know seen a ghost?'" I pretended to scrutinize him. "I guess that one would be right up your alley."

He pretended to be offended. "Excuse me, Mr. Aliens."

I laughed. "That one didn't make the cut either."

"Sounds wild," he said.

"*This is your chance!*" Tamar yelled.

I leaned in slightly. "It's supposed to be confidential, but do you want to take the weirdest survey of your life?"

"Honey, I went to art school. Someone did a thesis on the social relevance of the snot bubble in dubbed anime," he said, pretending to flip long hair over his shoulder. "I love weird surveys."

"*This guy personifies charismatic H-HIA,*" Tamar said with a laugh.

I could feel the same easy connection we'd made in our first conversation. I watched Tidus walk away to deliver the bill he had just punched in and to retrieve my drink. He stopped to talk with a couple and take an order.

"This place is nice," Wei said, coming over. He leaned against the bar, taking a candid close-up of me with his camera.

"This place or those women?"

He grinned. "Both." When he leaned in, he said, "There is nothing here at a quantum level that would indicate a rift. There is always a mix of particles, but you know it's probably just blow-over."

I nodded.

"Here you are," Tidus said, placing my drink in front of me. To my surprise, it was blood red.

"What is this?" Wei asked, picking it up and sipping it.

"Um, sir?" Tidus tried to intervene.

"He's fine. Wei, this is Tidus. Tidus, this is my coworker Wei."

"Charmed," Wei said. He slid his business card to Tidus with a wink. Then he slammed the rest of my drink and hissed in my direction, "Shit, that's hot. I'm gonna mingle."

"You're welcome," I called after him as he walked away.

"This business card is a mess." Tidus laughed. "What does the census need with a photographer?"

I took the card from Tidus. Wei hadn't lied when he said "scientist" was listed before "ladies' man." Photographer was first of his almost twenty occupations.

"*He's documenting meetings for internal news.*"

I repeated Tamar's words to Tidus, sliding Wei's card back to him. "Wei is a good friend, though. I don't like telling him that since he gets cocky."

"If drinking your drink isn't cocky, I don't know what is. You work at the capital? I love Denver," he said.

"Yeah, Denver's a beautiful city. I'm not sure how long I'm going to be here. I guess it depends on if I can get the South to drop tarot cards from their survey proposal."

Tidus grinned. "I want to take this survey even more."

I looked around the near-empty bar. "You have time?"

"It's slow."

I laughed. Then I pantomimed pulling out a piece of paper. "This is a sample of the Rejected Annual Census. Do you—state your name—"

"Tidus Allen Avery."

"—consent to answering the following questions knowing they'll be used for scientific research and analysis and that, while all the results are public, the details of your identity will be private and protected?"

"I do. 'Cept you know me. Does that break the rules?"

I adjusted fake glasses, pretending to look at him over the rims.

He nodded and laughed. "Right. Yup. I do."

I liked how animated he was. He was like his big dog, their long limbs and sinewy bodies exaggerating their movements. He leaned in toward me, his long arms coming close to mine as he rested them on the bar top.

"Oh, wait. I'm gonna get you a new drink since your friend…you know," he said, then strode away.

I waited, feeling my nerves rise. I hated how I felt about him. I hated how easy it was. I would have made up hundreds of questions if it meant talking to him for as long as possible. I hated how far away the multi-verse instantly seemed. Tamar's voice came through, just in time to refocus me.

"*Ask about dreams since that's what Dugan mentioned. Ask about ordinary multi-verse things like Mandela effects—or King Henry effects, as his verse calls them.*"

I tried not to nod in answer. I didn't want to look like the crazy guy talking to himself. I turned instead to Wei. He was scanning the books on the wall, looking for who knows what.

"Here," Tidus said. To my surprise, he was on the customer side of the bar, and he sat on the stool next to me.

"Is it blood?"

The look of shock on his face was miraculous.

"The espresso," I said, trying to recover.

"Oh, shit. I mean, yeah. It's a book about murder, and the red velvet flavor makes it that color."

I laughed. "I really should've read the descriptions."

"I have never had a more trusting customer," he said with a grin.

"*Martin, stop fucking flirting and ask the man the fucking questions*," Tamar yelled in my ear.

"Um, so anyway," I said, pretending to pick up my pretend survey.

"Oh, right," Tidus said. He sat up and crossed his legs at the knees, straightening his apron.

"Question one. Do you believe in a deity?"

"No…kind of," he said, thinking.

I blinked at him.

"I believe in energy. It's like if you put out good energy, then you get good energy and bad for bad. But also I believe in ghosts, because they are just the residual energy of someone's life. Energy can't be created or destroyed, right? So I think a god could be the accumulation of the energy people put into believing in it. But that's probably supposed to be a yes or no question, isn't it?"

I laughed. "Yup, and that's why it was nixed."

I stared at him. He made a dismissive gesture, then waved his hand at my fake paper, prompting me to continue.

"Do you believe in the existence of other universes?"

He made a scrunched face. "Like outer space or like parallel realities?"

I shrugged as if I didn't know. "They didn't specify before we canceled the question. So, either, I guess."

"Well, I believe in space, I mean obvs. But I hope there's other beings out there. I'd be disappointed if we're alone. I read once that scientists were able to create primordial ooze in a lab, and it's only a matter of a few millennia or so before animals start sprouting or whatever. I mean, if we can do it in a lab already, then some other planet somewhere has to have some of this."

"I agree."

He smiled and continued. "As far as parallel realities, I mean, probably. I know much less about how that works, but since I'm one of the people who thought there was a cornucopia in the Fruit of the Loom logo, I guess I must believe. Right?"

"I guess so. I mean, I was never sold on the cornucopia, but I did think Kit Kat was hyphenated."

"*See, that wasn't so hard*," Tamar said. I think she was pleased Tidus landed on Mandela effects on his own.

He looked at me slyly. "What about you?"

"What about me?"

"What do you think? How would you answer these questions?"

I sighed. "Honestly? Almost exactly the same as you. Only I think a lot of it is beyond our science still, especially in outer space. I don't know if there's a god, but I think something has to be holding the foundation elements together."

"God is in the quarks?"

"Something like that. Add in a statistical element and you're nearly there," I said, trying to be as honest as I could. I hated lying to him more than I hated spying on him.

"*Follow up on the cornucopia thing*," Tamar said.

"So, you believe in King Henry effects?" I asked.

Tidus nodded. "I do."

"What do you think causes them?"

"I don't know. I think the popular idea is that one forms when alternate universes collide. I like the 1984 notion that the government just uses them to reinforce their gaslighting. I mean…not the *government* as in the part you work for."

I laughed. "Tidus, it's fine. That's not the worst thing I've heard someone say. What about the power of dreams?"

He raised an eyebrow. "What about them?"

"One of the questions was that dreams show you the future."

"If that was true, I would be married to all five guys in the Backstreet Boys," he said, a real hint of ruefulness in his voice.

"Fair enough. I used to dream of being a professional baseball player."

"Really," he said, appraising me. "You could pull off the uniform."

I laughed.

"*Martin*."

"I think some people can do it, though," I said. "Aren't there cases of people solving crimes and shit through dreams?"

Tidus shrugged. "I guess. I just assumed they were more intuitive or empathic."

"*All right, follow up on that idea*."

"Like ESP?"

His eyes went wide, and he grinned. "I believe in ESP. It's like energy. Some people are more sensitive. They have better energy receptors than others. I don't, but I wish I did. I'm not a very good judge of character or predictor of things. That's why I got a dog."

"A dog?" I said, completely entranced.

Tidus smiled. Leaning on his elbows, he propped his chin in a nest of perfect fingers. "Oh yeah, dogs are amazingly energy sensitive. I knew Bowser was going to be helpful because when I went to pick a pet from the adoption place, he walked right up to me and put his head on my left foot. I had twisted my ankle that morning and was limping a little. He wouldn't let me move, he just kept lying right on that foot. My ex thought I was crazy, but then one day that asshole came over, and B wouldn't stop growling at him. Turns out that morning my ex had cheated on me."

"Bowser knew that?"

"He did."

"*H-HIA are amazing. Dugan didn't have a dog, though.*"

"Do you have any pets?" Tidus asked.

"No, my dad is extremely allergic to animals."

"You live with your parents?"

"No, I mean I do, kind of. I travel a lot for work, as you know, and I'd have to leave the pet with my family." I laughed and shrugged. "I guess I maybe also internalized Apollo's allergy."

"Apollo?"

"My stepdad is Apollo King."

"Crazy. Did you take his name? Are you Martin King? I guess I never thought to ask."

I laughed. "Yeah. Martin Logan King. It's more of a coincidence than a choice."

I thought of what Luca said just then. He said it was hope, chance, and choice. I had chosen my name, since it was my choice to ask Apollo to adopt me. Thinking about Luca reminded me of work.

"One of the questions on the survey was about strange experiences, things like extreme déjà vu or coincidences."

"Why do they want to know this stuff?"

"Advertising," I said.

Tidus laughed.

"I think they're just trying to understand people, and sometimes that gets weird."

"Tell me about it." Tidus looked hard at me. "I keep trying to understand this one guy, and I don't think he's even noticed. Or he's trying to get me to leave him alone?"

"I…" I faltered. "He might not be that interesting."

"He already is," Tidus said. The way he turned his sad but hopeful eyes on me broke something inside. Then he stood. "But if he isn't interested, I can take a hint."

He was interested. *I* was interested. But my world was an impossible distance from him. It was as right next door as it was light years away. I opened my mouth to say something but nothing came out.

"*Get back here.*" The voice in my head wasn't Tamar anymore. It was Hugo, and he sounded disappointed.

Tidus just smiled sadly and walked back toward the opening that would let him behind the bar. I sipped the drink. It was good. I also put a handful of money on the counter.

"You're in trouble," Wei said, walking over.

"I heard."

I reached behind my ear and pulled off the communicator. I suddenly didn't want the rest of the lab to be a part of my experience. Wei pulled a magnet out of his pocket. I had seen Mason use one to pick up some spilled drones once. Wei swept it over the communicator, my neck and shoulder, and then over his own. When he showed it to me, I could see both our communicators and both drones. I hardly knew what privacy was, but Wei had managed to find us some.

"I think it's romantic," he said.

"Wei," I groaned. "Hugo's gonna fire me."

"Naw, he likes you too much. You make things more fun. I think he'll be sad, though."

"Sad?"

"He was rooting for Luca."

I felt my eyes widen. "What about Luca?"

Wei laughed and sipped my espresso. "We see you and Luca. I guess now we can see you and this guy."

"I…it can't be about either of them—or me, though. Right? I have to focus on work. I mean, shouldn't we all be focusing on work and not my complicated feelings?"

Wei shrugged. "If we focus on work, then all we end up with is work."

"MVP—"

Wei gave me a stern look. "MVP is MVP. People are why *we* are here. It's why we do what we do. I bet if you think back to why you said yes to this job, there's a person at the end of it."

I sighed. There was a person. I didn't tell Wei the story, but he nodded as if he could see my internal agreement.

"Wei."

"Martin." He sipped more of the drink.

"Did I really fuck things up?"

He laughed and flashed me a heart shape with his hands.

"That's not an answer."

I looked down the bar at Tidus. He was coolly making a drink in a blender. His hair had fallen over his face, and one side of his shirt was bunched in his apron. It was both dorky and attractive.

"Let's go," I said.

We walked in silence through the town back toward the extraction location. I didn't want to go back. I felt exposed. I had been thinking of Tidus, especially FOX Tidus, for a long time. And now everyone knew. I should have been worried about what Luca might think if word got back to him. I had just made all of these people my friends, and if that hinged on how they thought I treated Luca, I might lose them. I couldn't have both MVP and a life in the verses, but I wanted both men.

"Maybe I'm not cut out for research," I said.

Wei looked at me through the lens of his camera. He had been taking photos of the verse as we walked. He snapped another photo of me. "You wouldn't be the first person to be attracted to someone in a verse."

"But I'm supposed to be a scientist. Seems kind of unethical to think about dating your subject."

"Hugo'll probably make you lab janitor."

"That's not helping me feel better."

"If you did anything wrong, it was that you didn't tell us you were compromised by him when he showed up the first time."

"Great."

"Besides, we don't know that that's not important. It all could matter, or it all couldn't. Our experiments have been fucked this whole time anyway. It's a frontier."

"I hate it."

And for some reason, I looked into a shop window. It was a convenience store with magazines on display. If I hadn't seen the photo Tamar had shown me on the bus, I would have kept walking. But I knew the face on the cover.

I stepped back and leaned into the glass to inspect it. He wasn't Tamar's guy, and he wasn't Don, but he *was* one of the three men in the founders photo. He had a jockish look and was wearing a tux, shaking hands with the president. His headline read: *Scientist Cracks Code on Miracle Drug.*

"I need this magazine," I said.

"What?" Wei asked, looking.

I didn't explain. I went in, bought the magazine, and we went back to HQ. To his credit, Wei didn't ask. I didn't know what I would have said.

❖

"Hey," Tamar said when Wei and I walked into the lab.

"Hay is for the weak," Wei shouted.

Tamar was closing the laptops at the table. She was alone in the computer lab. She just blinked at Wei.

"Hugo wants to see you," Tamar said. "He's on the observation deck."

"Is it bad?" I asked, handing her the magazine.

"Maybe. What's this?"

I didn't answer. I just handed Wei my backpack and went to meet Hugo.

Hugo was leaning on the railing of the overlook. The wind was strong, his hat in his hands. He looked older for the first time in the months I had known him. He was also over thirty but younger than Luca.

"Hey," I shouted, the wind pulling at my loose shirt.

He looked at me, then gestured for me to follow him to a bench that was on the lee side of the stairwell housing, which created a wind blind. I looked up at the sky, but it was cloudy so none of the stars were visible. There wasn't even a moon.

"You like FOX Tidus?" Hugo said.

"I do."

He nodded. "Do you think your feelings for him compromised your work?"

"I don't."

"Not even tonight?"

I felt a defensiveness rise, but I knew he was just doing his job.

"No. I got the answers, didn't I?"

"Is there a chance FOX Tidus was saying what he thought you'd want to hear?"

"I doubt it. He was the one who brought up ghosts when we met. I think he's just into paranormal things."

"I wish you had said something."

"You knew I had met him."

"Yes, Martin. But not that you had feelings for him."

I sighed and rubbed my face. "I wouldn't call them feelings. I'd call it an openness to feelings. And there's more. We'd texted for a few days when I met him. Basically from the day of the rift until his name showed up from the data team. I haven't talked to him since that night."

He stared at me.

"I do find him attractive, but I know I can't pursue a relationship with him."

"Okay, Martin, is it just FOX Tidus?"

"What do you mean?"

"I mean you've observed eight other Tiduses closely."

"Yeah?"

"Does your openness to feelings carry to the others?"

I hadn't thought about it much. "I feel like FOX Tidus is my…is the top of the list."

"How are you analyzing your feelings?" he asked.

"What?"

His voice was closer to curious than frustrated or disappointed. "Assuming a scale of interest, what parameters are you using to rank them?"

I laughed. "Jeez, have you never dated?"

He laughed too. "I haven't really."

"With the other Tiduses, it's like watching remakes of a character in a story."

"Like Cinderella," Hugo said.

I squinted at him. "Sure. There've been many, but there's probably one you like best."

"I see. And FOX Tidus is it?"

"Yeah."

My heart was beating hard. I didn't want to talk about Tidus or Luca. I didn't know how to talk about them both. Even with Wei, I had been nervous. Everyone had too much at stake: friendships, research, career, heart.

"Well, I'm going to go over the data you collected on the Tiduses so far and do a week of my own observation. I have been mulling over biases in our data collection process anyway. I mean, you like the Tiduses and Tamar hates everyone, so if I'm going to be critical of you, then I must be critical of her. I feel like this'll help me kill two birds."

"Two?"

"I can check your work and see if the Tidus results are compromised, and I can make a comparison of your data with mine to see if the analysis overall would benefit from having us continuing observations but switch subjects. I was thinking about the law of averages."

"I don't know what that is," and before he could say anything, I added, "don't bother."

"Fair enough," he said with a laugh. His expression went serious again. "I'm also going to make Tamar lead on the next Tidus, ACE Tidus. You'll go with her since you're still the Tidus expert. And I figure even if either of you flirt with him, this one is both married and monogamous."

"Fair," I said.

"Let's get some rest," Hugo said, standing.

I didn't stand. "H?"

"Yeah?"

"I'm sorry if this is a setback or if…"

He patted my shoulder. "It's not a bag of nails yet."

I stood. I had to ask, even though I didn't want to. "Wei mentioned that you noticed me and Luca?"

He turned to look out at the rocking ocean, and suddenly he was a wizened frontiersman in one of his shitty westerns. "Now, a man's heart is his own business. And Luca and I have been friends for a long time. It's not my place to comment one way or another, but I think you learned a lesson about honesty today. Or maybe about timing. Either way, I do know it's nice to see him care about someone again."

Hugo started toward the door that would lead us inside. I followed.

## Section 11

### *It just became a bag of nails*

"Good morning, everyone," Hugo said, wiping his sleeve across his forehead. He'd been forced to give us Saturday off since he and most of HQ had food poisoning. Sunday had him on his feet, for better or worse.

Tamar went over to him and put her arm to his temple. "You're hot."

"I'm on a prescription from the medics. I'll be all right. We have work to do. I need a volunteer to go with Martin to the FAX universe."

"I went with him for ACE Tidus," Tamar said. "I've met my quota."

Kiki held up their hands. "I did RUE Tidus. I don't want to go back to Florida."

The way some of the days were starting to run together, I wished I could opt out too. I didn't know how many more Tiduses I could take, even though there were literally thousands to go.

"I'll go."

We all turned to the voice. It was Mason. He stood and shouldered a backpack. He still looked more goth than not, but he also looked approachable for any A-class universe.

"I'd be happy to have you come with me. You know you're awesome even if you stay, right?"

I trusted Mason to know his boundaries way better than I did, but I couldn't help feeling protective of him. PTSD was no joke. And maybe if he didn't go I didn't have to.

"I believe in us," he said. He crossed the room and put an arm over my shoulder.

Hugo couldn't do much but agree, especially since no one else wanted to go. We listened to Hugo's brief on FAX Tidus and how pleased he was that we were getting even anecdotal evidence.

❖

FAX Tidus was a student and bartender. He was also the least focused and most ambivalent of the Tiduses. Mason and I were going to the bar to hang out and get an idea of how to approach him.

"I haven't been to a bar in a long time," Mason said softly.

Mason had Wei's camera because Wei trusted him more than me to get a decent picture. He snapped a photo of me as we passed a shop. The universes felt like they were blurring. The street the bar was on was generally the same longitude and latitude as the coffee shop FOX Tidus worked in, but this version of the city wasn't a queer community.

"You ever wonder what it'd be like to live in the verses?" I asked.

He shrugged. "Yes. In my own verse I was pretty lost. When I was first recruited, I used to dream about going to another verse and living a different life."

I looked in the windows of a furniture store. "Why not pursue it?"

"I found people I care about. I found work I care about."

"*Take another photo of Martin*," Tamar said in our ears.

I turned and gave the camera the finger as Mason snapped the photo.

"Do I look weird?" I asked.

"*Always*," Tamar said. "*You're just brighter than usual. You must be picking up a lot of debris from universe hopping.*"

"I bet." Pieces of universes tended to stick as people moved through them, but they always found their way back to their home-verse somehow.

"*Wait, go back to that store.*"

I immediately backtracked.

"*Buy that magazine, with the woman on it.*"

The woman was a Nobel Prize winner, and I knew she had been in the photo of the founders. Mason followed happily and silently as I went into the convenience store and bought the magazine. I put it in his backpack, and we continued.

"What about you?"

"What *about* me?" I answered.

"Do you wonder about living in a verse?"

"I do. I'd probably live in my own if it came to that. I have family."

"That's nice. What would you do for a job?"

"I'd probably be a stripper."

Mason laughed.

"Or a singing telegram guy."

"Can you sing?"

"Nope."

We got to the bar early enough to beat the crowd to the counter. A bartender carded us and asked what we wanted. I ordered a beer I didn't plan to drink, and Mason asked to see a food menu. The bar was a corner shop under a tower of condos, all brick and spray paint. It was filling up with half-dressed tan men and women.

"I don't know why, but I expected this to be a gay bar," I said.

Mason looked at me sideways. "How can you tell it's not?"

I gestured around to what looked like mostly heterosexual pairs and groups of women. I had the distinct feeling of having stumbled into some kind of ladies' night.

"Hello," Tidus said.

He looked at Mason. Well, he looked at Mason's menu, disengaged. His hair was shiny and black, straightened and combed back. His T-shirt was black with the name of the bar in red spray paint across his chest.

"Have you made up your mind?" he asked.

"I'd like an order of street fries," Mason said.

Tidus nodded politely and put out his hand for the menu. Mason gave it to him and grinned at me. Tidus's gaze lazily followed, so I ordered the first beer on the big list on the wall. He looked away, but his eyes snapped back to my face almost instantly. They narrowed then widened. He looked like he wanted to say something, but someone from the other side of the bar called his name and he left. Mason and I looked at each other, shrugging.

"He seems like the black sheep," Mason said.

"Yeah, considering every other one we met embodies the phrase 'out and proud.' What're you going to say to him?"

"I'm probably going to ask about the bar."

I doubted this Tidus would engage with that. The Tiduses liked the paranormal, dogs, and gay shit. Nothing about the bar went to any of those topics. I watched this Tidus. He looked at the floor as some guy explained something to him, nodding along in that dead-inside way. Then again, maybe this bar was a safe bet with this guy, considering what he might be trying to hide.

I looked around the room. "I wonder if we could get him to recommend something. Tiduses like to recommend. I bet if we say we're new to the area, we might be able to get him to talk."

I watched a big, tan blond guy shove a bigger, tanner brunette dude. The brunette took a step back and bumped into a table of women. That seemed to have been introduction enough because both guys ended up leaning their humongous arms on the table, each engaging one woman, leaving a third to pretend to be on her phone.

"Here's your fries," Tidus said, placing Mason's food in front of him and a beer in front of me.

His gaze landed on me again. "Do I know you?"

I tried to play it off. "Naw, I doubt it."

Tidus seemed unconvinced. "You're so familiar. Did you go to Shepard University?"

"We're new to the area," Mason said.

I smiled at Tidus. "We're from Denver."

"Huh…I…" Tidus looked injured for a small moment. He turned a blank expression on Mason. "I'm going to go check on your fries."

We both tried to stop him, since the fries were in front of us. But Tidus was gone before we could say anything. Mason looked at me as soon as Tidus was out of earshot.

"He recognizes you too."

When Tamar and I interviewed ACE Tidus last week, he thought he remembered me, and the same thing with RUE Tidus Kiki and I met. It was starting to freak me out. We didn't get to discuss it, though, because Tidus was back. His eyes were locked on my face, and I saw a familiar determination. He had something in his head, and he was going for it.

"Martin," he said.

"What's up?"

Mason gasped, and Tidus cocked his hip in a familiar pose. I didn't realize what answering to my own name meant until FAX Tidus spoke.

"How'd I know your name if I don't know you?"

"I don't know. I probably said it." I shrugged, taking a sip of beer. It was too bitter for me, but it gave me something to do.

Tidus was a picture of emotions. I could read the surprise and hurt and confusion on his face. There was tension in his posture, and he looked hostile. My heart started to race.

"No…I…who *are* you?"

"What's your problem?" I snapped, hoping being rude would chase him off.

Tidus took a step toward me, staring into my eyes, waiting for me to explain. I said nothing.

"I *know* you. I swear to God, I…"

Tidus's eyes lost focus for a second as he tried to remember. Then without looking anywhere, he said, "The…the grays don't blow things up."

I didn't register anything after those words until Mason put his hand on my arm. I heard my name being said calmly, but I ignored that. I dropped the beer bottle, and it shattered. All I could see was the look of horror on Tidus's face. We backed away from each other, him into the barback, the glass bottles rattling as he pressed against the shelf. I backed into someone but didn't stop.

"Mason, we have to leave, right now," I practically screamed.

I turned and ran. I didn't stop running until I was barfing in an alley behind a dry cleaner's. I gagged, and my breath wouldn't catch. How? How could he have known that?

"Holy hell, Martin what was that?" Mason asked. He had run after me. He stepped closer, showing the pale of his palms. "Tell me what I can do. Is this a panic attack? Can you speak to me?"

I wiped tears from my face and doubled over again.

"I'm going to put my hands on you. I'm going to help you. You have to breathe, Martin."

I felt his hands on my shoulders. I heard a bottle rattle, and I felt the panic rise again. I looked up and looked around. It felt unnaturally dark. It looked closed off and sinister and unknowable.

"We have to leave, we have to tune away," I gasped.

The bottle rattled again, and Tidus stepped into the light of a street lamp just at the entrance of the alley. I saw another figure with him. It was shadow but it was so similar. The world was black around the edges, but I could see his face clearly in the light. I knew in that moment I had failed.

"Okay, here we go, okay?" I heard Mason say.

❖

I buried my hands in the sand. A gull, a breeze and the…clicking of texting? I opened my eyes and looked around. Mason was sitting nearby. The sound I thought was texting was exactly that. It was Mason typing into his sequencer.

"Where are we?" I asked. My mouth tasted as sandy as the ground we were lying on.

"Our HQ-verse. I let the boat know where we are, all we have to do is walk to the shore. What happened?"

"God, I can't even…how much of that was real, Mas?"

Mason shrugged and dug some water out of his backpack. "Start with what you remember last."

"I remember Tidus in the alley," I said.

He nodded, his face unchanged. When his eyes met mine all I could see was understanding. Mason was handsome. He reminded me of my brother when we were young.

"That part wasn't real, he was never in the alley."

"Okay." I rubbed at the spot behind my ear where the earpiece should have been.

"I took off your com," Mason said, holding up the magnet.

"Why?"

"Panic attacks are sometimes very public."

"No shit," I said thinking of the three or four people I plowed through in the bar.

Mason smiled. "I like to find as much privacy as I can when processing the super-public ones. I feel like I get to choose at least that much. I thought I'd offer it to you. We can turn them back on if you want."

I shook my head and drank more water. I lay back in the sand, knowing I'd be scratching sand out of my locs for weeks. "Thank you."

Mason let the silence sit. I stared up into the enormity of the sky. The stars had different names in some of the verses, but they were almost always where you expected them to be when you looked up.

"Did you hear what Tidus said?" I asked.

"The grays don't blow things up?"

I nodded.

"There were other Tiduses who thought they recognized you."

"Yeah, *thought*," I said. As I tried to say the next part, I could feel my guts turn over again. I wanted to throw myself into the water and sink. "Mas, I said that to FOX Tidus two months ago, at my last rift encounter. I just assumed they all thought I looked like someone else, but this Tidus knew me."

His eyes narrowed as he pieced together what I was saying. "But that would mean—whoa!"

I rubbed my face. "Yeah, I don't know what it means either. This one not only knew my name, but he knew what I'd said months ago to a counterpart. I've really fucked us over."

Mason put a hand on my chest. "You're not to blame. You might be involved, but that is correlation, not causation. Hell, maybe you even solved the damn thing."

I laughed. It helped.

"How the fuck am I going to explain to Hugo what happened?"

"They'll understand. I'm sorry the impact of this has made you feel alone. But you aren't."

"Thank you."

"The boat's here…well, about a mile over there," he said.

It took four hours to get back to HQ, which made it three a.m. when our boat docked. The whole team was waiting for us. I could see their shadows at the end of the gangway, huddling in the chilly night air. Their voices carried a little across the water. I had tried to formulate an explanation on the boat, but I couldn't really piece it together.

When we reached the others, Hugo greeted Mason with a nod and a pat on the shoulder. Then he hugged me. The physical portion of it was brief and slightly painful since Hugo was a dense guy and his grip was tight. The emotional impact was blunt and deep. When he stepped back, he put his hands in his pockets like he always did when he was dumbfounded. This gave room for Tamar and Kiki to step forward. Neither hugged me, but I could feel their worry.

"What the hell happened?" Hugo said, his expression pure concern.

"It just became a bag of nails."

# Section 12

## *Merde*

No one said anything. Hugo just tossed his arm around my shoulders and started back inside. I could feel everyone else's sympathy. It felt nice. It felt like being home. Everyone seemed to share my sense of exhaustion, so we went to the more relaxing common room in the research lab. Hugo let go of me as soon as we got there.

He went around turning on lamps, which warmed the room with gentle light. Then he offered to make everyone coffee or tea. I agreed to coffee with the majority. I went to the bathroom and brushed my teeth, then I came back out and sat at the piano.

"Martin," Hugo said as he poured coffee into a mug.

I blinked at him.

"Cream?"

For some reason that made me laugh. I was practically on the ground with hysteria. They let me laugh. When I was able to, I asked for cream and sugar. Hugo brought me the mug. He took his coffee and stood in front of the white board with so many weeks of notes on it. Weeks I had ruined.

"*Merde*," he mumbled mostly to himself, "I can't even say where we are anymore."

"He knew your name," Wei whispered to me.

"I know."

"How?" he asked. His voice was low. He was on the chair next to the piano, leaning so far over the armrest that he had to put a hand on the floor to steady himself. His face was pure curiosity.

"I wish I knew." I pressed a piano key.

"Why did you freak out?" Kiki said after a minute.

"Kix," Mason said.

"I just panicked. You all probably heard FAX Tidus say the thing about the grays and explosions," I said.

"We did," Kiki said, their voice gentler. "I agree, by the way. The grays are too sophisticated for explosions."

"Right," I said.

"It's the ones with tentacles who blow shit up," they added, sipping their coffee.

"Why not? It's worth it if you don't have hands," I said. I knew they were just trying to make me feel better, and it was working.

"What is that?" Hugo said, looking at everyone in the room. "Is that some sort of queer code?"

"What?" the rest of us said together.

"I'm just wondering." Then he practically whispered, "Is it a hook-up thing?"

We laughed, Hugo laughing with us.

"No," I said, "it's not."

I waited for everyone to settle before I told them about the exchange between FOX Tidus and me at the rift. They all gasped when I explained I had said those words to Tidus that day, and we had been joking together about aliens. I also explained the texts and the depth of everything between us. But it sounded shallow in the repeating. A horrible silence followed as everyone let my story sink in.

"This...wow," Hugo said. He put his mug down on the nearest table and stared harder at the white boards.

"I'm really sorry," I said.

"What for?" Tamar asked.

I pointed at the notes on the board. "Ruining the experiment."

"It wasn't an experiment," Tamar said. It wasn't a confirmation or a denial.

Everyone else seemed to be holding back their reaction. Hugo looked at the boards for a minute, then he pointed to a place in the middle of the notes, his finger making an audible thunk in the otherwise silent room.

"This...this is a *good* thing," he said finally. Then his face radiated happiness. "*Merde!* This is possibly *the* thing."

"How the fuck is it a good thing," I said, almost no volume to my voice. I was relieved but confused.

"He's done the thing, hasn't he?" Hugo said, tapping the white board urgently. "The Tiduses synchronized, somehow. A transference of memory. This is the exact thing we were trying to observe. We wanted to see this, and we just got so in the weeds we almost missed it."

"But we have no idea how it was done," Wei said.

"*Yet*. It gives us something to work with." Hugo was getting excited. He took the white boards by the tray and shoved them up, revealing a clean set of boards underneath.

"I didn't know it did that," Tamar said.

"We were tasked with observing universe-multi H-HIA and connections they could form that might impact the multi-verse. We knew it was a thing because of the Dugans. Now the Tiduses have just shown us that it is possible again. What we need to do is try and connect these moments with ACE and RUE Tidus, who also seemed to recognize you. We can try and see what FOX Tidus was doing and what was happening in the quantum realm. All during the event!"

Hugo wrote aggressively in French as he talked, detailing what I could only assume was his understanding of the facts I had lived.

"Might have to do it," he said, turning and looking at me.

"What?" I asked.

"Is it an issue for you to see FOX Tidus?" he asked.

I sighed. I didn't know if I could take seeing him again. FOX Tidus and I were so linked, the other Tiduses were picking up on it. It was changing them. It was changing me.

"That sounds dangerous," Tamar said.

"How so?"

Tamar went into the kitchen and found some chips before she answered. "When the Dugans synced, there was a catastrophe across a bunch of verses. This might be a good stopping point for the Tiduses. If we push them, who knows what damage could be caused."

Hugo pointed his marker at Tamar and nodded. "Fair."

"Plus, we might break Martin," she added.

"Also fair."

"I think my gal Beverly shows promise," Wei said. "She lives near a rift in Arizona. She probably has crossed it once or twice."

"Bet," Hugo said. "So, for now maybe we focus on trying to observe synchronizing in other subjects using the interview method. This has been compelling." He'd switched from a blue marker to a black one. "This could be the methodology we need to set up something testable."

"Should I tell you now that Beverly is kinda hot?" Wei said. "Just in case one of us wants to fall in love with her?"

"Fuck off," Tamar said.

"It's not love," I snapped.

Mason looked at Wei. "Is she the one with the pet puma?"

Wei laughed. "Maybe the power of love is what causes people to synchronize. I volunteer—"

"Are we done here?" Kiki said. "I would like to get some sleep before—"

The common room door opened, and Luca walked in. Something inside me relaxed at the sight of him.

"It's a bit early for a lab meeting," he said shyly, tucking his hands into his back pockets.

Kiki, Mason, and Wei rushed to him, exchanging hugs. At first, he looked perfect to me, his black hair long and shaggy on his forehead. He had on his usual light button-down and dark slacks. But the longer I looked, the more I noticed the damage. He had stitches down his right arm, visible where his sleeve was rolled up. There was a series of cuts on his forehead and a bruise darkening his cheek and eye.

"What happened?" Wei asked with all the expected tactlessness. He held up Luca's stitched arm as if to show him his own wounds.

"Uh, my mom and I were in a car accident. That's why I stayed longer. I'm okay, but she got the worst of it since it was on her side. I wanted to make sure she was okay."

"Why didn't you tell us?" Mason said.

"There's a lot going on here and not much you could do."

I wasn't sure of the feeling, but I think my heart broke slightly. I felt for a moment like I had overestimated our relationship since he hadn't reached out. Not that our relationship was the only one that mattered. He hadn't seemed to have informed anyone.

"What'd I miss?" he asked, trying to take some of the focus off himself.

His eyes landed on mine, and he gave me a dimply smile and a wave. I waved back, but I don't think I smiled. His face fell.

"We had a breakthrough," Hugo said. "How'd you know we were here?"

"I messaged Kiki when I got to the dead-verse. They said you'd be working late, but no one was in the data lab, so I came here. A breakthrough is good. And just in time."

We all stared at him. He flushed a little under the gaze of everyone in the room. "I mean, when we meet with Don tonight, we will—"

"We meet with Don *tonight*?" Hugo screamed. He raced to his desk and shuffled pages, looking for who knows what. He repeated the word "shit" under his breath in English *and* in French.

"Balls," Tamar said. "It's the progress meeting."

"I didn't know there was a meeting," I said. I'd been so bludgeoned by the disaster with FAX Tidus and learning about Luca's accident that the news about having to meet with a founder almost felt like good news.

"The meetings are standardized to be the first Monday of the third month of the projects," Mason said. "So no one has to *remember* them."

Hugo went into a tailspin of activity and bounced between muttering and announcing things to the room. He handed some papers to Luca and then some to Wei. Once one set of pages was out of his hand, he went in search of the next. He mentioned putting together reports and extracting data and said something directly to Tamar. I ignored him. Instead, I stood and went over to Luca.

Luca smiled slowly when I stopped in front of him. I didn't know if I was allowed to, but I went for a hug anyway. He hugged me back in a way that let me know he welcomed it, not just tolerated it. The top of his head came to just under my nose, and his hair smelled like a forest.

"Hi," I said.

"Hey."

"I have something to talk to you about sooner rather than later," I said.

I wanted him to hear about everything from me since it involved my feelings for Tidus. I wanted him to know I had feelings for him too. I didn't know how I would explain any of it, but I didn't want to leave it to anyone else to do.

"I'm assuming you mean privately," he said.

I nodded. Wei had his head down on the coffee table and was probably more asleep than awake. Tamar was leaning against Mason but watching Hugo rush around picking up files and making notes. Kiki was reading the magazine Mason and I bought. Mason looked nervously content to sit as long as Tamar leaned on him.

"Hugo," Luca said finally.

"Yup?"

"It's six a.m. I think we should try and get some sleep. Even just a few hours. The meeting isn't until seven tonight. We might not be organized, but we're ready."

Hugo suddenly looked wrecked as he surveyed the room. He probably wasn't completely over his stomach bug.

"All those in favor of Luca's plan, say aye," Tamar said. As the room agreed, she stood and approached Hugo. She shoved him and all the stuff he was holding toward the door of his room.

"I'm going to drug you and put you to bed."

"Is that an invitation?" Hugo said.

Wei wasted no time stretching out on the couch. He pulled his arms into the big tan sweatshirt he was wearing and was probably dead asleep before his head landed on Mason's lap. Mason laughed and extricated himself.

"Good night," Mason said, passing me and Luca on his way out the door.

"Boss," Kiki said, giving Luca a kiss on the cheek as they passed. "It's good to see you."

Soon we were alone, save for the sleeping Wei.

"You look kind of worse for wear," Luca said.

"I feel it. Um, is there somewhere else you want to go?"

"Go to your room," Tamar said as she went from Hugo's to her own.

"He's already asleep," I called back, thinking she meant Wei.

"Not him, dipshit," she said before her door closed.

"Oh. My room," I said.

Luca followed me. My room looked different once I had stuff out of boxes. I'd hung the photo he had given me on the wall along with several movie posters and pictures of my family, but it still looked spacious.

"Sit anywhere," I said, opting for the least comfortable of two chairs. Luca sat on the bed. He looked at me, waiting. "I wanted to talk about what happened tonight."

And I told him everything. He listened, not looking up from the floor until I had finished. Then he looked at the poster of the rift.

"Why didn't you tell me before?"

"When?" I asked, sounding more confrontational than I wanted. "I never expected to talk to him again. It was kind of hard observing him, but that felt more like crushing on a celebrity than on a person. I was trying to let it go. And I was trying to focus on what I feel with you."

He didn't say anything.

To make a point, even though I wasn't sure what that point was, I asked, "Why didn't you tell me…*us* that you were in an accident?"

He looked at me. I couldn't read his feelings, but I didn't push.

"I honestly didn't think to. For as long as I've known everyone, it never felt this personal. I always felt like everyone's boss. Except this time around. We all actually hang out together, beyond just transferring reports. It hasn't even felt this close between Kiki and Mason and me. With you here and this project—I don't know, something clicked."

He looked back at the poster and smiled. "Why are you *also* telling me about how you feel about Tidus?"

I hesitated. "I respect you. I feel…have feelings for you. I feel like if you're involved with me and my multiple attachments, you should know."

He looked at me. I tried to look at him, but I ended up looking at a bunch of other stuff.

"Would you pursue something with him?"

"That isn't feasible."

He laughed a little. "That wasn't the question. Holding all other circumstances constant, only thinking about your feelings—would you want to be in a relationship with him?"

"Pfft," I said. Then I thought about it. "Yes."

He nodded.

I waited.

"And me?" he asked after a moment.

I felt the implications of the question deep in my heart. I wanted to jump at the chance, say yes, go all in. But I could tell the question wasn't an offer. He was asking with the objectivity of a man who had made a career of gathering information.

"Holding all else constant, yes," I said, even though it wasn't the total answer I had wanted to give. "Yes…holding nothing constant too…I think."

He nodded and stood.

"Wait where are you going?"

"To bed," he said.

"Is that an invitation?" Then I felt annoyed with myself and took it back. "What I mean is, what about…I…how do you feel about it all? And me?"

He shrugged. "Honestly, Martin? I'm so tired I couldn't even tell you how I felt about breathing."

I understood that. "Fair enough."

He did close the two or three steps between us and put his arms around my waist. I let myself be hugged.

"Good night, Martin," he said, pulling away.

"Night."

# Section 13

## *Honey—Oh shit!*

"I don't really want to go in there," Tamar said. She was standing outside the door to the computer labs with me and Wei.

I didn't need to ask what she meant. We had so much more of everything now. There was more information about universe-multi people. And about the founders. We had magazines and newspapers with their faces across multiple universes. It wasn't a lot, but it was enough to give me that prickling feeling.

"There's still a lot unanswered," Wei said.

I looked at him, but his sleepy face was unreadable. He had managed to shower and change into a brown turtleneck and green corduroy slacks. He looked nice.

"True," I said.

We keyed in the code, and Kiki retrieved us from the hall. No one said anything as we walked to the data lab. Hugo was already there, hole-punching pages and stacking them into eight neat piles.

"Hey, everyone," he said.

We just grunted.

"I know, but the good news is I think we're in a solid place. First of all, we have summaries of what information we've collected." He held up the unfinished report. The first section on blue paper was summary statistics for all universe-multi people we found using the altered algorithm, then on white, some base information about our methods. The gray section at the back was detailed reports for each individual we observed.

Hugo picked up a stack of pink pages not yet incorporated into the report. "This is a summary of the interviews with Dugan."

Then a stack of green papers. "This is the interviews Martin and company collected."

He flashed us the freshly hole-punched lavender pages. "I finished writing up my observations, and Mason was able to do a quick comparison of your observations and mine. He wasn't able to measure any statistically significant difference. Well, I mean there was one, but it's not crucial. Besides, I didn't have as many data points as I would've liked."

"What difference?" I asked, feeling a sense of panic. Did I fuck it up?

"You didn't mention anything about FOX Tidus's cereal problem," Hugo said, carefully realigning his papers.

I thumbed the forty-page report that occupied the space where my laptop usually sat. I thought it out. Sure, the guy liked Honoy-Os cereal. But I wouldn't call it a problem.

"So what if he eats cereal for dinner sometimes?"

Hugo nearly laughed. "I guess, but I wouldn't spend thirty dollars in one go on it."

That was at minimum ten boxes. I squinted at Hugo. "What?"

"I mean cereal is almost as uninteresting as paper in the multiverse, but he's obsessed. *Reconnaissez le maïs*."

"Because he buys BOGO cereal?"

"He had seven boxes on his counter two days ago, and he bought six more by the time I checked in on him this morning."

"That…no. Show me," I said.

Hugo pointed to the laptops set up on a new square folding table. I went to mine and opened the site. I went straight to Hugo's notes. Every time Hugo observed FOX Tidus, he counted an increasing number of cereal boxes.

"What the hell is he doing?" I said. "Something is up, because he didn't have anywhere close to this many when I was watching him."

"Really?"

Hugo looked over my shoulder. Actually, everyone did. I had been standing, but I sat and pulled the joystick closer. I activated the video feed on FOX Tidus's drone and drove it out for a long view of Tidus sitting at his kitchen counter.

Seven boxes of cereal were on the counter. Tidus was eating some out of a bowl he held under his chin as he overstuffed his mouth. He glared at the box. Then he jabbed it with his spoon. The box rocked, slid, and ended up on the floor. Tidus jumped up and raced after something behind the counter. Then Bowser trotted around to the visible side of the island with the box in his mouth, cereal spilling all over the floor. He dodged Tidus and trotted back around out of sight.

"Why is he doing that?" I wondered out loud.

"You think it matters?" Hugo asked.

I did. I couldn't say how or why. I flew the drone around to the front of the column of boxes. The front box was in a language I couldn't read. I drove down the side of the boxes, then I turned it around to try to find Tidus. He had managed to get the box back from the dog and was watching as the Great Dane lapped up the mini-donut shapes off the floor.

I clicked back to Hugo's notes:

*HDM FOX TIDUS: Purchases eggs, frozen veggies, three boxes of H.O.*

*HDM FOX TIDUS: Four more H.O. purchased. Two from Latino market. Two from kosher market.*

*HDM FOX TIDUS: Consumed one box of H.O. in one sitting.*

"Jeez, H, did you have to abbreviate Honoy-Os to H.O.?" I laughed. "Tidus buys a lot of Hos."

"I got hoes in different universe frequencies," Wei sang.

"*Merde!* I didn't even notice—damn it, it's like that in the report," he groaned. I could feel him move off.

The boxes on the counter were the ones purchased from the ethnic grocery stores. I couldn't read much off the boxes. I flew around as Tidus moved back toward his room. Bowser followed him, momentarily abandoning the cereal on the floor. I turned toward the open shelves that served as a pantry.

"Maybe it's a taste test," Tamar said.

"Doesn't everyone know what Honoy-Os taste like?" I wondered.

"He might be—"

"I don't think it's him." Tamar looked annoyed that I had barked at her. "I'm sorry, I just mean…I don't think it's him."

I found three English boxes of cereal on the shelf.

"Honey-ohs?" I read. Those words, gold lettering on a red box, were so familiar children could identify them. And yet it didn't look right. I squinted and tried to read it again. "Honey-oh-*oh shit*. It's the brand. It's the *brand*!"

"What?"

"I can't say for sure, but I don't think it was called that before. I mean it was always Honey-ohs in sound, but I don't think it was spelled that way," I said. I was trying to talk and think at the same time. I clicked back to my notes. I had tried to write down foods we had watched people eat. Some foods were decent at crossing rifts, some weren't. I wondered where and when I had noted the cereal.

"Really?" Tamar asked, leaning in. "That would be amazing. A real Mandela effect. I mean they're real, but in real time?"

"Another one?" Kiki said.

"What does that mean?" Tamar asked.

Kiki and Mason explained the alleged Mandela effect I thought I had experienced while at home.

"Why didn't you tell the rest of us?" Hugo asked. "That would've been great for the report!"

"I'm sorry, I didn't have evidence. But I have some for this, I just have to find it."

"What can I do to help?" Hugo asked.

"I need some cereal. Go down to the Hub get a box from every universe you can. Make sure they tell you which verse it's from."

"I'm on it," Tamar said.

"I'll help," Mason said. They left in a blaze of plaid.

"This is crazy," Kiki said.

"Kix, is there a way to search my notes for a keyword?"

"I think so," they said. I switched places with them at the table. They keyed in a backdoor code for the program, then they did some digital magic.

"This could be huge," Hugo cried, hole punch still in hand. "Could you imagine what we could know from observing a King Henry effect in real time? Could you imagine if we could pinpoint the exact moment it changed?"

"We don't *know* that it changed. I just really, really think it did. I can't remember for sure. The last time I saw a box was with Luca."

"What box?" Luca said, stepping into the room. We all turned to him and I heard the others breathe, readying to explain.

"*Nobody tell him*," I practically screamed.

Kiki, Wei, and Hugo looked at me like I was nuts. Luca looked amused.

"What is it?" he asked.

I found a pen and paper. "What's your home-verse?"

I poised the pen to write. I heard Luca clear his throat. He put his hands in his back pockets in that nervous way he did. He didn't look like he wanted to say.

"I…um…2940F…OX."

I stared at him. It was a moment of weightlessness. My brain couldn't process the idea that Luca and FOX Tidus shared a home universe.

"Wow, what're the odds?" Hugo said, expressing half of what my brain was thinking.

"Martin has a type," Kiki said, supplying the rest.

I glared at them. "Focus."

I looked back at Luca. I abandoned my pen. He just shrugged, a little apologetic.

"I…well, how you answer this next question has the potential to change everything."

"No pressure," Luca said.

I took a breath. "You know that donut-shaped oat cereal."

"Of course."

"How do you spell it?"

"What?"

I wanted to laugh with excitement and suspense. "Please, just spell it, the brand."

"H-o-n-o-y-o."

"I can't believe it," Hugo said, collapsing into a chair.

"Are you sure?" I asked. My heart slammed against my ribs. I had to be sure. I needed him to be sure. "How do you know?"

"Martin, I live there. There were jingles. 'We put the O in honoy, honey. We put the O in honoy, honey. Can't ever have too many Os, so we spell it h-o-n-o-y honey,'" Luca sang. His conviction was clear. "What's this about?"

"Look," I said, pointing him toward Kiki.

He looked at the video, still showing the boxes of cereal in the 2940FOX universe that were labeled Honey-Ohs.

"I don't get it."

"That's in your home-verse," I said. "That's FOX Tidus's house."

I watched his face, waiting for understanding to slot into place. The bruising on his cheek was hardly there, and he looked less tired than he had the day before. His dark eyes scanned the image and then looked at me.

"I—" Then his eyes snapped back to the cereal. The moment of understanding was so clear on his face, it was almost audible. His mouth dropped open and a hand came up to cover it.

"What in the hell?" he breathed.

# Part Two

## *Trying to rewrite the conclusion*

# Section 14

## *Who hates dogs?*

"I have to go there," I breathed, staring at the photos.

Kiki had printed every image of the cereal we could scrounge from different universes. Hugo was ready to dig into all the footage MVP had, but Luca put a hold on that since we still had the meeting with Don. Mason and Tamar also came back with seven empty boxes, each with varying names. Hugo and I searched our notes and were able to collect some seriously telling information about the Mandela effect.

We were sure four universes experienced the name change and a handful of others *maybe* had. Of all the questions in my brain, one kept repeating: what did FOX Tidus know about it? We checked on the Tiduses in universes where we could verify the change. FOX Tidus was the only one who noticed. What about FOX Tidus made him see it?

"Go where?" Hugo asked. He was ferociously writing on his lineless paper. I watched as one page of notes turned into three before I remembered what I had been talking about. He was inexhaustible.

"FOX universe. We should talk to that Tidus. Why is he the only one who noticed? Maybe it started in his verse. His memory was transmitted to FAX Tidus, and all the changes seem to be in universes that are close to his in quantum frequency."

"Should *you* really go back?" Tamar asked.

Even though there was nothing in her tone, the question stung a little. I blinked at her. "What else could we do? Send someone else? I guess he knows Wei, or maybe a stranger would be better?"

"Send Luca," Kiki suggested. "It's his verse."

"I don't think that's a good idea," I said.

The room looked at me, and I could feel the question. Was I trying to keep Luca and FOX Tidus from meeting? It wasn't that. I had no ground to stand on to defend my feelings toward FOX Tidus, especially not when we were on the brink of something. I couldn't stop Luca, nor would I. It was his home, after all.

"We don't know what'll happen if he goes back. Will he forget the change? Are we willing to risk it?"

"I never thought about that," Wei said. "Can you be impacted by your universe after something changes when you aren't in it?"

"We'd risk his memory of it."

"Good thinking, Martin," Hugo said. He put a hand on Luca's shoulder.

"Interesting," Luca said.

"I don't care who you send. We need to ask Tidus about this."

"Don't forget Don will be here in three hours," Luca said.

Hugo started swearing in French. He marched around the room flapping his hat against his thigh and running his hand through his long hair. I looked at the chart we had made documenting the changes. I could feel my connection to it all. I thought about Dugan and the drawings he had given us. I had the haunting feeling we were making a mistake.

"I'll go," Kiki said, "*with* Martin."

I looked at them. We all looked at them.

"Don doesn't like me anyway. I think Martin is the only one who can get close to FOX Tidus fast enough," they said. "Hugo said we shouldn't go to a verse alone, so I'm volunteering."

There was a full minute of silence.

"All those in favor of Martin's plan?" Hugo asked after chewing one of his thumbnails.

Hands rose into the air slowly, carefully. It wasn't unanimous, but I was going back to the FOX-verse.

"Okay, how will you do this?" Hugo asked.

"It's going to take five hours to get to Florida," Kiki said. They opened their sequencer and pressed a few buttons. HQ was on its way back south from its routine northern trek, but we were still far from the Florida area.

"That will make it eight-ish when we land, eight thirty by the time we get to FOX Tidus's part of the city."

"How will you find him? You'll scare him if you just walk up to his house," Mason said. "He doesn't work today."

The answer was simple. "Bowser."

"The dog?" Kiki said. "I hate dogs."

"Who hates dogs?" I asked.

"Someone who's been bit," Kiki snapped.

I sighed. "You won't have to engage with the dog. You don't have to do anything. The important thing is Tidus walks Bowser around nine. There's a popular park along their usual path. I can wait for him at the park."

"What'll you say?" Hugo asked.

"I'm not sure."

"Stick with the government thing. Say you're investigating something," Tamar said.

I was tired of lying to him. But what other way could there be? I couldn't explain everything. Not in one night, one moment, and have him believe it enough, trust me enough, to answer my questions.

"That's probably what I'll go with," I finally said, not knowing what else to say.

"Okay. Right, Tamar can be on the com, and the rest of us can finish getting ready for Don. This is really exciting. We're finally getting somewhere," Hugo said.

"Can't wait," Tamar grumbled.

Kiki and I split up to gather our equipment. We were on a boat heading south within twenty minutes. I closed my eyes and tried to think about what I could say. I thought about the lie that I was a government employee. I thought about the truth.

"Don't hurt yourself," Kiki said.

They sat across from me in the small, interior cabin of the boat. Their arms were crossed, and their face was shadowed. Their knee bounced.

"You okay?" I asked.

"Yeah, I'm just not sure what I hate more. Being there to face Don or leaving the others behind to do it. He sucks. All the MVP founders do."

I nodded. My brain cycled through the photos I had found for Tamar. I wanted to ask Kiki to say more but I knew I couldn't. "What would you say?"

"To Tidus? He's weird, so I'd probably go with the truth."

"Ya think?"

"Yeah. He's a dingus."

I laughed.

"*It would probably work,*" Tamar said in my ear. "*Hugo is worried we'll change a subject by observing it. I told him that it's quantum physics…so duh. Do what you need to. Plus, he seems super into talking to you about conspiracy shit. The worst thing that would happen is you punch a few more holes in the multi-verse.*"

"I'm not very good at punching, I'm all chub and no bite," I said.

"*Fucking focus.*"

I arrived in the park just past eight forty-five. I found a bench and pulled a book out of my backpack. Tamar was tracking Tidus and said he would pass me in ten minutes. Kiki wandered off to a coffee shop across from the park. They said they didn't want to watch me be weird with my in-universe boyfriend without a latte. From the bench, I watched women in sundresses take photos of each other against the hibiscus. I thought it was too dark to get good photos. Even though it was warm, it was winter, and the sun was long gone by now.

"*Do you remember the Mandela effect?*"

"I do," I answered, flapping the book's pages. "I didn't think it would impact me since this isn't my home-verse."

"*Couldn't hurt to check. It's kinda scary, right*?" Her voice dropped into a whisper.

I nodded. My heart was pounding. I thought of the last thing Tidus said. He was interested in me, and I had walked away from that offer. But there I was trying to get in his good graces again. I watched a collie catch a Frisbee and run a victory lap around a drinking fountain. The more I watched, the more I decided my cover story was trash. I didn't really have a reason for being in the park. If I was on a government job, I would probably just read in my hotel room.

"*Ten o'clock.*"

"It's only nine," I said without thinking.

"*Martin*—look."

I looked around. I didn't see him.

"*Other ten.*"

I swiveled and saw Bowser before I saw Tidus. The dog bobbed along, coming around a corner, his nose sweeping the path, but he never followed it into the grass.

"That's like four o'clock."

"*No, Martin, it's 'I don't give a shit' o'clock.*"

I shook my head and thumbed to a random page and pretended to read. I looked hard at the book, not seeing any of the words. I had read it over and over, so it's not like I didn't know what it said. It was from my home-verse. I used to think the book was universe-unique but now I know it's just a book, bundled paper. The book and my backpack ended up on the ground as Bowser climbed into my lap.

"Shit, I'm sorry I—" Tidus stopped mid-sentence when he realized it was me. He was holding his phone. He had been looking at it instead of where Bowser was going.

I petted the dog and tried to look remorseful. "It's fine. I…hey."

"Hi," he said in a voice with exceedingly little tone to it.

"I…uh, came here to read. I didn't come here to run into you again. I mean, I knew you came here, because I saw you the last time. I watched you leave…well, not *watched*, but I recognized Bowser and… um…well, here you are," I babbled. I also stood up. Bowser tried to put his huge paws on my shoulders, but Tidus carefully pulled him down.

"Well, it's a nice park. Bowser, let's go," he said with a polite smile. The dog heeled and they started to walk away from me.

"Wait," I said, grabbing my stuff off the sidewalk.

"Yeah?"

I caught up, and I looked at the book rather than at him. "I…am sorry. I'm…it's not…look—"

"I get it, Martin. You aren't interested, it's no big deal."

"It's not that I'm not interested," I said before I thought better of it.

He crossed his arms over his chest and looked at me through dark purple curls.

"You changed your hair."

He fought a smile and said, "You're not off the hook."

I laughed. "Okay. Fair, but I'd like the chance to explain. It's not going to be easy to understand most of it. It's complicated. I'm…if… well—"

"*Ask him to dinner*," the voice in my head offered. It wasn't Tamar.

It was Luca, his gentle, even tenor a surprise. "*Don's here, so it's just me now, I already got myself kicked out of the meeting. A restaurant will give you cover to talk without being overheard and it's neutral. Besides you're better over food.*"

I laughed and shook my head. I looked up at Tidus, who was looking at me like he was on the verge of walking away.

"You ever have Honey-Oh cereal?"

There was a flash of confusion on Tidus's face. His eyes narrowed. "Of course. Why?"

"I have been living off it for three days. If you let me, I'll buy dinner and explain myself. Let me prove I don't suck."

"*But you do suck,*" Kiki managed to add.

Tidus considered me. Bowser nuzzled under my hands until I had his big head cupped in my palms. I knelt down, and the dog flopped over to let me rub his belly, thumping his tail against my thigh.

"Bow, you're such a traitor. Let's go," Tidus said.

The dog rolled over and took his place at Tidus's side. They started walking away.

"I said let's go," Tidus called to me with a genuine smile. "I'm picking the restaurant, and we have to drop Bowser off at the apartment. I'm going to send your picture to my mom so if you murder me, she knows who to look for."

"Deal." I practically cheered.

❖

Tidus lived on the third floor of a condo complex he rented from an old couple who he used to housesit for. They moved to Boca Raton last year, and he agreed to keep the apartment until one of their grandkids wanted it. Paradise wouldn't last since a grandkid was set to graduate college next year.

"Sounds like a great deal."

"I'm a barista living alone in South Florida. I'm unashamedly taking advantage of them. But they don't care. They love me." He took out his keys and let us all into the apartment. Bowser bounded to the living room and started rolling on the floor, leash and all.

"Very cool," I said.

"I'm going to find a shirt with sleeves. Just have a seat," Tidus said. He hurried toward his room, and after a second, a door closed.

The boxes of cereal were all still on the counter. I sat at the island, one stool over from where I had observed Tidus sitting that morning. I picked up the box from the kosher market. Mason said the lettering was Hebrew.

"This is kinda intense," I called.

"What?"

"The volume of cereal you have."

I could hear him half laugh, half groan. "It was an experiment."

"On what?" I asked.

I wondered if it was going to be that easy. I could just stay on this line of questioning. But there was no immediate answer from the bedroom. I pulled a different box toward me as I waited. The boxes were completely full, but I knew Tidus wouldn't waste the cereal.

"What was the experiment?" I asked again louder, figuring his lack of response was because he hadn't heard me.

"*That's weird*," Luca chimed in. I didn't respond to him. I just tapped near the communication device three times to signal I was listening.

"*His location changed?*"

I stood, nearly knocking back the stool. Bowser slowly moved toward where Tidus had gone. His low growl was surprisingly scary. We stood side by side looking down the hall. By location Luca could only mean in the multi-verse, which was nearly impossible for Tidus.

"Tidus?" I called.

"*Martin!*" Luca's voice was unfiltered panic.

"Tidus!" I screamed.

The door to the bedroom opened, and a huge shadow filled the hall. It was too wide for Tidus. Bowser and I seemed to have the same thought, and I stomped on the dog's leash as he inched forward, growl rising.

"Hello, Martin," the shadow said.

I knew that voice. Bowser snapped and pulled on his leash. When he realized I wouldn't give him ground, even though he could have easily taken it, he crouched. The shadowed man came into light, and I stared into the face of Don Brady.

"Who the hell are you? What did you do to Tidus?"

"I think you know who I am," Don said. He looked like the MVP founder, except he had a full head of sandy hair and was dressed in a polo and slacks. He gave the vague impression of being a floor manager at a mattress store.

"That doesn't answer the question," I said. "I'll let this dog go."

As if he was just waiting for me to make a threat, Bowser growled louder.

"*Who is that?*" Luca said.

"Tidus is alive and well for now. In fact, they both are."

I blinked. "What does that mean?"

I had asked the question more to Luca than Don. If Luca could still see him, if the drone was still transmitting his longitude, latitude, and frequency, then Tidus was in the observed multi-verse somewhere. That meant Luca could find him.

"*Shit, I don't...he...his QD says he is in A-Class universe 2942GOZ.*" Then Luca said what I was thinking. "*That shouldn't be possible.*"

"Don't play dumb, Martin. I came to talk to you. Tidus is just going to be a little insurance so I can be sure you understand how seriously you should take us. We only have a few questions. I know you have a way of locating him, so for the Tiduses' sake, I would recommend you come. You have ten minutes."

I heard what Counterpart Don said, but my brain had stalled out on the idea that Tidus was in another A-class verse. This Don had somehow found a way to get Tidus in a universe with another Tidus without them converging. Don moved toward the living room, and Bowser shifted to keep him in his sights.

"What the hell could you possibly want to know from me?" I said, refocusing on Counterpart Don. But Don just looked at his watch, then adjusted what at first appeared to be a name badge on his shirt. Then he was gone.

# Section 15

## *Sounds like a trip to therapy*

"What the fuck was that?" I screamed, racing to stand where Don had disappeared from.

"*I don't know. Don—our Don, is still here. That is a counterpart. I can't see him in the data.*"

I took a breath. The air was clear. It smelled like Bowser and canned air freshener. The lack of peanut butter smell, my tell for people crossing the multi-verse boundaries, told me he hadn't tuned into or out of this verse.

"He didn't tune to get here," I said. "He had a device. It's multi-verse tech but different from ours."

"*Convergent evolution,*" Luca gasped. I could faintly hear frantic typing in the background. I suddenly wished he was with me in person. I wished I could see his face. It felt silly and new to want him in that way.

I raced down the hall to the bedroom, Bowser at my heels. The door was open, and the room beyond was empty. The shirt he had been wearing was on the bed. Bowser nosed around the room. When he didn't find Tidus, he ran back down the hall toward the bathroom. We both heard the front door open at the same time. He bounded past me back to the living room, leash whipping around my ankles. I followed and was able to see Kiki enter the house just before Bowser leveled them. Bowser was happy to see Kiki, as if he knew they would help. Kiki, on the other hand, was practically shrieking.

"Jesus, stop," I said. I tried pulling the dog off, but that was beyond my abilities. I took a step back and repeated a command in the most Tidus voice I could muster. "Bowser, let's go."

The dog heeled instantly. I picked up the leash.

"What the actual fuck?" Kiki said, rolling off the floor.

"Sorry. He's worried."

"Not the dog, Martin, you dip. What in the fuck? Was that really a Don?"

I sighed and ran my hand over my face. "Shit, I have to go after him."

"Martin—" Kiki said.

"*Martin*—" Luca said.

"No, listen. This is a big deal."

"I'm not stopping you, but what can I do? What can *you* do?" Kiki said. Luca was silent.

"I don't know. I need to think."

Kiki looked around and looked at the dog. "Think out loud."

"I need to get Tidus out of there. I need to hear what they want. A, it's a counterpart of a Don, so I have no doubt that he'll find me again and he'll find anyone he needs to get what he wants. Then, B, there's tech out there that can move people through the multi-verse, but it's not controlled by us and that's a problem. And three, he knows me by name. Or was that C? Four?"

"Martin," Kiki said. "You're going to hurt yourself."

"*Don't rift repair technicians have escape procedures?*" Luca said, his voice low and bland. "*Shit, someone is coming. I'll be back.*"

"He's right," I shouted, remembering.

A few years ago, rift technicians started going missing, dozens by the time we could get the coordinators to do anything about it. The real turning point was because Margo, the founder who recruited me, disappeared. The coordinators put together a team and designed escape protocols. I had a feeling the other founders cared more about Margo than the technicians, but we got our safety system anyway. I was part of the protocol design group. We must have done a great job, because no technicians have gone missing since.

"Right," I said. "Pull out your sequencer."

Kiki did as they were told. I took mine out and practically dumped my backpack on the floor to get to the Tupperware with the drones in it. I hurriedly typed code, waking the drones.

"Okay, Kix, I'm going to release a few thousand drones. I want you to sync with them and then sign your phone over to me."

"So, I'm without my sequencer. Am I staying here?" They did as they were instructed, but their voice made it clear how little they liked that idea.

"Yeah, I need you here to keep talking to Luca. Besides, I don't think Counterpart Don knew you were in this verse with me. And if he doesn't know you're here, all the better for me. If you need it, Luca can snag your drone and pull you out of here."

"*What do you mean?*" Luca asked.

"Good, you're back. Do what I tell you."

"*Okay, make it fast. There's an issue in the meeting, and I don't know how much time I have. They might be coming back to the lab.*"

"Right," I said. While I talked, I programmed a few escape protocols on my sequencer. "Each sequencer has enough power to tune a human what, ten times at the most, if you're not using the other features. Well, it's the same process drones use. If you shut off all a drone's functions except location and then burn the total sum of its energy, you can tune a person at least once, twice if it's freshly charged and the person is small enough. Luca, all the Tidus drones are linked to the computer in your lab. I want you to release Fox Tidus's drone to my sequencer. Then I want you to pull up the there-verse Tidus. We'll tune him out of there if we have to and send him to a nice empty verse until the danger is over."

"Sounds like a trip to therapy," Kiki said.

I looked at them and laughed. I felt like crying, but I was glad I wasn't alone.

"*On it,*" Luca said.

"Also, pull Kiki back if you need. Keep my drone on standby, but don't pull me out till I say so. As a signal, I'll just say your name since I doubt anyone there will be called Luca. I'll also have two sequencers. I have a few tricks up my sleeve."

I set Tidus's drone to its own escape protocol. Then I programmed each protocol to a speed dial option on my phone. When Kiki handed me their device, I did the same as I had done with mine. And that was it. That was all I had at my disposal to impact the situation.

I considered my plans. In my guts, I knew it would be dangerous. This Don threatened to obliterate two Tiduses and maybe even a handful more people just to get me to talk to him. The image of the painting of one Dugan staring at another one drowning under the ice came to mind. Don could and would destroy two universes if he needed to. And that kind of person knew my name.

"Man, I hate being popular," I said out loud. I put Kiki's sequencer into the bun of my locs and tightened my hair tie.

"Can you see it?" I asked them.

"No, but also why?"

I grinned. "If you were about to be searched by a white person, do you think they'd check your hair?"

Kiki smiled and shook their head. "What about the other one?"

I thought about putting it in my pocket, but that seemed both obvious and inaccessible. I couldn't risk Don getting it since half my plans depended on it, not that he could use it with the security protocols being as extreme as they were. My only option was to hide it. And I realized I should hide the drones, too. Nothing was more suspicious than my empty-looking Tupperware container. I considered the room. There was Bowser. There was the kitchen island, a bowl of fruit, a coffee cup, the boxes of cereal—*the boxes of cereal*!

"I got it," I said, snapping my fingers. I got a box and opened it. Tidus had started eating that one, the mangled plastic bag doing little to keep the cereal from spilling out into the cardboard. Before I reconsidered, I dropped the sequencer inside.

"You're insane," Kiki said.

I shrugged. "Escape training was about two things: hiding in plain sight and bluffing."

"Absurd."

"You would've been great at it," I said with a wink.

"I'm ready," I said.

Kiki made a dismissive gesture. "What? Don't want to pack a butcher knife or something fucking useful?"

I laughed. "Naw, it's fine. I wouldn't know how to use that anyway."

In a last-minute impulse move, I poured all the drones into the cereal box. It probably looked weird, pouring a near vapor of humming microcomputers into sugar O-shaped cereal.

*"Martin, you're going to be on your own for...well, I don't know*

*how long. I can hear them coming. Please be careful. I'll be listening. God, this is stupid and I hate it...good luck."*

"Wait, two more things," I said.

"*What?*" Luca asked.

"Go on a date with me," I said, feeling alive and worked up because of the adrenaline. Kiki's eyebrows jumped practically off their face. I heard Luca's warm laugh.

"*Ask me again when this is over. What else?*"

"When I say go, tune me to that verse."

"*God. You just said that will burn out your drone!*"

"Luca, it's okay. I have ten thousand more. I also just sent you a link to a second one for me. If all else fails, you'll know what verse I'm in, and I still have my com so you can track that. I just don't want to risk messing up my programing—"

"*Shit, fine.*" There was a beat where all I could hear was typing. Then he breathed. "*Okay. Ready.*"

Kiki stepped up to me and hugged me. I hugged them back. Bowser tried to get between us.

"Okay," I said when Kiki was back at a safe distance. "Go."

# SECTION 16

## *Think of me as a keynote speaker*

I blinked and found myself in an apartment. It was nearly empty and still smelled like paint. Well, like paint and peanut butter now. Maybe the building was new. The first thing I saw was Don standing by the windows. Tidus was sitting in one of five metal folding chairs. He jumped, visibly stunned, when I suddenly appeared.

"Martin," Tidus said. His face was pale and his eyes enormous. I could feel his panic. I tried to smile at him.

"All right, you have my attention," I said, going for cool, turning slowly clockwise to take in the rest of the apartment. I didn't let Don out of my sight, keeping him in my peripheral. "Seems to be a few people missing."

"Really?" Don asked, turning finally from the window.

I reached inside the open cereal box. I wondered what it would look like to ingest a handful of drones. I didn't try it. I shuffled the contents of the box and turned on my sequencer, pretending to eat some by putting my empty hand to my mouth. I could feel the drones buzzing through the cardboard, waiting for my commands.

"You said *we* would like a word with you."

The only hallway in the apartment led off to my left. I stood at a forty-five-degree angle to both Don and the hallway so I could see him and down it at the same time. That meant I was looking straight at Tidus. His eyes didn't leave me, but I couldn't let mine linger on him.

"I don't know shit," Tidus said. "And frankly, I don't want to know. I don't even know his last name. Wait. I remember it, but that's cheating because his name is what it is. I don't know anything about how I got here or who you are."

"It's all right, Mr. Avery. We didn't suspect you did. We're here for Mr. King."

"*We* again. So, let's see 'em," I said, gesturing to the room at large with the box, cereal crunching inside as it shifted. Tidus and Don were mostly in a living room. I was mostly in an entryway, and there was a kitchen behind Tidus. I could see five doors down the hall, but the weird part was the place was carpeted.

"Who has carpets in Florida?"

"That's what *I* said," Tidus said.

A high voice came from one of the bedrooms. "Let's move this along."

A woman stepped out and started down the hallway. She was a brunette with short, flat hair and thick makeup. She reminded me of a Twiggy-era model. She was wearing a pencil skirt with a gray hoodie and tennis shoes. She looked like she was going to brunch rather than a kidnapping. I knew her right away as the counterpart of the founder Josephine Hudson.

It almost wasn't a surprise. But it was interesting. Founder Don discovered a rift on the back acres of his home in Alaska, then he recruited lead scientists to help him investigate it. Founder Josephine was top in the field of quantum physics. Like the founders, these counterparts were working together. I could see counterpart Don, like founder Don, experiencing a multi-verse event. Then he found counterpart Josephine to help him.

I assumed they were here-verse. Josephine wasn't wearing a badge, so she didn't have whatever tech had allowed Don to find me in the FOX-verse. Tidus had a badge pinned haphazardly to the back of his shirt collar, though. I looked back down the hall. They needed two more founders to complete the team. A heartbeat after Josephine took a seat, two sets of arms emerged through the door, and two men tried to leave the room at the same time.

"Damn it, Justin," a warm tenor snapped.

"Sorry, after you."

Carl Payne came down the hall. He was another quantum physicist, but focused more on theory than actual technology. He was a dark brown man and wore a ball cap, blazer, and jeans. He actually smiled at me as he came into the room. On his tail was a tall, linebackeresque man. Justin Crawford looked like he'd had a career in high contact sports before he retired to be a social scientist. He stayed close to Carl but looked at me with obvious curiosity.

I had expected those four, so I almost turned away from the hall. Then another person stepped out of the room. And more surprising than the woman walking toward me was the man following her.

"Margo," I said before I could stop myself.

She looked at me with surprise. Her voice, however, was not surprised. "You knew my doppelganger."

"I did," I said, even though I more than knew her. She was the only reason I had a career in the multi-verse.

"We knew that," Justin said.

That earned him a few glares, but I tried to act disinterested. Margo had been one of the more crucial founders early in MVP history. She was not only a logistics specialist with a focus in cartography, but she'd also had the foresight to do a few computer science classes. I modeled my own education after her. Here-verse Margo was dressed in a tan suit and turquoise and silver jewelry, a long lazy braid of salt-and-pepper hair pulled over one shoulder. She looked so much like my Margo, I almost put up a hand for a high five. She just nodded and passed me.

It was lucky Margo had been first. My surprise at seeing a Hugo counterpart would've been enough to blow my whole cover. I doubted they knew MVP had a Hugo, or that I knew him. Until they revealed that, I would pretend not to know him. He looked at me and nodded out of politeness, his hands in the pockets of his jeans. His hair was shorter, and his face paler. But it was Hugo.

"What, is your grandma back there, too?" I tried to joke.

For good measure, I put my hand back in the cereal box, way to the bottom, past the hovering drones and actually pulled out a handful of cereal to munch. I let most of it fall to the floor in a way that would've made Mason pass out. They all watched the pile build at my feet.

"That's very funny," Don said, looking unamused.

I sighed and sat on the floor near the pile, my cereal box in my lap. "All right, if this is everyone, I'd like to start off by saying—"

"*You'd* like to start?" Don said, incredulous.

"Yeah, you invited me here to talk, so I'm talking. Think of me as a keynote speaker."

"We do have questions," Justin and Hugo said in unison.

"Bet, but there's something particularly important you need to know about me before this continues. And it involves that man right there." I pointed at Tidus.

"I'm not anyone," Tidus said, looking horrified. His expression was pure betrayal, like I was about to throw him under the bus. And I was, but I was mostly bluffing.

"We know that's not true," Josephine said.

"Yeah, we've watched you two together," Margo said coolly.

"Watched us?" Tidus said. "Nothing has happened between us—wait. Watched how?"

They looked where I pointed, and they looked back when I started talking. They weren't professional kidnappers, or criminals or whatever. As Hugo would say, this rodeo had too many cowboys and not enough horses. They were distractable by their own importance. While they were looking at Tidus, I put my hand back in the box and typed the speed dial code to start one of the escape protocols I had programmed. It would take a moment for the drones to get in place, so I needed to make a speech.

"Hey, whoa now, can I say something?" I said.

"What is it?" Don snapped.

"Thank you. Damn. Get invited to give a talk and all you get is heckled. What is that? Anyway, you aren't wrong. I care about that guy. But he has no idea what's going on, and I think it's important you send him home before we get started."

"Why would we do that?" Josephine asked.

I was happy with that question. I looked at everyone. Carl and Justin had on badges, Margo and Hugo didn't. The badges looked like something out of a TV show. They also said *doppelganger* instead of *counterpart*, which meant there were things about MVP they didn't know. Convergent evolution, like Luca said. I blinked to refocus.

"Seems to me that y'all think I'd rather talk than let you hurt the multi-verse or Tidus."

"That's true, no?" Hugo asked, his French accent thicker than the Hugo I knew.

"That just means you think I'm a heroic person, right? Well, I'm not. I'm the petty type."

"Really?" Don said, his annoyance clear.

"Really. That means I don't want Tidus hurt, and I don't want the multi-verse hurt, but threatening me, him, or it won't get you what you want. That'll do the opposite, actually."

"How does that work?" Justin asked.

I could have thanked him. I needed only a few seconds more. When we practiced, the protocol setup took a minimum of thirty seconds because it had to tap into the learning technology built into the sequencer. I also wanted to give the drones time to get out of the cereal box. Justin was providing time I needed.

"Any threat you make is going to inspire me to keep my mouth shut. I'm down to talk and all, but I won't do it if you threaten the things I love. See, out of sheer spite, the more you hurt him, the less I say. You've expended a lot of resources to find me, so I get that you need this information. But if you so much as look at Tidus or the multi-verse in a way I don't like, I'll shut up and you won't get another word out of me."

"I see," Don said. He looked at Tidus, then at me, then back.

"I guess we can just kill him," Don said. He took a step toward Tidus.

"Are you kidding?" Tidus screeched.

Don's comment divided the room, though I doubt they noticed. Margo and Hugo tensed, probably trying to hold back their shock. Justin shifted and Carl almost imperceptibly steadied him. The only one who seemed to agree with the plan was Josephine.

I stood and sighed. "See, that's the wrong answer."

I put my hand in the box and pretended to shake it, but I engaged the escape protocol I had set for Tidus.

"Well, I think you brought cereal to a gun fight," Don said with a laugh.

He drew a gun, real and scary, from the back of his belt and aimed it at Tidus. I hoped my face didn't betray my wildly beating heart. Tidus had just enough time to scream before he disappeared. The smell of peanut butter wafted. I couldn't tell if the others noticed their version of the tuning tell. They were all too surprised.

"What the fuck?" Don shouted. He stormed toward the empty

chair and kicked it across the room. He stared at the place it had been as if he expected Tidus to come back.

"How'd you do that?"

I sighed and tried to keep standing, though my relief almost sent me crashing to the floor.

"Escape protocol exorcist," I said, giving them an honest answer.

"Where did you send him?" Don asked.

I didn't say anything, I shrugged like I had no idea. Tidus, confused and scared shitless, was back in his own living room where Kiki could talk him down.

"God damn it," Don screamed. He leveled the gun at me. I tried not to flinch.

"Stop! We need him," Margo cried, trying to put her hands on the gun.

"Go get him," Don said.

"Who? Martin?" Carl asked.

Don looked around the room as if no one in his vicinity had a brain. "No, go get Tidus or his mom, get Martin's fucking dog for all I care."

"Why?" Hugo said. "He's not going to talk to us if we threaten him. So let's just—"

Don crossed to them and roared. "I said go get him."

"Well, I think we all need a minute to regroup," I said.

In their chaos, they again forgot to pay attention to me. I dropped the cereal box, pulled out my hair, and held the two sequencers in my hands. I pushed the call buttons on both at the exact same time. The group looked at me just as I tuned them out of the apartment. Then in a blink, the gun and the badges Don, Carl, and Justin had been wearing tuned back, thunking on the carpet. I collapsed to the floor too. I screamed with happiness and rage and excitement and terror. I kissed the phones and laid face down on the new carpet, breathing.

"Thank God for escape protocol pest and DWMP."

After calming my nerves, I stood and walked through the apartment. I picked up my cereal box, the fallen cereal, and the badges. I didn't pick up the gun. There was a charger for a phone in one outlet. I took that and put it in my pocket. Aside from the folding chairs, the place was empty. I wasn't sure what I expected to find. Whenever I engaged with the multi-verse, I carried a backpack full of gear, but apparently, I could get a lot done with nothing more than two phones and a box of cereal. If they had more equipment than the badges, they hadn't brought it here.

I went back to where I had been standing in the doorway and tuned back. When I opened my eyes, I was looking right at Tidus, who was on one side of the island. Kiki was standing on the other side of the room. Tidus had a knife.

"What the fuck was that?" Tidus screamed, leveling the knife at me, then Kiki, then me again.

"It's a lot to explain," I said, walking toward him.

"Don't move."

I stopped. "I'm sorry, Tidus. Like I was trying to tell you, my shit is complicated."

"That wasn't complicated, Martin. That was fucking impossible. Did I die? I mean, that can't be real. Was it magic? What was the point of that? I mean, fuck, I was just kidnapped by magicians. He had a gun. That is way beyond complicated. What the fuck do you want with me?"

"I'm trying to tell you," Kiki said. Despite being on the business end of a knife, Kiki looked calm and annoyedly empathetic. They didn't want to, but they understood Tidus.

"Well, do a better job," Tidus said. We all stared at each other, then he huffed tiredly and lowered the knife.

"What the hell *was* that?" he asked again.

"I hate to say it, but you know about as much as I do as far as them kidnapping you. This is Kiki, by the way."

"We've met," Kiki said in that weirdly polite way people did when people talked about someone they didn't like but had to be nice to.

I nodded. "Okay. Good. I bet you have questions, and Kiki'll answer them. I have to go."

"Wait," Kiki said, turning on me. "I'm not answering shit. What do you mean you have to go? Martin, what the fuck?"

"I mean I dumped Don and the others in a dead-verse, and I'm going there to talk to them."

Kiki stammered. "You...No...Why?"

"What's a dead-verse?" Tidus asked.

I looked at him. And despite everything he looked great. His hair had been half tamed into a curly faux-hawk, and the shirt he had picked out for our almost dinner was black and floral. He looked perfectly handsome.

"Wow, you look great," I said, realizing I had only stared and not answered his question.

He looked down at himself. "Stop that…but thank you."

Kiki practically climbed over the couch to shove me. "Martin Logan King, you better fucking explain yourself before I beat your ass and tune you straight to the center of hell."

Their face was pale and flushed and their eyes wide with panic. They were worried about me. I was surprised.

"Kiki, look. They know my name—I've got to find out what else they know. All of the founders' counterparts were there, even Margo."

"Oh, no."

"They even have a Hugo," I said.

Their expression turned from fear to unfiltered horror. "A Hugo?"

"Yeah, and they know that Margo and I knew each other. Someone has to get answers, and that someone's me."

They squinted at me. "I'll be murdered if I let you go alone."

"No one will murder you. Besides, you have to make sure someone comes to get me."

They looked even more outraged. "I do?"

"Yeah. You're the only one who's going to know I'm in dead-verse zeta-six."

Kiki sighed. "I don't know anything about the dead-verses."

"Don't worry, Mason'll know. All you need is a name."

Kiki flapped their arms. "What do you want me to do? Go back to HQ like nothing happened, explain all this to them then, what, come all the way back here to tune to there to get you?"

I blinked at them.

"You really don't have a plan, do you?" Kiki said.

"I have a plan to make a plan." I tried for a laugh.

Kiki crossed their arms and glared. "I don't like this."

"I don't either," Tidus said. We both turned to him. He took a step back surprised. "I…well, I might not know what you're talking about, but that guy had a gun, and that sounds dangerous. It seems like there's a lot of tension in that room and some high stakes. Once I was at the bar and one of my coworker's ex-bosses came in and exposed him for theft and fraud, and our boss explained my coworker had changed his ways, but the other guy wasn't having it, so he demanded my boss show him his margins or something, but they ended up in a fistfight, and in small claims court it turns out the other guy was my boss's ex-brother-in-law and was trying to steal his business secrets."

Kiki and I said nothing. Tidus shrugged and casually put his knife back in the rack.

"See? Tidus gets it," Kiki shouted, throwing their hands toward him. Tidus just saluted like he had done Kiki a favor.

I sighed. "I get that, but I can't just *not* do something. A lot of people could end up hurt, and we need a first responder. That's me. Besides, he doesn't have the gun now."

Kiki didn't look convinced. They were standing with their side to me, their arms crossed. Bowser flapped his tail against the couch when Kiki looked in his direction.

"Kix, if they could see how much I like him in three visits, what would they do if they found my parents or anyone else I care about? I can think of a thousand ways to use the multi-verse to fuck up someone's day, and I'm not even that creative."

Kiki groaned. "You might've been bluffing about being petty, but I'm not. I swear to God, if I get in trouble over this, you better get yourself killed before I get to you."

I laughed. "Deal."

"Does it have to be now? Can't it wait for help?"

"They have access to multi-tech and a Hugo. Think about how many people work for MVP. It's too risky to think someone isn't looking for them. I don't want to hunt the multi-verse for them later."

"I hate you."

I put my arms around them. "Even if I can't get information, I can distract them long enough for you to get reinforcements."

I put the badges and phone charger into Kiki's hands.

"The fuck?" they said.

"Tidus has one too," I said, pointing.

"I *what*?" Tidus yelped.

I walked over to him. He only took one hesitant step backward before letting me close enough to remove the badge from his shirt.

"Shit, I thought it was a security tag."

"I think Don put it on you. Where was he? In your closet?"

"Yes!" Tidus screamed. "I opened the damned thing to get a shirt, and he grabbed me. We went to that other place and then…well, you know."

"It's magnetic," I said, rolling the silvery disk and white plastic tag in my palm. "I'm sorry," I told Tidus.

He scanned my face and nodded.

I stepped back, and Kiki offered their hand. I shook my head. "Naw, wait. I'm gonna keep this one."

"Why?" they asked.

"Peace offering. If I did my job right, I essentially marooned them in the dead-verse. I'm going to give this one back so at least one of them can get help. I won't do it right away, but at some point."

"You sure have a lot of ideas for someone with no plan," Kiki said.

"The best offense is a good defense?"

"Shut the fuck up."

"What about me?" Tidus asked.

"What *about* you?" Kiki said.

Tidus threw his arms out. "I was just fucking kidnapped. What if they come back? I don't know shit about you all, and here I am having guns pointed at me. I can't stay here. I like you, Martin, but this seems a little toxic, so maybe you should both go? Or should I go? I don't know. What's a dead-verse?"

He paced around the island, ending up back where he had started. He ran both hands through his hair, disheveling the attempt to style it.

"Let me talk to him," I said to Kiki.

"You just said it was urgent."

"Kix. Give me a few minutes with him, okay?"

I signed their sequencer back over to them and placed it in their hand. They looked at it like they hardly knew it. It looked like them, though. In those days, when the phone was new, it had fun plastic faces and buttons that could be changed out from the generic black and white. Kiki's had a bright green plastic face with translucent buttons that lit up with different colors when pressed, and it had an antenna charm, a middle finger dangling from a bright pink cord.

"I'm going to the corner for air and coming straight back. That's all you get," they said benevolently, walking toward the front door. Bowser followed them and seemed sad when Kiki left. I looked at Tidus. He was leaning against the counter.

"I'm sorry. I really wanted to explain."

"Can you tell me what the fuck a dead-verse is?"

I laughed. "It's a universe without humans or human-intelligent animals."

"How does that work?"

I sighed and rubbed my head. "Uh, pretty much every moment, every choice, every event has the potential to develop a new universe—a reality that is fundamentally different from any other. It's founded on quantum physics and probability. In the dead-verses, something usually didn't happen when the earth was really young. In the one I sent the others to, humans just didn't survive a few ice ages. Maybe it lasted too long or was a few degrees colder than the ones that happened here, but all that's left is bugs and plants and a few kinds of animals."

"Damn, I was thinking it was some kind of underworld. Seems less scary." Tidus sighed. Then he thought about it all. "Any decision? Really?"

"In ways. There's a multi-verse where a Tidus agreed to go on a date with that *one* guy from his gym."

Tidus looked scandalized. "I didn't!"

"Not you, but another Tidus."

"I can't. He's so…ew—get me on the phone right now. I need to talk some sense into me." Then realization crossed his face, "How do you know that?"

"The answer'll make you mad."

"Try me."

"We were spying on you—"

"You *what*?"

"I know, I know it's not good. There's a lot more. I think you have the right to decide if you want to be involved in all this." I gestured to the multi-verse by sweeping my arm through the air. "You deserve an explanation, but I can't do it right now. Get answers from Kiki. You'll probably hate me for everything you learn."

He nodded. I had seen that nod before. It usually came after the sentence: "Sorry, sir, your car repair is going to cost more than the car is worth." Then his look shifted, but I couldn't decide to what. I felt obligated to keep talking.

"I give Kiki permission to answer any question you have about the multi-verse or me or whatever. But I wanted you to hear this from me—I didn't lie when I said I care about you. If this all weren't the way it is, I would've never walked out of the bar or away from your invitation by the river. I would've never stopped texting. No matter what you hear or learn about me, that was always real."

Tidus seemed to consider this. His expression was a mix of mad and scared and worried and elated and curious. He was going to have plenty of questions for Kiki.

"If I hadn't just teleported—twice—I would call the police." Then he thought about it. "Well, not the police, but someone."

"Thanks. Also, it wasn't teleportation. That's when you move from one point to another in the same verse. You just visited a whole alternate reality. We call it tuning."

"One where they carpet apartments in Fort Lauderdale," he said, disgusted. "You would've really dated me?"

"I would. Um, well…even that is a little complicated. See, there's another guy."

"You're polyamorous?" he asked, his tone too casual.

"Kinda. More like pre-polyamorous."

"What does that mean?"

"It means displays symptoms but not formally diagnosed."

He was biting his lip, trying not to laugh. "How long have you been with that guy?"

"It's kinda the same as you. I work with him. I know I met you first, but I work for a top-secret organization, and I didn't think you and I would ever see each other again. Then I met him and then you both kinda kept showing up."

"Is it a love triangle, then?"

"Not unless one of you make me choose, I guess."

He nodded. His nods were very telling. He had a nod for mad and disappointed, and he had a nod for amused but not amused. This latest one was pure scientific understanding. I could have just explained how the earth was round because of gravity and he would've given me the same nod. I felt suddenly like I had been seen, decoded.

"You can ask Kiki about that too. They know everything. His name is Luca, and he knows I have feelings for you. I don't know why I'm telling you that, unless you want to know."

"Is this the guy that came to the bar?"

"No, that's Wei. He's more like a brother. And I think he's straight. Honestly, if mystery were a sexual identity, that would be Wei."

Tidus smiled. "LGBTQIPA, why not add an M?"

"There's not already an M?"

"Oh, shit is there?"

"I don't know. I live in a dead-verse, and we don't get the news."

Tidus squinted at me, suppressing his laugh again. He had already figured me out, so his squint was probably to see if he liked what he saw. "You're so…"

"Weird? Bad?"

Tidus relaxed. "I'm kind of annoyed by how charming you are."

I laughed. "If I had a dollar for every time someone said that."

Bowser nudged Tidus, nearly knocking him over with the force of his head. Tidus looked at the clock. "Shit, buddy. Sorry."

He passed me and picked up a bowl off a stand on the floor. Then he held it up to a dispenser on top of the fridge. Dog food rained into the bowl. Then Tidus put powders and goop on the food and gave it to the dog. Bowser chomped happily.

The whole action brought Tidus closer. I was backed into a small corner the fridge made with a counter. Tidus stopped across from me, leaning on the island. He was still squinting. I looked at my shoes so I wouldn't have to watch him decide if he liked me. Not that I'd blame him if he didn't. Nor did I really expect him to know.

"You're really going back?"

"Yup."

"Really alone?"

"Yup."

"So, you were bluffing about not being a hero?"

I shrugged. "Is it heroic if you're sort of cleaning up a mess you helped create?"

Tidus looked like he wanted to ask about that. Instead he said, "So, if I ask enough questions, I might hate you in the future?"

"Probs."

"Well, you better kiss me now while I still like you."

I tried to regroup so I didn't look as desperate and excited as I felt. There was a flutter in my guts. His feelings had always been so tangible. I could feel his interest in me from the first day. In a burst of movement, he stood, met me halfway, and slipped his hands around my neck. His thumbs brushed along my jaw as I turned up to meet his mouth.

And it ended too soon. I heard myself breathe more than I felt it. It was like a time release pill of lust and joy and fear and happiness, my body only able to react to his mouth on mine after we parted. I was afraid that when I looked at him again, I would only see regret, but it wasn't there. Instead I saw sad confusion and warm pleasure in his eyes. I tried to think of something to say, but nothing came to mind. Fortunately, Kiki saved me.

"I hate stairs," they gasped, a shopping bag hooked into their elbow. I bet they noticed me and Tidus step away from each other, but they didn't say anything.

"You're a saint," I said.

Kiki gave me a look that was all venom.

"Right, okay, thank you anyway," I said. "Now."

I quickly shoveled my stuff into my backpack, including the remaining drones and my sequencer. As I zipped it, I carried the backpack over to Kiki. They didn't take it, just watched with annoyance as I set it on the floor near their legs. I checked that the counterpart's badge was in my pocket and stood in the middle of the room.

"I'm ready."

"No. Look, I had time to think about this and I can't," Kiki said. They tried to hand me back my sequencer.

"You do it or I do. I just would prefer if they didn't get their hands on our tech," I said.

"Hugo and Luca are going to have my ass."

"They'll be okay," I said.

Kiki growled loudly and pulled out their phone. "Fine, but I'm not going to your funeral."

"That's okay. I'll survive this." I gave them a wink and some finger guns for good measure. My laughter and unfounded confidence was the only way to make everyone believe it would work, to make myself believe it would work. I was scared shitless.

"Bye," I said to Tidus. He just waved.

Kiki looked from him to me then to him. "Welcome to the fucking shit show, Tidus."

"Thanks?"

Kiki flashed a fraudulent smile and held out their phone. They looked at me. “Tell me what to do.”

“Call up a single drone, set it to max power, attach it to me, set it to the dead-verse, then press call.”

I didn’t need to fill in any details. Kiki knew exactly what to do. They were probably just asking me for comfort. Or to have someone else to blame when it all went wrong. I took one last look at Tidus and at Kiki before the room blinked out.

# Section 17

## *I call it negotiating*

The Dugan universe, when it healed, if it healed, would look like the dark, starry pasture of this dead-verse, with tall grass and patchy trees. This was one of the first dead-verses Margo and I had visited. According to her, we were mapping, but I think she just needed to get on dry land. It was dry, but that was technically because it wasn't the Florida area. The longitude and latitude on the planet were the same, but the ground beneath our feet was not. Some of the tectonic events hadn't happened in this verse, so it was probably closer to the west coast of what most people knew as Mexico. I watched from the grass. The others were moving around and yelling at each other. It looked almost like a weirdly staged play.

"What were we supposed to do?" Carl shouted at Don.

"I'm starting to think there isn't anything to eat here," Justin said.

He was looking up at the sky as if the stars would drop a steak on him. I looked up at the sky too, thinking of that night on the roof with Mason and Luca.

"Why are you worried about food?" Josephine asked. "It's only been like ten minutes."

She was pacing perpendicular to Don's path, forcing him to occasionally go around her. Don seemed to be the source of most of the damage to the pasture. He was marching around, swiping at the grass as he passed it. Carl took a step or two after him but didn't follow all the way.

"I'm just trying to survive," Justin said.

Margo and Hugo stood off to the side, distinctly away from the others. Well, Margo was standing. Hugo was crouching, his head barely visible above the wheat. It was time to get this over with. Or started.

"Hello," I shouted.

All six counterparts turned to look at me.

"*You*," Don screeched. He started barreling toward me, the grass whipping back as he slapped it out of his way.

"Hi," I said.

I didn't bother backing up. I knew coming here meant taking whatever he had to dish out. He stopped only a few inches from me, grabbing my shoulders. He jerked me hard forward and then shoved me hard back, shaking me. He was taller than me by an inch or two, and I was not a skinny guy, but he shook me like I was nothing.

"Get us out of here," he said, his breath hot on my face.

"I can't." It was like he was shaking the words from me.

"Don," one of the others said, but I couldn't tell who.

"The fuck you can't. You sent us here, un-fucking-do it before I strangle you."

"I don't…have…enough…" He tried to get his hands around my neck, but I squirmed free. I almost fell backing up. When I was far enough from him, I righted my clothes and flipped fallen locs out of my face.

"I swear," Don shouted, trying to come after me. Justin and Carl got in his way.

"Come on, give us a second with him. Jeez, you can't go around trying to strangle kids," Carl said.

"Yeah," Justin added.

"I'm not a kid."

They all stared at me.

"I'm twenty-eight. It's a blessing and a curse. Look, I came to talk, just like you wanted. So, get talking."

"*No*," Don shouted, "No more. You had your chance, now we're leaving. Get us out of here."

"I told you I can't. I didn't bring any of my tech. Better start liking yucca's distant ancestor. We'll be here a while."

Don roared and charged at me. He was able to plow past Carl and Justin. He got to me in less than four steps, and before I noticed how close he really was, his fist was rounding on my face. It collided with my lower jaw and pain laced into my brain, turning everything black for a second. As I swayed and worked to get my bearings back, Don came after me again. No one else was close enough to stop him from landing another punch. I was knocked out after that.

❖

When I opened my eyes, I expected an endless field of grass and a bright sky of stars. I saw a water-damaged plaster ceiling instead. It was unwelcoming, familiar, but with none of the comforts of familiarity. I blinked at the ceiling and thought *hospital*. The room had the usual array of beeping and dings. I tried to move my head, but the sudden pull of medical tape across my face panicked me.

And I couldn't speak. No, that wasn't right, I could hear my voice in my head and trapped behind my teeth. I pulled a hand up to try and uncover my mouth, but another hand caught mine—a huge white hand with short fingernails and a wristwatch.

"*Bonjour*, Martin," its owner said.

I turned toward the voice, the tape pulling hard, but I needed to look at Hugo. When I couldn't quite get my head to turn all the way, he stood and looked down at me. I knew right away that it was Counterpart Hugo. His hair was short but not without volume, piled like yellow fluff on his head. He was wearing a black turtleneck and light jean jacket. He looked so French, it hurt. I made some incomprehensible noise I hoped sounded like the *fuck you* I had intended.

"I'm sorry, Martin," he sighed. "The doctors have wrapped your head. Don hurt you very badly. Your jaw was dislocated, but you've been two days under medication, and they say the splint will be removed very soon."

I groaned and tried to bring my hands to my face. Again, Hugo restricted my movements. I couldn't feel my face anyway. I mean, I could feel some of it if I thought hard enough, but I figured I was on some serious painkillers.

"Also, there's broken ribs and hairline fractures, but those are healing too." He smiled. And it looked so much like my Hugo's that it felt genuine.

I took his hand in my left, turning it palm up. Then with my right I wrote into his palm with my finger *y u?*

"Ah, *oui*. Well, we found our badge in your pocket, and we were able to get some help. Don wanted to leave you there, but Margo and I thought you would talk to us. We brought you here."

I had plenty of questions, but I couldn't keep my eyes open.

"I doubt he's up for this," Margo was saying.

It had been a few days, and a few doctors had come to see me. They said I was healing fine, so they were unwrapping my jaw. Nothing had been broken, but the swelling was enough to worry them. I didn't say anything and, unless my room was empty, I kept my eyes closed. When I was alone, I watched the TV mounted in the corner or I thought about my mom. Hugo had been in and out the whole time, always sitting quietly, sometimes reading. This was the first time Margo had come. I didn't open my eyes yet. I just listened.

"He came to us, so why shouldn't he be?"

"He just got the shit beat out of him," she said. They were doing a poor job of whispering.

"Well, soon then."

I could hear the clank of chunky shoes as Margo paced around me. "We don't really *have* much time."

I flexed the muscles in my face, scrunching it and un-scrunching it. I could feel more of it, mostly the right side. I could also feel the tightness in my chest as I breathed. It reminded me vaguely of top surgery.

"Margo, you can't have it both ways. You can't want him to give all the answers immediately and be worried that he's too injured to speak," Hugo said.

"Don't tell me what I can and can't do."

"Just," I said. Speaking sent a dull ache around the left side of my face, like someone spreading pain icing on my face cake. I also wondered for a moment what kind of painkillers they had me on.

"Martin?" Margo said, coming over to the bed.

I was sitting up a bit more than I had in previous days, so I could see them both standing near my feet. I put a hand up, and she stopped moving.

"Just ask your stupid questions." The words sounded slurred but were louder than I planned.

"I…it…how are you?" Margo asked, her face going from surprised to worried to compassionate.

"Fuck you."

And much like my Margo would've, she smiled. "Fair enough. My God, that was risky. What the hell were you thinking?"

"I was thinking how nice it would be to have my jaw wired shut," I said, closing my eyes again.

"That's not funny. It was very stupid."

"Call it what you want. I call it negotiating."

She sounded annoyed. "This was all beyond what we were trying to do."

"Does it matter?"

"Martin, we really didn't know it would be this way," Hugo said.

I didn't answer. I just stared into the void of my own eyelids.

"Maybe tomorrow," Margo said.

"I'm awake right now," I said, opening my eyes to prove it. "Who knows, I might just sleep through tomorrow."

Margo was wearing light tans and flowy cotton, her silver and beaded jewelry standing out like drops of color and refracted light.

"Well, shit. I don't know what to ask first." Margo scrambled for her bag on the floor by the door. She pulled out a laptop, pens, and paper. As she dropped items on the foot of my bed, Hugo moved them to the rolling tray they put my ice and water on.

I laughed. "Sounds about right. Who are you all anyway?"

"What do you mean?"

I closed my eyes again, "We're called Multi-verse Protection Corporation—MVP—and I've been calling y'all the Counterparts. Bet you have a name."

"We work for the Validation and Investigation of Parallel Universe Organization," Hugo said.

"Bet. I'm going to call you VIP for short."

Margo scurried around the bed and sat in the chair Hugo usually sat in. "Martin, our primary questions are simple."

"You mean what Don or Josephine want to know is simple. You look like you're ready for me to give a college seminar."

"You would tell me that much?" she asked.

"I guess it would depend on how you answer my questions."

"I didn't know you had any," she said, tapping her pen on her computer.

"Who wouldn't?" I was starting to feel tired. "Let's go."

"Right. First question—what universe is your company's headquarters in?"

"I...what?" I almost jerked forward, as if seeing Margo better would allow me to understand her question.

"What universe is your company's headquarters in? Or maybe the right question is where is your company's headquarters? I figured the way you account for both space and time is the same as the way we do when it comes to—"

"Margo?" The conversation was already a dumpster fire, and we hadn't even got past the first question.

"Yeah?"

I looked at Hugo, whose face was completely unreadable.

"Why do you want to know that?"

Margo looked at Hugo. And that look said she either didn't want to tell me or she wasn't allowed to tell me.

"Listen, I'm in a hospital bed with zero resources to contact my company. And if you wanted to, all you'd have to do is top this off with bleach." I made a point of rattling the tubes to my IV. "What's the worst I could do? Either start at the beginning or spare me."

Hugo laughed and sighed. "I'm going to go get some coffee. You want?"

"Yes," Margo and I both said.

"No, not you. Margo, come, so we can talk."

"*Toute peine mérite salaire*," I said in bad French before closing my eyes.

Hugo smiled. "Ah, rude even in French."

They left without another word.

# Section 18

## *That sounds like a real fucking problem*

I must have dozed off. When I opened my eyes again, the sky was growing black and the only one in the room was a nurse. I watched her looking at whatever it was nurses looked at. She was a wonderful older black woman. Her braids were pulled back under a wrap, and her scrubs had little elephants holding balloons. She caught me.

"Aw, see, you had us fooled there for a few days," she said, her voice light and warm.

I blinked like I didn't know what she meant. I didn't.

"You weren't talkin' to us, but we heard you talkin' to your friends today. Naw, now don't blink at me like ya don't know what I'm sayin'. Now, that French fellow is easy to pick out of a crowd around here. And your Indian friend—"

"Indigenous."

"Aw, see?" she said, snapping her fingers. It was as if she knew she could trick me into speaking by using the misnomer for Margo. "Now, tell me how that feels."

"Um, can't feel much."

She nodded like she knew that too. "Well, that's fine. The local anesthetics are wearing off. You'll feel it when they're gone, but we're gonna try to keep you comfortable. You ready to talk to the police?"

"The police?"

"Yeah, your friends told us it was a hate crime. Don't you remember?"

I sighed. "It was only a hate crime because the person who did it hates me. It's not identity related."

"Still a crime." She squinted at me. "How much memory have you lost?"

"How am I supposed to know if I don't remember?"

She harrumphed but smiled.

I smiled too. "Here, how about I ask you questions? You tell me the answers, and I'll tell you if I remember or not."

"That's not how it works."

"What day is it?" I asked, forcing lightness into my voice.

"It's Friday." As she answered, she maneuvered around me doing nurse things. Friday meant it was one day earlier than I expected. I figured it was Saturday.

"Who's the president?"

"Donald McMahon." Her voice betrayed her annoyance.

"Oh, dip, right."

She looked at me with a little more concern than she had before. "You forgot that?"

I shook my head. "No, but reality's unbelievable sometimes."

She nodded. "Who you tellin'? Anyway, try to get some rest. Like I said, once the local anesthetics wear off, you might be in a bad mood about the pain for a while."

"I would rather the pain. I'm not one for heavy painkillers if I can help it."

"Go to sleep, suga'."

"Thank you."

She dimmed the lights and left. I turned toward the window and thought of the stars, but I couldn't see any because of the light pollution. The important thing was that I now knew where in the multi-verse I was. Only one verse was screwed up enough to make Donald McMahon president. I was in A-class universe 346BGH, the hell pit that remained from the collision of two verses. And I knew how to get back home from here. I could see the whole multi-verse arranged around this one.

But the nurse was right. I was in a bad mood the next day. I woke up early enough to watch the sky turn colors as the sun rose. Everything I did caused the dull ache in my mouth to spike with sharp pain. And the absence of the locals also sharpened my rib pain. So if I did something like swallow, breathe, or think about my mouth, pain would lance through my teeth. When that happened, I would jerk and then pain would shock my ribs.

"Maybe I do want more drugs," I said to no one, looking at the slow drip of saline into my arm.

"Martin," Hugo said, knocking on the door.

I looked at the clock above the door. It was nine in the morning.

"It's nine in the morning," I called, causing pain all over my body. I sighed and tried to breathe through it, closing my eyes.

"*Oui*, but I come every morning at this time."

I watched him make himself comfortable in his chair. I was on the verge of asking why when Margo walked into the room, her laptop already open in her arms.

"Why bother having a twenty-four-hour waiting room if visitors are only allowed in from nine to five?" she said.

"God help me." I closed my eyes and counted until the pain in my chest was a dull roar and the ache in my teeth was bearable. On top of that, I was starting to get a headache. When I opened my eyes, the other two were staring at me.

I blinked at them. "Well?"

"We thought you had fallen asleep," Margo said.

"Look, I have, like, ten units of patience left, and seven of them are devoted to not offing myself with the IV tube. Let's get this going. You asked me where MVP HQ was, and I wanted to know *why* you want to know. Where is any of this coming from?"

Margo sighed and closed her computer, resting her forearms on top of it. To my surprise, she looked at Hugo. He was studying the point where his fingers met, laced together on his lap. He just nodded along in a sort of grandpa way, as if the story were continuing in his head and he agreed with it.

"Eleven years ago, Don found a fissure in his yard," Margo started slowly, first to Hugo then turning to me.

I had a running list of things that separated VIP from MVP. So far there was an interesting difference in technology, and MVP was a decade older than VIP, but there was also a difference in language. MVP used counterpart and rift but VIP used doppelganger and fissure.

"Don found the others and myself, and we set about understanding the multi-verse."

I pointed at Hugo. "When did you join?"

"From the start. I was a graduate student of Josephine's."

"Okay," I said, "carry on."

Margo seemed perturbed but pressed on. "We ventured only so far into the fissure, studying it on a number of levels. I took about two years' leave to have my daughter. And while I was gone, they developed the anchor."

"Is that the name of your tech? How does that work?"

"Well, it's…" She blinked at me and changed her mind. "I don't think that matters."

"Fair enough."

"Anyway, when I returned, we had just started venturing through other fissures, determining the differences between universes. Then we had a setback."

"What kind?" She squinted. I put my hands up in a shrug of innocence. "Hey, I might be your prisoner, but I'm still a scientist. I'm just curious."

She made a face, then continued. "We stopped exploring after that and refined our technology. That was about six years ago. Five years ago, I received a package in the mail. It was from Margo, my doppelganger."

"Margo! Shut the front door. What did it say? How did she get it to you? Why? Can I see it?"

"Martin." Margo stopped me, her expression a mix of amused and annoyed.

"Come on, that's a big fucking deal—ow!" As I got more excited, my ribs started to send lancing pain over my chest. It both hurt and gave me dysphoria.

"Relax, damn it, I'm going to explain. Stop interrupting," she said.

"Fine."

Margo said she received the package through the mail on an ordinary day. She didn't believe it at first. MVP Margo had apparently landed on the same idea that Tamar had. She figured out the founders weren't universe-unique. MVP Margo said she didn't think she was, but she hadn't been given a lot of insight into the human studies aspect. That had been left to Justin. But one day, she took the risk of stepping through a rift to send a little girl home.

My heart started to race, crescendoing in my chest until all of my ribs ached, broken or not. That little girl MVP Margo helped had been Nichelle, my sister. That day had changed my life. Nichelle and I had gotten bored at a family dinner, and I told Mom and Apollo we were going on a walk. I had been thirteen at the time. Five-year-old Nichelle and I walked up a hill behind our house into a cemetery. We weren't afraid, and I really liked the view of the mountains from it.

Then I stopped hearing Nichelle walking around. I looked for her, but she was gone. I panicked and started searching all the graves because I had read that bodies caused sinkholes when they decayed. I was practically crying into the soil when I heard the click of the beads at the ends of her braids. And a woman was with her. Margo had been my first contact with the multi-verse, and I was obsessed. She talked to me for a little while, explaining that my sister had stepped through a door in the universe. She remembered me when I applied to work for her.

"She mentioned your name," VIP Margo was saying.

I blinked at her. "She what?"

"She said you were her protégé. Anyway, after she encountered you, she started visiting that verse regularly and found pictures of Don and the others. She said as she explored for her job, she also looked out for evidence of doppelgangers. Eventually, she had collected a lot of evidence of multiple versions of all of us. But five years ago, she figured out that the founders were more than just multi."

"What does that mean?"

"Margo discovered that MVP founders were murdering their doppelgangers."

Well, that made zero sense. The words she had just strung together meant nothing to me for a second. "They were killing doppelgangers?"

"Yes."

I had to talk this one out. "You're telling me Margo basically figured out that the others, Don and Josephine and so on, had somehow located their doppelgangers and were murdering them."

"Yup."

"What the fuck for?" I nearly laughed.

"Your Margo said the MVP founders would just slip into that person's life and take it over."

If my face wasn't a broken pile of waning drugs, my mouth would've hung open with shock. "That's absolutely…how…even if the body was there and dead, they would still converge, wouldn't they?"

"Would they?" Hugo said.

I thought about it. *Would they?* Like a flash bomb going off, I suddenly knew the answer. I don't know *how* in the quantum sense. I couldn't even begin to pretend to explain the quantum differences between a living person and a dead person, let alone if they were the same person from different universes, but I knew, with complete certainty, a person wouldn't converge with a dead counterpart. And I knew that because I had been to Mikyea's universe over and over. Mikyea, like Luca and Tidus, was from the FOX Universe. And here I still was, un-obliterated. I hadn't put all the pieces together until just that moment. Luca had told me he shared a verse with Mikyea but never said which. Then when we needed proof of the Mandela effect, we found out his home verse was the FOX-verse.

"Martin?" Hugo said.

I blinked and looked at him. I realized I had frozen. I hadn't responded to what Margo had said. "Sorry, I was just trying to think about it."

Margo and Hugo looked at each other, their expressions suspicious. I decided to move on before they started to ask questions.

"How did Margo figure it out?"

"She noticed the infrastructure the others built to hide their fraud. They were getting rich around her and claimed it was the company, but she was a part of it and nothing had changed for her. One day she followed Carl into a lecture hall at MIT in a universe he didn't belong in. In their original universe, according to Margo, MVP leaders had basically become nonexistent. But in other verses, they were senators, professors, and so on."

I thought about the multiple photos Tamar and I had gathered in our own suspicion of the founders. I thought we found photos of just ordinary counterparts. Maybe we had been looking at one of the founders living someone else's life, assuming I believed this Margo. I also considered the missing financial pieces. They could easily funnel wealth from one verse to another and pay their way to the top. Even I kept money in a few bank accounts across a few verses.

"Wait a minute," I said. "Margo wasn't a killer."

"I know that," Margo said.

"Okay, but what I mean is that her details and accusations are centered around Don, Josephine, Justin, and Carl, right?"

"Right."

"In your book, Margo is not a killer?" I asked.

"Right."

"And the others are?" I asked. "All of them?"

Margo nodded.

I looked at Hugo. It sounded so real, even though I knew it should sound unbelievable. I lived and worked in the multi-verse, and my mentor was explaining the situation from beyond the grave. Just an ordinary Saturday. But there was a way to suss out motivation. Hugo was the wild card.

"What about him? Is he in the book?" I pointed at Hugo.

"I'm not a killer," he said.

"All our doppelgangers except Margo," Margo confirmed.

"How many?" I asked. I wasn't completely interested in that. I mean I was, but I was hung up for a second on the idea that anyone could think my Hugo could be a killer. I wanted to throw them off. "How many have died?"

"Martin, we want to stop them." Margo was an expert at deflecting questions. I could tell the answer would be either too revealing or she didn't have it.

"That is why you want the HQ verse?"

"Yes."

"You want to find them just because you don't want to die?"

She side-eyed me.

"They're also harming the multi-verse," Hugo said. He ignored a look from Margo. "MVP Margo said the founders would find technology in one verse and take it or the idea to a verse where it doesn't exist and sell it there. Anything from socks to cars."

"They're homogenizing markets?" I asked, not really following.

"More than that. When things exist in more than one universe, they run the risk of bringing on greater similarities between the universes. That can lead to more fissures and instability."

"Oh, I get it. If universe A has a thing and universe B doesn't, the quantum energy of universe A is different by at least the quantum energy of that thing. Once universe B gets the thing, the two universes lose that distinction. And enough loss means they could converge."

"Exactly."

"Christ, Margo. Open with that next time. That sounds like a real fucking problem."

My mind raced through all the weeks of rift news with the horrible accidents and the rising numbers. I looked hard at Margo. She seemed annoyed and maybe mad, and she stared back. I didn't care. I could feel the exact pressure of my top teeth on my bottom teeth, and I could feel my heart racing.

Then the Dugan image came up. That image had become a signal that something was off. Something was missing. Saying one verse and its nearest neighbor were similar was like saying humans shared DNA with bananas. We do, but there is enough space between us and a banana that one or even a hundred changes would still result in something that is not quite a banana but is also not human. I wish I had Mason or Luca to crunch the numbers. As I thought about it, I could see there was something more to that story.

"All right, assuming the multi-verse is converging because of the founders and that it's important you live, why didn't MVP Margo tell you how to find the dead-verse?"

"I've asked myself that over and over for five years. I think she just wanted us to protect ourselves, and I don't think she knew how. All she gave us was the facts she could gather."

I nodded. "Sounds like her."

"Can you tell us now?" Margo said.

I was spared from having to answer because a nurse came in the room. Apparently, it was breakfast time. The nurse asked if I wanted to try it on my own or if I wanted the feeding tube. I chose on my own.

"Can you guys like go out there in the hall?"

They blinked at me in shock.

"Now wait, what about—"

Hugo put his hand on Margo's shoulder and stopped her. "I think he needs a break from us."

I nodded and watched the nurse assemble mostly liquid food on the tray thing, then roll it over my bed. I didn't say anything or move. Margo waited to see if I would verify what Hugo had said. Hugo took my nonresponse as an answer. He stood and Margo reluctantly followed.

"We too shall get some lunch. See you in, say, an hour?" Hugo asked.

"Sure."

Margo pushed past Hugo and left. Hugo strolled out, and the nurse shut the door behind them. I closed my eyes, relieved to just feel my pain. It was a lot. I reached out for the liquid painkiller on the table, a ripple of pain pouring down my ribs.

"Fuck my life."

The problem was that I trusted MVP Margo and Hugo, but I didn't know whether or not to trust these two. This Margo and Hugo were supposed to be the bad guys. Trusting them felt like betraying something. I was suspicious of anyone who trusted a Don from any universe, especially if what they said was true. But even then, I felt my Margo in this Margo. Same with Hugo. And I felt like I was losing sight of the differences.

I guess I trusted them in part because they confirmed what Tamar and I were noticing. But no one else noticed? I wanted to see MVP Margo's evidence. I believed a Don or even a Josephine capable of hurting people. But the story collapsed with Hugo. I knew Hugo was not a killer.

The painkiller tasted like cherry-flavored ass, but I felt it right away. I crumpled the paper cup it had come in. The Jell-O had the same cherry-ass flavor, but it was sweet. I threw it back like a shot, only slamming one cube into my nose. I let it melt in my mouth before I drank it. There was some sort of mush in a bowl. It was too beige and too lumpy to be distinguishable. Oatmeal, mashed potatoes, grits, pureed shoes. It was a tossup.

Maybe it didn't matter. The end result would be the same. I mean for the multi-verse, not the mush. If I wanted the multi-verse healed, I needed things to be different. The whole team wouldn't have far to reach to believe MVP was doing harm. So, to protect the multi-verse we needed to stop MVP. VIP might be a big enough force to change it all. But then what? What would VIP do with the multi-verse?

"What, indeed?" I asked myself.

I used the spoon to scrape the mush from the edges of the bowl. I was hungry and I'd probably eat it if it was anything but grits. But I wasn't willing to risk a whole mouthful. I put the spoon in my mouth tentatively.

Mashed potatoes.

❖

VIP Hugo kept Margo away for a few hours somehow. I don't think they even returned while I took a post-food nap. I was awake and freshly dosed with painkiller by the time they marched back in the room.

"Right, where'd we leave off?" Margo asked as soon as she came in the door.

"Lunch was fine. I feel like shit, though. Thanks for asking."

"Martin, I'm sorry. I'm glad you're feeling…a…way," Margo said with a shrug.

Hugo eyed me. He half grinned as he said, "You don't look so great."

I almost laughed, but the pinch in my chest made me stop.

"Look," I said, "it doesn't matter where we left off. I'm down to talk to Don."

Margo blinked. "What do you mean?"

"Y'all want to know where HQ is. I have a few questions to ask before I tell you, but I think I'm on board, solid seventy percent."

"Really?" Hugo and Margo asked together.

"Yeah."

"That's great. Don and the others can be here tomorrow."

"Why?" Hugo asked. His tone was reserved. He didn't seem suspicious, but something in his voice made me second-guess myself.

I said it to him, not to Margo. "I've been worried for a minute MVP was doing more harm than good. If they're doing what you say and Don has a plan to right things, I should hear him out."

"Even after all he's done to you?" Hugo said.

"Maybe bring a bodyguard. But look, I'm not going to hold a grudge if it gets us somewhere."

Margo nodded as if she was getting the finer details of the conversation, but I don't think she was. I could tell Hugo could see through my bluff.

"Now go away. I'm tired."

"I'll stay," Hugo said.

"I'll go make arrangements."

"Margo," I said, stopping her. "Can you please find me clothes other than a hospital gown? I don't want to talk to Don with my ass hanging out."

"The booties are very professional," Hugo said, referring to the hospital socks at the end of my bed.

"Thanks, Hugo. I'll remember that when I professionally kick your ass."

He only laughed.

"I'll find something," Margo said, nodding goodbye to Hugo.

I knew then they'd agreed someone should be with me as much as possible. They must have been close by when eating lunch, maybe even right outside the door. Margo left and Hugo slumped into his chair. I pressed the button on the remote attached to the bed, and the TV popped on. A western was just starting on an obscure local channel.

"Let's watch this," Hugo said, turning his chair.

I turned up the volume.

# SECTION 19

## *What a waste of time*

Hugo and I ended up watching that whole movie and another. And we ate dinner together. He ordered delivery to the hospital and was gone just long enough to pick it up. I had more broth, but this one had bits of stuff in it, maybe chicken, and some sort of mushed vegetable. It was orange, but I wouldn't put money on it being sweet potatoes or carrots or pumpkin or from earth. I watched Hugo eat Pad Thai.

"H," I said when it was getting close to the end of visiting hours.

He grunted more than answered. His eyes were glued to the TV. The western we had finished earlier was playing again, and he was as riveted as he had been the first time.

"Have you seen MVP Margo's notes?"

He looked at me, but I couldn't quite figure out his expression. "No."

I closed my eyes. "What happened? I mean, what was the setback?"

"What do you mean?"

"VIP Margo said your company had a setback, and you had to refocus on the technology."

"I'm not sure. Josephine and I built the anchor, but Carl and Justin worked with Don and volunteers to test it."

"And they didn't explain what the problem was? How could you fix it?"

"I…I can't talk about this with you," he said with a small amount of regret.

I looked at him. "Well, it sounds a little sus to me."

"I can imagine it would."

"Naw man, I'm serious. You're important enough to be here and be a part of this, yet you don't know everything that happened in your organization? Why?"

"Do you know all that happened in yours?"

"No, but they don't think I'm important."

He almost laughed.

"Listen, Hugo. I…I know your doppelganger. I know MVP Hugo."

"You do?"

"Yeah, better than I knew Margo. He wouldn't kill anyone. Y'all only have a handful of doppelgangers, and he never leaves the lab. If he's done what they say, if he's taken over someone's life, then why have I seen him literally every day for two months? Wouldn't they notice him missing?"

Hugo considered what I said by pretending to watch TV. I watched too. I watched knowing it was one of MVP Hugo's favorite movies. He usually had it playing in his room or in the common room when he thought no one was around. I knew it almost word for word.

"There are ways around it, no?" he said softly. "He could've told the others he was on a trip."

"Sounds fake, but I guess."

He looked at me, half smiling. "You know, you're surly. The way Margo says the other Margo talked about you, I wouldn't have thought this."

"You know, you're a dummy if you believe VIP. The way Hugo talks about himself, I never would've thought this," I said, mocking his accent.

He really laughed that time. "You remind me of someone I knew in my original verse. He was surly too."

"Oh, yeah?"

"Yes, he was a homeless man."

My own snort caught me by surprise. I knew laughing would hurt, so I tried to ignore it.

"He would be outside the gas station and he would come up and ask for your shoes. He never wore shoes, but he would demand yours. And when you said no, he would say, 'Why not? You have two, what do you need two for?' Then you would have to tell him you have two because you have two feet, and he would follow you around the store and tell you all the reasons you don't need two feet."

I laughed. It hurt my whole body to laugh, but it felt good. He looked pleased with himself.

"And that's who I remind you of?"

"Yes, except I think you would tell people they don't need *any* feet."

"They don't. That's ableist propaganda."

Hugo shrugged. "Thank you for proving my point."

We settled again into silence, watching the town in the movie rally as the female lead explained it would be up to them to protect themselves.

"Is this not your home-verse…er, original verse?" I asked when I thought I might fall asleep.

"No."

"Why'd you bring me here?"

"It was nearby," Hugo said. Then a flash seemed to go off behind his eyes. "Do you know where you are?"

"Yeah," I said.

My eyes closed. And if he asked me a question, I didn't hear it.

By noon the next day, I was impatient to hear from Margo. Neither she nor Hugo had been to the hospital, which normally would've made me happy. But I had assumed my willingness to participate in their plot to overthrow MVP would've been met with some urgency. My bad mood didn't help. I figured I must have been healed enough for the hospital to want to kick me out since they pulled all their equipment. I was still wearing the hospital clothes and sipping meals, but a nurse had walked me through exercises for both my jaw and my ribs. After that they left me alone with my pain.

Rain like only Florida could produce slammed against the window, and the world was dark. I wondered how far I could get before Margo or Hugo found me. I could have left before, but the hospital seemed safer than being in the world. Don had found me in a universe none of us belonged to, and yet I knew he wouldn't come to the hospital.

I could walk my happy ass to the heart of Fort Lauderdale and step through a rift that formed every day for three minutes at five forty-five. You had to crawl into some shrubs to get to it, though. I imagined bending over just slightly, and my ribs cried out in pain. Plus, it was raining. Finally, I heard Margo's knock—three gentle taps then three hard ones.

"Hi, Margo."

"How'd you know it was me?"

"I listened to a you knock on doors five times a day for four years."

Margo had been casually crossing the room but hesitated when I referenced the other Margo. She smiled sadly and put a pile of clothes on the bed. "Here, you're going to need these for your meeting."

I pulled the stack over. "You bought me new clothes?"

"What did you expect me to do? Just dig something out of my closet?"

"I think I could rock one of your long-ass skirts."

She laughed and swished her skirt. Then she seemed to correct herself, her smile fading.

"I can manage the pants, but I'll need help with the shirt," I said.

"Do you want me to leave?" she asked, backing toward the door.

"No. You'll just knock again, and I hated it the first time. Just turn around."

She did. The hospital gown tied on the side and wrapped around my body, so it was easy to undo. I did manage the pants. I remembered the tricks I had needed while I healed from top surgery almost ten years ago. I used my first six months' pay from MVP to have the surgery done. Now I was wondering if MVP needed to exist at all. I have come a long way, I guess.

"These pants seem too big."

"They have drawstrings, so just…you know."

I cinched the laces on the forest green denim joggers. They were actually pretty cool clothes. Even though they had an elastic waist, they looked professional. Still felt big, though.

"I know I'm a chub, but what size did you think I was?"

"Martin, shut up."

"I'm ready now," I said.

She turned and reached for the light blue short-sleeve button-down. She undid the buttons and helped me get it on the arm I couldn't lift, then held the other side while I got my other arm in. The whole process made me feel sad.

"Do you know what happened to the other Margo?" I asked, not really knowing why.

"No, only that she's dead. There is one other Margo I know of."

"Weird."

"You're unique?" she asked.

"Yup."

"Does it feel lonely?" She blinked and brushed away the question with her hand. "Never mind."

"Shoes?"

She nodded and pulled some tan flip-flops from her bag.

"Respect the drip! You have taste, lady," I said, slipping on the shoes. "I wish I had some lotion and deodorant, though."

She laughed and pulled a grocery bag out of her backpack with all the toiletries I could want and then some.

"Well, damn."

I went into the bathroom to wrap up getting ready, and she said she would wait down the hall by the nurse's station. I didn't look too hard at myself in the mirror, just inspected the black patches where my brown skin was mottled with bruising. I hurried through the bag and tied it closed before I went out into the hall. It felt like all I had in the world, even though I had a lot in a lot of worlds. I wondered for a moment if being universe-unique really was lonely.

"Let's go," I said, finger-gunning the nurses behind the desk. They all rolled their eyes.

Margo nodded and led me out of the hospital to a waiting car. She went around to drive.

"Where are we going?" I asked. I felt instantly carsick, but I just put my head back and closed my eyes. I didn't need to see the rain beat against the windows as we drove.

"We have a meeting with Josephine."

"Not Don?"

"No. We all thought it was best you meet with Jo."

I didn't feel like getting my teeth smashed in again, so I wasn't going to argue. "Where?"

"We rented an office in a building near a college. Everyone wanted to continue their work"

"What're you working on?"

"Martin."

"Right, right. Finding MVP, I get that, but don't you do anything else? Aren't you trying to explore the verses or something?"

"We are and do. But we think the damage to the universes is most important. I focus on rift formation triggers."

"That's a fun game," I said, thinking of Luca and Mason staring at longitudes and latitudes and time signatures and other things only they could see in the numbers.

"It was for a while, but we've been having trouble lately…we…" I could feel Margo's eyes on me. She was wondering how much to tell me. I didn't bother looking at her or reassuring her that I really didn't care what they were doing save the part about searching for the founders and threatening the people I cared about.

She looked at me for a second too long and had to slam on the brakes as we came up to a badly submerged road and the slow line of cars trying to wade through it. I jolted forward. I was smart enough to have slipped the shoulder strap of the seat belt around my back, but my ribs screamed anyway. My vision swam, and I felt pre-vomit cold sweat form on my face. My instinct was to open the window, but with the downpour of rain I couldn't crack it more than an inch.

"Fuck me," I said. "Shit, I might barf in here."

"I'm so sorry, Martin, I really didn't—"

"Naw, we're good. Maybe we should listen to the radio instead." I turned my face into the AC vent.

"Right."

Margo must have taken that to mean that I didn't want to talk at all. We spent the rest of the hour-long drive in silence. The building we came to was a tall complex of offices. The name of the school was listed amongst the names of businesses that also used the building. I followed Margo through the rainy parking lot. The cool water was more refreshing than annoying for once, and at least I could look rain drenched instead of sweaty.

"We should've picked up your prescription before we came," Margo said as we stepped into an elevator.

The pain was rising, but I didn't want the painkillers. "I'm fine. Someone's bound to have a pocket of NSAIDs somewhere. Prescription drugs are boring."

"You just look uncomfortable."

Margo was watching me. I tried to look in front of me, but the doors of the elevator were reflective enough that I could see my face. So, I looked at the floor. I watched her white sneakers as we walked down the hall. The door she opened led to a bright and slightly crowded room. Boxes lined the walls, and there were several tables with computers on them. People moved around. At the far end of the room, Josephine stood with Hugo.

"This is the temporary lab," Margo said.

Several people called to Margo. Josephine and Hugo looked up. I scanned some of the items as we walked by. There were bits of mechanical devices I couldn't begin to reassemble even if I'd known what they were. There were charts that looked like they could have been for any data, hand-drawn diagrams on white boards, circles with arrows flowing through them, and time signatures by each circle. That much I did understand. It was a rift map linking several universes together.

"Martin," Josephine called, waving me over to her desk. She was dressed the opposite of how I saw her last. She had on dark gray sweatpants with the elastic on the legs pulled to her knees, and a dark blue blazer with a white satin blouse underneath.

"Hi," I said in a neutral voice.

I nodded at Hugo, who gave me a nod back. There was nothing else in his expression.

"Right, well, this is the lab. Why don't the four of us head into my office? We have some lunch waiting."

I couldn't eat even if someone paid me. I could still feel the jostling of the car in my bones. I nodded anyway and followed her as she marched into a small, less crowded room. There were two couches facing each other and a desk off to one side. Stacks of papers and books sat in a handful of places. It reminded me of the common room back on headquarters.

"Have a seat. Hue says you're still drinking meals, so I had this delivered," Josephine said, unpacking several paper bags on a coffee table.

If she wanted me to like her, she was doing it right because she set a bowl of warm bean and meat chili on the table in front of me. I smelled it and my mouth watered, but my stomach clenched.

"I'm not ready to eat at the moment, but thank you."

Hugo and Josephine sat across from me. Margo took the lunch container Josephine handed her and went to the desk. Josephine picked up a cup of coffee and slipped her yoga mat sandals off her feet.

"First," she said as she shuffled her feet under her, "I wanted to thank you for coming."

"I thought I would be meeting with Don."

"Yeah, but after…well, Don was disappointed, and we've had enough issues for him to be a little frustrated. I have a different method, that's all. I'm glad you've agreed to help us."

"Well, I have agreed *to* agree. If…"

"If?" she asked. Her voice was cheery, but her eyes weren't.

"I have questions," I said. I pulled one of the waters to me and sipped it to see if it would help the nauseous feeling. I looked at Hugo, but he seemed distracted either by his thoughts or by the nature of the wall behind my head.

"What are your questions, Martin?"

"What do you know about MVP?"

"We know enough, thanks to your Margo. We honestly wouldn't be as far as we are without her."

"Why do you think she didn't tell you where HQ was herself?"

She blinked, surprised. "I'm not sure. But I guess we'd need a medium and a Ouija board now to know why."

She laughed at her own joke. She was so different from Don. It was like a good cop/bad cop thing, but instead there was just bad cop and whatever Josephine was. I didn't trust her, but I didn't *not* trust her, either. I didn't laugh.

"What else?" Josephine asked.

"Why now?"

These weren't my main questions, but they were good ones. I wanted to ask her what they would do with the multi-verse once they had it, but I didn't think opening with that would get me very far. She phrased things tactfully, so I would have to be tactful too.

"What do you mean?"

"I mean why now? You've had Margo's info for, what, five years."

Josephine rolled her eyes and made a frustrated sound. "Don't get me started. It wasn't that we haven't been trying."

She put down her coffee and tiptoed to the back of her couch, pulling up a box. She put it in front of me with all the joy of a third cousin giving someone a graduation gift, pleasant but removed.

"That's why Don was so frustrated," she said.

I pulled the box over and tipped it toward me. It was about a quarter full of phones. I slowly picked one out of the box, resting the cardboard on my knees.

"What do you mean?" I asked.

"We have been trying for years to talk to someone from MVP, to get help. It took us a while to pin down anyone, but once we knew who to look for, we were able to find a few. Don tried talking to them, he tried explaining it, he tried bribing them. No one would talk to us about themselves or you or Margo or the multi-verse. So, when we found you, he thought we should try something more direct."

"You spelled *threaten* wrong," I said.

As soon as I had the phone in my hand, I regretted touching it. The phone was a generation before my own sequencer. It was a flip phone with a pink snap-on case and black flame stickers. It was MVP tech, and it belonged to one of the missing rift techs. She had disappeared four years ago. I looked at Margo, then Hugo, then Josephine. None of them looked surprised. I resisted the urge to shove the box away. Instead, I tossed the phone back in.

"Couldn't have been that bad if they gave you their tech."

"So, you recognize these devices?" Josephine asked.

I was being tested. I didn't know what she was trying to learn, but I knew any reaction I had would tell Josephine something important. To MVP, the technicians who owned these devices were missing. Seeing that box gave me an impression of a fate much worse, but I said nothing, I only righted the box on the table and leaned back against the couch.

Josephine moved on. "You would recognize the tech, wouldn't you? Anyway, no one talked to us. And the phones weren't so much a gift as a…well, we stole them. We needed to find answers. But even that was a dead end. Now you're here and know what a problem MVP is. You'll be able to right everything."

I shrugged and picked up the chili. I wondered how Hugo had known chili would be perfect right now. I thought about eating chili like this that first night MVP Hugo mapped out our experiment.

"I have one more question," I said, bringing the bowl to my lips instead of using the spoon.

"All right."

She was back in her place on the couch, eating the grapes out of a mixed fruit bowl.

"What are you going to do when you get to them?"

She smiled, but she didn't say anything. Then she looked at Margo and Hugo.

"Well, we're going to stop them."

"How?"

"By any means necessary."

I sighed and rubbed my eyes. I was getting a headache, regretting not picking up the prescription I told Margo to forget about.

"All right, I'll level with you," I said. "Assuming you banish the founders to their home-verse to live out the rest of their days or whatever, what would you do with the six thousand employees that work for them?"

"There are six thousand? Margo's notes said there was only three."

"What were her exact words?" I demanded, the annoyance in my voice obvious. Even at her disappearance, there had been five thousand.

"She said she'd trained three thousand technicians," Margo answered.

"Okay, three thousand techs, four founders, three hundred research teams, three hundred HQ staff, one hundred running their legitimate business, and the rest are trainers, graphic designers, internal reporters, and three morale advisors who plan birthday parties and shit."

The three of them looked stunned.

"I suppose we'd retrain those people who wanted to work for us and send the rest home," Josephine said.

"Is that what Don wants to do?"

She blinked at me.

"Whatever, fine. Assuming that happens, what would you do with the verses that the founders took over?"

"We'd leave them alone."

"Alone?"

"Yes, they should've never been interfered with in the first place," Josephine said.

I almost laughed. I wasn't buying it. "Really? You're just going to give up your chance to be a Nobel Prize winner?"

Josephine's mouth opened. "How do you know that a doppelganger of mine was a Nobel Prize winner?"

"You weren't the only ones suspicious of the founders."

"That universe will go on without her," Josephine said.

"But think of all the good you could do with her resources."

I wondered if I could get her to waver. Any Don would happily take power wherever he could get it. In all the versions that Tamar and I found, he was a senator or top lawyer or judge or CEO. He founded several tech companies, probably with stolen ideas. And all of the Josephines were tops in their fields, not working in a two-bit company like VIP, multi-verse notwithstanding.

"Are you saying you condone what the founders did?" she asked, raising her eyebrows.

I sipped my chili. "No, but there'll be holes, and the damage is done."

"Martin, that's not what we're about."

"What was the Nobel Prize in?" Hugo asked.

"Quantum transportation theory," Josephine and I said together.

Hugo nodded. He had helped. It had been a trick, and Hugo had helped me play it. The Nobel Prize–winning Josephine was from FAX verse, and VIP Josephine was watching her with something other than benign interest. I doubted FAX Josephine was really MVP Josephine. If she was, the quantum transportation research would've already been assimilated into MVP, and we weren't using it. But what was Hugo's game?

"Martin, my life and the lives of the others aside, the founders are doing damage. The multi-verse is growing more and more homogeneous. The pending disaster is astronomical. If that isn't enough, I guess you're free to go."

"Chill. I'm still in this, but I have questions. You just want to know where HQ is?"

"I do." She shifted and held her hands in her lap as if she were about to snatch away whatever I offered.

"How do you plan to get there?"

"What do you mean?" She sat back, her eagerness becoming annoyance.

"Unless you plan to walk there, you have to give me some idea of how you're measuring the damn multi-verse."

"Just tell us what you call it," she demanded.

"Dead-verse seventy."

She blinked at me then scowled. "Martin, I'm serious."

"So am I. Look I've figured something out. There's a language barrier going on here, and you haven't even noticed. How am I supposed to get you to HQ? The fastest way would be for you to tell me how you measure the multi-verse, and we can figure out the math from there. But if you can't do that, I would literally have to take you fissure by fucking fissure."

"So? Do that."

"That would be a waste of time. You know how vast the multi-verse is? If we started today it would take seventeen states and countries and four years to walk there."

"Four years?" Josephine asked.

"Seventeen states and countries?" Margo asked.

"Yeah. This is stupid. There's only one fissure into HQ, and it's only there every four years."

"*S'il peut fournir la route panoramique, nous pouvons construire l'autoroute*," Hugo said.

"Highway? What are you going to do, cut a tunnel?" I laughed.

"He speaks French," Josephine said.

"I have apps."

I looked at their faces. And the answer snapped into place.

"You guys really did plan to use the fissures," I said.

Josephine was on her feet. "How do you figure that?"

I laughed. "My God, the math doesn't matter since I'm right. Fuck, if you had said you just planned to walk into the dead-verse, I would've told you to fuck off from the start."

"I'll have you know—" Josephine said, pointing a warning finger at me. Then she changed her mind. "You literally just said there was a path."

"If you haven't found it by now on your own, you have bigger problems."

I liked defensive Josephine. She was a scientist who valued her reputation enough to kill. The offensive her was too clever, too manipulative; defensive her, though, was raw and exposed. If I could insult her intelligence and her work long enough, she would answer any question I wanted.

"What do you mean?" Margo intervened.

"I mean, do you even have a map of the multi-verse?" I cried.

No one answered.

"Ugh, okay. How are you categorizing the universes?" They didn't answer that, either. "How many universes have you even found?"

"We've found thousands and are discovering more every day," Josephine answered, her voice loud with triumph.

"Weird flex. Wait…what? *Discovering?*"

"As we branch out, we locate new universes," Hugo said.

"By thousands, you mean what? Seven or eight?"

"There are as many as eight thousand universes?" Margo said.

"Eight thousand?" The number seemed to shock Josephine too.

I wasn't really surprised. MVP Margo always said the other founders were cart-before-the-horse people and would rush headfirst into new information. I could see that in this group since VIP hadn't finished mapping the multi-verse yet, but wanted to take it over. This group was also confused by dead-verses, but if they had explored the totality of the multi-verse they would've known about hundreds of them. They probably hadn't made it to one yet, not if they were walking. I couldn't even tell if they were out of the A-classes. If they really needed the fissures, then a dead-verse was as near to an A-class universe as a recorder was to a sixty-piece orchestra.

I amped up the drama. "Are you kidding me? No, you know what? I'm out. You're no match for them. They have three times as many employees and tech that can move them to any universe in the multi-verse instantaneously. This is a *streaming* game, so take your VHS tapes and figure out something else to do with your time."

"Well, then," Josephine said. She was standing, and I watched as she calmly put her sandals back on. She didn't look at me, but I could see the thoughts turning behind her eyes.

She knew what was up. I could tell. A top-ranking scientist like Josephine should have been beside herself with embarrassment at the very least. I had done as much as I could without flat out calling her stupid. Margo and Hugo had the humbled expressions I was expecting, but not Josephine. She had recovered from her shock and was now on to her next plot.

"It was a little hard to tell where MVP was with tech as outdated as this," Josephine said. She pulled on the hems of her blazer, then fished a phone out of the box.

"It served its time."

"Would you really let the universe fall to ruin by not helping us?" she asked, laying the empathy on thick.

"What can I say?"

"You've spent so long trying to clean up the mess MVP was making. I'm offering to help you and everyone in the verses." She put the phone in my hand. "There's an alternative to *walking*."

*Ah.* She wanted into the sequencer. There was enough in any one of those to make even cavemen multi-verse advanced. I almost didn't know what to do for a moment. I looked around and felt exceptionally tired. Talking so much had irritated the bruises on my face, and my torso was on fire. I didn't have anything left physically.

And what had I learned? Who would I tell? I still had my com and my drone. If either was still charged and recording, then the others could know what I know. Since they had a box of phones, I figured VIP was responsible for as many deaths as MVP, and they were ready to add my death to their tally.

I sighed. It wasn't checkmate, but neither of us had gained. They knew a bit more about MVP, and MVP would know just as much about VIP once they recovered my devices—whether I was dead or alive.

I looked at the phone in Josephine's hand. I had roomed with the person that had owned that phone. Poor Mateo. I shook my head. "Even if you could turn it on, those have been discontinued for years. They were dumped from the system. They'd factory reset and just be janky old flip phones."

"Fine." Josephine said, tossing the phone in the box. "Are you finished with your lunch?"

"I am."

"Hugo, take Martin to our main lab. I'll be down in an hour, and we can wrap this up."

Hugo stood but said nothing. Instead, he led the way out of the office. The room we had passed through earlier was now empty. It felt almost staged, like the employees I had seen were actors, and now it was time to break down the set. The only people left were a handful of security guards. One of them stepped in to guard my other side. I guess pushing Hugo down and running for it wasn't an option.

"Where the hell did everyone go?"

"Same place we're going, the lab. I just need to grab some equipment from my workstation."

"The lab doesn't sound like I'll like it."

"You'll hate it." He said it so quietly.

I watched him shoulder a backpack and pin a device to his shirt. This badge was slightly different from the white tiles the others had worn. Those tiles were clean and contained. The one Hugo had on had wires crisscrossing the front and pouring out of the back.

He put a normal badge on my shirt. "Let's go. Lab, Benny," he said to the guard.

"Aye, boss."

Hugo had two smart watches along his arm and he pressed a code into each. I assumed one watch was for his tile badge—anchor—and the other for mine. Benny, the security guard, pressed some buttons on his own watch. I hadn't noticed the watches when I had executed my big escape plan in the apartment. It meant I had sent Kiki back with half the device. The anchor could have been just as useless without the watch as a drone was without a sequencer.

Hugo nodded to Benny. We started walking as a group toward the door.

Then I was in some other office.

## Section 20

### *It's fucking raining*

"Let's hurry," Hugo said.

"How did you do that?" I said. "I thought you used the fissures. There wasn't one there. Was there?"

"There was, of sorts," Hugo said. "I don't have time to explain."

A shiver traced my spine, and my body tingled slightly. We were in a dark conference room. I could hear other people but nothing distinct.

"What happened to Benny?" I asked.

Hugo pulled the badge off my shirt and the tingling stopped. "He's gone."

"Gone? Did you kill him or something? Transport him into the ether?"

Hugo shook his head. "No. Well, in that language, *we're* gone. He went to the lab."

"Where are we?"

"Come."

My anchor in his hand, Hugo started walking toward the door.

"What the fuck, bro?" I shouted.

"You can come with me or you can go where you want, but I promise you it is the same place. I'm going to find MVP Hugo."

"Are you insane? Are you defecting?"

Hugo opened the door. "*Oui*, Martin. Now shut up."

Leading us out into the hall, he straightened and walked like he was supposed to be there. I tried to follow his example. My brain was clouded with pain and confusion, but I kept my mouth shut.

"Hello, do you need help?" someone asked as we passed a desk.

"No, thanks. We came to see my brother, but we're leaving now," Hugo said in a surprisingly good American accent. I just nodded and followed out of the building.

On the street, he started marching down the sidewalk. I was having a hard time keeping up, but I didn't say anything. As we walked, he tapped his smart watch, and I could tell he was navigating. We walked for almost an hour, snaking through the city away from the office building. When we rounded a corner, I spotted a food truck.

"Oh yeah, I want food," I said.

He looked at me, "That's not why we're here."

"It could be."

He rolled his eyes. "Okay, what do you want?"

I cheered and ordered two bean and chicken burritos and two waters. Hugo ordered a soda. As he waited to pay, he dropped the anchor I'd been wearing into the semi-open window of the truck. The watch followed. Then he paid, and we left.

"So..." I said as we walked down the street at a much slower pace.

We were almost exactly tracing our steps back, only we were on the other side of the block. His pace was almost relaxed, even if his face wasn't. He had a scrunched expression and the skin under his eyes was dark. He looked exhausted.

"So?" he asked when I didn't follow up.

"All that was to throw them off the trail?"

He nodded. "Well reasoned."

"I've had good training," I said. "I knew a Margo and have, like, three degrees."

He just grunted. "Your reasoning skills are why I've decided to find your Hugo."

"How're you planning on finding him?" I wasn't interested in why at the moment. I had spent a week in a hospital and gotten zero straightforward answers to that question.

He smiled. "I had planned on you sticking with me, finding him for me."

"Fair enough." Then I thought about it. "Wait. How do I know you aren't going to try to kill him?"

"You didn't believe him to be a killer, but you think I am?"

I shrugged and tried to chew a burrito. I was lucky it was pulled chicken and not chunks. My headache was bright, but the food helped.

"I'll find him either way," Hugo said with finality.

"Okay, okay." I stopped walking and looked around the city. "What universe is this?"

"We call this universe five."

"So, you were just numbering them as you discovered them?"

He nodded. I looked around again. Nothing immediately placed this universe. It wasn't like the last, which was unique in a million different ways. This one gave me a vague sense of familiarity, but of course it would. I had been to so many universes.

"How many universes would we have to go through to get back to the FOX universe, I mean the universe that Don stole Tidus from?" I asked.

"I don't know. I wasn't totally sure where that one was. I've never been there."

"What about the one we left Josephine in? Are we next door?"

"That one is three universes from this, but the path between there and here is narrow, succinct, like passing through a deck of cards. Do you plan to go back to the one Tidus was from? I don't think it's safe."

"I agree. No, there are only two universe that fissure naturally with that verse."

I didn't feel like cluing Hugo into my idea. I was thinking I could get back to my own verse. There was a beacon in my house. With a broadcast signal back to HQ. Every tech had one hidden in a universe we could always find so we could be retrieved. Considering the limits to their exploration of the multi-verse and where I suspected they had started, I doubted VIP had found their way to my home-verse.

"FOX universe?"

"It's part of MVP universe designation."

"We knew that, though it seemed arbitrary to us. You were right in that we're reliant on the fissures." Hugo's voice was curious. "What do you call the one we took Tidus to?"

"The letters are GOZ."

"Our explorers were in GOZ not long ago and were trying to use our device to cross into FOX, but the parameters of the fissure decayed. They reported that your team was there, on the other side. We were trying to open it, but you succeeded in closing it. When we investigated more, we knew it was you. We had been looking for you, and we tracked you from there."

"You hunted me? Wait! I thought that fissure was weird. You were trying to open it at the same time as I was closing it? Wait, it was…did you *create* it?"

"Yes."

"Damn," I said. "How…you know what? Never mind. I can't even with that right now. I just want to go home."

"I can get you to GOZ if you would like," Hugo said.

"Do it. I can get us help from there."

"Voilà, a plan."

Hugo hired a car to take us across town. The rain started. Even though it made absolute perfect sense, it was annoying how rainy all Floridas were. I was starting to feel nauseous again, but I wasn't about to barf in some stranger's car. I counted my heartbeats as they pulsed through my skull.

"Are you feeling okay?"

I swallowed my sarcastic comment and shook my head. He left me in peace for the rest of the drive. The driver let us out at a government building two blocks from the location of the rift. Hugo explained he could create a rift for himself using his anchor and watch, but since he got rid of mine, I needed a natural rift.

"I think we should go to the location and make sure we can do it without being seen. I'm just gonna need a pit stop soon," I said, going for casual.

"Right," Hugo said as he typed on his watch. We had been walking with our heads down to keep the rain out of our eyes. My locs were already dripping down my back and the sensation of wet clothes was starting to piss me off.

"I—*fuck*!"

I didn't see what I slammed into. It felt like hitting a slightly pillowy wall. I did see an array of blue and white lights as pain raced into my skull. I felt the rain and the cement and the fire in my chest. I heard voices, but the words didn't register. When I opened my eyes, I saw two sets of shoes, then a set of thighs as someone kneeled on the puddly sidewalk.

"I'm so sorry," the voice attached to the thighs said.

"Martin," Hugo said.

The pain was hot and flowing all over my body. I could feel it in my blood like an electrical current. My muscles tensed as each pulse brought a new wave. The image of the thighs went static in my head, and the edges started to frame in black. I couldn't hold still enough to stop the pain.

"You have to breathe," the voice said.

Wasn't I breathing? His voice was familiar and soothing. The fear of taking a breath was real and petrifying. If I took a breath, the pain would increase.

"Martin," the voice said, and there was a hand on my shoulder. I felt my lungs fill with air.

"Oh my God," I gasped.

"Just breathe calmly. I'm so fucking sorry. What the hell happened to you?"

"He was attacked and has bruised ribs—"

"Why isn't he at a hospital?"

"He was, but he needs to get home," Hugo said.

"I'm okay."

Breathing had forced my lungs against my bones, and the fresh pain, different from the collision, different from the injured bones, brought tears to my eyes. I tried to lie on my back instead of my side. I didn't like the rain on my face, but I liked the solid feeling of the concrete.

"You can't just lie in the street," the other man said.

I finally looked at him, squinting through the pool of tears and rain.

"Tidus?" I could have shouted.

"Hi," he said. He looked at me from under a hoodie, just as tired and bored as the last time I had seen him.

FAX Tidus. "So we're in that universe?"

He gave me a curious look, then glared. "Well, I'm not ecstatic to see you either."

"No, no," I said, coughing. "I meant I'm surprised to see you. I just didn't realize how close we were to you."

"Look, I have to start opening, but you can come in the bar and sit down for a second. Or you can drown in the street. I don't care."

"I drowned once—zero out of ten, won't buy again," I said, mostly to throw him off. I put my arms around my chest as gently as I could. "I need help."

Hugo and Tidus worked together to right me. My body wanted

to black out again as they lifted me, but I forced myself to stay awake. Because of that, my next sensation was to throw up. I didn't do that either.

"You need painkillers. I'll go get some," Hugo said.

"I…I'll be okay, I don't—"

Hugo helped Tidus put me in a booth near the back of the bar, and then he left. I lay on the cool leather for a few minutes while Tidus moved around the bar.

FAX Tidus. I couldn't believe it. My brain tried to work out the puzzle. I should have been able to get home from here, rift by rift. But I couldn't think. The pain in my side had reduced to a numb throb. My headache was back, right behind my eyes. I had almost forgotten about my jaw, but I had smacked into Tidus with my face, so it ached too.

"Water?" Tidus asked. He put a glass down at the table without waiting for me to answer.

"Tidus," I said.

"Yeah?" he asked sadly.

"I'm sorry about the last time we saw each other."

"Martin, it's fine." He looked down at his feet. "I can't say I remember what happened between us."

"What do you mean?" I asked. I rubbed my eyes as if that would clear some of the pain I felt all over. "Nothing's happened between us."

He side-eyed me. It clicked. As closeted as he was, FAX Tidus hooked up with strangers from time to time, usually after getting shitfaced with his friends.

"We didn't hook up," I said.

That seemed to catch his interest because he slipped into the booth. "So, what then?"

"I can't explain."

"If you can't remember, then how do you know nothing happened?"

I almost laughed. "Naw, nothing like that. I…you wouldn't believe me."

"What're you, an alien? Did you abduct me?"

I sighed. I was too tired. I could also see I was doing damage. He'd spent a lot of time regretting his actions. He looked brighter than when I had met him, though. The bar was empty. The crowd of tan bodybuilders and models may have suited the bar, but it hadn't suited him. His black hair was down, curling like a greaser's around his eyebrows. And in his eyes was visible regret.

"I'm not an alien. We don't deal with space," I said.

He rolled his eyes. But he didn't get up from the table.

"Have you heard of the multi-verse?"

"Who hasn't?"

"There exists a universe where I'm close to a version of you. Something is wrong with the universes, and you picked up on something he and I had talked about a while ago." I tried to sound as casual as I could.

"What, so you had a crush on me a long time ago or something?"

"See? It's unbelievable."

He looked at me. I tried to sip the water and got maybe three sips down before I gave up. I put my head back and held the glass to my cheek.

"They really did a number on you," he said.

"Tell me about it."

"Why didn't you go to the hospital?"

"Like Hugo said, I have to get home."

"You're going all the way to Denver like that?"

"Yup."

He went silent, and I closed my eyes.

"I've never had purple hair," he said after a minute.

I looked at him.

"I dye it, sure, but not purple."

"You don't have purple hair, but the Tidus I know does."

I watched the emotions cross Tidus's face as he decided whether or not to trust me and his own memory—or non-memory—about that moment. He was recalling the purple of Tidus's hair the same way the words in that conversation had come to him.

"How did you get out of that universe?" he asked skeptically.

"It's a long story."

"Have you been to a lot of universes? Are there more of me?"

"Yes."

"How many more? How many universes are there?"

"A lot. And because there are so many of you, it's dangerous for you to travel around them."

He laughed. "Ah see, now I know you're full of shit."

"Why does that make me full of shit?"

"It's hard to believe that only *you* can travel through these universes. It's like when a guy tells you he works for the FBI but won't show you his badge. No proof, you know."

I shrugged. "Fair assessment."

I could see, though, that he still wasn't sure that I was full of shit. He had the details in his mind: my name, my conversation with FOX Tidus, FOX Tidus's purple hair. But it was hard to believe.

"How do you get to them? A spaceship?"

"No, it's not space. See, all the galaxies and shit are in this universe. And all other universes have a space with planets and stars and galaxies."

"How?"

"The quantum foundation is different for each. It hurts to think about. I mean, scientists in most universes agree space is expanding, right? But those who study the multi-verse know the volume of the container that holds the multi-verses is finite. Space is infinite but the space for spaces is limited."

Tidus blinked, but then he smiled. "You're right. That *does* hurt."

"You also didn't explain it very well," a familiar voice said.

Both Tidus and I jumped. And Hugo grinned at me.

"Hugo!" I cried.

"How'd you get in?" Tidus said. "I thought I locked the door."

"What are you doing here?" I asked. "How'd you know I was here?"

"He came with you. Are you having amnesia?" Tidus asked. We slid out of the booth at the same time, but I let Hugo hug my head while Tidus crossed his arms.

It was Hugo, MVP Hugo, *my Hugo*. I took a step back and looked at him. In all my suffering, I had completely missed the tell for someone tuning into the verse.

"Wait, who are you? You can't just bring people into the bar. I'm going to get in trouble for even letting you in here." Tidus was talking to someone over Hugo's shoulder.

I almost didn't recognize him. I had only known him at HQ, surrounded by plain gray walls and computers. But Luca was there in the bar. He looked tired and excited and perfect and was exactly who I wanted to see. Tidus stopped talking when Luca stepped closer and let me kiss him.

"I'm sorry," I said to Luca.

"You're a dumbass."

"Can't argue with that."

"Well, since your friends are here, maybe you can leave?" Tidus said, his annoyance obvious.

"Yeah, let's go. We can talk later," Hugo said.

Luca turned my hand over and placed my sequencer into my palm. "Come on, the code is—"

"I can't go yet," I said. Hugo and Luca stared at me.

"I can't go without—"

Someone knocked on the door of the bar. All of us turned and watched a soggy VIP Hugo staring in through the glass. He knocked again and cupped his hands to try and look in. MVP Hugo said something in French I couldn't understand.

"He's with you?" Luca asked.

"Yeah. He wants to talk to you," I said to Hugo.

"What in the fuck is happening?" Tidus looked from the Hugo standing in the bar to the one on the street.

"Tidus, someday I'll make it up to you," I said. Then I took Luca by the hand and started toward the door. Tidus said nothing.

Hugo followed me and Luca. I unlocked the door to the bar and stepped out into the rain. VIP Hugo let out a relieved sound.

"You're upright," he said. Then he saw Luca. "And met someone?"

"Hugo, this is Hugo," I said, and I stepped out of the way so they could see each other. VIP Hugo said the same thing in French that MVP Hugo had.

"Oh jeez," another voice said over my shoulder. Tamar and Wei were standing on the street. I felt my eyes burn with tears at the sight of them.

"Don't do that ever again," Tamar said before putting her hands on my shoulders and her chin on my head in an attempt at a hug. Wei was too busy with the Hugos to look at me.

"This is the part in the movie where we learn they were separated at birth," Wei said. "I need popcorn."

"Hugo," MVP Hugo said.

"Hugo," VIP Hugo said.

"I understand you want to talk to me," MVP Hugo said.

The other just nodded.

"Let's get out of here, it's fucking raining," Tamar said.

In a move that startled VIP Hugo, Tamar put a phone into his hand and pressed a button. He was gone. The smell of peanut butter was brief but comforting.

"We really shouldn't do that on the street," Luca said.

"Why not? It's all fucked anyway," Tamar said just before she disappeared herself.

Then we all went.

## Section 21

### *If knowing you both*

"What verse is this?" I asked as I followed Tamar down a different Florida street.

"This is Wei's retirement verse," Luca said. "It's C-class."

"His what?"

"I spend my money here," Wei said.

I blinked at him.

"What?" he said. "Techs don't spend all their money in one verse?"

"No, we don't spend *any*. What do you do here? What do you buy? Why here?" I looked around at the aesthetic of the late 1990s.

He laughed. "Better exchange rates. Most people I know buy a house and a few things. Can't take the money with you, after all."

"I honestly hadn't thought about it," I said.

"I've invested in a B-verse," Tamar said.

I looked at Luca. He shook his head. "I send my money to my family."

I smiled at him.

"Where in the universes is this?" VIP Hugo said.

"It's complicated," I said. "And far from any verse you know."

He was trailing Luca and me, who were trailing the rest. MVP Hugo marched ahead. I could tell he was uncertain and trying to keep as much space between himself and his counterpart as he could. I don't know what I would do if my counterpart kidnapped my best friend and then returned him, demanding to speak to me.

"Do you need a hospital?" Luca asked me gently.

"No," I said, trying to smile. "I was in one for a week. They can't do anything else. I need to just rest."

"I have just the thing," Wei said, letting himself drop in between Luca and me. He put an arm around Luca and tried to put one around me, but I winced as the weight of it made my side hurt.

"Sorry," he said.

"I don't think I support giving Martin drugs," Luca said.

"Which kind?" I asked, mostly to annoy Luca. He gave me his best I'm-annoyed-but-also-charmed glare. Wei laughed.

I glanced over my shoulder. VIP Hugo had stopped about a block away and was staring into a shop window. I gave Wei and Luca a look and then dropped back and went after him.

"Scared?" I asked him.

"Confused. And worried," he said. It was a bookstore, and a series of magazines were displayed in the windows. The headlines were pretty grim.

"Come on, I got your back," I said. "They are not the gun-pulling types."

Hugo looked right at MVP Hugo. He seemed even more exhausted than when I had observed him in Josephine's office. I think we were both totaled. I tried not to tune in to my own body, to all the places I ached.

"It's gonna be all right," I said. "Besides, you've come this far."

He shrugged, nodded resolutely, and we started again. The walking lasted about twenty minutes. We went to a car service. Wei flashed a pretty fancy credit card, rented a car, and shuttled us to a nearby luxury airport where a plane was already waiting. I sat between Luca and the window and tried to keep my eyes open. It wasn't until we landed that I realized I hadn't been successful. Luca nudged my leg to wake me. I looked out the window. The area was beautifully wooded and green. And it was bright, the sun low but powerful. I looked at the seat across the aisle where VIP Hugo sat alone, sleeping too.

"Where are we?" I yawned. Then I made the dumb mistake of stretching. I winced.

Luca answered the question even though I knew he cared more about how much pain I was in. "Central Ohio."

"This is a weird airport," I said, looking out the window. The plane rolled toward a private hangar. Less than one hundred yards away from the hangar was a huge Tudor-style mansion.

"This is where Wei lives," Luca said.

"When I'm not with my parents. They're only a few dozen universes away, though."

Looking at the house, it was easy to see Wei's touches. It was warm browns and cool grays, colored to look the most luxurious. A sand-colored SUV was in the driveway. There was a waterless fountain in the front drive, overrun with vines. We exited the plane before the pilot rolled it into the hangar.

"Okay, even I'm not this rich," I said. "You live like a super villain."

"My father manages mutual accounts," Wei said, "and my mother was a professional piano player, movie scores."

"Bet she wrote your villain theme," I said.

"I have a piano in there. You should take it for a spin." Wei smiled, unfazed by my teasing.

We had been walking, shivering in the Ohio cold, but I didn't look at him until he mentioned the piano. His face was half hidden by a sepia beanie, but he kept his eyes on me. I wanted to ask him what he was looking at, but I wasn't sure I wanted to know. I was wearing borrowed clothes and was fresh out of the hospital. I had been in a rainstorm and had been shoved to the ground. I wondered what my most pristine and fashionable friend had to say.

"Stop looking at me like that," Wei said as we stepped onto his porch.

"You started it."

"Oh my God," a voice cried. The front door to the house had been thrown open, and Tidus was standing in the entry. Mason was a pace or two behind him.

"Tidus?" I said, surprised. I had wondered what had become of him, but I never would've imagined he had come to the multi-verse, here with me, with them, with Luca. I blinked at him. And he blinked back.

"Hi," I said.

He laughed dramatically. "*Hi?* I think you better say a whole lot more than 'hi.' We were worried."

"You were?"

"You're an idiot," Tamar said, pushing past me and Tidus into the house.

"I guess I'm just surprised you're here."

Tidus rolled his eyes and crossed his arms. "They said there'd be pizza."

I laughed. He smiled, and his expression softened. "We all probably have a lot to talk about. I'm glad you're back…and alive."

"I'm fucking amazed," I said.

Tidus stepped closer and stooped to kiss me. It was a fundamental moment. Kissing Luca, even with my friends around, made me feel giddy. I hadn't thought about what it would be like kissing Tidus with them around, with Luca around. But there I was. I felt like I had an answer I couldn't question. As he stepped back, I heard a bellow from somewhere inside the house.

"Was that Bowser?"

Tidus shrugged. "Or Kiki. Mason is beating us at Scrabble, and it was their turn when we heard the plane roll up."

"Hey, Mas," I said, waving. He waved back, his face welcoming with its usual serene expression.

While I had been talking to Tidus, everyone except VIP Hugo had gone into the house. Tidus winked at me and turned to follow the crowd.

"Well," VIP Hugo said, "*Est-ce que tout cet univers est si affectueux ou est-ce juste vous? Deux gars? Sensationnel.*"

"It's complicated," I said, feeling only a little embarrassed.

He followed as I stepped into the house. Everyone else had disappeared somewhere. MVP Hugo was taking off his boots in the vestibule, hanging his hat. He had also straightened out everyone else's shoes.

"Is there a sign-up sheet, or do we have to stand in line to kiss you?" MVP Hugo said.

VIP Hugo laughed.

"Oh my God. If knowing you both means I have to hear the same joke in English and in French, one of you is going back to the Hugo factory."

"It wasn't exactly the same," they answered together.

I blinked at them as they turned to look the other over. "It really is like a twin movie," I said.

"Didn't you think this with the Tiduses?" MVP Hugo asked.

"No, they're different."

"*Quand même!*" VIP Hugo laughed, then he said something to MVP Hugo in French that sounded suspiciously like he was calling me out as the love interest.

"Stop that."

They laughed together.

"Let's go get some pizza," I said.

"There's no pizza," Tamar said.

Wei sounded disappointed. "Aw, why not?"

"But Tidus said—"

Mason tossed in, "Wait, what?"

I could hear Tamar sigh, defeated, from what I guessed was the kitchen.

"Woot, I want pineapple bacon," I shouted.

As I came into the living room, I saw Kiki. But instead of showing me any kind of affection, they walked right over to VIP Hugo and punched him in the stomach. He landed on the floor, crying out loud enough to bring everyone running.

"Jesus," I yelled. I stepped between Kiki and Hugo, but they didn't look like they were going to do anything more.

"How dare you threaten my people," Kiki said in a low, cold voice. "I swear on every god in every verse that if you're here to fuck with us or fuck us over, I'll you use your lower intestines as a noose and hang your entire home-verse. Do you understand?"

"*Oui*, I understand. I'm sorry," Hugo said. No one else helped him up, so I did the best I could. No one except Kiki had been willing to come into physical contact with him.

"I'm sorry, everyone, too," I said.

They all looked at me.

Luca's voice was even and compassionate. "Look, I think you two should settle in, clean up, and we'll order pizza. Then we can talk about it."

"There are plenty of rooms. Wei, if you don't mind, maybe some clothes?" MVP Hugo said.

That was an endorsement. If this was a feelgood-nineties-friendship-sports-movie, then the team captains had spoken and the rest of us had to trust them.

Wei pulled the brown suspenders on his wide-leg suit pants and waggled his eyebrows. "A tour!"

We followed him.

"Maybe *my* rib is broken now," Hugo said quietly, rubbing his stomach.

"They don't like you," Wei pointed out.

"*Merci.*"

Thankfully, Wei's tour was short. He mostly opened doors and pointed to things. He had a home theater and a pool and some other luxuries, but I didn't pay attention to most of it. Something was shifting. I felt like I was melting, thawing. It had to be the loss of adrenaline. I was back with the only people in the worlds I cared about besides my nuclear family. I felt safe and at home. I just wanted to curl up in the warmth and sleep.

"Here, my friend, next door to me just like at home," Wei said. He smiled and pointed at his door. "There are clothes in my room, so take whatever you want. The bathroom connects the rooms."

"You don't have a private master in your own mansion?"

"Well, when I don't have guests I just sleep on the couch, so…" Wei shrugged. He bowed dramatically to Hugo and gestured back down the hall.

Hugo looked at me with worry, as if being alone with Wei was dangerous.

I laughed and waved. "See you over pizza."

He nodded, and I went into the room.

It was simple, classic, and clean. I followed Wei's advice and found gray sweats and a tan shirt in his room. There was also an unopened package of assorted boxer briefs, so I took those too. I showered as best I could with bruised ribs and changed. It felt like I had been so much farther away than a few universes.

I sat on the bed. And then I lay back. I thought about the classic ant on a tightrope. Physicists loved that dumb ant. It was a way to convey dimensions, because beings as big as people on a tightrope can only experience so many dimensions, but an ant can go three hundred and sixty degrees around the tightrope. What I really wanted to know was how far they had to go. I wondered if it was between two buildings like in old movies. Why doesn't anyone do that anymore?

I forgot what I was thinking about.

❖

It was almost four a.m. before I woke. I slept hard and probably would've slept until I was forty except I was starving. I wandered back through Wei's house with a surreal and comforting feeling. The whole team was a bunch of insomniacs, so I wasn't surprised to see a light on in the kitchen. I *was* surprised, however, to find Tidus there. He was sitting at a table reading a book and writing notes.

"Hey," I said.

He jumped. "Christ almighty."

"Sorry."

He smiled.

"What're you doing?"

"Um, playing catch-up, actually. Hugo gave me this manual for the multi-verse, and I was just trying to understand what the hell everyone is talking about."

"That's hot," I said.

He rolled his eyes. "How do you feel? No one had the heart to wake you, and they didn't want to move on without you."

"Better. It's nice to be back. Why haven't I seen Bowser?"

"Because he weighs a hundred and seventy pounds and likes to greet people by knocking them on their ass."

I felt the nausea rise as I thought of the pain that kind of greeting would cause. My jaw seemed to have healed aside from the dull blackness of the lingering bruise, but my ribs were all too happy to remind me they were still damaged.

"Fair enough. And thanks. Is there still pizza?"

"Of course. Your bacon pineapple was untouched. Want me to get you some?"

"Naw, I got it. I get studying and shit, but why so late? Or so early?"

"I work in a coffee shop bar, so I'm either up through the night or up early enough to see the sunrise. Sometimes both. There's no such thing as sleep."

I laughed and tossed a few slices of pizza on a plate and stuck it in the microwave. Tidus was looking down at the book again. His hair was so glossy and light. I had a new urge to run my fingers through it.

"It's weird," I said.

"What?"

"Seeing you with them, seeing you here. I mean, they've always known about you and whatever, but now you know about them and talk to them. Y'all look so comfortable."

"You're funny. We spent a whole week together looking for your ass. It's easy for a group to bond over a mutual missing friend, though I doubt any other group had to deal with him deciding to yeet himself into a gangster verse, get the shit beat out of him, then fall off the radar. Real hero shit."

I laughed. "Too bad I'm a shitty hero."

"You're a hero to me."

"Ugh, don't tell him that," Luca said, coming around the corner. "He's reckless enough. We shouldn't encourage it."

He had a pad of paper in his hands and sat at the counter next to Tidus. That was when I noticed the two coffee cups and what looked like Luca's writing on a few loose pages. He was coming *back* into the room, not just showing up.

My brain shut down. "Um…"

"I'm helping him," Luca said, reading my confusion.

"Are you guys friends?"

They both stared at me, and I suddenly was unsure of every decision I had ever made. I never thought about what it would be like to see them in the same room, to experience them together. I suddenly didn't know how to act.

"Martin, your pizza's done," Luca said as he sipped his coffee. The microwave was beeping, probably had been for the minute I was staring. I opened it but didn't look away.

"Is this weird for you two?"

"Not really," they answered together.

"Um."

Luca smiled, his dimples going a long way to make me feel less tense. "Martin, it's all good. We've talked."

"Talked about what? About me? About what?"

Tidus laughed. "Duh. You're the only thing we had in common."

"Now?"

"We're from the same verse, so…" Luca said with an edge of teasing to his voice.

"Fine, fair. But is it weird? I mean I haven't—couldn't…between who…Do you know what I mean?"

"No one's asking you to choose," Luca said. It echoed what I had said to Tidus in his kitchen before he kissed me.

"Okay. So, what then? Are we dating?"

They both blinked at me, then at each other.

"I mean date you, sure. But it's not like we're going to date each other," Luca said.

"Huh."

"I told him I'm down to give a triad a shot," Tidus said. "It's exciting and romantic. I was mad at you like you said I would be. Kiki really didn't hold back. You know, it's fucked up that you spied on me and shit, but I tripped into understanding. Well, when Kiki and I met up with the others, they were worried those assholes would try and get to your family or some other Tidus and I was like, not a *me!* We have to follow 'em or something, and then it clicked. Unethical but well-intentioned. I understood where you'd come from thinking secretly studying people would help them. I guess if I was willing to do it, I couldn't feel too mad about you all doing it. What I really learned from that, though, was that when I was done being angry, I still wanted you with me. Besides, it's exciting. I've watched a lot of sci-fi, and when the hot guy says get in the car, you get in the car."

I blinked at him, but I felt my smile. He seemed bashful but not embarrassed.

All I could think to say was, "Wow."

"And you, Luca?" Tidus asked.

"I'm in."

Tidus laughed.

"Yeah?" I asked.

"It's not like I haven't had a crush on you for months, but I won't let this kid stand in my way. I feel like this multi-verse issue is more important than our personal shit. But, yeah."

"Baw, that's cute," Tidus said, looking between me and Luca. Then he turned on Luca. "I'm not a kid."

"You're ten years younger than me."

Tidus gasped. "You're thirty-*four*. Your skin is phenomenal! What do you do to it?"

Luca rolled his eyes, embarrassed. I laughed and retrieved my pizza. I sat at the other end of the counter, both in between and away from them. “Can I sit in? I don’t want to interrupt.”

They smiled and Luca turned back to Tidus. Tidus immediately opened his mouth and held up his hand. “What if it was aliens, but they time-traveled *and* came from a different universe?”

Luca’s expression of gentle joy melted into pure loathing. “I wouldn’t have to worry about what impact they had on the multi-verse.”

“Why not?”

“I’d destroy everything.”

That made Tidus giggle. I listened to them discuss the multi-verse and its various dynamics for another hour. Tidus got hung up on the idea of certain quantum particles existing both in the present, past, and future simultaneously, and he decided it was bedtime. Tidus gave me a good-night kiss and left. I watched Luca clean up the coffee mugs.

“Are you going to stay up?” he asked, adding my plate to the dishwasher.

I shook my head. “Luca.”

“Martin.”

“Am I weird to want this? I mean, doesn’t everyone look for that *one* person? You and Tidus would consider me potentially that *one*, right?”

He laughed, then leaned against the counter near me in that familiar and perfect way he always had, slipping his hands into his pockets.

“I guess the way I see it, statistically, even if a lot of people were looking for the *one*, it would still just be a mean, some *average* way that people did things. But, like with most averages, you have statistically relevant groups on either side of the peak of the bell curve. Somewhere on the left are people with less than one person: serial relationships, people who fall for pieces of people, or single people who want to stay that way forever. And on the right side, above the average of one are all the people like you.”

I smiled. Perfectly explained. “So, you’re saying I’m above average?”

He rolled his eyes just like I wanted him to. “No, Martin. What I’m saying is good night.”

I caught his arm before he got too far away and kissed him. I sat alone in Wei’s kitchen for another twenty minutes, just thinking about the state of things. Then I went upstairs to sleep.

# Section 22

## *I wouldn't say losing*

"Everyone get up now," I heard someone scream. The voice was both far away and right in my ear.

I jumped out of bed faster than my body could take. The room lurched to the left, and I found myself on the floor. It took a heartbeat for the pain to subside and for my vision to clear. I didn't know where the voice had come from, but I knew the nearest person was Wei. I stood up, holding my breath to stifle the pain, and plowed through the door to Wei's room.

"The fuck was that?" I said as he struggled to get pants on.

"It was Mason on the speaker."

"Where are you?" Hugo asked over the intercom.

"Game room."

"A game room?" I said as Wei and I left his room.

"Sounds better than war room."

Wei led the way through the house, VIP Hugo joining at some point as we ran down the hall. My boyfriends came around a different corner with Kiki at their heels. The game room was in the basement and was almost as full of computers as the data lab had been, only all the equipment was newer.

"You relocated the labs," I said.

"What's going on?" Wei asked, ignoring my comment.

"Two rifts are forming," Mason said.

He didn't look up from the computer he was sitting at. Well, he was actually sitting at six computers. He glided from one laptop to the next in his rolling chair, typing and adjusting the images on the screens. Along the other side the table were six more computers, facing away.

"Where?" MVP Hugo asked, pushing past the crowd. He leaned over Mason's chair.

"Martin's parents' house," Mason said.

"What?" I screamed, rushing forward to look at the image on Mason's screen.

It was around four a.m. in Colorado. The house was dark and eerie. There were two drone video feeds, one in my parents' living room and one in what everyone generally considered my room. Two computers showed the video feed and two more the quantum maps. The map showed the slightest blue tear on the gray background of the room.

"It's VIP," VIP Hugo and I said together.

"How'd they find them?" I said, turning on VIP Hugo.

"How do you know?" Kiki asked.

"Not all of us keep rifts in our living rooms, Kix," I said, immediately feeling bad for snapping at them. I would apologize later. I kept my eyes on VIP Hugo. "How'd they find them?"

"They always knew."

"What does that mean?"

"Can you get video like this from the other side of the rift?" MVP Hugo asked, moving on to resolve the problem.

Mason tossed Kiki a joystick and they each sent a drone through the rifts. Each rift was roughly the size of a marble, but they were clearly growing. The widening holes of color on the quantum screens was ominous, like burns on paper. On the other side of each rift was a person. They were a bland pair and looked like the workers I had seen in Josephine's lab. Nameless, faceless, and dangerous.

The quantum activity on that side of the rift was extreme. A hurricane of particles was being hurled at the rift, and each person was the center of the storm. It was like watching a sawblade hack at glass. Kiki and Mason brought their drones back on my home-verse side.

"How are they doing this?" I asked VIP Hugo. "Is this how you create a rift?"

"We find weak places where the walls between universes are thin and use electromagnetic energy to push through the barrier, but we have to have visited that universe first, crossing through existing fissures. Then we can calibrate our technology and reenter it safely."

"So, there are weak universe walls in my house?"

"No, this is different. When we first started developing this technology, we would try to cut through the walls at any point. That's what they're doing here. They haven't been to this universe, but they knew where it was, or knew they could find it because of details your Margo provided. They're breaking in. And your address was on the ID in your wallet."

"How does that work?" MVP Hugo asked, his voice too curious for my liking. "How does this tech prevent convergence?"

"I don't know how to explain," VIP Hugo said, the pressure of the question, of everyone demanding answers from him, making him lose track of the science. "I can't."

I had never seen a Hugo panic. It was hard to see the usually optimistic and cool scientist struggle.

"And they knew how to find my parents all along. You and Margo lied."

"I cannot speak for Margo, but I did not know until last night. I thought there would be more time. You have to stop them."

"What do they want with my parents?"

"They don't want them, they want you. Your Margo made you seem like you have the answers they need. They can't start over. And since you're supposed to be trapped in one of their labs, they're retaliating."

"How do I stop it?"

"It's dangerous." VIP Hugo took a deep breath then said, "Fissures made this way are like forcing metal bars apart. They don't always bend back to the way they were. You have to close it and make sure it is closed all the way. You've done this before."

I remembered the rift I closed at my interview for the research team. That rift, the size of a hula hoop, had been one of the hardest rifts I ever closed because it felt like it resisted. Now I understood. Someone had been trying to open it while I closed it. I had managed, but now there were two. I turned away from VIP Hugo and tried to wrap my mind around the work I had to do.

I looked at the quantum screen. These rifts were weird in the same way the first had been. Particles weren't flowing into my parents' house from the other verse. The particle seemed to flow toward the VIP goon. Their tech was sucking particles toward it like a tornado.

Luca went around to the computers on the other side of the table. He tapped a few buttons on a keyboard. “According to this, they’ll have a person-sized rift in three minutes and seven seconds.”

I took another deep breath. “Fuck me.”

I pulled my sequencer out of my pocket. That seemed to be a signal to the others to move. They scattered to help me, claiming computers. If any team could get it done, it would be this one.

“Tell us how to help,” MVP Hugo said.

I did my best to type code and give orders at the same time. “Mason, I need access to the relay to my home-verse. We’re going to have to do it from here.”

“Got it,” Mason said, going to a bank of computers on the card tables set up along the left side of the room.

“Wei, I need a laptop and a cable to connect this,” I said, flashing him my sequencer.

“You got it.”

“There are only like three drones in that verse,” Luca said. “It’ll take you longer to close one rift than the time we have by a factor of a thousand.”

“We could tune some there,” Tamar said, “but they’d be in Ohio.”

“I got it covered. I’ve been leaving drones in my room for years.”

“You’ve been losing highly scientific and secretive equipment in your parents’ house?” Kiki said.

“I wouldn’t say *losing*. Kiki, Tamar—monitor the VIP guys. Find some way to distract them.”

“Got it.”

“Hugo, can you link into my parents’ security system? They have cameras. I want to make sure none of them wake up and wander into another verse.”

“They aren’t unique,” Luca said as Hugo agreed.

“I know that. I had a counterpart,” I said as I roused the drones. The rifts being created didn’t lead to the FOX-verse, where my family’s counterparts were, so they wouldn’t converge, but I still didn’t want them wandering across the multi-verse.

“No, Martin,” Luca said, looking at his computer. “Apollo has a counter in the universe this guy is breaking in from. He has a lot of counters actually—how was he not in our study groups?”

“That fucking sucks,” I groaned.

Wei put my computer down on the table and flapped open a folding camping chair. I dropped into it and connected my sequencer. Slowly, the number of drones grew from four hundred to six thousand.

"I don't think this computer can handle you closing two rifts at once," Wei said.

"I don't think I can handle it either."

"One of us could close the other rift," Luca said.

I looked around the room, and then my eyes landed on Tidus. MVP Hugo seemed to have the same idea.

"He's probably as fast as you as far as dexterity and reflexes," Hugo said.

"Agreed."

"What, me? I've never—I wouldn't know how."

"Bae, we have footage of you playing thirteen straight hours of video games. For once, put that skill on your résumé," I said.

"I can teach you on the fly," Kiki said, tossing their joystick to Tamar. VIP Hugo dropped into the seat Kiki left and offered to drive the other joystick. Tamar hesitated but handed it over.

"I think I can disrupt what they're doing," VIP Hugo said, concentrating on his screen.

Wei got Tidus a computer, and Kiki hooked their sequencer to it.

"Mas, I need the drones under my total control in case something major happens, but I want to give Tidus some so we can work simultaneously," I said, hoping he would find some way to make it happen.

"Player two coming up," Mason said.

I liked the sound of that. I could see Luca's computer from where I sat. The diagrams of the rifts were displayed with a bar showing their size. I could also see the countdown until someone could reasonably cross the barrier. I had less than a minute.

"Which one is opening faster?" I asked.

"Living room," Luca said.

"I'll take that one," I said, sending code to the drones. I set the parameters of their field to an approximation of my parents' house layout, keeping a straight line to the living room.

"You're go on player two," Mason said. "And the relay is coming online now."

I couldn't imagine what he must have done to make it happen, but the drone signatures on Tidus's screen were half solid and half blinking. Mason came over to my computer and typed code into the interface. My screen buffered for a harrowing nanosecond before the feeds came back up. I had slightly more than half the drones under my direct control and Tidus had the rest, blinking to show they were his.

"Right, Ti, you got this," I said. "Just do what Kix says."

"How?" Tidus said, looking at my fingers moving over the keys. "I don't type when I game."

"Maybe this will help," Wei said, connecting a Zbox controller to the computer. He typed a quick code to organize the drones into a few groups and assigned them to the controller.

Tidus's eyes went wide with excitement. "Oh, this is better."

"Hey, I want one of those," I joked, trying to alleviate my own stress.

"Not now," Wei said with a laugh.

I looked at Tidus. "It's like Hungry Hungry Hippos meets Tetris."

"We got this," Kiki said, leaning over Tidus. "Mind your own shit."

I laughed and focused. I jumped straight into a sixteen-group pattern. I must have caught the VIP person off guard because the stability of the dinner plate sized rift shrank by half before I noticed any resistance.

"Forty percent closed in B-room, eighty-five in L-room," Luca said.

I split the drones again into a thirty-two-group pattern.

"Eighty-eight, eighty-five," Luca said. "There was a charge increase on their end."

"They noticed the fissures closing. They doubled their power input," VIP Hugo said.

"Eighty-four," Luca said. "You're losing ground, Martin."

I watched the edges of the opening as my drones worked. The tears at the edges of the rift were almost instantaneous. The edges sheared away as quickly as I could repair them. The hurricane on the other side of this rift seemed more powerful than my drones.

"Shit," I said.

I considered my pattern. It was large eclipsing rings like an atom, a technique signature to me. I wasn't sure suddenly what was more dire, watching the VIP tactics work or watching my foolproof patterns fail.

"How much power is needed on this thing to tune a human?" I heard Tamar ask.

Mason went to her. "You don't have enough."

"What *would* I have enough to tune?"

"Um…a book?"

"What size?"

"What?"

"Like a coffee table copy of *Moby Dick* or what?"

"Like a normal-sized *Great Gatsby*," Mason said, nearly shouting back.

"The watch! You're trying to send something away, like Martin did? The watch is the thing," VIP Hugo yelled.

Tamar must have done something because two seconds after VIP Hugo's comment, the rift stopped expanding. There-verse particles started pouring in through the rift. My drones chased back as many of the there-verse particles as they could, but the closure of the rift had dropped to less than thirty percent. I was in a worse place than when I started. But that didn't matter. No way one of them could come through without the watch.

"Goddamn," I sighed. "I can see why these rifts stay open if they aren't closed right."

"It's a nightmare," VIP Hugo said. "We've been trying to move away from this. It's better now."

"The VIP techs are disabled," Luca said. "Now it's just a matter of getting it closed."

"Not out of the woods yet," I said.

"This is so hard," Tidus said. "He does this for a living? He's literally a beast! What did he do, study badassery?"

I don't think he was talking with the intent of me hearing.

"He studied swarms," Kiki said, answering the question the way I always had.

"We have a problem," Tamar said.

"The person couldn't have gotten the watch back," I said. "What is it?"

The particles pouring into the rift moved with the same intensity as they had when in the artificial orbit created by the VIP technology. As they swept in, they shredded the rift edges like bullets through tissue paper. I had too few drones to do this, so the idea of another problem was immeasurably irritating.

"Martin, Apollo's awake."

I looked over to Luca, all code abandoned. His computer wasn't on video of the house, so I turned to Hugo. He had tapped into my family's security, and I watched Apollo scratch his ass as he went into the bathroom on the lower floor. My parents' room was in the basement.

"Maybe he won't come up," I said.

"Is that…what's that?" Tidus asked, still talking to Kiki.

"The gray is all the quantum stuff for the here-verse, and the blue is the shit from over there. Color designates a particle of a different frequency."

"It's so creepy, it looks like the simulations of a bulkhead breach on the *Titanic*," Tidus said.

I looked briefly away from the code to the feed and shrugged. It did look like that. I had never seen anything like it. Maybe I should have studied leaks—

"Oh shit," I said, nearly jumping out of my seat. "It's a leak."

"Duh," Kiki said.

"I need a fucking patch," I nearly screamed at them. It was time for a tactic change.

"What does that mean?" Luca asked.

"I'll explain later."

"You better hurry the fuck up. He's coming up the stairs," Tamar said.

I stood up and watched my stepdad sleepily climb the two flights of stairs.

"How long until he crosses the rift?" I asked as I set to work on giving the new instructions.

"Martin," Mason said. I could see on his face that I was in trouble.

"Tamar, you have to stop him," I said.

"How?"

"I don't know. I'm taking back all the drones. We'll deal with the second rift later."

I took one last look at the screen with my stepfather on it. Then I looked away. I had to type. I aborted player two and finished my instructions as I waited for the other drones to catch up. They were fast, moving stealthily across the ceiling to avoid Apollo.

"Is it so bad if he bumps the barrier?" Tidus said. "It's not like he could fit."

I didn't listen to the answer because I knew it. Even if just his hand crossed to the next verse, it would be enough to converge with his counterpart. That had the potential to melt down both universes. Not only that, but it would destroy him.

"In ten," Luca said.

I tried to ignore him. I hit send on the code I had written and then started on the next sequence of information. The drones tuned out of my home-verse and appeared on the other side of the rift. I had told them to form a grid spanning the gap of the rift on the there-verse side.

"Five—"

"Christ, Tamar, do something."

"I just…I don't have…shit."

"Two—"

I saw a flash. I didn't know if it was Apollo or what. I had never given much thought to what it would look like if someone converged with a counterpart. I thought of Dugan and the piles of dust, a pile for each of my family members starting with the man who had saved my life.

"Martin," I heard someone say.

I concentrated on my grid of drones. By putting them on the other side, they formed a grate. As particles tried to flow through, the charged drones stopped them. Within a second, the particles had backed up on themselves, and the flow into my home-verse was almost a trickle.

"Martin."

I was so close. When the flow of particles measured less than two percent, I sent the second set of code. The drones tuned again, taking with them the particles that had been trapped in between to form the patch. The third and final instructions brought the drones out of the patch and spiraling around in small groups, filling in the holes they had vacated. Eight seconds. That was all it had taken to patch the rift. One hundred percent closed.

"Fuck, where is he?" I said, looking at Tamar.

Tears streaked down her face, ruining makeup that was already messy because she had fallen asleep in it. Hugo's screen was empty, just my parents' living room. I nearly climbed over the table to look at her screen. It was blank, not empty but completely black.

"I can't see him," she said.

"Here," Hugo said, taking VIP Hugo's joystick from him. He drove the drone out of the bedroom into the living room.

It came up on the empty hallway, just like the security feed showed. My whole world stopped for a split second. Then I noticed the TV was on fire. A second later, Apollo rushed into the living room brandishing a fire extinguisher. He pointed it at the TV and pulled the trigger. My sister and mother came rushing from their rooms.

"What the fuck, T? You—oh my God—you *stopped* him! You did it! Why are you crying?"

She nearly laughed. "Because *you're* crying, dummy."

I touched my face. And I was. I pulled her into a very painful hug we both needed. Several other arms came around us, and we cheered.

"Oh, shit, the other rift," I shouted.

"It's patched," Mason said. He was sitting where I had been.

"What, by yourself?"

"Meh, I just copied your patch code," Mason said, pointing. "The MLK Patch!"

"Don't...don't call it that," I begged weakly.

"And both MLK Patches are holding," Luca said.

"Please stop."

Wei laughed. "You're a protocol now...sellout."

"I'm dying."

Luca looked both impressed and proud.

Kiki, however, looked irritated. They said, "Your house is flooded with there-verse particles."

"Mason, we should have a sweep protocol," MVP Hugo said.

"I don't get it," Luca said. He turned a scientific stare at VIP Hugo. "Tidus's apartment didn't look like this after Don had come. It was spotless, not a particle from the other verse at all."

"When done properly," VIP Hugo said, "the orbit is like a bubble around the person going from one universe to the other. Because of the inclusion of here-verse particles, the fissure closes as soon as the person is on the other side, as if it had never been a fissure at all. That's why knowing a verse before you cross is critical. You can start programing here-verse particles before crossing through. I've set my anchor to automatically do it wherever I go since I knew I would either travel through natural fissures or by your means. I just needed it to retain my atmosphere. Look for yourself, can you scan me?"

Wei and Luca did a handful of things and pulled up a quantum feed of VIP Hugo. Around him was a thin, almost imperceptible bubble of swirling blue, and then a layer of gray orbiting around that. None of the blue particles escaped the gray perimeter.

"If I put my hand in there, though?" MVP Hugo asked.

VIP Hugo shrugged. "I don't know, but probably not anything good."

"You motherfuckers," Luca said, scrolling through the quantum data from scanning VIP Hugo.

"Wow," I said, impressed. He didn't usually swear like that.

"This is why we couldn't see you! We literally stare at rifts all fucking day, but you shits wouldn't look like anything because of the outer layer of here-verse particles. Even through a natural rift."

"It all makes sense now," Kiki said, looking over Luca's shoulder. Mason went to stare at the data too.

"But look at that," Mason said, pointing.

"It's an energy signature," Luca and Kiki said together.

Kiki pointed right at VIP Hugo. "We got you now, fuckers."

"That was my intention all along."

"I bet," I said, thinking about the rift rates, "if you reanalyze some of your data, that signature might show up on enough rifts to account for some of the increased rates. If they don't close properly, they would reopen. Maybe there is a time delay or something."

"Yes," Luca said. "I like it."

"I guess we better have a meeting," MVP Hugo said. "We have less time than I thought we would."

No one said anything else. They went about their work at the computers doing whatever they needed to do to talk about how fucked the multi-verse really was. Tidus came to me and put his hand in mine as a show of support and comfort. I just watched Apollo survey the hot wreckage of his TV.

# SECTION 23

## *Is that…the result*

I decided to take a walk. And my partners decided to join me. Tidus got Bowser, and we went out into the early morning. Wei's yard was more like a small national park. He said there were a few hundred acres of forest, and I believed him. He had personally dug pavers into the relatively flat land, so a distinct maze of trails led all over the property.

"So," Tidus said. He had been strangely quiet for the first few minutes of the walk, finding sticks for Bowser to chase but not retrieve. "So."

Luca and I kept pace with each other, which was slower than Tidus was capable of naturally. He meandered around us. He was the only one in real clothes, jeans that were too short around the ankles and a flowy tank under a too-small winter coat. Luca and I were still in pajamas.

"Are we allowed to talk about what just happened, or do you need a minute?"

"You can talk about it," I said.

He turned to me, his purple curls bouncing in the bright sun. "That was insane! I feel like I ran a marathon—not that I've ever done that. That was like a heist escape room or something. Is it always like that?"

Luca and I laughed. "No," I said. "That was dramatic even for us."

"It's not *not* like that," Luca said.

"How does it usually go?"

I explained my former job. Luca filled in where he thought I was being modest.

"A commercial airliner?" Tidus said incredulously as Luca told him I had once closed a rift from the ground so a plane wouldn't go missing in another verse. It was a little hard to listen to what I had managed to do when the news of so many rift accidents lived in my memory.

"I swear it," Luca said, bragging on my behalf. As he talked, his fingers brushed mine until finally he hooked my pinkie and ring finger in a loose hold.

"After what he did in there, I believe it."

"I'm sorry," I said. They both looked at me. "If I was rude or something. I tend to get short when I focus."

"No apology needed."

"Love you anyway," Tidus said. Then he turned bright red and tried to talk his way back from it. "I mean, you know, as the expression goes. I just—Bowser, did you call me?"

Then he trotted after a confused dog. I laughed.

"He's right, you know," Luca said.

"About?"

"It was insane. It's a problem that they come out of nowhere. If Mason hadn't been watching, who knows what would've happened?" Luca crossed his arms over the hoodie he had been sleeping in. It was flannel lined and had classy-looking toggles instead of drawstrings. It worked in a weird, sexy, high-fashion way with his black pajama bottoms. "At least now we might have a way to track them."

"There really wasn't any other tell?" I asked. He shook his head pensively.

"What's a tell?" Tidus asked, but then waved his question away. "Never mind, I know what you mean. I hear something when someone tunes."

"What sound?" I asked.

"It's like someone beeping their car locked with a key fob. Only it's weird. It's so fast it feels like remembering the sound."

"Cool," I said. He looked at me, waiting for me to share. "Peanut butter smell."

"Someone taps me on the shoulder," Luca said. He was concentrating on his feet, trying not to get wet as the paving stones went over a brook.

"Weird, I know so few people who feel it," I said, amazed.

He made a face I couldn't read then shrugged.

"Well, I didn't hear or see or smell or anything when that guy abducted me," Tidus said.

"When VIP Hugo used his device to get me to the universe you picked me up in, I didn't experience anything either."

"Is that what you've been calling him?" Luca asked.

"Who? What?"

He smiled. "VIP Hugo, that's funny. I've been calling him Other Hugo."

"Valid."

"I've been calling him Hugo Two-go," Tidus said.

Luca and I laughed. The sun was warm even though the air was cold. I had lost track of so many days. I understood that it was probably near the holidays, but I hadn't seen a calendar in a while. The days I spent in Florida didn't help solidify the season for me either. I played with the zipper on my borrowed coat.

"Hey," I suddenly remembered. "What happened at the meeting with Don?"

"Wow, I forgot about that. Nothing probably as dramatic as it seemed. He was mad we hadn't made more progress. He threatened to give the project to another team. He threw a chair, damaged a bank of processors. The room caught fire, and they had to dock HQ at the repair overlap in Florida. It took almost three days for it to get there. Wei said we could move it all here. Mason set it up to look like we're still using the temporary lab. We couldn't stay on HQ. Mason was pretty triggered. We wanted to find you, anyway. He was so mad that we didn't have any answers. None of the progress we made mattered. He gave us three weeks or we were done—*fired* done."

"That's as dramatic as it sounded," I said, annoyed.

"How does docking HQ work?" Tidus asked. "And why Florida?"

Luca explained. I didn't listen. I found sticks for Tidus to throw for Bowser. Luca just strolled along. I could see the endless stream of calculations running through his mind.

"I mean, it's so improbable," Luca said almost to himself.

"What?" I asked.

"That their technology creates rifts and yet it's traceless, I mean unless they botch it."

"There's the energy signature," Tidus interrupted.

"Sure, but how'd we miss it? We can map the location of ancient rifts closed hundreds of years ago, but we didn't see *them* coming?"

"It's like there's no rift at all," I said, feeling that thought congeal in the back of my mind.

"Is it that weird?"

"Yes," Luca said. I could almost hear the statistics waiting at the end of his sentence.

"But we've seen it before," I gasped.

Dugan's event suddenly snapped into place with the clarity of a finished puzzle. Even the drawing of Dugan standing on the edge of an iced-over pond looking down at himself had a perfect and simple explanation. He could share universes with his counterparts. I must have stopped walking because when I looked at Luca we were still. I stared at him, but I couldn't speak. My thoughts raced. Suddenly his eyes snapped to mine, and I could see my own understanding reflected in them.

"Impossible," he said. And I knew he knew it wasn't.

"What's happening?" Tidus asked. "I get that you're both smarter than me, but come on. Let a guy in on one."

"VIP was behind Dugan's event," Luca and I responded.

"I have to tell Hugo," I said.

At the same time Luca said, "That bastard."

Luca and I turned and started back toward the house as fast as we could, which for me was a pained trot.

I heard Tidus grumble behind us. "It really doesn't make sense."

We barged through the side door to the kitchen. I wasn't about to chase everyone down, so I followed Mason's example and jammed the button on the intercom.

"Kitchen, now," I said into the mic.

"What're you going to say?" Luca asked.

"VIP Hugo made some hints about understanding something. Something changed him my last night in the hospital, and I know he came here to tell us. But of everything I could think, it was never that."

Luca nodded. Tidus fumbled with Bowser, who was trying to put his paws on the counter to see what was up there. The others meandered in from wherever they had been. Tamar and Kiki looked like they had been trying to sleep. Hugo came alone, his hands black along the edges where he wiped off the white boards. Mason and VIP Hugo came from the direction of the game room. Wei was last, looking fresh with combed hair and casual clothes.

"I need y'all to know that's *not* what that's for," Wei said, pointing at the intercom.

"What happened now?" Tamar asked.

"Hugo," I said. Both looked at me. "Shit, fine, you're Hugo, and you're Del Mar—Del."

VIP Hugo shrugged. "Del it is. What's your question?"

"What do you know about a man named James Dugan?"

Del blinked, then his eyes brightened with horror. "How do you know about him?"

I sighed and covered my face.

"He's behind that mess?" Tamar said, pointing at Del.

"Not me! But VIP, yes."

Hugo and the others erupted into a roar of discussion.

"Okay, okay," Hugo said over the crowd. "Let's not soak our beans before we harvest them."

"Ugh," Tamar groaned. "Yeah, yeah. A meeting, We know."

"I need food," Kiki said.

"The cook comes in an hour. Do you need something to hold you over?" Wei asked them.

They blinked at him. "You have a cook?"

"I hire one when I have guests."

"Mas," I whispered.

"Yeah?"

"Can you get drones to Dugan ground zero, I want to see something."

"It'll only take a few hours if I use the ones in CO since it's closer."

I nodded, and he set off to the game room first. Kiki and Wei grabbed a few things and assembled a sort of continental breakfast among the computers. It made my heart ache with affection to watch Luca and Tidus split a box of Honey-Ohs cereal. The cereal looked even more like a Mandela effect in an early 90s throwback box. To my surprise they sat on either side of me.

"Right," Hugo said. "Tell us about the Dugan event."

Del swallowed a bite of muffin. "When our technology forms a fissure, it might not close properly. When VIP was first exploring, they found Dugan's universe. It butts up against Josephine's lab in San Jose. They selected Dugan as a test subject for new versions of the device."

"Why him?"

Del shrugged. "Josephine's notes didn't say. Guessing, he was probably a nobody to her, a simple man who wouldn't ever catch on. He collected pins and silly things from amusement parks. They set up a fake wildlife charity, and when he sent in his five dollars every month, they would send him a new pin infused with the tech. Several of the Dugans made trips, but the one at the center of it all visited seven different universes dozens of times before the explosion."

"That explains what he said about dreams or what he thought were dreams," Tamar said.

"How could the Event be caused by a botched rift? There were no particles, not like in Martin's living room," Kiki said.

"Josephine's notes didn't say. She only told me to fix the problem with the fissures reopening. That's what I did. It was slower, but it was working. I don't even know the extent of the damage."

"We do," Kiki said. "God, if I could punch you again, I would without hesitation."

Del looked around the room, his eyes cloudy with regret. "I stole Josephine's notes. They're here. I wanted to share them with you. My Margo and I were convinced you and MVP were destroying the multiverse, that our science was safe and clean and our leaders were good."

He looked for a moment like he was going to say more, but he didn't.

"It happens," Mason said diplomatically. It's not like we were in a different position. MVP wasn't off the hook for damage.

"I have your Margo's original, unredacted notes too, not the paraphrased ones Josephine used for her own agenda."

"I'm sure they say MVP is hardly sanctified," I said.

"That doesn't answer the rift question," Kiki said. "I'm one hundred percent in on VIP being guilty, but how did it happen? Can it happen again?"

"I think I figured it out," I said. I looked at Mason.

"Oh, I was able to find a reserve of drones in a nearby verse. They just finished a repair there, and a tech was still around. I sent him a message, and he said I could borrow his stash. So, give me like three minutes to get to the Event Ground Zero."

"Right, while he's doing that," Hugo said, going to his white board.

"Let's just put shit we figured out in a place," he said, running his smeared hand through his blond hair. He wrote "MVP" on the board. "I'm going to give the marker to someone. Write what you know and then hand it off. Stick to the facts for now. We can get objective later."

He put the marker in Tamar's hands first. It took a while to get a list that felt complete but concise. I was surprised by everything that we were all able to put together.

*MVP:*

- *Founders were lying about being unique: evidenced by Tamar*
- *Kill counterparts to live in their verses: evidenced by Del*
- *Increases universe similarity: evidenced by Other Margo*
- *Being in a verse where counterparts had lived causes increased risk of convergence: theorized by Martin*
- *Increased risk of convergence: evidenced by Mandela effects*
- *Increased rift rates: evidenced by Data Team*
- *Martin may be a Mandela effect: theorized by Wei*

That last one made me laugh. I agreed with everything on the board except the rift rates.

"This one," I said, pointing to *Increased rift rates: evidenced by Data Team*, "is because of VIP."

"I agree," Del said.

Luca went to his other computer. "We're still waiting on some of the data, but so far one-fourth of the rifts observed in the last seven years have had the energy signature. It'll take time to figure out how many of these are related to events."

"VIP is responsible for a lot more than just that," Del said.

"Let's see it, then," Hugo said. He took the marker and wrote "VIP" on the board, then handed it to Del. Del detailed what he knew about his company.

"While he's doing that, let's see if we can get more information on the increased convergence rates," Hugo said.

"I already have it," Kiki said. "I couldn't find Martin's video game Mandela effect, but I searched for others. These events rely on the collective memory to prove them or give them merit. So I went to the primary source of collected memory."

"The internet?"

"Yup. I did some deep searches for effects across a few verses and put them on a timeline. I even included some events that aren't national or global, something people tend to write off."

"Ooh, like how everyone at my five-year reunion thought the 'A' logo for my high school had three wings but it only has two?" Tidus said.

"Sure, or how everyone in Battleground, Indiana, in universe DKS2381 remembers the statue in one of their parks pointing, even though the statue doesn't point now."

"That's scary," I said.

"Isn't it? Anyway, I was able to put a timeline to the discussion of several major effects and a hundred or so minor ones. In the last five years, people have reported statistically significant more events. And I have been able to verify some the same way we did with the cereal. If the change was reported in the here-verse, a neighboring there-verse had the original."

"Interesting," Hugo said.

"That's not the last of it. The MVP founder home-verse accounts for more than thirty percent of the originals. Martin's for five percent."

"Shit," I said.

"I don't mean to interrupt," Del said, "but I'm finished."

"Del, tell us what you got," Hugo said.

*VIP:*

- *Technology faulty, creates fissures/rifts that don't always close*
- *Cause of Dugan disaster*
- *Cause of death of MVP techs*

Del had drawn a line connecting the rift rates listed under MVP to the VIP side.

"Those techs were my friends," I said.

"I'm sorry, Martin," Del said, apologizing for so much more than he knew. He shook his head and looked back at the board. "I think MVP put you on the trail of VIP, and I think they wanted you to stop them."

"I mostly agree," Hugo said. "The research question was about universe-multi people and Dugan. It was connected, but not in the way we figured. MVP wants a solution to their counterparts, which happen to include VIP. I don't think they know the extent of VIP's work."

"What does VIP want?" Tamar asked.

"They want to stop MVP and stop the damage to the multi-verse," Del said.

"They couldn't answer Martin's questions, though," Tidus said. "We all heard the meeting recording. They wouldn't say what they were going to do with the multi-verse."

"I think we know what they would do," Kiki said. "They would just step in. They have the tech to do it. We know from observing universe-multi people that counterparts share motives and values even if their lives track differently."

"Really?" Tidus asked.

"Yeah, all Tiduses are somehow connected to dogs. They either have one, or work or volunteer with dogs in some way," Kiki said.

"All the ones we observed share the compulsion to give to those in need," Mason added.

"Don't all people?" Tidus said.

"No," Tamar answered.

"Okay, so you think the founders of both companies just want control of the multi-verse?" Wei asked.

"Let's not try to guess their motives," Hugo said. "*Chacun voit midi à sa porte*, no? Mason, Martin, didn't you have something to show us?"

"Yup," Mason said.

"Want to project it?" Wei said, excitedly tossing a cable to Mason. Mason attached the cable and Wei turned on a projector. After a few seconds, an image appeared. The landscape wasn't gray or white or barren because of quantum sameness. Mason was traveling using the video feed. The emptiness was Dugan Ground Zero.

"Is that the result?" Del said. No one answered him.

"Stop there," I said when the drone reached the alleged explosion coordinates.

I looked at Del. "The universe where VIP Don took Tidus was your original verse?"

He nodded.

I told Mason the name of the verse. "Tune there."

The image changed. The drone was hovering in an empty lab. Or what used to be a lab. It looked abandoned. Bits of things were left that let you know someone had been there once: a box of files, a cup of pens, a crumpled paper.

"Was this Josephine's lab?" I asked.

"Yes, but it's been years since we worked there."

"That's okay. I'm not looking for her. Let's see the quantum feed."

Again, the image blinked, only now it was a white landscape riddled with colored fog.

"What the fuck is this?" Kiki said.

"You *did* figure it out," Hugo said, open mouthed.

I nodded. "I noticed when the VIP device is active, the particles flow from one verse into the other, toward the device. For the sake of clarity, say this lab is the here-verse. The particles would flow from the there-verse into the here-verse. They flowed out of my parents' house to build the barrier around the VIP goons, right?"

"Right."

I stood and crossed closer to the image. The speckles of pink and blue and green wafted as the air in the room circulated. It had probably thinned over the last six years, but it looked like I expected.

"When I closed the rift during my interview, I noticed the same one-directional flow. Because of the way Dugan talked about moving through the multi-verse, I knew it was VIP tech. When Del explained that it started in Josephine's lab, it figured we would find particles there. I think in Dugan's case, the particles were flowing from his verses to this one, into the lab where the rift first formed. It was probably the flow of particles from all of the affected Dugan verses through ground zero and into the lab that caused the synchronizing."

"And we missed it because we didn't look in any non-B-Class universes adjacent to the Dugan verse," Tamar said.

"Right. This idea, that the particles in a verse cause some sort of synchronizing, is why I believe what I wrote on the board. 'Being in a verse where counterparts had lived causes increased risk of convergence.' I think the weird shit Dugan did, synchronizing and pantomiming, was the particles creating a convergence event between several Dugans as they flowed to ground zero. I think the Mandela effects Kiki is talking about are caused by this too."

I looked at the room to make sure I was explaining myself clearly. "I think the founders, and I—and maybe some other techs—are causing a convergence event. Kiki already said my home-verse accounts for five percent of originals in the Mandela effects. Then there's the Tiduses all remembering me."

"We what now?" Tidus said.

I smiled at him, then continued. "I think this Tidus was right."

"I what now?"

"Quantum particles are just energy at their base level and can't be created or destroyed. Well then, dead counterparts would still exist on some level, right?"

Everyone was looking at me like I was on the verge of insanity, so I restarted.

"Del said MVP founders live in their counterparts' verses, trafficking technology and ideas into new verses in order to profit, which I wouldn't doubt. VIP Margo seemed to think that was making the universes similar, but I don't think that's it. We've seen verses develop identical technologies to the nth degree and they all are distinct, right?

"Well, what if it's the founders making the universes similar? I think they're picking up particles from their dead counterparts and converging at the smallest level, becoming amalgam beings across all involved universes. And I think I'm doing it too. I think the particle flow did that to the Dugans."

"You?" Hugo asked skeptically.

"I've been to a universe where a counterpart lived and died. What if some of their quantum energy got on me, or I converged to that verse, without exploding or whatever because they were nothing but dust by then. Then I went to a different verse. Kiki said my home-verse accounted for originals, right? Well, in my home-verse Honey-Ohs were called Honey-Ohs, not Honoy-Os, and now in FOX-verse they are the same as in my verse. FAX Tidus knew me by name because FOX Tidus knew me. Even ACE Tidus said I was familiar. What if it's because I'm part FOX-verse now, what if I accidently almost converged him and his next nearest counterpart?"

"Seems like a leap," Tamar said.

"It makes sense to me," Wei said at the same time.

They squinted at each other.

"We need more proof," Tamar said.

"I have quantum photos of him, years of them," Wei said, "If Martin's right, we can observe how many FOX-verse particles are on him and compare it to known dust decay rates."

"Do it," Hugo and Luca said in unison.

Just then the doorbell rang.

"My chef," Wei said excitedly and was out of the room before anyone could say more.

"I guess it's break time." Kiki laughed.

# SECTION 24

## *It's a lower threshold than you think*

Wei and the chef agreed on a brunch menu since it was already twelve thirty p.m. Everyone else wandered off. Before I could get away, Hugo took another photo of me with Wei's camera. Then I wandered through Wei's house until I found the piano he mentioned. Eventually the chef informed everyone breakfast was ready.

"Here, boss," Wei said, getting overly excited about his work. He passed some pages to Hugo.

"What's this?"

"It's the photo analysis of Martin."

Hugo set aside his pancakes and looked at the pages. He nodded and passed the pages to the right as he finished them. Tidus was the last person to see them.

"These…aren't photos," Tidus said.

Wei laughed. "They are. See? His ugly face is right here."

He made a show of tracing his finger in a circle around the page Tidus was holding.

"Hey, fuck off," I said.

"It's a summary of the data in the photos," Tamar said.

"Oh," Tidus said, like that cleared everything up. Then he set the pages down and asked, "So, was Martin right or not?"

"This shows he retains a statistically higher portion of FOX particles in his latest photo than in previous photos. It's almost double from a photo Wei took at the rift closure. He's been to the FOX-verse twice since then. All of Martin's data shows that he has been retaining FOX particles since his first visit four years ago," Luca said.

"So, he's right," Tidus said.

"He's not wrong."

"There's still a million questions," Tamar said.

"Wait," Wei said. "There's more."

Mason pulled out a small packet of pages and passed those around. I hadn't looked too hard at the data of my own photos because I knew someone would explain it. The next packet I did look at.

"Once Luca told us a Don had kidnapped Tidus, I looked for every founder counterpart and attached a drone to them. This report confirms they've been taking the place of their counterparts and each has a list of verses they're living in, where their counterparts have died. There's a particle analysis for each founder."

I flipped to the pages for Josephine. MVP Josephine was responsible for the death of seven of her twenty counterparts. The summary of particles on her was consistent with those seven universes and her own home-verse.

"And finally," Wei said.

Luca passed around a summary sheet of his own. It was a more detailed look at some of the rifts caused by VIP, including the one that impacted the Dugans. "The energy signatures are still there. From what I can surmise, high-energy events cause the rifts to reopen using the pattern set by the anchor. In the first universe listed, there was a lightning storm that triggered a rift opening. In the Dugan verse, six years ago an experiment failed in Josephine's lab, according to her notes, causing an electrical surge."

"So," Kiki said. "This is a cluster fuck."

"More like a perfect storm," Mason said.

"So, now what?" Tidus asked. We all looked at him.

"I don't really know what," Hugo said.

The rest of us didn't know either.

After breakfast the group lost cohesion. There was a horrible sense of defeat. What we had finally figured out felt more like a mistake, like going too far. I decided to take a nap. I slept for a few hours, feeling rested but not necessarily better. When I woke, I went in search of one of my partners. I figured if I just wandered around the house, the odds were I would stumble upon one or both of them.

After looking around the main level, I went to the game room. Tidus was sitting with Mason and they looked like they were concentrating pretty hard. Del was sitting opposite them, Margo's notes laid out in front of him.

"What're y'all up to?"

"We're trying to build an interface for the drones that's better at using the controller," Tidus said. He let me kiss him, then went back to work on the simulation. I went up behind him to look over his shoulder.

"What rift is that?" I asked.

"It's the same one we did this morning in your living room. Mason built a simulation and I have been working on closing it with the drones," Tidus said.

"Why?" I asked.

They both shrugged.

"Why not?" Mason said. "It helps me think."

"I like video games," Tidus added.

"Why do you think this would be more efficient?" I asked.

"Mathematically a keyboard relies on numbers and letters," Mason said. "You can type code, but you're at the mercy of the totality of the keyboard. In the MLK Protocol, you used fifteen unique characters. I think we can shorten that by assigning basic meanings to different buttons. You use the command 'surge' a lot, so if we made 'surge' say 'x,' you wouldn't have to type it."

"Cheat codes," Tidus said.

"Neat, but wouldn't you lose nuance?" I asked.

"That's the part we're working out. How much nuance do you need?"

"Never thought about it."

"Done," Tidus said. "How long was that?"

"Three minutes," Mason said. Tidus made a face, but I couldn't tell if he was happy or not. He nodded once and then restarted the simulation.

"What about you?" I asked Del.

"Oh, I'm helping Mason."

I looked back at Mason.

"I was thinking the VIP tech could actually help us fix the rift issue.

Theoretically, we could use the relays we already have in the A-classes to amplify the frequency of each universe. That would strengthen the barrier. And we could close any rifts at the same time."

"What's holding you back?" I asked.

"Well, first of all, it's hard to estimate the number of rifts. I'd need something to emit the frequency of that verse in order to amplify it through the relays. And I don't know how strong to make the sound."

"Can't take the noise, get out of the concert," Tidus said.

"I'd need the emitted sound to be high enough to stimulate the particles, but too high and I could accidently suck everyone back to their home-verse."

"What do you mean?"

"We've seen it before," Mason said. "On the Hub, we call it the Other Sock Phenomenon. When a verse becomes overamplified naturally, an object from that verse gets sucked back. It's like the universe recalls parts of itself. Usually animal swarms do it, the emergence of cicadas, or pod whales singing."

"That's crazy. Would the relays be able to reach that high?" I asked.

"It's a lower threshold than you think," Mason said. He pointed at his computer and showed me the simulations he was running.

"Does your brain ever stop?" I asked.

Mason looked like he was going to answer, but then he paused. We all did. The room froze. The distinct and out-of-place smell of peanut butter told me someone had just tuned into the here-verse. We listened. As the silence crept, a small feeling started to grow in the pit of my stomach. Something was wrong.

The doorbell rang. The game room was directly under the hallway to the front door, so we could hear walking around over our heads. The silence stretched. Then there was the sound of something hard falling on the floor.

"What do you mean?" Hugo's voice boomed. Hugo must have turned on the intercom.

"It's like I said, Del Mar. You violated the security clauses in your contracts. We're here to escort you back to HQ," a stranger answered.

"We aren't going anywhere," Hugo said.

"You don't have a choice."

"Shit, this is bad," Mason whispered.

"What about our work?" Hugo said.

"Don't worry, it's coming with us." I didn't like the tone in that guy's voice. I knew it was HQ security.

"Mason," I said, putting my hand on his shoulder. He jumped with a small squeak but looked at me. "You have to dump everything."

"I *what*?"

"We can't let them have it. They'd know it all. They'd know where VIP is, how their tech works, that we know they're killing counterparts. I think it's a setup. Could you imagine what they would do with this?" I could hear the panic and worry in my own voice. "How did they find us?"

Mason seemed to think for a second. His eyes went sort of glassy, and I thought for a moment he would have a panic attack. But then his eyes focused sharp and clear on me, and he nodded. He went to his computers and started typing.

"Del," I said, turning next on him. We could still hear the conversation over the intercom, and we could tell everyone else was doing what they could to try to slow the security detail down. Even Bowser was barking in a menacing way.

"What?" he said. He was standing with Margo's book clutched to his chest as if it was the only thing he had left in the world.

"You have to go. Use your watch and walk out of here."

"What?"

"Listen, if they find you here, you're as good as dead. But you can leave now. Take Mason and Tidus with you."

"Martin," Tidus said.

"No, you have to." I thumbed a few commands in my sequencer, then tried to hand it to Tidus, but he didn't move.

"I won't leave you. I won't leave anyone. What about Bowser?"

"Come back for Bowser. Mason knows too much, Del *is* too much, and you're too important." Tidus let me step closer to him. He let me put the phone in his hands. "I'm not going to argue about this."

"Why do you keep doing this? The risk—"

"Yeah," I said, "It might be a risk, but this time it's you who has to come rescue me."

My pulse was like a thousand bees under my skin. The sound of footfalls overhead, moving down the hallways, branching and splitting off, felt like the most ominous thing in the world. "Mas, take them to the next universe over, wait it out, then come back. How long until it's done deleting?"

"Eighty percent."

"And it's going to be total?"

"Total. It'll be like no one ever used them."

"Okay, I can manage the last twenty percent. Leave."

No one moved.

"Leave," I nearly screamed.

They jumped, then huddled together.

"Damn it, Martin," Tidus said before he stepped forward and pulled me into a slightly off-center kiss.

The next second they were gone. I had just enough time to get into a chair, log into a computer, and bring my drones to life. I sent them to a different verse, selected an object randomly, and pulled it into this verse. The swivel chair from some poor soul's office was big enough that the quantum tell was activated. I was trying to cover the others tuning. I sent the chair back and pulled it again. The computer warned me it would reboot in fifteen seconds. I let my hands fall away from the keys. The door nearly fell off its hinges as the security guard kicked it open. I jumped and put my hands almost comically high in the air.

"What the fuck are you doing?" the guy in front demanded. Four others were behind him.

"Nothing." Just as I said this, all the computers in the room turned blue and flashed the restart screens. I and the five security guards watched the three seconds it took for them to blink back to life. All you could see was some generic MVP background.

"What the fuck are you doing?" the guard asked louder, emphasizing totally different syllables.

"Chillin'."

"Are you Martin King?" a different one asked.

I nodded. "Is there a problem?"

"Time to pack it in, Martin," the guard said.

❖

The security team herded us into the front room. Everyone stared at me as I came up alone from the basement. I shook my head to signal that the others weren't coming. I hoped they trusted me. I hoped they got the message. Their response was to look at the floor. Hugo was handcuffed and Wei and Luca were standing nearby. Kiki and Tamar were holding hands in a corner near the door. I was placed somewhere in the middle of the room.

The security guys were all wearing radios, and calls came in from all over the mansion that things were clear. No one said anything. Seconds after the all-clears, people started pouring back into the living room. They had us outnumbered three to one.

"Boss, there's a dog," one of the guys said.

"Leave him. There's a cook who comes in the evenings. She'll figure it out," I lied, hurrying to keep the others from wrecking the cover I had built. Bowser bellowed from a back room. The security guards shrugged.

"This is everyone?" they asked.

We nodded. They led us out of the house into the snowy evening.

# Section 25

## *A coup and I'm still a fucking prisoner*

Security confiscated everyone's sequencers. I lied and said mine was in my room back at HQ. Then they ushered us into the yard and into a different verse. The trip back to HQ was almost uncomfortably short. There was a private jet and then a private bus to a dark section of beach. It was isolated for the most part, a stretch of sand trapped behind private summer houses. Then we tuned into the dead-verse.

I spent most of the trip panic-strategizing things Mason, Tidus, and Del could do to help us. It was pointless. I didn't know what we needed help from. I just knew in my core that the fallout from whatever this was would be bad. I also didn't know where they would go. If Tidus stayed with them, their options were limited. And even if I *could* come up with a plan, I had no way of communicating it. I clenched my teeth so much that by the time we stepped on the beach in the HQ dead-verse, the pain in my jaw was almost as bad as it had been when I was in the hospital.

The colossal carcass of HQ, dark and unyielding against the water's edge, was borderline horrifying. I knew that when damaged badly enough, the whole thing could be maneuvered to shore for repairs. I had just never seen it done. I was surprised by how little activity there seemed to be. It was even quiet inside. We crossed a few gangways working our way to the Hub, but we passed no one on the way in.

"Where is everyone?" I asked.

"Most people decided to go home because we're doing repairs and will be shored for a while," a guard said. She had a pleasant voice and had tried a few times to get one of us to engage with her. When that failed, she just offered us water. We didn't say anything to her or to anyone else. If it weren't for the cheap jokes from the guards, the trip would've been silent.

"It's creepy," Wei said.

"They'll be back," she said.

We were taken to the second level of the Hub. It looked like a storage room with big locking cages, like in a cheesy cop movie. They put us each into a cell. Mine had a cot, a blanket, and a table with water and food but no chair. I stepped inside, and they shut the gate behind me, locking the door with a padlock and chain. HQ had never prepared for a security threat as big as the one they were accusing us of.

"This seems like a lot," Hugo said as they removed the handcuffs. He was my direct neighbor. He rubbed his wrists and stepped into the cage without any protest.

"Hey, until we can figure out what you were up to in a B-class verse with MVP tech, we can't be too cautious," the main security guy said.

"When do we talk to someone?" I asked.

"The team extracting the tech from the house will be back tomorrow. And then it's just a matter of figuring out what you did."

It was funny. These people had been in the business too long. They had lived most of their lives in the dead-verse with the rest of us. Having shared so much of the same space made security less like sentries and more like bouncers for a local bar. Aside from the silence and the initial conflict, we had all been civil with each other. It made me wonder what they thought of the people giving them orders. How would knowing they worked for stone-cold murderers make them feel? Did they already know?

The group who had taken us from Wei's mansion left, replaced by two fresh guards who announced their names and that they would be just outside the door should anyone need them. They seemed less friendly than the others, so they were probably newer to MVP.

"What the actual fuck," Kiki groaned. I couldn't see them. They were farthest from me, on the other side of a cage full of metal lockers. In between me and the lockers was Hugo. Wei was across from me, Tamar across from Hugo, and Luca across from Kiki. Luca and I made eye contact at some point, and I tried to smile at him.

"God damn it, how'd they find us?" Wei asked, pacing back and forth. "I thought we had it locked in."

"No one is perfect, no use fussin' over a broken urn when what's inside is already dead," Hugo said.

"That doesn't help," Tamar said. Hugo shrugged and put his hands behind his head in that I'm-relaxed-but-only-for-show way he had.

"I agree with Hugo," I said. I lay down on my cot, which was like a stone slab. It was lying down, though, and I needed it.

"Martin, what do you think is going to happen?" Kiki asked.

"Someone has a plan," I said, trying to sound offhand. In reality, I was banking on Mason, Del, and Tidus. My only conclusion from the countless scenarios I tried to play out on the plane was to stall. I needed to buy as much time as I could.

"I hope you're right," Kiki said.

That was explicit enough. Kiki had basically asked if I knew what I was doing, and I had effectively said I did. Their last comment wasn't meant to convey any hope. It was a threat.

Most of us passed the night restlessly. I watched Hugo, Wei, and Tamar move around their cages. Luca sat near the door of his. I assumed he could see everyone else and the door to the room from there. I couldn't bring myself to move much. I just lay on my cot, which was only one one-hundredth of a degree better than standing. The pain in my chest was so bright, even yawning made me want to scream. I ate the food and drank the water, then called the guards at some point because I had to pee. A new guard came in a little after ten a.m. To my surprise, he stopped in front of my door.

"Hello," I said when he didn't say anything. This guy was tall and unremarkable looking.

"You need to come with us," he said. A second guy about half his size stepped out from behind him and went to Hugo's door.

"You too," the second guy said.

"Okay." I rolled myself onto my feet and went to the gate. Hugo shrugged and gave me a fake confused look. We had expected at least this much. I was already prepared for a long series of questions. I was just surprised Luca, the data lab leader, hadn't been included.

"Martin, Hugo," Luca said, coming as close as his fencing would allow.

"Don't worry," I said. "I think I know what this is about."

I smiled at him as Hugo and I followed the guards out of the room. Two more guards met us in the hallway, and we were led sci-fi-villain style through HQ to a data lab. The layout was exactly like Luca's, only it flowed in the opposite direction. A woman came out to meet us. She was about my height with blue eyes and red hair that was in a straight, severe-looking ponytail.

"Emma Elizabeth?" Hugo said.

"Hugo! My God, it's you?" she said, her face turning a bright red. "When they said—"

"Never mind that, ask your questions," Guard One said.

Emma Elizabeth was surprisingly calm and turned a steely gaze on the guard. "Hugo doesn't have the expertise to do what I suspect was done, not by half."

"No offense," she said to Hugo.

"Not him," Guard One said, pointing at me. "Him."

"Him?" Emma Elizabeth asked.

"Me?"

"Who are you?" she asked me in a friendly tone.

"Martin King."

She turned a pinker sort of red and grinned. "No, you can't be. You're him? Martin King as in *Martin King*?"

She pointed to a photo on the wall. I instantly knew it as a rift still, like the one Luca had given me.

"Oh jeez," I said, feeling a genuine amount of embarrassment. "Yeah, that's me. What rift is that?"

"That's the Chicken Problem Rift," she said. I groaned and covered my face. The Chicken Problem Rift was a rift I had closed on a farm, only the area was so overrun with chickens that I had to climb a tree to get away from them.

"All right, all right, stop with the circle jerk," Guard One snapped. "Well?"

"Well what?" Emma Elizabeth said.

"Your questions."

She nearly laughed herself to the floor. "Martin King is pretty amazing, but whoever did what they did to those computers was a genius. Also, no offense, Martin."

"None taken. Do you have our tech?" I asked.

Step one of the plan: stall. It seemed to be working. My gut had been right to have Mason dump the info on the computers. Emma Elizabeth would have had all the answers by now. But even she was reluctant to work with the guards, which only made the warning signal in my guts louder. I had to wonder what she knew. The evidence on the white boards and the notes we printed were incriminating enough, but I didn't know if that stuff was here. Or if she had seen it.

"I do," Emma Elizabeth said, putting her hands into her pockets. "I have the hardware at least. Whoever cleaned them did a seriously professional job. *And* as I have told these fools, there's nothing left and no way to recover it."

"Really?" Hugo said, sincerely impressed. I also had to wonder what he was thinking. I wanted so badly to fill him in, but I knew it was better if he knew nothing.

It was time to move on to step two: bluff.

"I might not've been the one to do it," I said, my voice as indifferent as I could make it. "But I gave the order."

"You what?" Emma Elizabeth said.

"What do you mean?" Hugo asked, his voice dropping as if he were trying to have a private conversation with me.

"What?" some guard said on top of that.

"Why?" Emma Elizabeth asked.

I sighed and then squared my shoulders. The next part of the plan seemed to divine itself as I spoke it. "The reason is simple. The information on those computers was the most damning information in MVP history. And if Don or the other founders want it, they're going to have to go through me to get it."

"What the fuck?" Guard One said. He took a series of menacing steps toward me. I tried to back up but only backed into more guards.

"I mean it, they talk to me or—"

"Martin," Hugo interrupted, stepping between me and the guard. "This isn't a time to be funny."

"I'm not. I gave the order to delete the work. Then I told the person who did it to wait for word from me. I'm going to get mine in all of this."

Hugo squinted at me, then his eyes went wide, and he gasped.

"You're going to sell us out?" he asked.

The emotion in his voice was real enough to make me want to take it all back. Instead, I took a page out of his book and modified my face to neutral. He either understood it or he didn't. Maybe he could tell I was bluffing, and he was playing along. Then again, he could really think I was betraying him. I decided it didn't matter. The outcome was the same, and his performance would be convincing.

"Jesus, Martin. Don't you see what damage that would do?" he said, placing his hands on my shoulders.

"That's half the point."

"And the other half?"

I took his arms by the wrists and pulled them off me. "Someone will pay for it. It's information, Hugo. The other half is and always will be what someone is willing to pay."

Emma Elizabeth gasped, adding to the drama of it all. "What the hell are you talking about?"

"If I wanted you to know, I would've left it on the computers," I said harshly, hoping to paint myself as a bigger threat.

"What the fuck does that mean?" Guard One said.

"It means," I said, trying to stay cool, "tell Don I'm waiting."

The meeting pretty much descended into chaos after that. Hugo insisted on trying to talk me out of it. A set of guards had to practically pull him off me. He struggled against them, but they won out. They escorted him out of the room and led me down a hallway opposite the one I had come from. I was not going back to the storage room then. Emma Elizabeth just stood there looking like a teenager who just found out her boy-band crush was just some middle-aged sellout. I could live with that.

The room they led me to was mostly an office. They put me inside and locked the door on their way out. I went to the desk. It was empty. The boxes in the corner, empty. The lamp on the desk at least turned on. It looked like the room had been staged. I immediately collapsed in the chair, the most comfortable thing I had sat on since being at Wei's, and tried to come to terms with the idea of being shot on sight when Don arrived.

❖

I lived in the office for two days. About an hour after they stuffed me there, some guards carried in my cot. I didn't miss it. But on top were my pillow and blanket from my room in the research lab. The black throw was usually tossed over my desk chair.

"Next time bring the Cheetos," I said to no one.

At first, I thought the guards were going through my belongings in search of whatever evidence they needed to find. But the next morning a delivery of my stuff wasn't random. In the box were my top two favorite outfits and my toiletries. I seriously doubted the Caucasian guards would think to grab the sack of silk I usually slept in to protect my hair. But there it was, blue and shiny, on top of the rest of my crap. Someone was looking out for me. I couldn't guess who, but I was glad I wasn't alone.

Don arrived the morning of the third day. I was sent to one of the gyms nearby to shower and change. I had to walk into the Hub and down another hallway to get to the gym, so I saw enough to know we were still on shore and that a lot of people were still gone.

I had an escort of seven guards this time. My heart raced as we walked to Don's office. Step three of the plan was still up in the air. Should I keep bluffing? Should I tell the truth? Should I sit down before he shot me, so I didn't fall like some sad sack in an action movie? I looked at the guard next to me as if she would know the answer. She just blinked at me.

We walked to the top of the Hub and went through a door that I had seen plenty of times as I went to the observation area. I had never been inside. The office was big, almost one-fourth of the whole circle of the Hub. Windows arced the crust side of the pizza slice of a room. I'd never noticed the windows since they were tinted. I could just see land as I stepped into the room.

I was surprised to find Don alone. I mean, he had enough security that I don't think he saw me as a threat. Still, I expected to find MVP Josephine or Justin or Carl. But it was just Don. He sat behind a huge oak desk I'm sure was bolted to the floor. It was in the center of the room, and a series of random things shared the space with it: a treadmill, a wall of filing cabinets, mismatched couches, and a glass coffee table. Considering the dated appearance of the furnishings, I knew this wasn't a regularly used space.

"Good morning," I said.

He had been looking down at his computer when I came in and didn't look up when I spoke. I wasn't the type to be annoyed by that.

I usually let people take as long as they needed to talk to me. And it's not like he was wasting my time. But I wasn't completely myself right then. Step three of the plan suddenly and irrationally called for provocation.

I walked up to the desk and put my hand at the back of the laptop. Then I slowly started to push it closed. Don's eyes shot to mine. His smile was horrible and tight, and the darkness under his eyes was noticeable through his makeup. Even his bald head was stubbly. He didn't like me touching his computer. My pulse jumped, but I didn't stop until the screen was flush against his knuckles. Then I backed into a seat and looked at him.

"If we're going to do this, let's do it," I said.

"In a hurry?"

I shook my head. "Quite the opposite. But *you* might want to be. At least I want to give you the chance to hurry."

"Enlighten me," he said through his teeth.

"Don, I know about your counterparts."

It was probably the most provocative thing I could say, but I wasn't looking for a reaction from him. I was looking for a reaction from the guards. Someone drew in their breath in a stifled gasp, someone else shifted their feet, and another's gear rustled as they turned their head to look at me, then immediately snapped it back forward. They were surprised, and that was good. Don's smile switched from annoyed to sinister, and he emptied the room with a gesture of his hand.

"That was a bold statement," a woman said. A panel gave way behind a wall and Josephine herself stepped out. Unlike her counterpart, who looked like she never knew what to wear, this Josephine was dressed in a black jumpsuit and heels. Her hair was short and slicked back.

"Oh, good. I was hoping to get the attention of the brains of this operation."

Don growled and stood. I remembered the horrible feeling of having VIP Don's hands on me, his fat fists grabbing my shirt. I blinked and took a breath. Josephine broke into a smile.

"That's why I came here," I said. "I have something to say."

"So do I," Don said. Then he stooped slightly, opened the drawer of the desk, and set a gun on the tabletop.

I wasn't really afraid of it. I had seen so few guns in my life that seeing one was like a deer encountering a hunter for the first time. The idea of being shot, however, was something I'd already thought about. I betrayed no panic, and I think that annoyed him.

"I told my accomplices if I was killed, they could sell the information to the other guys anyway."

"What other guys?" Josephine asked.

I understood something in that moment, and I felt so giddy I could have laughed.

"Oh shit," I said. "You really haven't found them, have you?"

"Martin, I thought you weren't here to play games," Josephine said.

"Naw, I'm not. Based on everything we found out, I just assumed you'd at least know about the others. Know what they knew about you."

"Listen," Josephine said with a sigh. "If you're going to be cryptic, I'm going to leave. Don and I don't have time for this."

I stood up too, feeling weird about sitting. Don straightened and twitched toward the gun, but I waved him down. "I knew you knew you had counterparts and I know you're picking them off one by one. Genius. Whose idea was that? Probably Don's, since he is the business, right? Anyway, I'm just surprised at how much you underestimate yourselves. Wouldn't you think that one of them, like you, would be able to do something like this?" I gestured with one arm, trying to capture the whole of MVP.

"There's nothing like this," Josephine said. Her pride in her work was clear on her face.

"The research team thought you wanted us to find them so you could stop them. I can see now you really were just looking for a way to keep replacing your counterparts until you were the last ones."

"Who are you talking about?" Don roared suddenly.

VIP knew about MVP, so why not even the score? "There's an organization that has multi-verse technology just like us. The only difference is they know all about you. They're looking for you. I had planned to make a deal with you, sell you the information the research team collected. But that's because I thought you had the advantage. I thought with all of MVP's wealth and employees and resources, they could easily slide me a few mil. And after learning that you were making billions across multiple verses, well…But now I'm not sure you do have the upper hand."

"This conversation is over," Don said. In a flash, the gun was in his hand and pointed at me.

"Don, please," Josephine said. "What do you mean by upper hand?"

"Their tech is untraceable, but you have numbers. They're more agile through each verse, but you know more verses. I don't know. Seems like a stalemate, now that I think about it."

"All right," Josephine said. "I have to admit, I'm not surprised."

"What do you mean?"

She paced around the room as she spoke. She pressed a button on the treadmill and pressed the conference call button on the industrial phone on the desk. A dial tone filled the air, and then she lifted the receiver and dropped it, ending the call.

"Someone else threatened to betray us," she said, "but we disposed of her."

She was talking about Margo.

"She thought our work was damaging the multi-verse. How could it when everything we do is to protect it? It wasn't until we stumbled upon the Event that we thought she might be right. And now that information is being withheld by her protégé," Josephine said. "That's unsurprising."

"I guess. But what are you going to do? Get rid of me like you did her? Fine, but I told you I have accomplices, and they'll release your info to the others."

"We'll stop them too," Don said.

"How? Until this moment you didn't know they existed. You know, it's hilarious that you believe you're untouchable and in the next turn you underestimate your counterparts."

"Well, this has been fun," Josephine said as Don leveled the gun on me.

"My accomplices will tell the others. They'll know everything, and you'll have to start from scratch just to pick up the pieces."

"Not before we work our way through your friends downstairs," Josephine said.

I know my face revealed my surprise. And I found myself cornered. I couldn't say they didn't know anything, because they obviously did. I couldn't even say I knew something they didn't. I was still searching for a response when the door banged open. A tall guard in head-to-toe riot gear stormed into the room.

"What?" Don roared.

The guard flinched. "Sir, something is happening on the beach."

All three of us turned to look out the window. Slowly, people wearing all black were walking out of thin air onto the sand. VIP Josephine was at the front of the pack. There was no tell, so I knew they were using their own tech.

"Oh shit, I guess I'm too late. They found you," I said, just as surprised as Josephine and Don.

"How's that possible?" MVP Josephine gasped, recognizing herself on the beach. VIP Josephine seemed to know where we were because she looked right at the windows.

"Told you they're just like you." I nearly laughed.

"We have to get you out of here," the guard said. There were more guards in the doorway.

Don looked at me for one cold, frustrated minute. Then he turned on his heels. He picked up the computer and left the room. In his haste, he left the gun. I knew a helicopter would be waiting for him on the roof. The guard gestured for Josephine, who was still staring down at the sand.

"Ma'am," the guard insisted. She strolled out of the room after Don. The guard who had come into the room first turned as if he were going to follow but then he stopped, shut the door, and locked it behind everyone else.

"What the fuck? A coup and I'm still a fucking prisoner?"

"Chill, bae, it's me," Tidus said, pulling off the guard helmet.

"What the hell are you doing here?"

He marched over and hugged me, laughing. "You said it yourself. It's a coup."

"That's not who I would've picked for the cavalry," I said, looking back out the window. Black-clad guards started to pour out of HQ, squaring off with Josephine and her technicians.

"They aren't the cavalry," he said. "They're the distraction."

I was about to ask when a voice came on the radio attached to Tidus's uniform. Now that I was closer, I could see the small ways in which it was different from the ones worn by real HQ guards.

"Clear on township." I didn't quite recognize the voice.

Tidus answered back. "Clear on decoy."

A third voice, feminine and familiar, said, "Bait and switch in three, two..."

Everyone on the beach vanished, VIP and MVP alike. And the smell of peanut butter was almost nauseating.

"What the actual fuck?"

Tidus just laughed. He told me we were to meet everyone in the Hub, so I led him down.

"That was some crazy shit," I said. "Where'd you send everyone?"

"I don't know. I put Mason in charge of that. My job was to get to you and announce that something weird was happening on the beach."

"You put Mason in charge?" I asked.

Tidus gave me a gigantic grin. "This was my plan! I'll explain it when we catch up to the others."

Meeting up with everyone in the Hub felt like a family reunion. Luca gave me a gentle hug. Kiki, Tamar, and Wei hugged me as a group. Hugo didn't hug me. He just shook his head.

"Your reckless behavior is starting to annoy me," he said. And I knew in that one sentence he had been the one who managed to get the stuff from my room.

"I'm starting to annoy myself," I said. There was a small cheer behind us. We turned in enough time to see Tamar step back from kissing Mason.

"How did you pull this off?" I asked Del when he stepped up to talk to me.

He laughed. "Your boyfriend figured it out. Mason said this place was like a castle. And Tidus told us about a bunch of strategies from a video game, and suddenly he had a plan. He said we three weren't a threat to anyone, but he had access to a threat big enough to put this place on the defense. And while they were looking the other way..."

"What did you say to VIP Josephine?" I asked.

"Basically, that I had tricked you all into trusting me so I could get the info and turn it over to her."

"I told our founders pretty much the same thing."

"Well, I did all the hard work," said the feminine voice I'd recognized, "so don't go thinking those three chuckleheads would've gotten this far without me." I turned and smiled at the beautiful woman walking toward me.

"*Fern!*" I shouted. The technician coordinator was accompanied by two of her techs. I knew them too, Kazz and Doug.

"What the hell, King?" she said. "Trying to fuck everything up all at once? Tired of doing it one job at a time?"

"You know it," I said, taking her hand. In another life, she would've been a fitness professional of some kind. She was jacked and could easily lift me, and I wasn't a skinny guy. She liked to flex, figuratively and literally, and spent most of her day in sports bras and leggings.

"How did they find you?" I asked.

"They messaged me on your sequencer, dummy," she said. "They told me what's been happening with those other guys, VIP and MVP and the damage. Is it as bad as all that?"

I thought about the Dugan dead zone. I thought about every message she herself had sent me about the state of the rifts. "Can't you tell?"

"Fern is actually the reason they found us," Mason said, stepping into the conversation.

"I…what?" Fern gasped.

"Martin opened a message from you on his sequencer. I had accounted for everyone else through expected channels, but I didn't know he was talking to anyone directly."

"Oh shit, that means the guards were really just following breach protocol," I said.

"Yeah, well, now everyone knows a lot more than they used to," Hugo said.

"It won't matter," Mason said. "I have everyone locked into their home-verse. I just reprogrammed some drones. We can at least try to talk to them. Someone is bound to listen."

"We can try," Hugo said.

"Well, what's next?" Fern asked. None of us had an answer for her.

"We need to figure out who is still here," Kazz said. "When we did the sweep, we missed a few people."

Wanting to get some air and not feeling needed, I headed for the shore, Tidus offering to come with me. We sat far back in the tall grasses that lined the beach. Tidus was systematically picking off pieces of guard uniform, making a neat pile on the ground next to him. I buried my hands in the sand and breathed in the wind.

"This has been a lot," Tidus said.

"Yeah, but now, we can do something about it."

"What do you mean?"

"We have to stop them both. I think that's the only way. I've talked to Don and Josephine on both sides. They don't see each other as equals, and as long as they're trying to beat out their counterparts, they'll never see the damage they're doing."

"I think I want a ten-inch Italian," Tidus said after a moment.

I laughed. "What's his name?"

"Christ, Martin, not everything is about men. You know what I mean. I want it on wheat bread, toasted, lettuce, tomato, an obscene number of pickles, and…"

"Salt and vinegar chips?" I said, having seen more than one Tidus down more than one bag of those chips.

Tidus laughed. "Please and thank you. God, this was so much. How are you all not exhausted?"

"Who says we aren't?"

If we weren't looking right at HQ, we would've missed it. It was getting dark, just losing the colors of sun set but not quite black. The wind was loud, and the grass blowing around us made hearing that much harder. There would've been nothing to tell us they were coming, except for the sheer luck that Tidus and I were sitting back from the water.

The sand took on a haze of shapes, mounds that moved, casting long shadows on the beach. It was slow and massive and almost incomprehensible. Once the shapes stopped appearing, they started to roll en masse toward HQ. If VIP Josephine hadn't stood up and turned to look around, I would have never picked her out of the crowd. And that is what it was, a crowd.

"Oh—" Tidus said, the panic rising in his voice. I clamped my hand over his mouth.

If they saw us, we wouldn't be able to help anyone. Somehow, VIP Josephine was about to take HQ. And I was going to let her. She had prepared for this, that was obvious. All of her techs had been dressed in dark colors when they showed up that afternoon. Now they were in jumpsuits the same color as the sand. It was an ambush. When VIP was inside, I sighed and uncovered Tidus's mouth.

"She tricked us! She knew! She—"

"Tidus," I said.

"What are we going to do?" he asked.

"Stay here," I said.

"What?" he cried.

"Stay here. I'm going in to see if I can help."

"Why do I—Martin," he said, grabbing both of my arms hard. "This again?"

"How else can it be?"

"I can help."

"Think about it," I said, appealing to his strategist brain.

He squinted at me. "I get it. I don't know the layout of HQ, and if we *both* go, there will be one less opportunity for a backup plan."

"Right. Still have my sequencer?" I asked.

He nodded, holding up the phone.

"Keep it," I said. "I bet you've figured out how to work it by now. Unless you hear from me, don't move. I don't know how long, either. Trust me."

"I hate this."

I didn't know what else to say to him. So, I stood and moved as fast as I could back into HQ.

# SECTION 26

## *Swim with their hands tied*

The entrance from the beach was a shipment receiving pod at the end of one of the primary gangways. It had a direct walkway to the Hub. No one was in either the pod or the hallway. As I approached the entry to the Hub, I could hear the rising commotion. I crouched just inside the door and scooted along a wall.

"Just make sure they're secure," Josephine was saying.

She was standing in the middle of the Hub cafeteria. Since no one had been using the tables, HQ staff had folded most of them and stacked the chairs along the edges of the room. Josephine paced in a circle. At her feet, my friends were being wrestled to the floor, their hands zip-tied behind their backs. Fern snapped through three sets of ties, then punched through three of Josephine's goons. The fourth got her with a Taser, and she sank to the floor. They used an actual set of handcuffs on her at that point. When everyone was down, Josephine turned to a guy who looked winded. He probably was just a scientist, not the soldier Josephine was asking him to be.

"See if anyone else is here. Martin King and that tall guy are missing," she said.

Since she mentioned me by name, I figured the tall guy was Tidus. Kazz and Doug weren't there either. They were probably still looking for others just like Josephine was about to do.

The scientist nodded and turned toward an equally stunned-looking group. "Let's go."

Five of the thirty or so VIP people moved off.

"What the fuck are you going to do with us?" Kiki said.

Josephine cackled. "Probably nothing."

"I don't understand," Del said, looking like he really didn't understand.

"I know. That's why it worked. Margo thought you might've turned on us." She strolled over to a shorter person still wearing a sand-colored helmet.

The person took off their helmet, and a wave of salt-and-pepper hair flowed down her back.

"Margo," Del gasped.

"I'm sorry, Hugo, but I—"

Josephine shoved Margo in a way that looked playful but really wasn't. "Margo, don't apologize. You were right. See, it seemed too good to be true that after escaping with Martin, you would just show up with a window of opportunity to finally get to Headquarters. We were party to his tricks before and somehow I knew, I knew."

"How'd you get back?" Del asked.

"I got back because I didn't go far."

"When we got to the beach, we removed the drones you attached to us," Margo said.

"How did you know they were there?" Mason asked.

"We've collected a few drones over the years, and after seeing what Martin could do with them, I designed a few tricks," Josephine said.

"It's a magnet," Wei said, "not a trick."

Josephine didn't like that. She walked over and kicked Wei hard in the chest. He crashed to the floor gasping.

"Stop," Hugo said.

Josephine and Margo both looked at him.

"Honestly, I never expected to see you," Josephine said to Hugo. "I wondered why Martin and our Hugo were so chummy. Margo told me Martin knew her doppelganger. It makes sense he'd know you too."

"What're you going to do with us?" Hugo asked.

"Well, you're a different matter. From what our Hugo says, you probably know the most about this place. I feel like my team could figure it out. And since Mason was able to trap everyone else, I feel like we have as much time as we need. However, I think you could help it go faster."

"What do you want to know?"

"I want everything," she said.

I needed to find a way to slow her down or stop her. I wasn't about to go charging into another direct conflict. This group seemed armed with only Tasers, so I guess it was harder to get guns than I thought. But that didn't make me want to face them. I'd also left Tidus on the beach. I wondered what tools I could use.

I scooted to a hallway, thinking if I could get out of the Hub and to any research lab, I could find gear I needed. Even better, if I could get to a technician supply room, I would be even more useful. When I was sure no one was looking my way, I slipped around the corner, stood, and started to run.

And I slammed chest first into two of Josephine's goons. I almost didn't feel them dragging me back to the center of the Hub. The pain turned my vision bright white, and I felt bile rising. I think I might have also jammed my nose, but the flare in my side was astronomically worse.

"Oh, there you are, Martin." Josephine laughed. They tossed me in with the others and put three zip ties on my wrists. I didn't say anything.

"There were some other people. We're bringing them now," the scientist soldier announced.

"You checked the whole place?" Josephine asked skeptically.

"Oh…you mean the whole…not just…okay," the man said.

Josephine looked like she would murder him, but he turned and gestured for the others to follow. I slumped and almost fell over, but Tamar braced me with her body.

"Are you okay?" Margo asked me.

I shook my head and tried to breathe without wincing.

"I did a good job, didn't I?" Josephine said, crouching to look me in the eyes. "You thought they'd have it over on me. But here I am."

"Congratulations," I growled.

She laughed.

"Let them go," Hugo said. He tried to stand but a VIP tech kicked him in the back of the knee, causing him to crash back to the floor.

"How like a Hugo," Josephine said. She rose and adjusted her sand-colored jumpsuit.

"Let the others go," he said, "and I'll talk."

She looked us over. A lot of people there had betrayed her, tricked her, and made her doubt herself, me chief among them.

"All right, but let's see if they can swim with their hands tied."

She nodded to some of her techs, and they started pinning anchors to our clothes.

"Jo," Margo said.

The look Josephine gave Margo clearly said *if you stick up for them you're next*. So, Margo backed down. They didn't give a warning or a countdown. One minute I was looking at Josephine's horribly prideful smile, the next I was in the water.

❖

I tried to breathe, like a dumbass. Water filled my lungs, burning my throat and nose. I wanted to cough. I knew better than to open my mouth again, but the pressure of the water in my lungs was overwhelming. I tried to kick, but my body wouldn't respond. I had learned to swim without panicking, but my head had to be out of the water. If I was submerged for even a second, I was paralyzed with fear. My eyes were closed tight, not that the darkness under the nighttime ocean would have made any difference. At least when I drowned the first time, it had been bright and welcoming.

I felt hands on my body and was sure they were meant to pull me down. I thrashed. Then stronger hands grabbed me on the other side. They did pull me. The instant my face breached the surface of the ocean, I was gagging. The waves rolled over my head again and again, and I learned drowning in the ocean was ten thousand times worse than in my neighborhood pool. My body tried to get me to throw up, misinterpreting the massive volume of ocean water in my lungs as something I had eaten. Luca and Fern pulled me onto the sand and placed me on my stomach. I could feel Luca inspecting me, trying to help me, but I couldn't do anything but force water out of my lungs.

"God damn it," Tamar screamed. She jammed her wrists against her knee and snapped the zip tie. She looked so young, stomping her feet and growling.

"What the fuck was that? Where are we?" Fern said.

"Some verse. There's a city, so at least it's not a dead-verse,"

Mason said. Tamar was helping him with his ties. He had two, which she carefully sawed with a pocketknife she kept in her boot.

"I'm so tired of losing," Wei said. He held his hands out to Tamar. She gave the knife to Mason and he freed Wei.

"Who's not here?" Kiki asked.

"The Hugos. That's it," Tamar said.

"Kazz and Doug," Fern added. She was pulling with all her strength against the handcuffs, but all she was doing was digging the metal into her wrists. Red started to seep out from the raw skin.

"Maybe no one found them yet," Mason said.

"Tidus," I said.

"What? Where was he?" Tamar asked.

I was done gagging, but I still felt like I was leaking water. Maybe I was just crying. "We were outside when we saw them appear on the beach, I told him to wait for me. I need to get a message to him."

"How? We don't have any gear! They took it," Fern said.

Wei looked around. "We could find something here, make something."

"That would take too long. Where even is here?" I asked.

"All right, everyone," Luca said, "Get up. We're going to figure this out. We already know some things. Of everyone here, I'm the only one with counterparts, so we know we aren't in one of those verses."

Luca pulled the anchor off his shirt and tossed it into the sand. He then stood and snapped through his zip tie like Tamar had done. I admired his will, but I couldn't really find any at the moment. My lungs burned, my eyes seared, my ribs ached, and everything seemed suddenly so much bigger than me. Luca took the knife from Wei and used it to free me.

"What else do we know?" Luca asked. I know the question was for the group, but it felt like it was to me. He helped me sit up and carefully inspected my face, wiping away sand.

"We know they couldn't send us just anywhere," Mason said.

"What do you mean?" Fern asked. breathing hard. She seemed to have given up on her handcuffs.

Mason stood and looked around. "We know they haven't explored the full multi-verse, so we know they need to have been to a verse beforehand for their devices to work properly, as fast as they had to get us here."

"There's always a way to know what verse you're in. We just have to look around," Tamar said.

"Then what?" I asked.

"Then we figure it out," Luca assured.

He pulled me to my feet and we started for the city. We decided to start with new clothes since we were soaked. There was a souvenir shop open nearby and Wei insisted on finding something for everyone to wear. I just followed Luca around. The storekeepers weren't really happy to see us, but Kiki won them over by speaking to them in their native language and Tamar overpaid for everything using an emergency multi-verse credit card she also kept in her boot.

Wei asked the store owners for a toolbox, explaining that Fern had lost a bet and we needed to help her. They gave us one, and Mason was able to free Fern without crushing or cutting her using a hammer and pruning shears. Wei threw clothes at me and Luca, and we went into a changing room together.

"You've been quiet," he said, helping me out of my shirt.

"What do you want me to say?"

He ran his hands through his beautiful wet hair and sighed. I leaned forward and kissed him. He smiled at me.

"Was it the water?" he asked in the patient, caring tone he used with Mason. I didn't answer. I just stepped closer to him and nuzzled against him. He sighed and put his arms around me.

"Martin," he said, pulling away, "I know it's hard right now, but we're going to get back."

I shrugged.

That made him laugh. "Oh, really? You've been balls to the wall since VIP showed up and now you're doubting?"

"Aren't you?"

"No, because you're *you.*" He kissed my cheek, then my chin, then my shoulder. It was some sort of clever compliment reward system. I got kisses when he wanted me to believe in me. "And I'm me, and they're them, and we'll fucking think of something."

"I don't know what to do."

"Take off your pants," he said.

That made me laugh. "Is that an invitation?"

"Joke all you want, but we're going to talk about your feelings," he said, but I could see he regretted not playing along.

"I should've never left him." It was as simple as that.

"Take your pants off," Luca insisted. He pulled his own shirt over his head. "You did what you thought was best."

I took my pants off. "So what?"

"Martin," he said, drying his hair with a towel Tamar had bought. "We know we're in an A-class verse."

"Right," I said, thinking about the smartphone the shop owner had and the make of electric car we had passed in the parking lot.

"So, what does that mean?" he prompted. I shrugged. He picked through the four shirts that Wei had given him, and he handed me one. I used it to dry my hair.

"It means," Luca said, exasperated, "there's a Tidus *here* somewhere. And if your Tidus had come with you to HQ, he'd have been dumped here too, and that would've been way worse than spending the last hour on a beach in a dead-verse. Also, I gave you that shirt to wear, not to dry your hair. That's what the towel's for."

I couldn't help but smile. "Towels are bad for hair."

He smiled at me too. He was looking particularly handsome. He hadn't shaved since we were escorted out of Wei's house. He had a lot of white in his beard, and his damp hair was regaining some fluff, making him look wild. And his smile creased his eyes in that perfect way.

"Um…Martin," he said. I didn't answer. "I need you to stop looking at me like that."

"Hey," Kiki said, throwing open the curtain to the dressing room.

"Kix, I'm not wearing pants," Luca said, sounding more exhausted than annoyed.

"So what?" They looked right in character in a bright blue floral print shirt and very short, blue beach shorts. They looked at me. "Did you say there's a Tidus here?"

"There's one in every A-class, so…"

"Right. So, if you saw him, would you know which one he was? Pinpointing this verse would be a great start."

"I think so," I said.

"How do we find him?" Wei asked, stepping into the doorway.

"Can we finish what we're doing here first?" Luca demanded.

Wei and Kiki exchanged a glance, side-eyeing me and Luca

standing around half dressed. Luca rolled his eyes and pulled the curtain closed. I put on different pants, and he changed, then helped me put on a shirt. Then we all wandered out into the street.

"They're all on social media. We just need a computer," I said, following up on Wei's question.

"I can do that," Wei said.

❖

I sat outside squeezing water and sand out of my locs while Wei and Tamar negotiated a phone at the first wireless store we found. We needed access to the internet right away. The hard part was that we had no bills in our name or credit history in this verse.

"You okay?" Kiki asked me. They plopped down next to me and handed me a small bag of Cheetos.

"Wow. Not very filling, but thanks."

They shrugged, then opened the bag beside them. It seemed like they had gotten one of everything the convenience store had to offer.

"You're a beautiful human," I said with a smile.

"Once we know the verse, we know all the rifts. Well, *you* know all the rifts."

"I also know the one natural rift into the dead-verse won't open for years," I said. I pulled the seams on the bag of Cheetos, and it tore, spilling Cheetos into my lap. Thankfully, the board shorts Wei had picked for me were bright orange. I ate what spilled.

"Wait a minute," Kiki said. They looked at Mason, who was nervously watching Tamar and Wei in the store through the windows. He looked so unlike himself in a black snap-back instead of the beanie. "What about the rift VIP used to get there? If they made it, then it's probably a weak spot, right? Because they had to force their way in. We could just trigger the rift with energy."

Mason winced a little and sighed. "No. It won't be there because I filled in their data in order to make their devices work."

"Damn it."

"Good thinking, though," Luca said.

"So we find this verse's Tidus," Fern said. She was eating several corndogs out of a paper tray.

"Then we'll at least know where we are," Wei said. He trotted to the curb, triumphantly wielding the latest model of smartphone in a gold case.

"Time to get to work," I said, holding my hand out for it.

"You're going to make it gross with your food hand," Wei cried, snatching the phone away.

I sighed and wiped my hands on some napkins from Fern. Wei placed the phone in my hands slowly. I sighed and thumbed it open. I started with the app store. The social media platforms themselves were all the same across the A-classes, but the names changed a lot. Sorting the app store by most popular social media always worked.

I made a new account, and I took a photo of me on the street with Kiki and our bag of trash snacks for the profile photo. Everyone else was mad, so I took a group photo for the banner. A few details later, and I had a new social media count. This site was called THRUSH and mostly shared videos. The nice thing about it was that people usually used their real names, or at least an accessible name, so I didn't have to try and guess at a screen name Tidus might use, not that it was hard since most of them used Titan.

I searched for Tidus Allen Avery and he was fourth on the list based on the area.

"There he is," I said. I opened the first video post. It was a short of him putting makeup on his eyes, and it was captioned *Every day is eye day.* He did have beautiful eyes. "It's FAU Tidus."

"Great. What's the next closest verse that parallels the dead-verse?" Luca asked.

"We should go talk to him," Mason said, nearly giddy with excitement.

We all looked at Mason.

"Why?" Tamar asked.

"To see if he recognizes Martin." Mason grinned and explained, "I have a theory. Martin suggested other Tiduses know him because he carries FOX particles and that he is sort of minutely converging the here-verse Tidus with FOX Tidus. But based on the prox—"

"Mason," Luca interrupted gently. "We aren't here for data."

Mason deflated.

"What if we could do something crazier than that?" Kiki said.

"Like?"

They looked around, the spell of their thoughts breaking. They rubbed their face and groaned. "It's a fucking long shot, but what if we could use this Tidus to send a message to our Tidus?"

"What?" several voices said, mine included.

"Let's do it," said Wei.

"That won't work," I said. "When FAX Tidus remembered what I said to Tidus, there were months between those moments. We don't have months."

"But I think it's speeding up," Kiki said. "What was the name of the bar you were rescued from with FAX Tidus?"

"Neon."

"When we were looking for you, we had pinpointed you to FAX-verse. Tidus knew that FAX Tidus had tapped into him before. And he joked about doing the same to try and help find you. He said you were probably with FAX Tidus at Neon."

"So?"

"We never told him the name of the bar," Kiki said. "I sent Hugo the name of the bar and that's where he said he just found you."

"That's lucky?" I said, feeling both completely caught off guard and unsurprised.

"Or is it."

"Sounds like a long shot," Luca said.

"Right now it's our only shot," Fern said, "so when you think of a better plan, we'll switch. Now find out where he is." For emphasis, she held all six corndog sticks between her fists and snapped through them.

Kiki took the phone from me. "Would he be dumb enough to leave his location tags on?"

❖

Apparently he was. We zeroed in on him at a club nearby. I didn't tell anyone that the club overlapped with Neon in the FAX-verse geographically. We paid the cover and strolled right in, lucky no one was carded. I searched for Tidus. The crowd was thick with people in various states of dress. The club was loud and pulsing with lights, music, and a dance floor below a DJ station. The floor was the source of the lights, white two-foot by two-foot tiles, blinking in rhythm with the music.

"This is a bit too much for me," Mason said.

"I'll wait outside with you," Fern said, and I felt them leave, their presence behind me becoming nothing but air.

"Oh, boy. I think I'm having a flashback," Luca said.

"This place is amazing," Wei said breathlessly. He tried to move away, but Luca caught him by the back of the beige and red parka he had decided to wear.

"Work, not fun."

"Over there," Tamar said, tapping my shoulder. I looked at where she pointed.

There he was. FAU Tidus. He was about a third of the way into the crowd on the dance floor, dancing with his eyes closed. He was barely dressed, wearing only a tight pair of shorts and fuzzy rainbow boots. I appreciated that the Pride flag on his shorts included the trans colors and the POC stripes. His face was painted with a green masquerade mask, and his hair flashed different colors with the lights, so it must have been dyed white.

"God damn," I said. Some in the group agreed.

"I never thought anyone could out-gay me, but *damn*," Kiki said.

"You have to go talk to him," Luca said.

"What am I supposed to say?"

"Does it matter?"

"Kinda…probably."

"Martin, every Tidus has been attracted to you, so it's not like he won't want to talk to you."

"Not FAX Tidus."

"FAX Tidus thought he had already hooked up with you."

I turned to look at Luca. He was standing in a very bossy manner, arms crossed over his chest, chin tipped up, still holding on to Wei's coat.

"What kind of boyfriend are you? Can't you be jealous or something?"

"The man is seven feet tall, of course I'm jealous, but that's not *your* Tidus, That's FAU Tidus, and we fucking need his help. When this is over, I'll be a better boyfriend. For now I'm your fucking boss, get the fuck over there."

"It's hot when you cuss."

"Agreed," said Tamar and Kiki.

"All right," Luca said, glancing at Wei. "I'm going to get this one an incentive to behave. You go over there."

"Send two drinks to that table," I said, pointing. "Anything with the word 'sunrise' in it."

"Deal," he said to me. He let go of Wei, who immediately launched himself toward the bar. Luca followed.

"Five bucks says Luca gets hit on before we leave," Tamar whispered to me. It wasn't his usual polished look, but he looked handsome and neat. He had picked a loose long-sleeve cotton shirt and blue pinstripe shorts. With his messy hair and scruffy face, he was very much the Mediterranean heartthrob.

I shook her hand and crossed to the edge of the dance floor. I stood at a high-top table to try and figure out a plan. I watched Tidus dance. He looked like he knew the group dancing around him, occasionally brushing up against one of them. All the other guys seemed more occupied with each other than with him.

Then he opened his eyes and looked straight at me. I sensed a moment of indifference, then a moment of consideration. I did my best to smile and look away. I made eye contact with Luca at the bar and he gave me a stern look and a shooing motion with his hand.

"Buy me a drink?" Tidus asked.

The sound of his voice suddenly so close made me jump, but I played it off by laughing. He leaned across the table, his bare shoulders shining with body glitter.

"I already did," I said. And thank fucking God the waiter appeared right on cue with both drinks. I would have to remember to tip him for amazing timing.

"God, I love this drink," Tidus said, sipping the yellow and red cocktail through the straw.

"I thought you might." I tried to lower my voice to draw him closer to me.

He took the bait and leaned in. "Do I know you?"

"Kind of," I said.

"From? School?"

"No, I…close your eyes," I said.

"What?"

"I'm going to describe the setting where we were last together, and you let me know when you know my name."

He grinned and shrugged, closing his eyes, turning the painted-on mask into something eyeless and mysterious.

"Imagine you're on a beach," I said. I needed to test the immediacy of the connection between him and my Tidus. FAX Tidus had recalled something with weeks in between, but I hoped that the right trigger would enable FAU Tidus to recall the events from just a few hours ago. My Tidus had said he believed in energy, and I knew he was trying to reach out to me across the multi-verse, beg me to return for him. I hoped this Tidus could find him.

"Okay," Tidus answered in a low breath.

"It's not far from here. We're sitting in the grass just at the edge of the sand. The sun is setting, but we can't see the horizon. You're wearing a costume that you take off piece by piece. We were talking about getting hoagies."

"An Italian," Tidus said.

"That's right."

His laugh died quickly, and his eyes snapped open. He put down the drink. The look he gave me was one of pure shock.

"What happened, Tidus? Did you remember?"

"No," he said. "No, I—that doesn't make any sense."

"It does. It's confusing, but a version of you remembers. A version of you is reaching out."

Tidus laughed maniacally. "Damn it, you *would* be a crazy one."

"You know I'm not crazy."

"I don't know you," he said, but the look on his face said he knew something.

"Please just tell me what you remembered."

"I didn't remember anything. I couldn't have. Leave me alone."

He turned and crashed into the crowd. He pushed into the bathroom just as a drag queen wearing a sash and swimsuit came out. I followed Tidus in before the door closed behind her. He seemed scared for a moment, then he rallied and turned a steady glare on me.

"Tidus…"

"No, I'll fucking defend myself," he said, standing to his amazing full height.

"You're right," I said. "Those aren't your memories. They're the memories of someone very important to me. He's particularly important to you too, and if you just give me a chance to explain, you'll understand."

He sighed. "Fine. Go ahead, tell me your crazy story and get the fuck out of my face."

"Okay. I'm from a different reality—a different universe where you and I are dating."

"That's a new one, boldest pickup line yet."

"It's not a line. My Tidus is alone on the beach I described, the beach you could see in your own mind. Bad people threw me and my friends out of that universe. I need your help to get back to him."

"Okay, I've heard enough. Do you really expect me to trust you?"

"No. I hoped you'd trust him."

"You mean the other Tidus trapped in a different reality." He ran a hand through his snowy blond hair. The glitter coating him created a gentle dust I could almost feel land on my skin. The look of irritation on his face was such a stark contrast to the pleasant sprinkle of shining color that I regretted coming.

"Okay, okay, Tidus. I'm leaving. I'm sorry I upset you. You—he—the other Tidus said once that in an adventure, when the hot guy says get in the car, you get in the car."

Tidus laughed and crossed his arms over his chest, looking at me with a face that gave away his lie as he said, "You aren't that hot."

It was a Hail Mary. I'd hoped using a direct quote from Tidus would trigger something for FAU Tidus. I didn't think it would work, but I had to be *sure* it wouldn't before I went to regroup with the others. I almost laughed as he raised his eyebrows at me in clear challenge. Instead, I turned and left the bathroom. I found Kiki at the bar talking to some muscular woman.

"Where is everyone?" I asked them.

"Tam went outside with Mas and Fern, Luca is over there somewhere watching Wei, who wanted to dance."

"It didn't work. We should get out of here and find a plan B."

"You can't go," the muscular woman said to Kiki.

Kiki laughed and shrugged. "Sorry."

While Kiki wrapped it up with the woman, I looked around for

Luca. He was at a table talking with a guy whose face was painted like Tidus's. He had on rainbow leggings and black work boots. I started to cross to Luca but was surprised when Tidus beat me there.

"For fuck's sake, Grayson, do you have to flirt with everyone's boyfriend?" Tidus said.

"Excuse me?" Grayson snapped.

I stepped in behind Tidus and was listening. I knew the name Grayson. That was the ex who had cheated on my Tidus, and Bowser had ratted him out. It was weird seeing that guy, a guy I couldn't understand at all with a Tidus. I clenched my fists so I wouldn't do something stupid.

"What are you talking about? How do you know he's dating someone?" Grayson asked.

"We have the same boy—" Tidus gasped and clamped his hands hard against his mouth. He spun around searching the crowd. When his eyes landed on me, only a step or two behind him, his eyes went wide.

"Martin," he said. Then he turned back to Luca. "Luca."

"Hey, Tidus," Luca said evenly.

# SECTION 27

## *What's the number again*

Tidus shoved Grayson away from Luca and considered him. "You're dating Martin. And so is…?"

"Yup."

"I think I need some air."

"What's going on, babe?" Grayson said, coming to his side.

Tidus considered Grayson as if searching his own memories. "Oh my God! You cheated on me—him—*me*."

Grayson looked confused but not necessarily innocent. "What are you talking about? We aren't together."

"Are you kidding me?" Tidus took a step back. "I think I need to sober up."

Instead of doing that, he took Luca's drink and chugged it.

"Ew, was that just soda?"

Luca laughed, nodding.

"You're so old," Tidus said.

Then he stared at me hard. I didn't move. I didn't even try to smile. I just let him think about whatever it was he was thinking about. In a flash, his mouth was on mine, the kiss clumsy and familiar and different and altogether surprising.

"Um…" I said when he backed away.

"Shit, the other me isn't going to like that. Tell him I'm sorry. I just needed to understand."

"Tell him yourself."

He blinked at me. "Can I do that?"

"I'm counting on it. You can hear him, right? You're picking up on him. Well, I'm hoping he can pick up on you too. I need you to relay a message."

"This...this is absolutely *insane*."

"What the fuck is going on?" Grayson said.

"It's above your pay grade, pal," Wei said, laughing as he approached. Tidus just waved Grayson off.

"Well, this is a thing. So what do you want me to say?" Tidus asked.

I blinked. "Shit, I don't know. I didn't think we'd get this far."

"He could call us," Luca said. He mourned the loss of his soda by picking up the glass and looking at it.

"Sequencers don't make calls."

"No, but the phones on HQ do. They can call into any verse if you put in the verse code before the phone number," Wei said.

"Wow, y'all are so serious about this," Tidus said.

"It *is* serious," Kiki said.

"The trick becomes finding a phone he can get to without getting caught," Luca said.

"I know one," I said.

"I think we should leave. It's distracting," Tidus said.

"Where are you going to go dressed like that?" Kiki asked.

Tidus laughed. "I have a coat."

I paid the tab and left a three-hundred-dollar tip. Grayson watched us leave, stunned. We followed Tidus toward the door. Tidus's coat was a white faux fur trench coat the same shade as his hair. He pulled it on and led the rest of us out of the club. Mason, Tamar, and Fern greeted Tidus as if they knew him, and he didn't shy away. I could tell he couldn't get a clear read on the others, but I could also tell something was telling him they were safe.

He led us to a diner around the corner, and the waiter greeted Tidus excitedly. They exchanged some small talk while we waited for a table. I asked for a kids' menu and a crayon pack. The front of the menu listed food and had some characters you could color. The back was an activity asking kids to draw a picture of their meal inside a cartoon gator's open mouth. I used that space to plan out the message to my Tidus. I needed it to be clear and short, so he could remember it.

"Follow me," the waiter said, finally taking us to a booth.

Wei nearly ran everyone over, excited to be in a diner.

"He's living his best life—a club and diner food," Luca said, laughing. I took his arm and slowed him down. He looked at me with tired, patient eyes.

"I'm sorry about here-verse Tidus kissing me."

"I was there. I know you didn't know it was going to happen."

I wanted to kiss him. Instead, I followed him into the booth.

"Look, I'm going to stand here till you order because if I move it'll be thirty minutes or more before I can get back," a waiter said, coming to the table.

"House special," Wei cheered.

We all looked at each other and then at the waiter. "Same."

We added a round of coffee and the waiter nodded and walked away.

"Do you dress like this all the time?" Fern asked Tidus.

He laughed. "No. Sometimes I wear pants."

"The other you has purple hair," she said.

"Fern, you act like you've never seen a counterpart, chill please," I said.

"I think you can make this shorter," Luca said. He took the blue crayon and started crossing off sections of my message.

"What is the house special?" Kiki asked Wei.

I didn't hear the answer because I was watching Luca restructure my message. It felt late. It felt like time was slipping by, and I had left someone I cared about alone for too long. I just hoped he trusted me enough to wait for me to get word back.

"I think that'll work," Luca said.

"Now, we just need a phone for him to call," I sighed. I looked around the diner. There was a greasy-looking black phone hanging on the wall by the dish return for the bar. I wondered if they would let me use it.

"Just use your cell," Tidus said.

We all looked at him.

"What, they don't have cells in other realities?" he said, then he noticed we weren't laughing with him. "Oh, *seriously*?"

"No, we have one. What was the number again?" Tamar asked Wei.

"I think it says it somewhere," Kiki said, pulling out the gold phone.

"One phone between all of you?"

"We were attacked, and they took our stuff. We bought these clothes around the corner," I said.

"They took your clothes?" Tidus said, looking particularly scandalized.

"No, I mean…look, never mind. It's a long story. Do you have a cell?" I asked.

He nodded and pulled a silver touchscreen from his coat.

"What's the number?" I wrote it on the designated place on the coloring page. Then I turned the whole page toward Tidus.

"Safe. Call. Phone where found me. Climb outside to roof. Door code 1907. Call…" Then he read the seventeen-digit number.

"That's a four," I said.

He blinked at me. "This is the shortest you could make it?"

I shrugged. "Attempt number one?"

Tidus sighed, adjusted in his seat, and did the fake hair flip. He read the note again, loud and with confidence. Then he looked at me. Then at his phone.

"Did that work?" he asked me.

"Does it feel like it worked?" I asked back.

The others sighed.

"This is my first time doing this," Tidus said.

Luca glared at everyone, then turned a kind eye on Tidus. "Hey, it's ours too. Let's try a few things to see what happens."

Tidus nodded. The next hour was spent with Tidus reading the note an assortment of ways. Luca went full scientist mode and turned a second coloring page into a data table where he recorded Tidus's response after each reading. By the end of an hour, the only column with the most data was labeled "inconclusive."

"What happened?" Tidus asked. He slurped a milkshake through a straw and looked at me. "To you all, I mean."

"It's hard to explain," I said.

"Not that hard," Kiki said. So, I let them tell it. I grabbed a third coloring sheet and started planning. Assuming we could get through to Tidus, he would need to find a way to get us some tech. I couldn't know how Josephine's guards were operating. I hoped Hugo went for maximum distract. From there, we needed a way to stop them.

I had an idea but I hated it. I remembered Mason saying he could heal all the rifts at once by amplifying the signal of a verse. I wrote out the details I could remember. I was counting on being able to create a signal powerful enough that it would snap everyone back to their home-verse. *Other Sock Phenomenon*. I wrote that on the page. If that worked, then everyone would be safely away from harm. But then what?

If the signal could be maintained, it could trap people in the verse. It was like the perfect marriage of the two companies: the amplified frequency would snap people home like tuning, and the relay could pulse an electromagnetic frequency that would keep anything from leaving. All we needed was a source for the signal. I listed a few things common to most verses: Cracker Barrel, the Mets, apples. None of that completed the plan.

I could feel Luca watch me write. And I felt a weird sense of love and admiration and amazement when he added to my sheet with his blue crayon. He filled in some things I didn't know like door numbers and pass keys. The more he added, the more it felt like it could work. Then he wrote a solution under the Other Sock Phenomenon plan that was so perfect it was almost poetic. I looked at him. And he looked back, completely certain.

"What happened to the dog?" Tidus nearly shouted, breaking my concentration.

"We went back to the verse to get him. Then we took him to Wei's parents, who live in Ohio," Mason said.

The phone on the table rang, lights flashing along the edge. Tidus picked it up and looked at the screen. He frowned, advanced it to voicemail, then set it back down. It wasn't until he looked back at Mason's horrified face that he realized what he had done.

"Oh my *God*," he cried. "I'm sorry. It's habit. It said unknown."

The table erupted in a series of affirming and scolding words. I, for some reason, wasn't worried. I just waited until the lights flashed again.

"Tidus," I said.

They all stopped at the sound of my voice. Tidus snatched up his phone and answered.

"Hello, this is Tidus," he said, his eyes locked on mine. The smile he gave me confused my heart a little. He cheered into the phone. "That's amazing, I didn't think it would work…yeah, I was at a club… ugh, with Grayson of a—I know, I know, I heard. Or I guess I saw into your brain. No, I don't know how it works. It's not like he explained. Martin. Yeah, they all are…No, I don't think anyone is called Hugo. Oh, right…hey, that reminds me, I maybe, totally kissed Martin, but you were thinking about him and I was just…oh, um…huh, I didn't really think that hard about it. I guess…of course…"

"Tidus," I said. He had shifted in the booth and was casually sticking and unsticking his fork in a puddle of syrup on his plate, talking to my Tidus as if they were old friends. His eyes snapped to mine, surprised.

"Oh, shit. Right. Emergency. I'm going to hand the phone to Martin," he said.

"Thank you," I said. I took the crayon plan and the phone out into the street.

"Hi, Tidus," I said.

"Martin," he half whispered, half yelled. "It's so good to hear your voice. That was genius. I didn't know we could do that—the Tiduses and me, I mean."

"You're really amazing."

The crowd around the restaurants and bars was dense but casual. That made me feel less out of place. No one would notice a guy on the phone. I moved to a table outside a closed café and sat down.

"Who, me? I know…well, I'm here, so what's going on? What happened to you?"

"Jesus, Tidus. I'm so sorry about all of this. I thought we had it, you know. I really thought it would've been that easy. Josephine caught me and dumped us in another verse. I think she expected us to drown or give up. I don't know. Are you okay? Is it safe for you there? We could find a different place—"

"Martin, I'm fine. I'm safe. Everyone is on the lower levels. I'm freezing my balls off. Fuck the ocean. I'm a Floridian. We don't really go in the water in October."

"I'm sorry."

"Martin Logan King, cut it out. I got in the car, remember? Stop apologizing. Tell me what's going on."

"You have a sexy phone voice," I said.

He laughed and groaned. "Fine. Apology accepted. Are you safe?"

"Yeah, but safe here is almost worse than being in danger there."

"It's a cluster fuck."

"Well. We have a plan."

"I have a pen," he said, his voice sounding far away for a moment. "And paper."

I carefully explained he needed to sneak down to Emma Elizabeth's lab and find as many sequencers as he could. I assumed that that was where they took the other's tech so Emma Elizabeth could try and get the data off it. He, of course, had my sequencer and could send me at least that much if there weren't others. Then he needed to get them back to the beach and send them to the FAU verse so we could come to him.

"Is there a plan from there?" he asked.

I nodded, but he couldn't see that. "Yeah, but it's a little bit more dependent on how the first few steps go."

"Right, well, I'm on it. Don't lose there Tidus, though. If shit goes down, I can try to get to another phone. I have the fucking number memorized, he repeated it so much."

"Okay."

The line went silent, but his presence alone was almost audible. I wish I'd heard what he had said to FAU Tidus about the kiss.

"Tidus."

"Martin."

"I'm sorry Tidus kissed me. I was caught off guard, and I didn't even have time to blink before it was over. I just don't want you to think that I'm like your ex, I'm not a cheater. Okay, maybe that's weird for a guy with two partners to say, but…"

I could almost hear the smile in his voice. "Martin, the worst part of that situation wasn't even the other guys. It was how much he lied. You haven't lied to me. You were up front about Luca, and that means more than you can know."

"Fair."

"Thank you, though, for talking about it." Again, he paused. Then he asked, "Martin, I have a weird question."

"Okay."

"Was kissing that Tidus like kissing me?"

"No."

"No? Just no?"

I laughed. "Tidus, do you know the odds of winning a five-number lotto jackpot?"

"Only to the fifth or sixth decimal," he said, even though we both knew he didn't.

"Good. Now imagine the feeling of winning that jackpot, of getting those correct five numbers and winning the whole thing."

"I've imagined it," he said, "who hasn't?"

"Right, now imagine getting four of the five right. You literally lose the game if one number is off by one value in either direction. All of the sameness except that one number. How would you feel?"

"Devastated."

"Naw, I mean maybe for that one day or for a minute but not really, because that astronomically unlikely win is only a feeling you can know when you know it. Anything else is just everyday."

"Okay."

"Tidus, you're that jackpot-winning combination of numbers. Here Tidus is just…"

"Off by one number."

"Yeah. I mean sure, I love every Tidus I've encountered, even the one who is the least like you. But you're the one I'm falling in love with."

"God damn it, man, you're so smooth."

"It wasn't meant to be smooth, just honest."

"Too bad," Tidus said with a laugh. I laughed too. Again, there was a silence. Then he huffed and sighed. "All right, I'm going to do my job. See you on the beach. Bring food."

"Be careful."

"I mean, there's a gun here, so I'm going to take that."

I remembered the gun Don had pointed in my direction. He had left it on the desk in his haste to grab the laptop and flee HQ. I hadn't thought too hard about where MVP Josephine or MVP Don had ended up. It wouldn't matter if my plan worked.

"Do you know how to shoot a gun?"

"Right trigger," he said. "I'm going."

"Oh, okay."

I didn't hang up, of course. I would never hang up first on that man.

"Martin," he said.

"Yeah?"

"I'm falling in love with you too."

Then the line went dead.

I was smiling so hard I had to wait a few minutes before going inside. It was embarrassing to feel so much joy and pain all at once. I looked back at the plan in my hand. I couldn't bring myself to tell Tidus about Operation Other Sock. Telling him would've meant telling him Luca and I had found the perfect thing in every verse to use as a signal source. It was so simple. Luca had really figured it out, and it gracefully overcame Mason's list of issues. There would be no need to track anything down, pin a drone to it, calibrate a relay. We had already done all of that.

I had written in green "what could be a universe signal source in all verses," and in blue, Luca had written "Tidus."

# SECTION 28

## *Suck it up, it was your idea*

I bought Tidus a burger and fries and paid the tab. I made sure to leave another gigantic tip. FAU Tidus decided to come with us to the beach. Tiduses all seemed to have a thirst for unusual adventure. I just didn't think he would trade his plans for the night so readily to stick with us. His excuse was that he didn't want to abandon FOX Tidus.

We placed ourselves on the sand and waited. I tried not to get involved in much of the conversation, but time passed slowly. It was hard to think the only plan I had would separate everyone. Tamar and Mason stayed close to each other, though they hadn't shared any more explicit affection. Tamar sat with her back pressed to his, speaking to Kiki. Mason was excitedly answering FAU Tidus's questions. Kiki was watching Fern try to bench-press Wei.

"Do you think we should tell them?" Luca asked me quietly, sitting near me.

"I can't make up my mind. Seems cruel to rob them of the chance to say good-bye."

"I wouldn't say good-bye if I knew. I mean, I do know, and I don't plan to say good-bye," Luca said.

"Why not?"

"I'll see them again."

"How do you know? Statistics?"

He laughed. "In a way. I know because I know them all. I believe the choices we made and make put us in favor of always being connected."

"We can tell them when we're back in the dead-verse. It feels like it'll make more sense there," I said.

An hour passed, then another. I was almost beside myself with anxiety by the time midnight rolled around. The beach was bright with city lights, but we found a semi-secluded section of shadow near a resort. I didn't think we were allowed to be on that part of the beach, but no one seemed to notice us.

I was about to try to conjure another message through FAU Tidus when he stood up. His gaze was on the ocean. We tried to see what he was looking at, but we couldn't. He stepped forward, moving toward the water slowly.

"Tidus?"

Suddenly just before he reached where the sand was wet, he turned and raced across the beach paralleling the surf. In a matter of seconds, he was just a white blob in the distance. We ran after him, but only Fern and Mason could keep up his pace.

"Tidus," Fern shouted. She looked like she was about to tackle him when he veered a hard right into a park.

He crouched and looked wildly around, then he laughed and put his hands on the ground.

"What the fuck," Kiki said.

Tidus stood and whirled on us. He looked at us in a way that seemed more present, like the last few seconds of him running was a dream. He blinked and smiled at us. He said, "He did it."

A reaction rippled through the crowd, and we all sensed something tune into the verse. Then on the heels of that, a second something followed. On the ground where FAU Tidus had crouched were two sequencers. My heart leapt at the sight of my device. Then it plummeted when no more devices followed the second.

"There's only two," Tamar said in a tone I couldn't interpret.

"It's mine," Luca said, claiming the second device.

Tidus inspected the phones. "The others were in pieces. I didn't know…I'm sorry. That was from the other Tidus."

"Shit," Fern said.

"Emma Elizabeth must have gutted them to get the hard drives out," Mason said.

"I guess it's up to you two," Kiki said with cheery finality.

"What?" I said. "We can find some other ones, decommissioned ones or—"

"No, it'll be okay. Martin, you have everyone you need," Kiki said. They stooped, picked up the phones, and put them in mine and Luca's hands. "You and Tidus have the mechanical skills to get Luca to a data lab. Ours would probably be the best since it's still connected to the Tiduses. Luca has more than enough skill to do what you need for Operation Other Sock."

"You knew the plan?"

"We can see. You don't write small and you write in all caps, so it's not like we couldn't read it."

"Why didn't you say something?"

They shrugged and batted their eyelashes at me. "I guess because I agree with it."

"Same," the others said. I just stared at them. But what the fuck was happening? They all even smiled a little.

"I don't know that I understand, but I trust you," Fern added, slapping me hard on the shoulder. I took a deep breath to counteract some of the pain.

I wanted to argue with them, but I knew it would be a losing battle. "I don't really want it to be this way."

"Who does? But this is our best plan. We're running out of time. The longer Josephine has access to MVP and to the Hugos, the more fucked everyone is."

"No, I…but—"

"Suck it up, King," Wei shouted. "It's power throuple time. That's what y'all are called, right? Tripple?"

Wei practically skipped over and placed his hands on mine and Luca's chests in some weird *Wei* way of saying good-bye. Then he made the bird shape out of his hands and flapped it away toward the street entrance to the park.

"Son of a bitch," Luca said. "You're all really going to make us do this."

"Wouldn't have it any other way," Kiki said. "Besides, it was fate. I'm going back to that club. I want a drink. Come on, Tidus."

"Oh, is this—what's happening?" Tidus asked.

"You'll know soon enough," Kiki said.

"I think I might like to try the club again. Maybe the crowd's thinned," Mason said to Tamar. He clearly meant it to be an offering of some kind. She smiled at him and took his hand.

"Y'all can't just leave," I said.

"Watch us," Kiki said, handing me the bag of snacks that also had Tidus's cold meal in it.

"What if we fail? How will you know?"

"Tell him to tell him," Kiki said, pointing to Tidus. Tidus just flashed me two peace signs and made a pouty lip face.

"I'll miss you," I said.

Fern shook my hand, then winked at Luca before she followed Wei and Kiki.

"Like Wei said, suck it up. It was your idea," Tamar said. She stopped and kissed my cheek, then Luca's, then she walked away. Mason hugged us both briefly, then trotted after his girl.

"I told you they wouldn't say good-bye," Luca said, watching them walk toward the city. His face was a bright sort of sad, the kind parents have at their kids' weddings. I felt suddenly homesick for all the moments I could lose with him if this plan worked. The feeling was immediately counteracted by the thought of everything everyone could lose if we failed.

"It was nice to meet you," Tidus called before they all disappeared behind a building.

"Fuck me," I said.

"Is that an invitation?" Luca said with a wink. It lost some of its shock value when I noticed the tears in his eyes. I didn't say anything. I just hugged him.

"We can do this," Luca said into my neck.

"I know."

"Come on, we should do this before I fall asleep. Maybe we should get coffee first."

"See, humor is a great way to hide your feelings."

He rolled his eyes, squared his shoulders, and looked at his sequencer. "Don't brag about being a bad influence."

I looked at my device too. He tuned to the dead-verse first. I took one last look around and followed.

We tuned into a sort of oak grove. It was thin where we stood because a massive magnolia tree had shoved everything out of its way. It created a secluded canopy from the beach.

"Tidus?" I said.

"Shh," Tidus said. "Come with me."

We followed him deeper into the grove. I don't think he really knew where he was going, but we followed without question. Ten minutes later, he stopped on the other side of the tree line in a clearing at the edge of a black field of water.

"Wow, this is kind of beautiful," Luca said.

"I wandered back here when the guards were walking the beach looking for people. They aren't the most proactive bunch."

"Tidus—"

But he didn't let me say anything. He just sat on the sandy bank and sighed. "God, I'm sorry I couldn't get more devices. They were all dismantled. I thought about putting some back together, but it was impossible. Are the others okay? What's happening?"

"Hey," I said, dropping into a crouch in front of him. This wasn't his usual excited rambling. It felt more intense and edgy. I put a hand out wondering if I should touch him at all. But he leaned into it without hesitation. He grabbed my hand and pulled it to his chest, rubbing it as if he was trying to comfort me.

He looked at me. "I'm sorry."

"For what? You did everything that was asked of you. It wasn't easy. You're the most amazing. I mean it. I don't know if I would've been able to do what you did."

He smiled and rolled his eyes. "Come on, you do crazy shit all the time."

I laughed.

"You were built for this job," I said. "You had to swim to the Hub and reach the ladder along the side, right?"

"Yeah."

"Well, that right there is a feat, because it's five feet up from the water, and then you have to pull yourself up…hum…"

"What?"

"Naw, now I'm kind of picturing it," I said in my flirtiest tone.

That seemed to do the trick. He laughed and leaned forward for a kiss. "Jeez, I can't even imagine what I look like. My hair is air-drying *gross*."

I reached up and raked my fingers through the impeccably soft purple curls that did have a sense of humid chaos. "You look amazing. You *are* amazing. I know the other Tidus was impressed."

Tidus laughed. "Do you know how weird it is to talk to yourself on the phone? How could Hugo and Del stand it?"

"I can't imagine. And I didn't forget." I put the bag of food in his lap.

"Oh, fuck me *yesss*," he said, pulling the Styrofoam container out of the bag.

"Good work." Luca held out his hand.

Tidus took a huge bite of the burger and high-fived Luca but didn't say anything.

He had meant the gesture to be praise, but he didn't want it to be too sappy. "No, I want a tiger cake."

Tidus laughed, dug around in the bag, and handed Luca a pile of snacks.

"What happened to you guys?" Tidus asked. Luca and I explained our trip to FAU-verse while he ate. He managed to eat the burger, fries, most of the snacks, and three of the waters in record time. I figured that was one of the burdens of being a giant.

"What now?" Tidus said after a few minutes.

"Well, we have a plan," I said.

"Good."

"But it's not going to be easy."

Tidus gestured to the dead-verse as a whole and then shrugged. "Where do you see easy?"

"No, not like that. We…do you remember Mason talking about the Other Sock Phenomenon and using the relays to heal rifts?"

"Yup."

"Well, that's the plan. We get to the lab. Luca brings all the relays online, and we snap everyone back to their own verses, then we seal the multi-verse so no one can move around."

"Sounds like a plan," Tidus agreed. Then he thought some more. "Wait. Won't that mean—won't we be separated?"

I nodded.

"Oh, from everyone," he said almost as if talking to himself.

"Not me," Luca said.

Tidus looked at him, blinking. Then he looked at me. "Okay, right. That's not easy. Why? Isn't there another way?"

"Not that we can think of," I said, "but if you think of one, we can try it."

"Honestly, I'm too tired to think."

"There's one more thing," I said.

Tidus groaned.

"You have to go home." It took a lot to say that. It felt like trying to talk in a room that was on fire, the heat ripping all the use out of my vocal cords. My voice didn't break, but I felt my throat close at the immense sadness.

"What? When? Why?" Tidus cried.

"The plan hinges on you being in your home verse," Luca said. "Part of the problem Mason had when developing his original idea was finding something in all the verses to use as a source signal."

"Oh shit, it's me. The Tiduses!" Tidus gasped, covering his mouth with his hands.

I nodded. It was so dark, with no ambient light from the sum of human evolution to cast everything in a gentle hazy yellow. We could see each other but only as blackish shadows in the blue of the moonlight. In this verse, the animal life was sparse, not even mosquitoes, so the silence was almost total. Only the crashing of the ocean behind the trees kept everything from being empty.

"I didn't get to say good-bye," Tidus said.

"You probably still can. They're all probably with FAU Tidus still," I said.

"They know what we have to do," Luca said.

"Can…can I stay a while longer? I can help still."

"Yeah, there's time," I said. "I just wanted you to know."

There was another stretch of silence. Then Tidus stood. "Okay, let's do this."

"You ready?" I asked.

"No, but I don't want Josephine to win. My petty ass would yeet myself out of a moving bus before I let someone I don't like win."

"That doesn't sound petty," Luca said. Tidus laughed, which only confused Luca more.

"Right, so we need to get into the data lab," I said.

Luca made a sound and put a hand on my knee. "All the individual units have doors on the roof, just like the Hub, but you'd have to get back in the water."

I groaned. "I'd rather risk walking through the front door."

"It's pretty shallow," Tidus said. "I could walk out pretty far."

"You're eighty percent leg. By the time you notice the water, I'd be in over my head," I nearly shouted. "Don't talk to me with your giraffe-ass self."

"Tell me about it," Luca said.

"Poor hobbits. I could carry you."

I made a series of terrible sounds that earned me a kiss of comfort from each partner. They started back through the trees, I followed. The water was shallow but not as shallow as Tidus made it seem. Considering where the data lab was, we had to swim out past the Hub. I managed not to panic.

When we got to the right pod, Tidus dove under and was able to swim up with enough momentum to grab the bottom rung of the ladder. Luca and I had to essentially climb him to get up. Luca went up first with little effort because he was so light. Then they both had to pull me up.

"Not too bad?" Luca asked me.

I shook my head. He nodded and climbed.

"On the way up, I got a handful of his ass. Your boy has some cake," Tidus whispered to me.

"Dang, really? I wanna feel," I said, watching Luca climb.

"I can hear you," he said.

"So slow down then, let me get a touch," I said.

I followed Luca, and Tidus followed me. Luca found the right trap door on the roof and flung it open. A distinct charred smell wafted up from the room below.

"Was the fire that bad?" I asked.

Luca shrugged. "We were evacuated. I haven't been back. I guess it must've been to bring the whole structure to shore."

"Where does this come out?" I asked, looking into the dark hole we were supposed to climb into.

"My room."

"I guess I didn't realize there were rooms in the data lab," I said.

"Where'd you think we slept? At our desks?"

"Mason did."

"True. No, this one drops into a corner in my room. It was supposed to be Mason's room, but we switched because it gave him too much anxiety. The ladder is bolted to the wall and goes to the floor, but you'll end up standing on my desk. There's a lamp. Here, I'll go first since I know what's down there."

Luca was lost to the darkness below and Tidus followed. I went last. Because of the damage, most of the main systems were offline, and this included the main lights and the lamp. The processors and emergency lights were on a backup system, so they were on.

"Just stay on the ladder. I have a flashlight," Luca whispered.

"A what?" Tidus said.

"A flashlight," I repeated.

Tidus laughed. "Oh right, yeah, that makes *way* more sense than what I heard."

We couldn't see Luca, so we listened to him rummaging around in his room before a light bloomed. The flashlight was a generic LED one from the afterthought section at a gas station, but it gave us enough light to know where to put our feet.

Being on the solid floor of the lab was reassuring enough that some of my anxiety and tension slipped. I felt pain and exhaustion wash over me, and I nearly fell as I tried to walk toward the lab. Luca caught me under an arm and I leaned on him.

"Too much," I said. Swimming and climbing without using my injured side as much as I could was so far beyond pushing myself that I couldn't even explain what was happening.

"Here, sit down," Luca said. He practically tossed the light to Tidus. I sat on the edge of his bed.

"You should rest."

"We have so much to do," I said.

"True, but there's nothing we can do if I can't get one of the computers to work or if too many of the processors are damaged. Stay here."

He went to a closet and pulled out towels.

"Luca…"

"Please," he said. His expression, amplified in the harsh angles of the flashlight, was so pleading I had to comply. I took the towel.

"I got him," Tidus said.

Luca shook out his wet hair and raked it in a criminally sexy way from his face. Then he nodded. Tidus tried to hand him the flashlight.

He declined, saying something about emergency lights in the lab. I wrapped the towel over my head like a nun and flopped backward.

"Luca is almost too tidy," Tidus said, opening a desk drawer. "Look at this, are these pencils alphabetized?"

"How's that possible?"

"They have sayings, like 'A penny for your thoughts,' and 'Capricorns do it right.' Well actually, it says 'Capricorns do it w-r-i-t-e,' but that is crossed out and r-i-g-h-t is written in. You must not love him for being a good time. I get it. Stable and boring is sexy. He does have great hair."

This distracted assessment of Luca's desk contents actually made me feel a little better.

"Why are you roasting Luca?" I said, trying to not encourage him by laughing.

"I'm kind of jealous."

"Why?"

He came and sat by me. "You guys have had so much time together. And now I have to say good-bye."

I put my hand out and he put his hand in it. "I'm jealous of the time he got with you too."

Tidus looked at me like I was crazy.

"The week I was missing. I don't want it to be over. He and the others insist we'll all see each other again."

"I mean, I guess you could kind of see me again. There must be a Tidus in your home-verse," he said.

I almost laughed. "I guess I hadn't thought about him."

"What would you do with me if you had more time?" he asked, lying back on the bed.

"We'd sit in your apartment, and I'd be on your squad for video games."

That seemed to mean so much more than I thought it would, because he started talking about playing with other people and wanting someone to play with sometimes. I passed an hour listening as he talked and traced patterns into my palm.

"All right," Luca said, coming back.

I sat up with some effort. Tidus shone the flashlight at him.

"It's up and working," Luca said.

"Is that an invitation?" Tidus and I said together.

"Yeah, it is. See?" Luca said. He reached for the button on his pants, then he put his hand up and flipped us off. "See, ready. Just for you."

Tidus and I cackled.

He took the flashlight from Tidus, went to the desk, and wrote out a list. "We only have two computers to use, so we can split the jobs. Martin should do a quick audit of the QDs and check that they're all still working and attached to a Tidus, then we'll have to get one attached to you. While he does that, I'll check the relays, then build the code that'll create the pulse and then the continued signal boost. Here are some concerns I have—"

"Luca," I said.

He looked at me.

"Can you slow down? I didn't get the first part."

His face was placid, but I saw a shine in his eyes as he said, "Sure, do you need me to backtrack?"

"Baw," I said, "You're having fun, aren't you?"

That earned me some dimples.

"Keep going."

"Right, so my concerns are the power source in the QDs or the relays will burn out too fast. They can recharge on their own, but if we shut one off, we risk opening the multi-verse again."

"*Une clôture fait deux travaux*," I said, almost feeling the presence of the Hugos.

"What does that mean?" Tidus asked.

"One fence does two jobs. It's from Hugo's cowboy movie. It means if you build a fence, you can keep things out *and* keep things in," I said yawning.

"I'm not saying that doesn't help," Luca said, "but that doesn't help."

"I think he means we could alternate the relays. Assuming the projected frequency of one verse is strong enough to keep things from getting out, then it is probably strong enough to keep things from getting in. So if you have A, B, and C verses next to each other, you can project B verse and keep out A and C verse, then you can project A and C verse and keep out B," Tidus said.

"That's genius," Luca said, turning back to his list.

"Thanks," Tidus and I said together.

"Good to know you two share a brain cell."

"I can help with the code. I saw Mason write it for his simulation," Tidus said.

"Let's do it," Luca said with a nod.

We went into the lab and started troubleshooting and investigating everything Luca thought might be important. Anyone else probably would've thought he was stalling or was being overcautious, but I knew him better than that. He was crafting something to last. He was going to give it everything he could.

It felt good to be in the lab with him across the table from me working. And it felt better to have Tidus there too. My heart didn't understand what my brain knew. It was likely the last few hours we would spend together till God knew when. I tried to focus as I checked drones on the Tiduses. The Tiduses would go on with their lives and never know what we needed their help with.

I was done first. The clock on the computer said it was five a.m. The sun would rise soon. It was hard to believe that this trial started with the setting sun. Everything might be over by daybreak, but there was still one thing I needed to know.

"How long until you're ready to launch?" I asked, stretching out my legs by pacing the room.

"Soon," Luca said, concentrating.

"Where are you going?" Tidus asked.

"Going?" Luca said, turning to look at him then me. "Going?"

"I'm thinking about going to find the Hugos."

They both stood. "Why?"

"I want to see how they are, see if they're okay. I can't just leave them."

They looked at each other, likely nonverbally scheming a way to talk me out of it.

"What if you're caught?" Luca asked.

I shrugged.

"Will you be back before…" Tidus asked.

I didn't have an answer for that either. "Don't wait for me."

They sighed.

"Here, take a com," Luca said.

"Why?"

"It'll make me feel better, and you can tell me if he's okay."

"Oh! Take the gun too. I left it in the office," Tidus said.

"What would Martin do with a gun? Do you even know how to shoot one?" Luca asked.

"Right trigger," I said, winking at Tidus.

"It'll look scary, and I'm sure Martin could hit something with it if he needed to."

"You don't know where they are," Luca said quietly, ignoring Tidus. While we were talking, he was sifting through the wreckage of the lab looking for a functioning communicator.

"It won't be hard to guess if I know Hugo like I do," I said.

"I need to get a different com. This one was burned. Mason has a stash in his room," Luca said. He went through the door at the back of the lab.

Tidus came over to me and wrapped his long arms around my head. I pressed my forehead into his chest.

"I'll miss you," he whispered.

"I'll miss you too."

"Jeez, I haven't felt this broken up over a guy I've only known for a few weeks since summer camp in high school. He was Scout leader for the Rooster cabin, and I was leader for the Peacocks."

I grinned. "I've never felt about anyone the way I feel about you."

"You better stop," he said. Then he leaned down and kissed me. Hard. But it wasn't final. There was no good-bye in it. It was desperate and hopeful.

"Here is…sorry, I can…" Luca said, starting to back out of the room.

"No, you're fine. Is there like a bathroom or like a closet, someplace quiet and soundproof where someone could, I don't know, cry?" Tidus said. He tipped his head back and fanned his face to protect makeup he wasn't wearing from his tears.

Luca came over to me and attached the com.

"I'll walk you out," he said, pointing to the door.

He followed me out into the dark anteroom. He was illuminated by a bright green exit sign, a stark change from the red emergency lights in the lab. He looked suddenly more vulnerable.

"Here is this," he said, pressing a new flashlight into my hands.

"Luca—"

"Don't say good-bye," he insisted, crossing his arms over his chest. He looked at the wall, then at the floor. "I won't say it back."

"Okay, how about this? I love you."

His eyes snapped to mine like I had said the craziest thing he had ever heard. "Don't, if you don't mean it. It's not a substitute for good-bye."

"I mean it. I think it's been true since the day you let me kiss you. There's been so much, I don't think I realized it until the dressing room tonight. You're so amazing and I—"

He sighed, took my face in his hands, and pulled me into a kiss. Despite not being altogether gentle, the kiss was mindful, savory. And I recognized a desperation in it he wasn't used to feeling.

"I love you too," he said when he stepped back. Then he narrowed his eyes at me. "Don't do anything stupid."

"Oh come on," I said, trying to play off the fact that my heart was beating through my chest. "When have I ever done anything stupid?"

He sighed and gave me a dismissive gesture. I laughed. He kissed me again quickly and softly, then went back into the lab. I went into the hall.

# SECTION 29

## *I think humanity will be okay for a while*

Me getting into the water alone was laughably impossible. Besides, I was too weak to even think about being able to climb a ladder, so I took the dark gangways from the lab to the Hub. People were in the cafeteria. I looked down at them from an upper-level balcony. They were all dressed in the sand-colored jumpsuits, lounging on tables or on the floor.

That eliminated the first place on my list of where to find Josephine and the Hugos. I didn't actually expect to find her there, though. I paused long enough to determine no one in the Hub was talking about anything useful, then I went to the office and found the gun. I bypassed the main section through a service hallway and then down another gangway to a different pod. I saw people, but again, it was just goons in jumpsuits. These ones had Taser-sticks, though. They weren't very vigilant; their conversation gave them away.

"I've never seen her like this."

"She's intense."

"But this seems out of hand. Even Margo—"

"Look, you know why we're here, so either deal with it or leave."

"You're just pissy because you think doing all of this for her will make her promote you."

"Don't start."

I went the opposite way around the pod to avoid them.

"*Martin.*" It was Luca in my ear. I tapped the device to let him know I was listening.

"*There's a collection of people in Main Control. I tapped into HQ security. It's not like anyone's here to notice.*"

I tapped again and started for that pod. Main Control was on the farthest edge of the web. From there, they navigated the HQ complex and monitored things going on inside. Allegedly, you could access every program in any department from that pod. HQ IT and HQ maintenance also operated from there. It made sense Hugo would take her there. It was literally the Holy Grail of MVP information.

I could see the gangway to Main Control from a side gangway as I ran into the pod that connected them. The pod was pitch black and empty, and I stared down the long tunnel as I hugged the wall. The people in the tunnel looked like guards. Their vigil was slack, though, and they leaned sleepily against the Plexiglas walls. Some were sitting on the walkway.

I stepped back into a shadow and thought. I wasn't going anywhere near the ocean. I could have used the gun, but that was beyond my planning skills. I didn't need them dead, just out of the way long enough to get down the gangway into the control pod. Then I could sneak into the room. I needed some ideas.

"What pod is control attached to down the center gangway?" I asked Luca, looking around the dark room. I didn't dare turn the flashlight on.

"*Nothing. It's just a pass-through pod. Main Control is attached to three gangways and all three are attached to pass-throughs.*"

"Well, that doesn't help me," I said. "I guess I could walk in. What's the worst they could do? Tase me? I'd survive."

"*Where? What? What are you doing?*"

"I'm sneaking around in the dark like a fucking idiot wearing bright orange board shorts. I don't know what I'm doing."

"*Martin?*"

"Naw, it's okay. I'm just tired."

"*We're almost done. Ten minutes, maybe less.*"

"Good. Just make sure Tidus gets home okay. He should have my sequencer, I left it on the table. I also left behind a bank card for his verse. The login is taped to the back."

"*Do you want me to tell him anything?*"

"Uh...naw, he knows. Wait, tell him to go to Ohio and pick up

Bowser. He'll probably be sent back too. Also, see if you can find Kazz and Doug."

Luca sighed. I decided I was just going to stroll down the gangway with the same unjustified cockiness I had when I tuned into the apartment where Tidus had been kidnapped. I put my hands in my pockets and tried to find a casual smile.

"Morning," I said, strolling past the first group of technicians.

They looked at me, then at each other, then back at me like I might be something they had dreamed up. They were probably as exhausted as I was. I kept walking, but it was the second set of technicians that stopped me.

"Who the fuck are you?" they demanded. They didn't raise their Taser-sticks. They didn't even block my path. They were scientists, not bouncers.

"I'm going to talk to Josephine," I said and kept walking.

They didn't do anything, just followed me. Maybe they couldn't believe my audacity. Maybe they didn't even know what they were supposed to be on the lookout for. How many of them would recognize me? The door to Main Control was broken and kicked open, so I didn't bother knocking.

The room looked like the control center at NASA, with banks of computers facing large monitor screens. There were thin windows along the ceiling of the pod, and a metal balcony encircled the room with a navigation station in the center. I squinted into the bright lighting. It was the only fully operational room in HQ.

Josephine stood with her back to me, hunched over a computer near the center of a row. She was pressing buttons loudly. Del was on one side of the room, closest to me. He looked asleep or worse, his head drooping forward, his chin propped against his chest. Hugo was on the other side of the room. I could just barely see him sitting on the floor. He looked alert and angry. Both Hugos were zip-tied and had several trickles of blood running from different parts of their faces. If I could get to my Hugo, maybe he could help me.

Josephine looked almost rabid as she turned to see who had come through the door. I didn't stop, even though the glare she gave me was horrible. Her hair was frazzled, raked through too many times. There were places where her makeup had been wiped away.

"How the fuck did you get back here?" she screamed.

I shrugged. “It’s a long story. But I wanted to come back and check on how you were managing.”

“We can’t get in,” Hugo said. He smiled at me defiantly. “She kept me because she thought I would know how to get in, but I don’t. I—”

Josephine walked right over to Hugo and kicked him in the side. He flinched, but that didn’t erase his smile.

“Well, that’s one way,” I said. I tried to step farther into the room.

“Grab him,” Josephine said. The technicians who were still standing in the doorway tried to grab me, but I dodged them and ducked into a row of computers.

“Look, I’m here as a courtesy. I didn’t want y’all to get stuck here,” I said.

Josephine took a deep breath and pinched her nose. “Fine. You, give me your stick. I’ll get him myself.”

She marched up to one of her technicians and snatched away the Taser-stick.

“Calm down. I’m here to talk.”

“I don’t want to hear anything you have to say. Ever again. I won’t fall for your tricks.” She turned to the technicians. “Get the others. Search the complex again. He never works alone.”

They scurried from the room. Only one remained, and that was because Josephine had his Taser-stick.

“What happened to Margo?” I asked.

“I said leave,” Josephine said, engaging the weapon. It crackled and buzzed. She started toward me with the very real intention of using it. I drew the gun from my shorts and aimed it at her. She stopped so suddenly, she almost tripped.

“I told you I’m here as a courtesy. I’m warning you. I’m shutting this down—you, them, VIP, MVP—all of it.” The gun was surprisingly heavy and hard for me to figure out how to hold since I could only get one arm up so high without hurting.

“You can’t do that,” Josephine said. “You wouldn’t shoot me.”

She started walking toward me. I pointed the gun at the ceiling and fired. The recoil was astronomically painful, and the sound was louder than they made it look in the movies. I leveled it back at her before I winced. On the edge of the smell of the gun firing was the smell that let me know someone left the universe.

“Ow, fuck,” I said, rubbing my wrist.

"You're so pathetic. Put that down."

She didn't move forward, though.

"No, I'm trying to help you."

Just then a voice piped into the facility, calm and feminine sounding. "*Hello, this is not a drill. A red-level emergency has been detected. Alarms will sound. Please evacuate to the nearest lifeboat and proceed to the nearest shore.*"

Luca clarified it, his voice breathy in my head, like he was running. "*It's a countdown. There's a subtle pulse to the alarm, every second. You have three minutes.*"

"The others?" I asked.

"*I got them. Just don't be dumb. Tidus is gone. Get out of here.*"

"What the fuck is this?" Josephine said.

"I told you," I shouted over blaring alarms. Luca was right, it was like listening to a rotating speaker, starting off loud then diminishing then rising again. Each diminish was at one-second intervals. "Everyone needs to get off HQ now."

"I'll kill you," she said, trying to run at me again. I held the gun up level with her chest. I had backed up until I was near Hugo.

"You get him, get to land," I shouted at the technician. He tried to cross to Del, who still hadn't moved, but someone stepped out of an alcove and shoved the useless technician aside. VIP Justin. The technician scrambled to his feet and raced out of the room before Justin could grab him.

"Martin," Hugo said, lunging in my direction.

Hugo almost tripped Carl, but he still managed to get to me. He grabbed me hard enough to make my body tense with pain. The gun fell to the ground, and Carl got to it before I did. He pointed it at me. Carl backed toward Josephine. Justin came forward, and I saw Margo behind him. She surveyed the scene, a look of horror freezing on her features.

"Now, I respect you coming after your friend," Josephine said, her voice back down to a sinister calm. "But how about you explain what's going on?"

I sighed and put my hand down to help Hugo to his feet.

"Leave him."

"Naw, it's okay. None of us have much time anyway," I said. I looked straight at Margo while I talked. "And you guys aren't killers,

I mean not all of you. The MVP technicians were one thing, a part of your masochistic rampage for power. But you wouldn't kill the Hugos, right? You didn't kill me."

"We didn't kill the technicians," Justin said.

And though her jaw tightened, Josephine didn't react to Justin's comments. Instead, she kept speaking to me. "You don't know what we have riding on this. You couldn't possibly understand."

"Oh, I get it now," I said even though it was something I had already suspected. "This is about Josephine's ego. Everything you do is for her."

It was hard to hear over the sound of the alarm, and I had lost count. I didn't know how much time was left, but I knew it wasn't much. Josephine, Justin, and Carl were all standing in the center row of computers, looking at me. They didn't see the decision Margo made. She put so much together in the time they had been in the dead-verse, and I could see it all congeal in her mind from across the room. No one was looking at her, and no one heard over the alarm as she helped Del to his feet and left with him, nearly dragging him out of the room. They wouldn't get far before Operation Other Sock commenced, but when everyone here dropped into the ocean, they would have a head start.

"We're all scientists, Martin. Can't you see how important this work is for the good of humanity?" Josephine pleaded. She was almost convincing.

I sighed. "I can and can't. I think humanity will be okay for a while without MVP or VIP fucking with the verses."

"What do you mean?" Carl said.

"I'm shutting it down. We rigged the system."

"How?"

"I don't really know. I'm not a physicist. I'm just a guy with super-smart friends."

Hugo looked at me. "Other Sock?"

"Fine, leave. We'll figure it out. It's not like you were any help," Josephine said, probably intending some sort of reverse psychology.

"Okay," I said.

I tried to lend Hugo my arm. He waved me down and was steady on his feet. We crossed to the door. I knew only seconds remained. I turned back as Josephine demanded Justin find a way to stop the alarm.

"By the way," I called, "when the alarm stops, you'll be sucked back to your home-verse, so…good luck cracking security in less than ten seconds. Hope you can swim."

Josephine gaped at me. I should have left it alone. I had time to regret stopping to brag, to see her displeasure when she understood I wasn't going to let her keep any of what she felt she had earned. The alarm pulsed, the volume dropping then rising, but the peak of it was lost to the sound of her roaring, her rage clear and focused on me. The gun was out of Carl's hands before he knew it. Hugo shoved me hard, my shoulder colliding with the jamb of the door. I lost track of the structure of the room, of the definition of reality. The corner of the jamb caught my ribs right where they had yet to heal. There was the added force of Hugo's body falling on mine, falling with me, falling into me as he pushed me out of Josephine's line of fire.

"Martin," Hugo cried.

"*Martin*," Luca said in my head one last time.

There was the sound of the gun, Hugo screaming, and then the cool rush of water all around.

# Section 30

## *You'll see me again*

It took the doctors a while to patch Hugo up. He had taken the bullet in the upper arm and then been dipped in the ocean. Some beach cleaners had come across our bodies around dawn, and they called an ambulance. I was treated for a hundred things that didn't matter. And Hugo made a full recovery after a few weeks. He invited me to his family's ranch in the Wyoming territory. He told his family I was a work buddy who needed a change of pace, and that was all they needed to know.

One Saturday after about a week on the ranch, we were willing to put all the pieces together for the first time. We had spent the morning chopping up a few trees that had fallen during the last snowstorm and were tripping up the cattle. I had never used a chainsaw before, and we didn't get very far because, healed or not, we were still bone-tired and weak.

As a treat, Hugo and his brother, Lyle, stacked some of those logs in a fire pit, and his mother, Tilda, made us coffee. We sat out under the stars by the fire, tucked into thick jackets and warm blankets. The family stayed around—Lyle, his wife and their three kids, Hugo's parents and his two sisters. But as the second round of logs were tossed on the fire, the others decided to go to bed. After an hour or so alone, Hugo tipped a flask into his coffee. I declined. We sat in silence for a long time. Then something in the firepit popped, and I found my voice.

"It's weird seeing you be a real cowboy. I thought the hat and boots were for show."

Hugo laughed. "Well, those were my good boots, not like these shit-kickers. I think the real unbelievable thing is getting you to look the part."

It was true. I fought him on wearing the French western shirts, but I couldn't say no to his father gifting me a hand-me-down coat and hat. I had impressed Pa Del Mar with my French cowboy-isms so much that he also gave me his favorite horse, a black monstrosity named Bien Joué.

"I can't believe it's going to be March," I said, warming my cold hands by the fire.

"Three months since…"

"Hey…H."

He grunted, his breath billowing around him.

"Why am I here? I thought the Other Sock Phenomenon was supposed to send me home."

He shrugged. "*Je ne sais pas*. There are still a million things we don't understand about the multi-verse. Why does tuning transport our clothes but not the ground we stand on? Or those around us? Or the whole earth? My best guess is that you're not all one verse, like your photos show. And because you were in contact with me during the event, perhaps the universe couldn't tell where you belonged. Since my frequency made up the majority of our amalgam, here you are."

"Huh."

"I'm sorry."

"For?" I asked.

He looked at me, his expression clear. "How lonely it must be without them."

I knew by *them* he meant both my family and my partners.

"I'm glad I have someone around, though," I said, hoping it conveyed my gratitude. "Not many guys'll take a bullet for you."

"You came back for me. It was the least I could do."

"What happened that night? What happened to you?"

We hadn't talked about it. I think we needed some time to heal. I know that thinking about it, working it out in my own head made my ribs ache and feel like they would never be the same. When I didn't think about it, I could nearly feel my body recover. I think Hugo felt the same. At the fire's edge that night, he explained how Josephine had demanded he let her into the system. He gave her the runaround by dragging her all over HQ, but she got the upper hand when Justin and Carl showed up with some more people. They had threatened to kill Del. Hugo couldn't let anyone get hurt, so he caved and took them to the Main Control room. He didn't say anything else after that, and he spent the rest of the night watching them try to hack into the computers.

"Do you think it worked? The plan, I mean."

"I know it did," he said. "This area of the country has a lot of natural rift activity, but I haven't seen evidence of one. You'll see. It worked."

I believed him. I hadn't used any of my rift-locating skills since getting to the ranch. I think I feared it working as much as I feared it not. I loved Hugo, but thinking about my mother and Apollo wondering where I was and what happened to me broke my heart. I liked to believe Tidus and Luca were keeping tabs on each other, but who knew.

After that Saturday, I passed time by doing whatever job Pa Del Mar and Lyle could come up with. I learned to ride a horse and learned how allergic I was to them, even though that didn't matter. I accompanied Hugo's uncles when they played the fiddle or the guitar. I learned to drive the oldest truck on earth. It was positive even if it wasn't happy.

I also mapped the natural rifts Hugo had mentioned. I spent hours walking or driving around their property and the ranches nearby, scouting rift locations. Hugo was right. There was no sign of them. But other signs confirmed our plan had worked. As time passed, we saw news reports about missing people being found or missing items being rediscovered. Sometime in June, Hugo and I watched a news series about the disappearance of world-renowned scientist Carl Payne. The here-verse Carl had been killed and MVP Carl had been living as him. And in the aftermath of Operation Other Sock, the Payne family was begging people for answers as to where he might be.

In my weaker moments, I thought about driving or flying down to Florida. I thought about looking up here-verse Tidus, asking him if he knew me, asking if he could contact my Tidus. I didn't, though. It wasn't even out of consideration for Tidus. No, I would've selfishly disrupted a new Tidus if I thought it would allow me any contact with mine. But I knew if I did, I wouldn't be able to let it go. So I just thought of the few moments we were able to have. I also knew it probably wouldn't work. I had asked Hugo a few times if he could sense Del, but he said he didn't. I thought of Luca. He usually snuck into my thoughts unexpectedly when I was working or just before I fell asleep.

I would say I was squirrelly and anxious and depressed during the first months I spent on the ranch. Hugo, on the other hand, was the picture of calm. He was as in his element helping goats give birth on the ranch as he had been detailing the structure of the multi-verse on a white board. He talked a lot about missing people even though he never explicitly said he did. He would just mention how much Wei had liked pancakes or how much Tamar would've hated some new movie. I missed all of them too.

He didn't start to get weird until August. He grew distracted and quiet, and I could hear him deriving equations under his breath. When I asked him about it, he just said he was thinking. When he started to go to bed early and wake up late I really started to worry about him. It was on a trip into Denver to the stock show that I had to demand an answer.

"Dude," I shouted.

He snapped out of his thoughts and looked at me.

"You missed our exit," I said.

He slowed the truck and stared at the next highway sign we passed. "Oh shit. Did I?"

"No, dude, how could you? It's a fucking straight shot to Denver. I just wanted you to realize how distracted you were."

"I'm sorry, I was thinking. Were you talking about something?"

I rolled my eyes. "No. But I want to know where you've been."

He looked at me and sighed. "We aren't going to the stock show."

I looked around feeling suddenly ungrounded, as if the mountains might suddenly shift. They didn't. I looked back at him. "Where are we going?"

"I have a gift for you. We'll be there in two hours. Can you wait? Just trust me."

I shrugged. "Okay. I guess."

I watched vigilantly as he drove into the Colorado territory and then pulled off the highway to a city I knew very well in my home-verse. My parents lived there.

"Why are we here?"

"Almost there," he said. He pulled the truck into a neighborhood and parked in front of a nice house.

"In my home-verse."

"Yup. This would be your parents' front yard."

"Why are we here?" I asked again.

He reached into the back seat and handed me a duffel bag. I opened it and it was full of the clothes he had bought me to live and work in on the ranch.

"Oh shit, you're kicking me out?" I said looking at the neighborhood. It suddenly felt as remote as the deepest woods.

"No…well, not like that," Hugo laughed. "The way I see it…we are running out of time."

As he talked, he reached into the glove box in front of me. He handed me the phone he pulled out of the compartment.

"Is this a sequencer?"

"*Oui*. I found it in the attic when we were cleaning for Mom last month. It turned on. Martin, the people we were up against were elite multi-verse scientists. That means the fence you and Luca and Tidus created won't hold forever. I wouldn't even give it another year."

"You don't think so?"

"No, but if that's all the time we have before those people have access to everything again, I want you to be able to spend it with people you love."

"I love you," I said.

"I love you too, but you know what I mean."

The surprise of potentially losing my best friend, of leaving him behind in this verse was scary. I had done a lot of healing with that man. I had lived in his house. I had been adopted by his family. Who was I suddenly without him? He was a brother.

I looked over the device, then tried to hand it back to him. "Hugo, this won't even work. The fence prevents tuning too."

"It won't tune you."

I stared at him.

"I modified it. If you use one hundred percent of its power, it'll recreate the frequency boost that drew things back to their home-verses. If you use it, it'll send you to wherever you were meant to be. I figure since we don't know which, I could drive here or I could drive to Florida. Either way, I have an equal chance of guessing right. This was closer."

I thought about what he was saying. If he boosted my frequency, I would either end up in my parents' front yard or I would end up in some stranger's yard in the FOX-verse, but then I could go find them. Either way, it meant walking away from Hugo.

"What if it doesn't work?" I asked. My voice caught, and I was surprised by my own fluctuating emotions.

"So what? We go back to the ranch. We're having corn chowder for dinner."

"God, I hope it works. I can't take any more chowder," I said with a wink.

He laughed. I looked at him. He had a subtle scar over his eye. He also looked older but in a healthy, vibrant way. Winter had suited him best, but the golden highlight to his skin from working in the sun wasn't a miss either.

"What if—"

"Martin, you'll see me again."

I sighed and looked at the device. "Really, you think less than a year?"

He nodded. The decision to try it was instantaneous and overwhelming. If I believed I would see him again, I knew I could press call.

"Okay," I said.

"Okay."

I reached over to the driver's side and pulled Hugo into a hug. We were both stronger than we had been, completely healed with a summer of hard labor behind us. But it was painful. I felt my eyes well with tears, but they didn't fall. I pulled away and held up the phone.

"Maybe you should get out of the truck. You'll end up on your ass if you do it sitting," he said. Hugo had teary eyes too, but he played it off.

"Oh, fair," I said with a laugh. I stepped out of the truck.

"If you end up in FOX-verse, give Luca and Tidus my best."

"Oh, I'll give them something all right."

Hugo laughed and cringed at the same time. I took a step back on the sidewalk and watched Hugo as I pressed call on the device. I saw him wave, then he was gone and the street was empty.

I turned around and looked at the house. It was dark, and there was a For Sale sign on the lawn.

❖

I knew where I had to go next. I took a taxi to the next city and looked up their name in the directory at the cemetery. When I got to their headstone, I knew exactly where I was. It was a flat headstone covered in bright flowers and toys. Someone still cared for it.

"You know, I wonder about you," I said to Mikyea Winslow's headstone. "I don't plan to live your life. I just wonder how you would've turned out. What name would you have picked? What job? Would you love Tidus too? Luca? I owe you, though. I wouldn't get to be here if it weren't for you."

Mikyea didn't seem to have anything to say. I straightened the toys on their headstone and walked away. The forces of the universes had sent me here, to them. I only need to find them.

Tidus was easier to track down than Luca since I already knew where he lived. All I knew about Luca's family was that they lived in Pennsylvania. It took an hour of discussion at the bank to get access to the accounts I had in the FOX-verse, especially since Tidus had made some changes. Then it was two flights to Florida, all just to find out Tidus had moved. Thankfully, the kid who lived there now was one of the grandkids of the landlords Tidus had been holding the place for. Without any suspicion, he gave me Tidus's new address.

Tidus was living in New York and going to school. I bought a phone, some new clothes, and another plane ticket. I wasn't surprised he was doing more school but was surprised he had ended up in New York. According to a map app on the phone, his house was a brick standalone duplex on a wooded lane. I rented a room at the only motel in town so I could clean up before I went to see him. I had no idea what I was going to say.

The walk over was pleasant enough, thanks to the quaint nature of the town. I had gotten used to the wide plains of the ranch, so the tree-lined streets made me feel crowded. I wondered if I should have looked up his phone number. Or looked him up on social media. Or bought a gift. It had been eight months. I guess I wouldn't have been surprised if he had moved on. If he could change states, he could change boyfriends.

My thoughts were interrupted by a blunt mass slamming into my body. I collapsed under the force and instinctually curled into a ball. I could only register the thing on top of me was solid, soft, and wet all at the same time.

"Oh my God, I'm so sorry. He usually doesn't do this," a husky voice shouted. It all snapped into place, and I found myself laughing. Tidus got Bowser under control about the same time I got my laughing under control.

"I'm really sorry, I—" Tidus offered me a hand. Then he snatched it away, screaming. When he realized it was me, he screamed again, only joyfully, and tossed himself on me like Bowser had.

"Are you fucking kidding me? How is it you? Is it really you? I mean, I guess it can't be anyone else, can it?"

"It's me," I reassured him. He pressed into me, trapping me between him and the sidewalk and rubbing his face against mine. His attentions quickly became an urgent and messy kiss. I lost track of everything in the breathless moments his mouth was on mine.

"I thought," I said when he finally freed my mouth, "I thought you might've moved on."

"Don't be stupid."

"I mean, you moved all the way to New York."

"I can't even. I had to do something while I waited for you to show up again."

We got to our feet, and I got a proper look at him. His hair was styled into an undercut ponytail and was dyed grayish blue. He had on an uncropped T-shirt from his school and tight jeans. It was so casually him, and it was perfect.

"You look amazing," we said at the same time.

He posed in a high-fashion way, and I tried to brush off the compliment.

"I'm amazed to see you," he said.

"Same. Have you heard from Luca? I was going to find him too, I just knew where you lived, but then you were here and—I mean, I had to look for someone first."

Tidus laughed. I sighed and tried to regroup.

"Chill, Martin. I get it. And yeah, I know where Luca is. We talk, I guess you could say. Oh, hey, you should come in and meet my roommate."

"Roommate or *roommate*?"

"Ew, no. He's old. Anyway, come on. We can talk about Luca inside," he said.

"Tidus," I said, grabbing his arm. "I missed you."

He smiled and kissed me much more gently. "I missed you too."

Bowser insisted on walking by my side as we went up the steps to the porch, and he sat on my feet as we waited for Tidus to open the door. Tidus stepped in and Bowser bounded inside. The hallway was wide, stairs going to the second level right inside the door. Then there was a long hallway to what I assumed was the common areas on the ground floor of the house.

"Hey, I'm back," Tidus called, practically running down the hall into the next room. I cautiously followed.

"Thank God, I need you to taste this. I'm afraid if I stop stirring it will separate and I—"

I stepped around the corner at the same time Tidus's roommate came out of the kitchen. When his eyes locked on me, the pan and whisk he had been holding clattered to the floor. The handsome, dark-haired man's hands covered his mouth in surprise.

"Luca," I said.

"If I didn't know better, I wouldn't believe it," he said, stepping toward me slowly. He didn't say anything else. He just walked and didn't stop until his mouth was on mine and his arms were around my neck. I pulled him as close as I could.

"You dropped something," I said when he pulled back.

He laughed, his head thrown back, tears in his eyes. I laughed too. In the background, Tidus was fighting the whisk away from Bowser. It was hard to tell who was going to win. With Hugo's words about the defenses we built around the multi-verse failing in the back of my mind, it was hard to imagine anyone counting any of it as a win. But looking at these two men, I was sure I had come the closest.

## About the Author

Sander Santiago enjoys his publishing home here at Bold Strokes Books. Wanting to see more of himself in fiction, he makes sure that his works feature LGBT+ characters and characters of color. This work is about a trans man written by a trans man and doubles as an absolute honor. He lives in South Florida with his partner, his best friend, and their many pets. Colorado born and raised, he still owns a windshield scraper… just in case.

## Books Available From Bold Strokes Books

**Fresh Grave in Grand Canyon** by Lee Patton. The age-old Grand Canyon becomes more and more ominous as group of volunteers fight to survive alone in nature and uncover a murderer among them. (978-1-63679-047-3)

**Loyalty, Love & Vermouth** by Eric Peterson. A comic valentine to a gay man's family of choice, including the ones with cold noses and four paws. (978-1-63555-997-2)

**Bury Me in Shadows** by Greg Herren. College student Jake Chapman is forced to spend the summer at his dying grandmother's home and soon finds danger from long-buried family secrets. (978-1-63555-993-4)

**A Different Man** by Andrew L. Huerta. This diverse collection of stories chronicling the challenges of gay life at various ages shines a light on the progress made and the progress still to come. (978-1-63555-977-4)

**Busy Ain't the Half of It** by Frederick Smith and Chaz Lamar Cruz. Elijah and Justin seek happily-ever-afters in LA, but are they too busy to notice happiness when it's there? (978-1-63555-944-6)

**Pursuit: A Victorian Entertainment** by Felice Picano. An intelligent, handsome, ruthlessly ambitious young man who rose from the slums to become the right-hand man of the Lord Exchequer of England will stop at nothing as he pursues his Lord's vanished wife across Continental Europe. (978-1-63555-870-8)

**Best of the Wrong Reasons** by Sander Santiago. For Fin Ness and Orion Starr, it takes a funeral to remind them that love is worth living for. (978-1-63555-867-8)

**Coming to Life on South High** by Lee Patton. Twenty-one-year-old gay virgin Gabe Rafferty's first adult decade unfolds as an unpredictable journey into sex, love, and livelihood. (978-1-63555-906-4)

**Death's Prelude** by David S. Pederson. In this prequel to the Detective Heath Barrington Mystery series, Heath discovers that first love changes you forever and drives you to become the person you're destined to be. (978-1-63555-786-2)

**His Brother's Viscount** by Stephanie Lake. Hector Somerville wants to rekindle his illicit love affair with Viscount Wentworth, but he must overcome one problem: Wentworth still loves Hector's brother. (978-1-63555-805-0)

**The Dubious Gift of Dragon Blood** by J. Marshall Freeman. One day Crispin is a lonely high school student—the next he is fighting a war in a land ruled by dragons, his otherworldly boyfriend at his side. (978-1-63555-725-1)

**Quake City** by St John Karp. Can Andre find his best friend Amy before the night devolves into a nightmare of broken hearts, malevolent drag queens, and spontaneous human combustion? Or has it always happened this way, every night, at Aunty Bob's Quake City Club? (978-1-63555-723-7)

**Every Summer Day** by Lee Patton. Meant to celebrate every summer day, Luke's journal instead chronicles a love affair as fast-moving and possibly as fatal as his brother's brain tumor. (978-1-63555-706-0)

**Everyday People** by Louis Barr. When film star Diana Danning hires private eye Clint Steele to find her son, Clint turns to his former West Point barracks mate, and ex-buddy with benefits, Mars Hauser to lend his cyber espionage and digital black ops skills to the case.(978-1-63555-698-8)

**Royal Street Reveillon** by Greg Herren. In this Scotty Bradley mystery, someone is killing the stars of a reality show, and it's up to Scotty Bradley and the boys to find out who. (978-1-63555-545-5)

**Accidental Prophet** by Bud Gundy. Days after his grandmother dies, Drew Morten learns his true identity and finds himself racing against time to save civilization from the apocalypse. (978-1-63555-452-6)

**Counting for Thunder** by Phillip Irwin Cooper. A struggling actor returns to the Deep South to manage a family crisis but finds love and ultimately his own voice as his mother is regaining hers for possibly the last time. (978-1-63555-450-2)

**Of Echoes Born** by 'Nathan Burgoine. A collection of queer fantasy short stories set in Canada from Lambda Literary Award finalist 'Nathan Burgoine. (978-1-63555-096-2)